Ganymede

Ganymede

Cherie Priest

A Tom Doherty Associates Book *New York*

GANYMEDE

Map by Jon Lansberg

Edited by Liz Gorinsky

A Tor Book
Published by Tom Doherty Associates, LLC
175 Fifth Avenue
New York, NY 10010

www.tor-forge.com

Tor® is a registered trademark of Tom Doherty Associates, LLC.

Library of Congress Cataloging-in-Publication Data

Priest, Cherie.
    Ganymede / Cherie Priest.—1
      p. cm.
    ISBN 978-0-7653-2946-2 (pbk.)
    1. Air pilots—Fiction. 2. New Orleans (La.)—Fiction. 3. Alternative histories (Fiction)—Fiction.   I. Title.
    PS3616.R537G36 2011
    813'.6—dc22

                                                                2011021569

First Edition: October 2011

Printed in the United States of America

0 9 8 7 6 5 4 3 2 1

Ganymede is dedicated to everyone who
didn't make it into the history books...

... but should *have.*

Like all my Clockwork Century books, this is a work of fiction. Its facts are contrived and improbable, its finer points are forcibly bent to serve my narrative purposes, and I am led to understand that its zombies are highly unscientific. But if you're okay with zombies shambling around New Orleans in the nineteenth century . . . then I'd like to think you can forgive some finessing of politics and geography.

So thanks for reading! And please don't send me letters about how wrong I've gotten this whole "history" thing. I assure you, my history is at least as accurate as my portrayal of the living dead.

Acknowledgments

This book would have never come together without the patience, assistance, and all-around awesomeness of the following (in no particular order): Liz Gorinsky—editor, diplomat, and advocate of the highest caliber; my husband, Aric, who keeps the home fires bright; Jennifer Jackson—agent and sounding board, who is worth her weight in diamonds; Bill Schafer, a friend and boss, who invited me on board with love, and saw me off with encouragement; and webmaster Greg Wild-Smith, for preventing personal Internet meltdowns by the score. . . . A thousand grateful kudos to all of you, for putting up with this Tiny Godzilla.

Thanks also to the community of writers who keep me company as I work from home. The Team Seattle crew of Mark Henry, Caitlin Kittredge (still a member in honorary standing, though she's moved), Richelle Mead, and Kat Richardson; my convention peeps Scalzi, Mary Robinette, Tobias, Scott, Justine, and many others, who keep this from being such a lonely gig. See also Wil and Warren, Ariana (the gatekeeper), and everyone else in the secret clubhouse that serves the world: I couldn't do it without you. Likewise, love to the Home Team of Ellen and Suezie, keepers of cats and purveyors of brunches and baked goods.

Mad props also to all the indie bookstores and chains alike across the country. You've been so extraordinarily helpful and supportive, and I can't thank you enough. Particular gratitude goes to the

Seattle-area folks who deal with me the most: Duane Wilkins over at the University Book Store, Steve and Vlad over at Third Place Books, and the crew at the Northgate B&N.

And finally, excessive, effusive thanks must go out to all the readers who have embraced this weird little franchise. Thank you steampunks, dieselpunks, clockpunks, steamgoths, and everyone else in the retro-futurist niche of your choosing. Thank you for reading these books, and for sharing them, and for giving them a place on your shelves and in your hearts.

You have made these books happen.

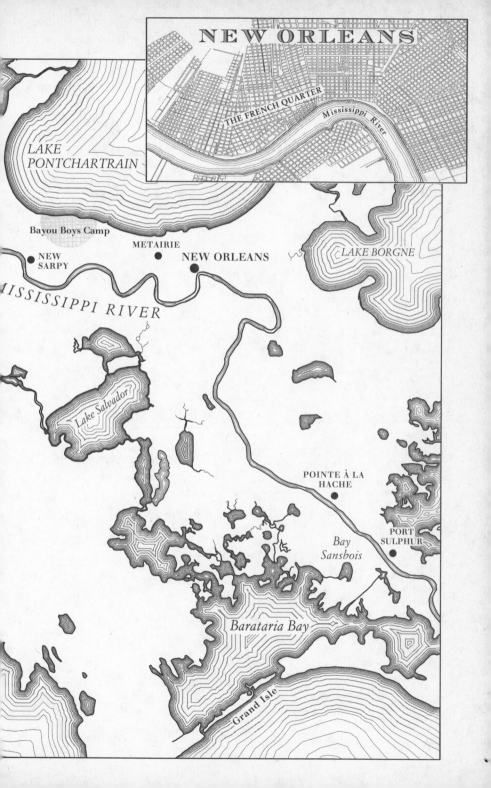

NEW ORLEANS

THE FRENCH QUARTER

Mississippi River

LAKE
PONTCHARTRAIN

Bayou Boys Camp

METAIRIE

NEW
SARPY

NEW ORLEANS

LAKE BORGNE

MISSISSIPPI RIVER

Lake Salvador

POINTE À LA
HACHE

PORT
SULPHUR

Bay
Sansbois

Barataria Bay

Grand Isle

Nor must Uncle Sam's web feet be forgotten. At all the watery margins they have been present. Not only on the deep sea, the broad bay, and the rapid river, but also up the narrow, muddy bayou, and wherever the ground was a little damp, they have been, and made their tracks.

—ABRAHAM LINCOLN
(From a letter to John Conkling, August 26, 1863)

Ganymede

 *One*

"Croggon Hainey sends his regards, but he isn't up for hire," Josephine Early declared grimly as she crumpled the telegram in her fist. She flicked the wad of paper into the tiny round wastebin beside her desk and took a deep breath that came out in a hard sigh. "So we'll have to find another pilot, goddammit."

"Ma'am, the airyard's full of pilots," her assistant, Marylin Quantrill, replied.

She leaned back in her seat and tapped her fingers on the chair's armrest. "Not pilots like *him*."

"Hainey . . . he's a colored fellow, isn't he? One of the Macon Madmen?"

"Yes, and he's the best flier I know. But I can't blame him for turning us down. It's asking a lot, for him to come so far south while he's still wanted—and we don't have the money to pay him what he's worth, much less compensate him for the extra danger."

Marylin nodded, disappointed but understanding. "It didn't hurt to ask."

"No. And if it were me, I wouldn't take the job either." Josephine ceased her tapping and shifted her weight, further wedging her voluminous blue dress into the narrow confines of the worn mahogany chair's rigid arms. "But I sure was hoping he'd say yes. He's perfect for the job, and perfect doesn't come along every day. We won't find anyone half so perfect hanging about the airyard, I can tell you that much. We need a man with excellent flying skills *and* absolutely no loyalty to the Republic or the Confederacy. And that, my dear, will be the trouble."

"Is there anyone else we could ask, anyone farther afield?"

"No one springs to mind," Josephine murmured.

Marylin pressed on. "It might not matter, anyway. It could be Rucker Little is right, and a pilot won't have any better luck than a seaman."

"It'd be hard for anyone, anywhere, to fail so spectacularly as that last batch of sailors."

"Not *all* of them drowned."

"Four out of five isn't anything to crow about."

"I suppose not, ma'am." Marylin lowered her eyes and fiddled with her gloves. She didn't often wear gloves, given the heat and damp of the delta, but the elbow-length silk pair with tiny pearl buttons had been a gift from a customer, and he'd requested specifically that she wear them tonight. Her hair was done up in a twisted set of plaits and set with an ostrich feather. The yellow dress she wore cost only half what the gloves did, but they complemented each other all the same.

Josephine vowed, "I'll find someone else, and I'll show Mr. Mumler that I'm right. They're going about that machine all wrong, I just know it. All I need is a pilot to prove it."

"But you have to admit," the younger woman carefully ventured, "it sounds strange, wanting an airman for a . . . for whatever it is, there in the lake."

"Sometimes a strangely shaped problem requires a strangely shaped solution, dear. So here's what we'll do for now: Tomorrow afternoon, you take one of the other girls—Hazel or Ruthie, maybe—and you go down to the airyard and keep your eyes open."

"Open for what?"

"Anyone who isn't Southern or Texian. Look for foreigners who stand out from the usual crowd—ignore the English and the islanders, we don't want them. We want people who don't care about the war, and who aren't taking sides. Tradesmen, merchants, or pirates."

"I don't know about pirates, ma'am. They scare me, I don't mind saying."

Josephine said, "Hainey's a pirate, and I'd trust him enough to employ him. Pirates come in different sorts like everybody else, and I'll settle for one if I have to. But don't worry. I wouldn't ask you to go down to the bay or barter with the Lafittes. If our situation turns out to call for a pirate, I'll go get one myself."

"Thank you, ma'am."

"Let's consider Barataria a last resort. We aren't up to needing last resorts. Not yet. The craft is barely in working order, and Chester says it'll be a few days before it's dried out enough to try again. When it works, and when we have someone who can consistently operate it without drowning everyone inside it, then we'll move it. We have to get it to the Gulf, and we'll have to do it right the first time. We won't get a second chance."

"No, ma'am, I don't expect we will," Marylin agreed. Then she changed the subject. "Begging your pardon, ma'am—but do you have the time?"

"The time? Oh, yes." Josephine reached into her front left pocket and retrieved a watch. It was an engineer's design with a glass cutout in the cover, allowing her to see the hour at a glance. "It's ten till eight. Don't worry, your meeting with Mr. Spring has not been compromised—though, knowing him, he's already waiting downstairs."

"I think he rather likes me, ma'am."

"I expect he does. And with that in mind, be careful, Marylin."

"I'm always careful."

"You know what I mean."

She rose from her seat and asked, "Is there anything else?"

"No, darling."

Therefore, with a quick check of her hair in the mirror by the door, Marylin Quantrill exited the office on the fourth floor of the building known officially as the Garden Court Boarding House for Ladies, and unofficially as "Miss Early's Place," home of "Miss Early's Girlies."

Josephine did not particularly care for the unofficial designation, but there wasn't much to be done about it now. A name with a rhyme sticks harder than sun-dried tar.

But quietly, bitterly, Josephine saw no logical reason why a woman in her forties should be referred to with the same address as a toddler, purely because she'd never married. Furthermore, she employed no "girlies." She took great pains to see to it that her ladies were precisely that: ladies, well informed and well educated. Her ladies could read and write French as well as English, and some of them spoke Spanish, too; they took instruction on manners, sewing, and cooking. They were young women, yes, but they were not frivolous children, and she hoped that they would have skills to support themselves upon leaving the Garden Court Boarding House.

All the Garden Court ladies were free women of color.

It was Josephine's experience that men liked nothing better than variety, and that no two men shared precisely the same tastes. With that in mind, she'd recruited fourteen women in a spectrum of skin tones, ranging from two very dark Caribbean natives to several lighter mixes like Marylin, who could have nearly passed for white. Josephine herself counted an eighth of her own ancestry from Africa, courtesy of a great-grandmother who'd come to New Orleans aboard a ship called the *Adelaide*. At thirteen, her grandmother had been bought to serve as a maid, and at fourteen, she'd birthed her first child, Josephine's mother.

And so forth, and so on.

Josephine was tall and lean, with skin like tea stirred with milk. Her forehead was high and her lips were full, and although she looked her age, she wore all forty-two years with grace. It was true that in her maturity she'd slipped from "beautiful" to merely "pretty," but she anticipated another ten years before sliding down to the dreaded "handsome."

She looked again at the watch, and at the wastebin holding the unfortunate telegram, and she wondered what on earth she was going to do now. Major Alcock was expecting a report on her mission's progress, and Admiral Partridge had made clear that it wasn't safe to keep the airship carrier *Valiant* too close to the delta for very long. Texas wouldn't tolerate it—they'd chase the big ship back out to sea like a flock of crows harrying an eagle.

She had until the end of May. No longer.

That left not quite four weeks to figure out a number of things which had gone years without having been figured out thus far.

"*Ganymede,*" she said under her breath, "I *will* find someone to fly you."

All she needed was a pilot willing to risk his life in a machine that had killed seventeen men to date; brave the Mississippi River as it went past Forts Jackson and Saint Philip and all the attending Rebels and Texians therein; and kindly guide it out into the Gulf of Mexico past half a dozen Confederate warships—all the while knowing the thing could explode, suffocate everyone inside, or sink to the ocean bottom at any moment.

Was it really so much to ask?

The Union thought she was out of her mind, and though they wanted the scuttled craft, they couldn't see paying yet another seventeen men to die for it. Therefore, any further salvage efforts must come out of Josephine's own pocket. But her pockets weren't as deep as the major seemed to think, and the cost of hiring a high-level mercenary for such a mission was well outside her reach.

Even if she knew another pilot half so good as Croggon Hainey, and without any allegiance to the occupying Republicans or the Confederates, a month might not be enough time to fetch him, prepare him, and test him.

She squeezed her watch and popped it open. The gears inside flipped, swayed, and spun.

But on second thought . . .

She'd told Marylin she didn't know any other pilots. The lie had slipped off her tongue as if it'd been greased, or as if she'd only forgotten it wasn't true, but there *was* someone else.

It wasn't worth thinking about. After all, it'd been years since last she saw him—since she even thought about him. Had he gone back West? Had he married, and raised a family? Would he come if she summoned him? For all she knew, he wasn't even alive anymore. Not every man—even a man like Andan Cly—survives a pirate's career.

"He's probably dead," Josephine told herself. "Long gone, I'm sure."

She wasn't sure.

She looked back at the wastebin, and she realized that with one more telegram, she could likely find out.

Croggon Hainey frequented the Northwest corners, didn't he? And Cly had come from a wretched, wet backwater of a port called . . . what was it again? Oh, yes: *Seattle*—out in the Washington Territory, as far away from New Orleans as a man could get while staying on colonial turf.

"No coincidence, that," she said to the empty room, realizing she flattered herself to think so. Well, so what? Then she flattered herself. She wasn't the first.

Downstairs, something fell heavily, or something large was thrown and landed with a muffled thunk.

Josephine's ears perked, and she briefly forgot about the wastebin, the telegram, and potential news of long-ago lovers from distant hinterlands. She listened hard, hoping to hear nothing more without daring to assume it.

The Garden Court Boarding House was different from many bordellos, but not so different that there were never problems: drunk men, or cruel men who wanted more than they were willing to buy. Josephine did her best to screen out the worst, and she prided herself on both the quality of her ladies and the relative peace of her establishment; even so, it was never far from her mind how quickly things could turn, and how little it would take for the French Quarter to remember that she was only a colored woman, and not necessarily entitled to own things, much less protect them, preserve them, and use them for illicit activities.

It was a line she walked every night, between legitimate business-woman performing a service for the community of soldiers, sailors, merchants, and planters . . . and the grandchild of slaves, who could become a slave herself again simply by crossing the wrong state lines.

Louisiana wasn't safe, not for her or any of her ladies. Maybe not for anybody.

But this was Josephine's house, and she guarded it with all the ferocity and cunning of a mother fox. So when she heard the noise downstairs, she listened hard, *willing* innocent silence to follow, but suspecting the worst and preparing herself accordingly.

In the top left drawer of her battered, antique, secondhand desk, she kept a .44-caliber Schofield—a Smith & Wesson revolver she'd nicknamed "Little Russia." It was loaded, as always. She retrieved it and pushed the desk drawer shut again.

It was easy to hide the weapon behind her skirts. People don't expect a left-handed woman, and no one expects to be assaulted by anyone in a fancy gown—which was one more good reason to wear them all the time.

Out past the paneled office door she swept, and down the red-carpeted runner to the end of the hall, where a set of stairs curved down to all three lower levels, flanked by a banister that was pol-ished weekly and gleamed under the skimming touch of Josephine's hand. The commotion was on the second floor, or so her ears told her as she drew up nearer.

The location was a good thing, insofar as any commotion was ever good. Far better than if it were taking place down in the lobby. It's bad for business, and bad for covering up trouble, should a cover-up be required. At street level, people could squint and peek past the gossamer curtains, trying to focus on the slivers of light inside and the women who lived within.

At street level, there could be witnesses.

Josephine was getting ahead of herself, and she knew it. She always got ahead of herself, but that's how she'd stayed alive and in charge this long, so she couldn't imagine slowing down anytime soon. Instead she held the Schofield with a cool, loose grip. She felt the gun's weight as a strange, foreign thing against her silk overskirts, where she buried it out of sight. As she'd learned one evening in her misspent youth at the notorious pirate call of Barataria, she need not brandish a gun to fire it. It'd shoot just fine through a petticoat, and knock a hole in a man all the same. It would ruin the skirts, to be certain, but those were trade-offs a woman could make in the name of survival.

Down on the second-floor landing, she stepped off the stairs so swiftly, she seemed to be moving on wings or wheels. She brought herself up short just in time to keep from running into the Texian Fenn Calais.

A big man in his youth, Mr. Calais was now a soft man, with cheeks blushed pink from years of alcohol and a round, friendly face that had become well known to ladies of the Garden Court. Delphine Hoobler was under one of his arms, and Caroline Younger was hooked beneath the other.

"Evening, ma'am!" he said cheerfully. He was always cheerful. Suspiciously so, if you wanted Josephine's opinion on the matter, but Fenn was so well liked that no one ever did.

With her usual polite formality, she replied, "Good evening to you, Mr. Calais. I see you're being properly cared for. Is there anything I can get you, or anything further you require?"

Caroline flashed Josephine a serious look and a sharpened eyebrow. This was combined with a quick toss of her head and a laugh. "We'll keep an eye on him, Miss Josephine," she said lightly, but the urgent, somber gleam in her eyes didn't soften.

Josephine understood. She nodded. "Very well, then." She smiled and stepped aside, letting the three of them pass. When they were gone, she turned her attention to the far end of the corridor. Caroline and Delphine had been luring Fenn Calais away from something.

From someone.

She could guess, even before she saw the window that hadn't been fully shut, and the swamp-mud scuff of a large man's shoe across the carpet runner.

With a glance over her shoulder to make sure the Texian was out of hearing range, she called softly, "Deaderick? That'd damned well *better* be you."

"It's me," he whispered back. He leaned out from the stairwell. "That Fenn fellow was passed out on the settee with a drink in his hand. I thought I could sneak past without waking him up, but he sleeps lighter than he looks."

She exhaled, relieved. She wedged Little Russia into her skirt pocket. "Delphine and Carrie took care of him."

"Yeah, I saw." He looked back and forth down the hall. Seeing no one but his sister, he relaxed enough to leave his hiding place.

Deaderick Early was a tall man, and lean like his sister, though darker in complexion. They had only a mother in common, and Deaderick was several shades away from Josephine's paler skin. His hair was thick and dense, and black as ink. He let it grow into long locks that dangled below his ears.

"You're lucky it was only Fenn. He's easily distracted and probably too drunk to recognize you."

"Still, I didn't mean to take the chance."

She sighed and rubbed at her forehead, then leaned back against the wall and eyed him tiredly. "What are you doing here, Rick? You know I don't like it when you come to town. I worry about you."

"You don't worry about me living camped in a swamp?"

"In the swamp you're armed, and with your men. Here you're alone, and you're visible. Anyone could see you, point you out, and have you taken away." She blinked back the dampness that filled her eyes. "With every chance you take, the odds stack higher against you."

"That may be, but we need soap, salt, and coffee. For that matter, a little rum would make me a popular man, and we could stand to have a better doctor's kit," he added, looking down at an ugly swath of inflamed skin on his arm—caused, no doubt, by the stinging things that buzzed in the bayou. "But also, I came to bring you *this*."

From the back pocket of his pants, he produced an envelope that had been sealed and folded in half. "It might help your pilot, if you ever find one."

"What is it?"

"Schematics from a footlocker at the Pontchartrain base. It's got Hunley's writing on it. I think it's a sketch for the steering mechanism, and part of the propulsion system. Or that's what Chester and Honeyfolk said, and I'm prepared to take their word for it."

"Neither one of them needs it?" She slipped the envelope down into her cleavage, past her underwear's stays.

"They've already taken that section apart and put it all back together. It doesn't hold any secrets for an engineer, but a pilot who wants to know what he's getting himself into . . . this might come in handy. Or it might not, if you have to trick someone into taking the job."

A loud cough of laughter came from upstairs, and the *whump* of heavy footsteps. The siblings looked up to the ceiling, as if it could tell them anything; but Josephine said, "Fenn again, heading to the water closet. Listen, we should go outside. Out back it's quiet, and even if someone sees you, it'll be too dark for anyone to recognize you."

"Fine, if that's what you want." He pushed the back stairway door open and held it for her, letting her lead the way.

Down they went, her soft, quiet house slippers making no noise at all, and his dirty leather boots trailing a muffled drumbeat in her wake. At the bottom, she unlocked the back door and pushed it. It moaned on its hinges, scraping trash and mud with its bottom edge.

It opened, letting them both outside into the night.

The alley itself was dark and wet, smelling of vomit, urine, and horse manure. Overhead the moon hung low and very white, but they barely noticed it over the grumbling music, swearing sailors, drunken planters, and the late-night calls of newspaper boys trawling for pennies before closing up shop. The gas lamps on Rue des Ursulines gave the whole night a ghostly wash, leaving the shadows sharp and black between the lacy Old World buildings of the Vieux Carré, and leaving Josephine and Deaderick as close to alone as they could expect to find themselves.

Josephine swatted at her brother's vest pocket, the place where he always kept tobacco and papers. He took the hint, retrieved his pouch, and began to roll two cigarettes between his fingers. "It's a good thing that dumb bastard let himself be dragged away so easy."

"Like I said, you were lucky. Some of the younger men lounge around armed, and after a few drinks, they're quick to draw. Fenn's not dumb, but he's harmless. Even if he'd seen you—even if he'd recognized you—we might've been able to buy him off."

"You'd trust some old Texian?"

"That one?" Josephine took the cigarette he offered and waited for him to light it. She gently sucked it to life, and the smell of tobacco wafted up her nose, down her throat. It took the edge off the mulchy odor of the alley. "Maybe. I don't think he'd make any trouble for us. He'd die of sorrow if we told him he wasn't welcome anymore."

Deaderick lit his own cigarette and stepped onto a higher corner of the curb, dodging a rivulet of running gutter water. "You making friends with Republicans now? Next thing I hear, you'll be cozying up to the Rebs."

"You shut your mouth," she whispered hard. "All I'm telling you is that Fenn spends more time at the Court than he does at his own home, assuming he has one. He's sweet on Delphine and Ruthie in particular, and he won't go talking if he thinks we'll keep him from coming back."

"If you say so." He sighed and asked quietly, "Any chance you heard from that pilot friend of yours? The man from Georgia— could you talk him into it?"

"He can't make it, so now I've got to find someone else. I'm working on it, all right? I've already talked to Marylin, and tomorrow she'll take Ruthie over to the airyard to look around."

"There's nothing but Republicans and Rebs down at the airyard. You'd have better luck in Barataria. Not that I'm suggesting it."

She snorted, and a puff of smoke coiled out her nostril. "Don't think I haven't considered it. But I want to check the straight docks first, all the same. Times are hard all over. We might find foreigners— or maybe Westerners—desperate enough to take the job."

"How much money you offering?"

"Not enough. But between me and the girls, we might be able to negotiate. There's always wiggle room. I've talked it over with those who can be trusted, and they're game as me to pool our resources."

"I don't want to hear about that," Deaderick said stiffly.

"I suppose you don't, but that doesn't change anything. If we can get this done between us, it'll all be worth it. Every bit of it, even the unpleasant parts. We're all making sacrifices, Rick. Don't act like it's a walk in the park for you and the boys, because I know it *isn't.*"

Life was hard outside the city, in the swamps where the guerrillas lurked, and poached, and picked off Confederates and Texians whenever they could. It was written all over her brother's flesh, in the insect bites and scrapes of thorns. The story was told in the rips that had been patched and repatched on his homespun pants, and in the linen shirt with its round wood buttons—none of which matched.

But she was proud of him, desperately so. And she was made all the prouder just by looking at him and knowing that they were all struggling, certainly—but her little brother, fully ten years her junior, was in charge of a thirty-man company, and quietly paid by the Union besides. He drew a real salary in Federal silver, every

three months like clockwork. Out of sight, at the edge of civilization, he was fighting for them all—for her, for the colored girls at
the Garden Court, and for the Union, which would be whole again,
one of these days.

And just like her, he was fighting for New Orleans, which
deserved better than to have Texas squat upon it with its guns, soldiers, and Confederate allegiance.

Deaderick gazed at his sister over the tiny red coal of his smol-
dering cigarette. "It can't go on like this much longer. These . . .
these—" He gestured at the alley's entrance, where a large Texian
machine was gargling, grumbling, and rolling, its lone star insignia
visible as it shuddered past, and was gone. "—*vermin*. I want them
out of my city."

"Most of them want out just as bad."

"Well, then, that's one thing we got in common. But I don't
know why you have to run around defending them."

"Who's defending them? All I said in behalf of Fenn Calais is
that he's an old whoremonger with no place left to hang his hat.
I have a business to run, that's all—and I don't get to pick my customers. Besides, the better the brown boys like us, the safer I stay,"
she insisted, using the Quarter's favorite ironic slang for the soldiers who, despite their dun-colored uniforms, were as white as
sugar down to the last man. "I can't have their officers sniffing
around, looking too close. Not while I'm courting the admiral, and
not while you're running the bayou. As long as we keep them quiet
and happy, they leave us alone."

"Except for the ones you treat to room and board," he sniffed.
"You let that old fat one get too close. You call him harmless, but
maybe he thinks like you do. Maybe he watches you send telegrams,
or pass messages to me or Chester. Maybe he sees a scrap of paper
in the trash, or overhears us talking some night. Then you'll sure
as hell find out how far you can trust your resident Texian, won't
you?"

It was something she'd privately wondered about sometimes,

upon catching a glimpse of Fenn Calais's familiar form sauntering through the halls with Delphine, Ruthie, or a new girl hanging on his arm . . . or drinking himself into a charmingly dignified stupor in one of the tower lounges. Occasionally it occurred to her that he could well be a spy, sent to watch her and the ladies. Spies were a fact of life in New Orleans, after all—spies of every breed, background, quality, and style. The Republic of Texas had a few, though as an occupying force, they were all of them spies by default; the Confederacy kept a number on hand, to keep an eye on the Texians who were keeping an eye on things; and even the Union managed to plant a few here and there, keeping an eye on everyone else.

As Josephine would well know. She was on their payroll, too.

She dropped the last of her cigarette before it could burn her fingers, and she crushed its ashes underfoot on street stones that were slippery with humidity and the afternoon's rain. Her house slippers weren't made for outdoor excursions of even the briefest sort, and they'd never be the same again—she could sense it. Between her toes she felt the creeping damp of street water and regurgitated bourbon, runny horse droppings strung together with wads of brittle grass, and the warm, unholy squish of God-knew-what, which smelled like grave dirt and death.

"I don't like it out here," she said by way of changing the subject. "And I don't like you being here. Go home, Rick. Go back to the bayou, where you're safe."

"It's been good to see you, too."

"Just . . . stay away from the river, will you?"

"I always do."

"Promise me, please?"

Down by the river and roaming the Quarter's darker corners, monstrous things waited, and were hungry. Or so the stories went.

"I promise. Even though I'm not afraid of a few dusters."

"I know you're not, but I am. I've seen them."

"So have I," he declared flippantly, which meant he was lying. He'd only heard about them.

"They aren't dusters," she muttered.

"Sure they are. Addicts gone feral, like cats. And you worry too much."

She almost accused him of lying, but decided against starting that particular fight. If anything, it was good that he was ignorant of the dead—or that's what she told herself. She'd be thrilled if he went his whole life without ever seeing one, even though it meant that he wrote them off as bedtime stories, designed to frighten naughty children.

He last lived in the Quarter ten years ago, before he'd headed off to fight. Back then, there hadn't been so many of them.

Deaderick didn't want to argue any more than Josephine did. "I'll stay away from the river, if it'll make you happy. And maybe I'll head out to Barataria myself, one of these days soon. We hit them up for discreet mechanics and supply fliers every now and again. While I'm there, I'll see if I can't spot any potential pilots for you."

"All right, but if you find anyone, be careful what you tell him. It's dangerous work we're asking for, but anybody we have to trick too badly won't do us any good, when push comes to shove. That's why I'm sending another few telegrams tonight. I've got somebody else in mind."

"You do?"

"I know of a man who might be good for the task. If I can find him. And if he's still alive. And if he can be persuaded to come within fifty feet of me."

Deaderick grinned at her. "Sounds promising."

"It's *not* promising, but it's better than nothing. We have to get that thing out of the lake. We have to get it out to sea, to the Federal Navy. Once they get a crack at it, it's just a matter of time. *Ganymede* could change everything."

"I know," her brother said, putting his arms around her. "And it *will*."

In the distance, a cheer went up and so did a small flare—a little rocket of a thing that cast a pink white trail of burning fire into the sky. A second cheer followed it, and the clapping of a crowd.

"Goddamn Texians," Josephine said wearily, the words garbled against his shoulder.

"What are they doing?"

"Tearing up the cathedral square, gambling on livestock, and shooting off fireworks. It isn't right."

Deaderick nodded, but noted, "You haven't been to church in half a lifetime."

"Still," she said, "that doesn't make it right, what they're doing over there."

A faintly burning chemical stink joined the city's odors, trapped in the humid fog of Gulf water and river water that crept through the Quarter like a warm, wet bath. Gunpowder and animals, men and women, alcohols sweet and sour—bourbons brought from Kentucky, whiskeys imported from Tennessee, rums shipped in from the islands south of Florida, and grain distillations made in a neighbor's cast-iron tub. The night smelled of gun oil and saddles, and the jasmine colognes of the night ladies, or the violets and azaleas that hung from balconies in baskets; of berry liqueur and the verdant, herbal tang of absinthe delivered from crystal decanters, and the dried chilies hanging in the stalls of the French market, and powdered sugar and chicory.

Josephine leaned her head on Deaderick's shoulder as she hugged him good-bye. She breathed, "We're drowning like this, you know," and she saw him off with tears swallowed hard in the back of her throat.

Two

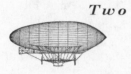

Andan Cly folded the telegram shut and said, "I'll be damned." He slipped it into his shirt pocket, then changed his mind and set it instead on the bar—as if he were reluctant to touch it, but didn't want to let it out of his sight.

"What for?" Angeline drew her feet up onto the stool's bottommost rung and looked at him expectantly. She was dressed in her usual preferred attire, a man's shirt and pants cut down to size. A slouch-rim hat sat atop her head, crowning the long gray braid that hung down her back.

The pilot and sometimes-pirate cleared his throat and signaled the bartender for a glass of something stronger than what was already in front of him. "It's . . . it's a message. From someone I used to know, a long time ago."

"Must be a woman."

"I didn't say it was a woman."

"If it wasn't, you wouldn't be hemming and hawing like a schoolboy."

"Hush, you," he told her, not for a moment expecting her to do so.

Lucy O'Gunning slipped a shot in front of him and then put a bottle of whiskey beside it. "One for you, too, Princess?"

"Since you're offering."

Lucy poured another drink, using her one mechanical arm as deftly as any bartender ever used two of the usual kind. "And what have we got here?" She reached to pick up the cheap slip of transcription paper, but Cly snatched it back, crumpling it in his hand.

"It's a note from a woman," Angeline informed her. "He won't admit it, but that's what it is. Telegram came up from Tacoma. Freddy Miller brought it in his sack with the last batch of mail; I just brought it along, 'cause I was passing through anyhow."

"A woman?" Lucy gave Andan Cly a suspicious squint. "You airmen, all the same. A girl in every port."

"It ain't like that," he insisted. "I haven't seen this woman in . . . I don't know. Eight or ten years. She's a few thousand miles away, and she didn't dash off a note because she missed me." Under his breath he added, "I can promise you *that*."

"Ooh." Lucy leaned forward, planting her matronly bosom on the countertop and propping her chin in her clockwork palm. "Sounds *interesting*."

"What does she want?" Angeline asked bluntly, unconcerned by the blush that climbed the fair-skinned fellow's neck. Cly's hair was cut close to his scalp, and it was light enough to plainly show the pink when embarrassment made it all the way to the top of his considerable frame.

"She wants to hire me."

"For what kind of job?" Lucy asked.

"She wants me to come to New Orleans. There's a craft she wants me to fly, but I don't know anything more than that. The telegram is thin on details."

Angeline harrumphed. "Sounds like a trumped-up excuse to bring you out for a visit."

"She's not that kind."

"You don't sound so sure of it," Lucy said. She waited for him to down his shot. When he did, she poured him another before he had a chance to ask for it.

"I'm plenty sure of it, and now you're just trying to liquor me up so I'll tell you more."

"You complaining?"

"No. Keep 'em coming." He cleared his throat again and said, "There's got to be a catch. New Orleans is a huge place—big port, big airyard. She could get a perfectly good pilot by setting foot outside her front door and hollering for one." Unfolding the paper, he reread a few lines and said, "All I know is, it's got something to do with this thing, the *Ganymede*."

The bartender asked, "What's a Ganymede?"

"A dirigible, I assume. She needs someone to take it from Pontchartrain to the Gulf, and she's willing to pay . . . but it's only a few miles, from the lake to the coast. Why she'd want me to go all the way out there to move it for her, I just don't know."

"Ask her," suggested Angeline.

"Not sure it's worth the trouble."

Ever the practical one, Lucy asked, "Is it enough money to make the trip worthwhile? That's a long way to go, to fly a ship a few feet."

"Almost, but not quite. She's offering low, asking it like a favor for old times' sake."

Angeline smiled. "Old times must've been good."

Lucy straightened up and grabbed a towel. She pretended that the bar needed a good wipe-down and said, "I never been to New Orleans."

"Me either, but I done heard about it," the older woman said, her smile still firmly in place—and now with a playful gleam twinkling in her eyes. "I hear it's a city for music and dancing, and drinking, too. I hear it's all Frenched up."

Cly swallowed his beverage but put a hand over the glass when Lucy used her bar rag to nudge the bottle his way. "New Orleans is one hell of a city, or it was last time I saw it. Even though Texas had been sitting on it for years."

Angeline's smile contorted into a puzzled frown. "What's Texas got to do with it?"

He picked up his glass and fiddled with it, tipping it this way and that between his fingers. "Early in the war—back in 1862—the Union went after the city. They thought if they could control the port and the river, they could get a good choke hold on the Confederate supply line. So they took the place. Trouble was, they couldn't keep it."

"Texas took it away from them?" Angeline guessed.

"Yeah. The Rebs couldn't pry the Federal troops out on their own, not for trying; but the Texians didn't like having the Union presence so close by, so they agreed to lend a hand. They freed up the city in '64, I think. But once they'd booted out the Union, they had a problem: The Rebels didn't have enough people on hand to keep the city secure, and the Union wanted back inside it real bad. That's the biggest port this side of the world, you understand? So Texas could either hold down the fort, or it could withdraw and risk an enemy stronghold right outside its eastern border."

"So Texas stayed," Angeline inferred.

"Texas stayed. And nobody likes it much."

Lucy nudged the bottle Cly's way again, and this time he picked it up and poured another round for himself and the princess.

"Texas did some rebuilding, and they set up shops of their own to take advantage of all the trade and travel—trying to make the best of it. Nobody knew how long the war would last, though. Nobody knew it'd straggle on twenty years. Even back when I was there, in '71 and '72, the locals were fed up with the occupation. It must be worse now, worse by all these extra years."

Andan Cly ran his fingers around the lip of the still-full shot glass, thinking about the French Quarter, and about a woman named Josephine. Neither of his companions interrupted, but both leaned expectantly toward him, waiting for more.

"New Orleans," he said slowly. "It's not like other places, in the South or anywhere else. I mean, all over the South you've got a whole lot of colored people—not surprising, since they went to so much trouble to import 'em; but in New Orleans there's a goodly number of *free* negroes, and mixed folks, too. They own property there, and have businesses, and get married and make families and run households just like the Southern white people do in other places. The whole state is organized different, and that city is especially different, that's all I'm saying." He scratched his head, trying to find a good way to explain the place, and not coming up with anything that sounded right.

"What do you mean, it's organized different?" asked Lucy.

"Oh, like they don't have counties and such. They have parishes, left over from when France was running the place, and their elections are different—the people who get into power are different. It's hard to explain. But as you could guess, the free colored people don't have much interest in being run by the Confederacy . . . or any of its allies, either. Hell, being unhappy with Texas is the one thing the colored locals have in common with the Confederates. You'd think it'd give them something to bond over, but that's not how the world works."

Angeline's frown deepened. "Don't the Rebels want to keep the city open for their own country?"

"Sure, but Texas holding New Orleans—it's a permanent reminder how the Rebs couldn't hold it themselves. They talk like it's about honor, but it's not. It's just pride, same as anything else."

The princess shook her head. "Honor, I understand. Pride, I've got a handle on. But sometimes you white folks are crazy as a snake-loving rabbit."

"Aw, come on Angeline." Cly grinned.

Lucy laughed and said, "*Surely* you mean present company excepted."

"Nope!" She spun off the stool, swallowed her drink, and saluted them both with a tip of her hat. "Both of you are well included, I fear." As she dug around in her pockets, she added, "And I thank you for the history lesson, Captain, that was real enlightening. But I need to be on my way. I have a train to catch tonight, from Tacoma."

"Where are you going?" Andan asked. "Maybe I could give you a lift."

"Portland. But don't you worry about it, much as I appreciate the offer. I'm headed down there to see an old friend, and sometimes

I don't mind a nice train ride. It's only half a day's trip, and he's meeting me at the station." She tossed some coins on the counter and winked. "I'll catch you two when I come back around."

"All right, Miss Angeline," Lucy said with a wave. "You have a safe trip."

When she had exited through Maynard's sealed, filtered front door, Lucy shook her head. "I swear to God, that woman . . . I don't know how she comes and goes so free and easy, like it's nothing at all to get inside or out again."

Andan examined the telegram some more, shielding it from Lucy's curious hovering. He scratched at his ear and revisited the letters again and again, in case a fourth or fifth reading might squeeze some extra meaning out of the few brief lines.

"Captain?" she asked, pretending she was offering another drink.

Without looking up, he said, "Hm? Oh, I'm sure Angeline has her methods."

"No doubt. But what about you? What about that telegram?"

"What about it?"

"You taking the job?"

He shrugged and finally looked up. "I could use the money, and there are lots of things I can pick up in New Orleans—things I can't get just anyplace. I could bring you back some absinthe, Lucy. You ever had any absinthe? You'd be the richest bartender in the Territory if I could fetch you a few barrels."

"Oh, you'd do it for *me*. And here I was thinking maybe you wanted to go strike a match on an old flame."

"You've got it all wrong."

"I bet I don't."

"It was complicated."

"I bet it *wasn't*."

Just then the front door opened, sliding stickily forward on its rubber-coated seals. Everyone in Maynard's—Lucy, Andan, and the three men playing cards at a round green table in the back corner—turned to see the newcomer. After they looked him over, Cly shifted his weight on the stool, putting one foot down on the floor, and the men at the green table became engrossed in their game, their eyes darting back and forth over the cards.

"Yaozu," Lucy both announced and greeted him.

The white-clad oriental man surveyed the underground saloon. His attention skimmed past the drunks and the gamblers, settled briefly on Andan Cly, and returned to Lucy. "Mrs. O'Gunning. I'd like to try some of that beer you brew. The local selection," he clarified in precise, flawless English.

She blurted, "Are you sure? It's . . . an acquired taste, or so I'm told."

"Then allow me the opportunity to acquire it."

"As you like." She stepped away from Cly, grabbing a clean mug off the second plank shelf and toting it over to the tap. "But if you don't care for it, I have some *huangjiu* on hand. Mrs. Wong gives me a bottle every now and again; I think she takes them away from her husband. A barkeep should have something on hand for all her customers, don't you think?"

"Yes, but there's no need to assume. Today I'd like to try this beer . . . about which I've heard so . . . *much*."

Though the pub was more empty than full and there were many seats available, Yaozu chose the stool next to Andan Cly. He sat upon it with a graceful swish that let the tail of his jacket fall perfectly behind him. A black braid snaked back and forth between his shoulder blades when he turned his head to examine the state of the fixtures, the stock on the shelves, Lucy O'Gunning as she filled his mug, and his own reflection in the mirror behind the bar.

Then he regarded Andan Cly. Their eyes met in the glass.

Cly adjusted his position on the stool, a frequent occurrence, for it was about a size too small for him. "So . . . what are you doing here, Yaozu?" He aimed for a cautiously friendly tone and more or less hit it.

To what Cly considered the Chinaman's credit, he did not stall the conversation with disclaimers or pleasantries. "I'd heard you were inside the walls—that your ship is docked at Fort Decatur. I thought I might find you here."

Lucy arrived with the beer and placed it before Yaozu with a dubious look in her eyes. Seattle's home-brewed beverage was distilled from blight-contaminated water, and though it was safe to drink, it was rarely anyone's first choice. Or second. Occasionally, it came in third.

"Thank you, Mrs. O'Gunning," he said. Without so much as a nervous sniff, he lifted the mug and began to drink. Two or three swallows into the draft, he paused and cocked his head to the right. "It certainly has a *distinctive* flavor."

"You're too kind," she said, still not convinced she wasn't being humored. "I'm glad it suits you, and I suppose I'll leave you to it." Taking up her rag once more, she ambled to the far side of the bar and started cleaning anything that looked like it might hold still for a wipe-down, whether it needed it or not.

When Lucy was gone, Yaozu set the beer aside. He said to Andan Cly, "I need a ship."

"What are you moving? Big sap shipment going out?"

"On the contrary, I want to bring goods *into* the city." He gave the beer a hard stare and a moment of philosophical inquiry. He took another drink before continuing. "I've been reorganizing Minnericht's operations—a task which needed to be done *long* before his demise, might I add—and I've discovered that Seattle is running perilously low on the basic necessities. Between you and me, Captain, I'm not sure how much longer the city can remain habitable. Such as it is."

Intrigued, Andan Cly nodded. "So what are we talking about?" he asked. "Pitch and the like, for seals? Masks? Pump equipment?"

"All that and more. We need canvas, lumber, charcoal for filters, coal for the furnaces, and that's just the beginning." He sighed. "Last week we ran out of coffee, and I thought the chemists would start an uprising."

"It can be a lifesaver," Cly acknowledged. "Sharpens the mind, and the hands, too."

"That's what they tell me." Yaozu abandoned the beer glass, now more empty than full. "This will be an enormous undertaking, and I'm happy to finance it. Minnericht was an able tinkerer, but some of his works are not so stable or permanent as one might wish."

The ensuing silence in the saloon was so thick, you could spoon it into a bowl. Cly realized that everyone had been listening in, but he was still startled to feel the eyes of everyone present glued to himself and Yaozu.

In a normal speaking voice, intended to be overheard, his companion added, "For now, things are as safe as always, of course. But there's room for improvement, don't you think? Here—" He pulled out some coins, one of which appeared to be pure gold. Placing them on the counter, he added, "Let us take a walk. We can discuss your fee."

Andan Cly wasn't sure how he felt about taking a stroll with Minnericht's former right-hand man, but there was more to be said, and Yaozu was unwilling to say it in front of an audience. The captain couldn't blame him, so he shot Lucy a two-fingered wave and followed the Chinaman out the sealed door, into the dark, mulch-smelling spots beneath the city.

Both men carried gas masks for convenience or emergency, but the masks were not required in the unfinished basement wonderland. There, forests of brick created a dank labyrinth that unfolded with bends, kinks, and curves under the streets as far as the Seattle wall extended, in every direction. It would have been an impenetrable place, blacker than any night without a moon, except that lanterns were hung on hooks at the spots where corners crossed, and at the mouths of the tunnel entrances.

Yaozu unhooked a lantern and turned the knob to raise its wick. He offered the lamp to Andan Cly, who lifted it above his head. Courtesy of his prodigious height, the whole quarter was bathed in a yolk-yellow glow.

"This way, Captain. Toward the vaults. If we take the long way around, I can show you what I mean."

The corridor was wide and flanked by the exposed wet bricks that characterized so much of the underground's topography. Its floor had been packed, but it was not paved in any way; the surface was soggy from the atmospheric moisture—seeping rains above, drizzling down long-dead tree roots and filtering past the houses and businesses of the polluted city.

The air captain and the oriental man walked side by side, their feet struggling slightly with the mucky path. And as they pushed onward, back farther and deeper away from the buried saloon called Maynard's, Yaozu explained.

"I am fond of this particular passage. It sees little travel, partly because"—he gave his dirty boots a rueful gaze—"no one ever installed flagstones or slats. And up ahead, one of the walls has crumbled across the path."

"Then why do you like it so much?" Cly asked, doing his best to keep the lantern steady. But with every step, shadows danced and kicked to the sway of the light, up and down the moss-covered walls and along the black-mud footway.

"Because it very nearly connects our Chinatown to your vaults, and to the storage quarters back beneath Commercial Street."

Andan Cly said, "Huh. I can see why that would be useful. So you want to clean it out? Shore it up?"

"I do. However, two walls will need to come down in order to make the way passable by track and mining cart," he replied, referencing the handcarts and buckets by which some of the residents moved supplies and toted important items. "And above those walls, new sections of street-level buildings must be sealed against the blight."

"Gotcha."

"Also, if we expand and fix this passage, we could turn one of the offshoot basements into another pump room."

"Do we *need* another pump room? The air's plenty breathable down here."

"So far," Yaozu agreed, "but in the last few weeks, the workers have been keeping longer hours, and more coal is being used to power the pumps. My engineers suggest that it's a maintenance issue. Therefore, I wish to invest in maintenance procedures. I want to clean the pump tubes, all two to three hundred feet of them, one after another."

Cly made a low, worried whistle. "That sounds like a big job."

"Yes—a job that will require the pumps to be shut down for cleaning, one at a time. But before we can begin such a chore, supplementary pumps must be operational. Do you understand?"

"I do," he said thoughtfully. Then he stopped and said, "And this must be the brick pile."

Yaozu nodded. "You first? Since you're holding the light."

They scaled the bricks and slid down the other side. Cly dusted off his pants and observed, "The kind of thing you're talking about . . . big renovations, big improvements . . . is going to take time. And money."

"Money we have, and time, too—though less of the latter than the former."

The path split before them, and Yaozu urged Andan Cly down the right fork.

"How much time?"

"Impossible to say. The tubes and pumps have held for years, and might hold for years to come. Or they might not."

"What about those engineers you mentioned?" Cly asked. "Can they give you a better idea?"

"They're trying, but they are new to the city and still learning the finer points of its workings. I have recruited them with *generous* paychecks. And I am trusting your confidence on this matter when I tell you—" He paused and looked up into the giant's face. "—I'm burning through Minnericht's coffers at a rather alarming rate. He left a fortune, of course. He hoarded it like a dragon, underneath King Street Station. But it is *costing* a fortune to keep this place livable."

The captain asked, "Then why are you going to all this trouble? Does the sap really make that much money, to make it all worth this?"

A thin, slow smile spread across Yaozu's face, and it was not entirely pleasant. "Oh, *yes*. And the potential for more money still is *staggering*. The gas—this punishing, brutal substance that killed the city above us—it offers us the means to save it. With better processing and more efficient means of survival underground, these doornails"—he used the white men's slang for the underground citizens—"could make more money than Californians have ever dug out of their rocks."

"And you."

"Me?"

"You stand to make a bundle, too, don't you?"

"Absolutely. But as I was sometimes forced to wonder, with regards to my former . . . employer, what does it profit a man to be wealthy, but to live in the midst of such . . ." He hunted for a word, and settled on one. "Instability? It was obscene to me, how much he could have done for this place—and how little interest he showed in doing so."

"So why don't you make your money and leave? With what's left of Minnericht's stash, you could live like a king outside these walls. Everybody knows it. Everybody wonders."

"Everybody knows it?" Yaozu asked, his understated smile fixed in place. "I wonder what else everybody knows." He gazed down the pathway and once more struck out for it. "But to answer your question, I stay here because I want to. I like this settlement where a man like me, or like you"—he gestured one long hand toward Cly's chest—"can live undisturbed by others."

"But *I* don't live here."

"You could if you wished; you'd fit right in. Perhaps," he said, watching Cly duck to dodge a low-hanging support beam, "less so in the literal sense. I've often thought it must be strange to be a man of your size. Like Gulliver in Lilliput, at times."

Cly was familiar with the tale, and Yaozu wasn't the first to make that comparison. The captain shrugged as he ducked another beam. "I've been big my whole life. You get used to it. I've known a few dwarfs—a couple of them pirates, and damn fine ones—and I've wondered the same thing about them. I expect it's not so different, living in a world where nothing is the right size."

Yaozu murmured, "I know what you mean."

"There's nothing strange about your size," Cly observed.

"Not my *size*, no. But outside these walls, I could be treated as a monster, evicted from my home, my property seized and my family sent away. It happens all the time in Portland, you know. Strange persons such as ourselves, Captain Cly . . . we may be very different from one another, but we recognize a kinship all the same."

In silence they traversed another few blocks, and all the while, Cly considered this. Finally he said, "I suppose that answers my question well enough."

"Speaking of fitting in . . . you've spent a good deal more time in the underground than before these last few months."

Cly flushed, and even the rattling lantern couldn't hide the creeping color. "I'm not . . . Well. Maybe a *little* more."

"You protest too much, Captain. And look, here we are at the cross-paths before the vaults."

It was true. Their conversation had brought them all the way to the edge of a set of living quarters, the entrance to which had once been a great bank vault with a reinforced door in a reinforced room.

Here, where people came and went more frequently, the labyrinth opened and the streets were packed cleaner, lined with planks or stepping stones held aloft from the perpetually moist floor. More lanterns hung, dimmed, from the end of every wall, and containers of fuel were stationed beneath them, left ready for any passers-through who might require them. Painted signs were affixed to walls or mounted to posts between the corners where mine-cart tracks split the right-of-way. These weathered rectangles held messages in hand-written black lettering and clearly marked arrows.

UNION STREET, THIS WAY; SENECA STREET, OVER HERE; COMMERCIAL AVENUE, TO YOUR RIGHT.

"So," Yaozu said, clapping his hands together. "My appeal for your services."

"Yeah, that," Cly said. "Sure, I'll make your supply run. I'll need some details, and a list, and a budget—"

"Absolutely. I'll draw up all of these things, and we'll discuss your rate."

"Oh, that's easy. I ask—"

"Whatever it is, I'll double it. I'll need you back by the end of next month, and I'll need my instructions followed to the letter. I'm fully prepared to pay for speed and quality service."

"That's good, that you're giving me a few weeks. Because I've been thinking . . ."

"Yes?"

"About making a trip to New Orleans."

"When?"

"Soon. Real soon."

"That's . . . quite a ways off, for a jaunt. May I ask why you've chosen such a destination?"

"An old friend wants me to run an easy job, down there on the Gulf. It wouldn't interfere with anything you're asking—not at all— and New Orleans has everything you're looking for."

"And then some, I'd bet."

"You'd bet right," Cly said. He was surprised to hear himself selling the idea, but he sold it anyway. "It's huge, and with all those Texians on the premises, you can bet I'll find plenty of good industrial-quality wares. They've got the best machine shops on the continent."

"I've heard as much," Yaozu said, considering the possibilities. "I wouldn't have thought it'd be worth the trouble, to send you so far away. But if you're already going . . . it might work out well for us both. Two of my engineers are Texians, or they *were*. They've been known to complain about things I can't provide them—instruments and tools they wish they had, or equipment they can't necessarily find on the West Coast."

Cly said, "Ask them what they want. I'll get it for them. I'll kill two birds with one stone, Yaozu—yours and mine."

"And you'll collect two flight fees for a single trip."

"There's that, yes," the captain admitted, counting up the coins in his head. Between what Josephine was offering and Yaozu's bold statement that he'd double the usual asking price . . . there was enough money in the trip to make major plans.

Life-changing plans. Settling-down plans.

The Chinaman contemplated the pros and cons, staring alternately into space and into the captain's eyes. After a few moments of deliberation, he declared, "I like the sound of it! I'll speak with my engineers, and you and I shall confer again shortly."

With that, he made a short, dipping bow and excused himself down the far passage to the right. He disappeared on the other side of a sign that said KING STREET. Before long, even his shadow and footsteps were lost to the buried city.

Captain Cly stood in the moldering chamber, chewing over the conversation, replaying it in his head—trying to figure out how much to believe, and how much to accept regardless of whether it was true or not.

Yaozu had been an unknown quantity back in the bad old days, suspicious for the obvious fact that he kept so close to a capricious madman. Even his fellow Chinamen didn't trust him, for they had suffered too much at Minnericht's hands. And Angeline, last surviving royalty of Chief Seattle's reign, had made concerted efforts to kill him. Under the best of circumstances, it would have been difficult for the primarily white, working-class doornails to warm up to the oriental man with the educated voice and a millionaire's manners. And now that he was running the empire that remained— whether it was by default, ambition, or some other power mechanism yet undetermined—the enigma of his presence was both a blessing and a curse.

On the one hand, he managed an operation that peddled poison to willing takers. On the other, he'd done an admirable job of holding the underground together while leaving the doornails in peace. Therefore, complaining was kept to a superstitious minimum, as if Yaozu might change his mind or vanish, only to be replaced with someone worse if too much ill were spoken of him.

"Strange persons such as ourselves," Cly recalled out loud.

He resolved to await the list with an open mind and an open pocket, and he approached the great vault door.

From the outside, it looked like the portal of an enormous bank— which it had been, once upon a time. The spinning lock jutted like the spokes of a wheel, and though the combination to this lock had been long-since lost or forgotten, it had been rigged to open to a different key. Now, when a visitor wished to come inside, all he had to do was pull a lever hidden beneath the panel. Unless the door had been barricaded from within, it would open with a tug.

Cly lifted the panel and pulled the lever with its rubber grip and rusting hinge. With a creak and a low moan, the heavy door swung out, and Cly descended the uneven steps down into Briar's living quarters in a basement beneath a basement, two cool, secure stories deep underground.

 *Three*

Night at the Café du Monde was illuminated with strings of hanging lanterns anchored to gas lamps on pillars; candles in jars made the small tables bright enough for beignets and coffee blended with chicory root. These small bubbles of light pocked the darkness and gave the impression of privacy in public, a place where people might be seen, but they might not be observed. It was never quiet, always bustling with the kitchen fryers and workers calling back and forth, taking and filling orders. The café always hummed with the noise from the river off to one side, and the street on the other—ships' horns and paddle wheels, horse carts and singing, drunken partiers, the patrols and bickering of soldiers, and the music of a dozen bands playing for their supper within half as many blocks.

Josephine Early was careful to keep the lace from her gloves away from the candles, and the napkin in her lap was covered in powdered sugar—but not a drip of coffee. She was joined by Marylin Quantrill and Ruthie Doniker, both of whom nibbled and sipped along with her. Together they chatted about virtually nothing, and at length, until the four slowly sobering Texians at the table beside them finally rallied and staggered back to their barracks.

Marylin raised the white mug to her lips, blew at the steamy mists of the still-warm beverage, and said, "We aren't meeting much luck at the airyard, ma'am. Lots of fellows are interested in us, but only for the usual reasons."

"And we aren't finding useful foreigners, either." Ruthie, darker and by some accounts prettier, sighed and discreetly adjusted her bodice. She was thin as a waterbird, and twice as graceful. "Nothing but Rebels and Texians. And a very pretty Spaniard, but he wasn't a pilot. Perhaps a new customer, though?" She lifted her mug and an eyebrow at the same time, and hid her smile behind her coffee.

"A new one for you?" Josephine asked. "Be careful, love."

"A new one for me, maybe. He is very beautiful, and the Spanish . . . they are almost as easy as the French in these things."

Marylin asked, "What about you, ma'am? Have you found anyone to fly for us?"

Josephine wrapped both hands around her drink, even though the night was almost hot and the beverage's steam might've been too much for a woman who wasn't accustomed to it. "I sent off a telegram to a man who might help us, if he's willing to make the journey."

"For you? I cannot imagine a man would say no," Ruthie insisted.

"Hainey said no."

"But he had, how would you say? *Extenuating circumstances.*" Ruthie's French was stronger than her English, but she practiced at every opportunity, working to expand her vocabulary. She said *extenuating* with the accents in all the wrong places. She was a voracious reader who had seen the word spelled, but never heard it spoken.

Josephine corrected the pronunciation with context, rather than rebuke. "This other pilot comes with extenuating circumstances of his own. He's terribly far away, for one thing. And for another, I suspect he does not wish to see me."

"Why?" Marylin frowned.

"We haven't spoken in many years." That was all she offered. "It doesn't matter. We need a pilot, and he's a good one. If he'll come, we'll be lucky to have him. But it's only been a few days, and the telegram had quite a distance to travel. I had to send it through Mr.

Hainey, and wait for the message to reach the Washington Territory."

"Washington?" Marylin gasped. "That's practically the other side of the world!"

"Practically, yes. Realistically, it's only two or three thousand miles."

Ruthie's eyes narrowed with cunning, and a hint of mirth. "He must have a very impressive ship."

"Pirates usually *do* have good equipment, and last I knew of him, that was how he earned his living. And I know you don't like pirates," she cut off Marylin before the protest could be mounted, "but we can trust Cly if we have to."

To return to their previous conversation, Marylin asked, "Is he *perfect*?"

Josephine considered the question. "No, he isn't perfect. He's just about the biggest man you'll ever lay eyes on—if he hadn't gone into raiding, he could've had a career in a circus, easy as you please. He could've been the world's most amazing strong man."

Ruthie noted, "A very big man would not be good. The craft we need him to pilot . . . it was not made with a giant in mind."

"No, but he'll fit. He was always good at working around his size, and unless he's collected sufficient money to custom-build his own ship, I expect he's still flying in cramped quarters today."

Marylin pondered aloud, suddenly sounding more optimistic. "You said he's from Washington, ma'am. He's not a Rebel or a Texian, but not a Yankee either—so the airyard will let him come and go, and that's something."

"Furthermore, Cly never cared about the war, and he's friends with Hainey, so he isn't in a rush to kidnap runaway negroes home to the Rebs, not even for the money they offer these days."

After another sip, Ruthie said, "Good to know he's not *that* kind of pirate."

"I wouldn't employ *that* kind of pirate. It's a goddamn ridiculous thing, too," the madam complained, picking at the edge of a beignet.

"Except for Alabama and Mississippi, there's no difference between free coloreds and the rest anymore. It's nothing but spiteful, Georgia putting up bounties and insisting on their return."

"But, ma'am, wasn't Hainey one of the Macon Madmen?"

"Oh, even if Hainey weren't a bona fide crook, they'd want him back regardless. Nothing but spite," she repeated. "I just can't abide it. Anyway, Captain Cly isn't that sort."

"I hope he decides *soon*. It'd take him a week just to get here, if he's that far away—and if his ship is half as good as we could hope. And how much longer until you-know-who wants his report?" Ruthie meant Major Daniel Alcock, who intended to make a final decision on the *Ganymede* project within the next weeks.

"End of the month. I could probably beg a few extra days through the start of May, but I'd rather not have to. It'd look desperate."

Softly, Marylin asked, "Ma'am, are we desperate yet?"

Josephine bought herself a few seconds by taking a bite of beignet and savoring its fluffy sweetness. She washed it down with coffee and replied, "No. Not yet. But if Cly doesn't respond within the week, I'll have to assume he isn't coming—and *then* we'll be desperate."

She opened her mouth to add something, but closed it again when she spied two men walking toward the café. They were speaking in low tones, their heads too close together for either of them to be up to any good, and they both wore the brown cotton "summer" uniform of the Republic of Texas.

"Ma'am?"

"Don't look now," she murmured. "I mean it—*don't look*."

"Who is it?" Ruthie wanted to know. She lifted her mug and pretended to drink—while she only whispered from behind it.

Josephine did the same. "I'll be damned if it's not Colonel Betters and Lieutenant Cardiff."

Not only were they two of the highest-ranking Texians stationed in the city, but Lieutenant Cardiff was one of the investigators leading the search for the *Ganymede*. It was an open secret. Any

Union spy or sympathizer knew about Cardiff and his wheedling into the affair of the "missing" craft. His name had become a watchword for the guerrillas in the bayou and out at the lake. They knew he was looking, and knew he was coming.

For the time being, all they could do was hide from him.

The look on Marylin's face said she was exerting superhuman willpower to keep from turning around. "What are they doing?" she asked.

"Conspiring."

Ruthie said, "They are going the wrong direction, yes? Barracks are back the other way."

"Hush." Josephine lowered her eyes and leaned forward to touch Ruthie's arm. She laughed lightly, and the other ladies joined in for the sake of show. Still wearing her pretend smile, she said in an ordinary voice—in case anyone should overhear them after all— "Perhaps you two had better run home without me. I have some business to attend to before I settle in for the night."

"Ma'am, are you sure?"

"Oh, yes. Besides, we left Hazel in charge. She does all right when things are slow, but she'll want your help if business picks up."

Marylin and Ruthie understood, but they didn't like it. Marylin fretted with her coffee mug and whispered, "But, ma'am, they're headed—" She could only guess, since she was forbidden to turn and see for herself. But they weren't coming toward her, so they must be walking away, in the other direction. "—down to the river, I think."

"Then that's where I'm going, too. Chins up, ladies." She slipped her hand down to her left thigh and patted a bulge that no one could see. "Little Russia and I will be just fine."

She rose from her seat and placed her half-empty mug on the table, then folded her napkin and put it beside her plate. Nodding coolly at her companions, she set out in the wake of the two Texian officers, who had now passed beyond her sight . . . but Marylin was right. Josephine knew where they were going. There was nowhere else to go, not if they'd taken that turn she'd seen—down the steps and away from the city lights.

Down to the river.

Josephine always made a point to wear quiet shoes. Even if she sported the most fashionable boots in the whole city, she'd glue wool felt to the bottoms and replace it as needed. It was a small precaution, but never had it served her quite so well as when she stepped along the damp-swollen stairs and along planked walkways that flanked the river's banks between the piers.

Her dress rustled as a matter of course, but it was the sort of sound that was easily lost in the Quarter, beside the water most especially. The noise of her skirts blended seamlessly into the soft rushing of the Old Man as he worked his way to the Gulf. Her passage was masked by the calls and wings of night birds, and the dipping paddles of rum-runners coming in for the night, unwilling to crank the diesel engines on their small, flat crafts. It was lost in the sound of low, loose waves lapping up against pilings and the broad sides of the larger boats that were moored along the way.

She followed the Texians' footsteps and the grumbling trail of their conversation—too distant to be heard with any clarity—down along the rickety wharves and alongside warehouses that no one examined too closely—not even the Republicans, unless they had strict orders to do so. And even then, only in the daytime.

This was a dangerous place, dangerous to any given group of men—armed and strong and unencumbered by corsetry or ankle-length skirts. No one knew this better than Josephine, and no one liked it less.

As the city glow was eaten by distance, and the banks, and the taller buildings that cast devious shadows thicker than ink, the only light to be seen bounced off the river in splintered fragments and skinny ribbons. It sparkled along the currents, cast by the lights on mercantile ships and riverboats chugging through the night, or sometimes by a quickly shuttered lantern or a smattering of torches left lit but fading at the edges of civilization.

This gray space between the city and the river . . . it was dying, and it was not a place to be visited frivolously. But not for fear of the rum-runners, smugglers, and other assorted criminal fiends. Even the worst of that motley lot shuddered and moved carefully along this borderland.

No, the banks were avoided for fear of something else.

Josephine wasn't sure how long she'd been on the Texians' trail, or how far she'd walked in silence. She must be coming up on Rue Canal soon; it must be there up ahead, over the nebulous edge where the city was so impossibly far away and out of reach. Even the music from the saloons, lounges, and gentlemen's clubs was muffled here, or snuffed out altogether. Stray notes drifted in pairs and clusters, their tunes lost to the thick, wet air and the increasing distance.

Gradually, by carefully conducted shuffles and short, brave sprints, Josephine came near enough to catch their words. She could not see their faces, and for that matter, she could not tell them apart. She watched them in glimpses, around the side of a stack of crates stuffed with straw and heaven knew what else.

She shivered despite the warmth, pressing her back against the crates as firmly as she dared, as if she could will herself closer than the crates would allow. The stays of her corsetry jabbed into her hips, and her bosoms were thrust uncomfortably high as she compressed herself as tightly as her clothing would allow.

At first the conversation was idle office gossip, complaints about a stenographer, and then it moved on to concerns about money, troops, and supplies. Finally they both paused, like men who had been avoiding a topic and were now forced to confront it.

"I don't like it out here, especially since I don't know what we're doing—so why don't you help me out and tell me what's going on?"

"I'm sorry to lead you so far out into the boonies, sir, but I have my reasons. I can't trust the barracks, or the office on the Square. We're being watched, sir," the speaker announced. Josephine's heart nearly stopped.

It calmed again when she heard, "Of *course* you're being

watched—we're all of us being watched, all the goddamn time. It comes with the territory." This man—Colonel Allastair Betters, Josephine gathered—made an impatient noise and crossed his arms. "Listen, son. I realize the locals are none too forthcoming, but you've *got* to scare up some results. General Dwyer knows it's out there. Shit, we *all* know it's out there, in the water someplace. I don't understand why you're having so much trouble getting your hands on it!"

"Sir, do you have any idea how much *water* they've got around here? That's why I'm bringing you down here, because look—look at this old wharf. You can see, can't you? Somebody's been here recently, and moving something real big. And I think I know what it was."

"I can't see any indication of anything except mud, dust, and a few fornicating turtles."

Seconds later, a brilliant flare lit up the wharf—so bright that it felt like an explosion, but it was only the striking of a lamp. Josephine turned away, deeper into the shadow, and hoped that she vanished. She also thanked her lucky stars she was wearing a dark blue dress, which, except for its cream trim, may as well have been black, so long as she stayed out of the light.

"Jesus Christ, my eyes!"

"Sorry, sir. But it's important that you see this. They're doing something, on these pilings—on this dock. Look at the boards, sir. They're scraped up all to hell, and freshly so. You can see, it looks like a huge team of men has been stomping all over the place."

Josephine dared another peek around the corner and saw the two men huddled over a long drag-mark that did in fact look very recent. A few of the weaker slats had splintered and now jutted up, making for a truly treacherous landscape, and others were merely scuffed clean of the mildew, rot, and the discoloration of a century.

"All right, all right," said Colonel Betters. "I do see about a thousand footprints. It looks like a bunch of men have been running around, back and forth. What makes you think it's tied to one of the Hunleys?"

"Sir, I think we've had it all wrong. I think they've already got it on the move—that they've unscuttled it, fixed it, and they're sending it down the river."

This was news to Josephine, insomuch as it wasn't true—but she didn't mind the investigator being so very wrong. The farther off-track he could be drawn, the better.

The colonel said, "Hm. I don't know about that. This is a mess, but is it a mess that says a military watercraft has been man-hauled around? We know the scuttled Hunley holds nine men. Would something that big and heavy fit up here? Wouldn't this whole wharf just come folding right down? Hell, Cardiff, this thing's so fragile, I'm half-afraid to stand here and bounce on my toes after a steak supper."

"Sir, you're right. And no, I don't think this set of matchsticks would hold a Hunley . . . not all in one piece. I think they've disassembled it. They're moving it in parts. They're sneaking it off, bit by bit, onto barges. Dozens of flat-bottoms go by every day. We could never search every craft that comes through the delta. It just isn't possible; we don't have the people. And these bayou boys, they've got friends in Barataria. They could buy help, if they needed it."

From her spot behind the crates, Josephine considered their incorrect theory.

It wasn't a half-bad idea, and just this once she was glad that her brother's crew had been so slow moving the craft. If it'd gone any quicker, they might've disassembled it—and then what? Then the Texians would be on to them. Still, it was cold comfort.

The Union had said outright that they wouldn't spare extra money on a recovery mission until it could be demonstrated that the Ganymede actually *worked*. And worked without killing anyone inside it.

To date, such a demonstration had not been achievable, not on

56 ....

any serious scale. The controls were a mystery to every sailor the guerrillas had brought aboard, and the bayou engineers had only just discovered how to rig up makeshift ventilation pumps. No one had died on board since the ventilation had been installed, so progress was being made. It just wasn't progress enough.

Not yet.

Deep down, Josephine knew it was possible to move the *Ganymede,* and move it safely. She believed it with all her heart—she'd seen the elegant schematics left over from the Confederate Hunley's last, best efforts before he'd drowned in an earlier prototype. She'd held the secret rolled-up blueprints in her hands and read all about the machine's destructive capacity, as laid out by its now-dead creator.

And she was confident to the point of obsession that if the *Ganymede* could be given to the Federal government, and reproduced, and brought into the war . . . then even Texas would back away, and at last the Rebs could be choked into surrender.

Much earlier in the war, the Anaconda Plan—an attempt to blockade the supplies to the whole southeast—had failed. But then, it'd been tried only with ordinary warships. Imagine how much more effective it could have been—and might be again!—if the blockade were undertaken with craft that swam below the water's surface. Just consider the possibilities of such extraordinary machines, hidden and powerful, able to destroy ships from the Gulf or the Atlantic without having ever been seen.

It could end the war. Maybe the simple *threat* of it could do so. How much more could the Rebels really stand, anyway? Any idiot could see they were living on the cusp of what was sustainable; any fool could pick up a newspaper and understand in seconds that this couldn't go on much longer.

Of course, everyone had been saying so for years.

"Tell me, then. What does this mean? How do we respond, in case you're right?"

"First, I think we should clear out the bayous. Make a huge

push—just wipe those bastards out of the wetlands for good. We'll round up a few, twist some thumbs, and find out what they've done with the ship. Maybe if we're lucky, they haven't finished moving it off yet."

After a pause, the colonel asked, "The damn thing failed, and failed again. Do you think the Union really wants it?"

"Mr. Hunley was a genius, sir, and so were the fellows who took up his work after he died. If the blues think they can start up that machine, they'll pay for it, and pay top dollar. If they aren't funding the operation already."

"We may as well assume they are. Those swamp rats, they don't have the money or resources to make such a stink on their own. Out there in the sopping wet middle of noplace, there's not even any-thing worth stealing. *Someone's* keeping them in guns and ammo."

"Sir, I—"

"Wait. Hush."

"Sir, what—?"

"*Hush,* I said." He dropped his voice so low that Josephine could scarcely make out the words. "Do you hear that?"

The lieutenant whispered back. "Hear what, sir? . . . Oh. I think . . ."

"What is it?"

"Sir, I'm sure it's nothing."

Josephine Early wasn't sure. She heard it, too, very faintly—it was coming from the far side of the men, from below the wharf, nearer the water. Crouching down, she reached for the Schofield under her skirt and retrieved it from the heavy-duty garter where it had been fastened. She removed her gloves and stuffed them into her pocket, then grasped the gun carefully, readying it, adjusting her grip.

"It sounds like . . . like someone having a hard time breathing."

"Yes, sir, something like that. Where's it coming from?"

"There . . . no. Over there. Or maybe over *there*." He indicated several directions, none of them certain.

The woman behind the crates closed her eyes, in case it'd help her listen harder. She concentrated and breathed as shallowly as she could—until the pounding of her heart was nearly as loud as the distant wheezing. Her hips and lower belly ached against her foundation undergarments from maintaining such a cramped posture, and her head was beginning to throb.

"Cardiff, I don't like this."

"Me either, sir. Maybe we should be on our way."

The colonel wasn't quick to move, but he *was* quick to reach into the gun holster he wore hanging off his shoulders. Josephine couldn't see what he carried, probably a Colt service revolver—something loud and high caliber, being a Texian and a man of authority. Very likely, it was the kind of gun that could take somebody's head off in a pinch.

Against all reason, she was glad to see he had it. He was going to need it, but not to defend himself against any hidden Union spies like herself, crouching behind crates. She was sickeningly confident of that much. She knew it from the rushing sound of broken breaths being dragged in and out through rotted throats. She knew because the sound was coming from everywhere and nowhere at once, drawing closer, coming toward the lantern light on the dead-end wharf.

The lieutenant drew a handgun as well, more nervously than the colonel. He instinctively retreated until his back was nearly pressed against the commanding officer's—and he held the lantern high, throwing the light as far as he could, hoping to get a glimpse of whatever was approaching from the darkness.

Josephine didn't want to see it, but she needed to.

This had all been a terrible idea—on everyone's part, and at least the colonel ought to have known better. Maybe he *had* known better, but he was cocky with his guns and his rank; maybe the lieutenant had been the ignorant one, seeing the place during the day when the sun had chased off the worst of the shadows.

If only they'd left the light off. If only they'd kept their voices down.

Every muscle in Josephine's body was tighter than a violin string. She watched around the corner, crouched on one knee, gun held up at the ready, almost next to her face as if she were praying. She considered running, back out the way they'd come—but no, they'd see her, or hear her. They'd open fire, not knowing she wasn't the most dangerous thing on the wharf, and not knowing she only meant to escape.

Besides.

She jerked her head away from the corner and listened.

Coming down the walkway, up from the river in staggering, shambling steps that didn't keep time like an ordinary walker. . . .

Josephine retreated away from the crate's edge, shrinking herself to the fullest extent possible, down at the bottom edge where the angle was sharpest and the shadow was deepest.

It wouldn't help. They didn't have to see her to know she was there.

The ragged, sickly gasps grew nearer. Josephine tried to sort them out—to determine how many were coming. She detected three on the far side of the Texians, who were sweating with fear; she was sure of two more, from farther back on the wharf; and one more . . . no, two more coming up the back way, cutting off the only obvious means of retreat.

"Sir, we should go!"

"Put out that light, you idiot."

"We won't be able to see!"

"What'd you walk me into, Cardiff?" The colonel's voice was rising, not from panic, Josephine didn't think. She'd give him credit there—he was holding steady, feet planted and firearm level. Texians were repugnant, problematic, occupying, Confederate-allied bastards down to the very last man . . . but she couldn't accuse them of being cowards.

"Sir, we should be quiet—"

"Turn it out!" he ordered. "I've heard about what goes on here, I've heard what people say."

"People say a lot of things, sir."

Lieutenant Cardiff struggled to hold his gun and turn down the lamp without dropping it, a prospect that flooded the watching woman with horror. What a thought, burning alive or being eaten alive—a choice no one should have to make.

His voice quivering, the lieutenant said, "So many people have made reports. Word from Austin says they're sending a specialist—some Ranger with an interest in strange . . . *things.*"

Josephine began to calculate how far she was from the wharf, and if she could run past the men without them shooting her, and if she could swim in what she was wearing—if she made it over the side of the walkway and into the Mississippi where there were snakes, to be sure; and alligators, maybe; and bad men up to bad things, but none of it was as awful as what was coming.

"Sir, there are stories," the lieutenant gulped. "But they're only *stories*—goddamn locals, they think we ought to be afraid."

"Goddamn locals aren't always out to snow you, son. I don't know about you, but I'm *plenty* afraid right now."

Out of the darkness, up the walk that led to the wharf, something rose out from the murky night. It moved more slowly than a person should, and its posture suggested that something was broken, deep inside. When it stepped, it stepped unevenly, and with effort. Harder and faster the loud, harsh breathing came; for when it spied the Texians—or possibly Josephine, who was nearer to the thing and in its direct line of sight—its efforts rose. It let out a loud, hard cry, a noise that shredded the wharf and summoned more of its kind.

Faster it approached, one foot in front of the other, gracelessly, but with a purpose. Now it saw fresh meat and loped ever faster toward it—toward Josephine, who held out her gun but held her fire.

If she squeezed the trigger, the Texians would know she'd been there hiding, listening. If the hideous man-shaped thing reached her, it wouldn't make a difference anyway—she'd be dead or worse by dawn. She held off as long as she could, waiting until the last moment . . . until the feeble moonlight sparked off the thing's wet mouth and she could've almost counted its teeth.

One shot, two shots—both of them blasted like cannon fire in such a close space.

But not from Josephine's gun.

The Texians had seen the incoming monster just in time, and it was their fire that took the thing down, and took it to pieces. Its head split in two, and the top half landed at Josephine's feet. Its quivering torso went left, right, and toppled backwards to lie still upon the wharf's edge.

She clapped a hand over her mouth and fought for composure.

Another one was coming. She wouldn't be so fortunate twice in a row. She lifted the gun again and waited. The sloughing scrape of dead feet, the horrible rhythm of dead lungs.

More of them, incoming.

The first brute had only located and declared the prey. The rest would come in for the kill.

"Dear God!" the colonel barked. He opened fire again, two more shots that exploded and left the madam's ears humming. The bullets landed with squishy thumps, the sound of arrows hitting melons, but Josephine didn't dare take her eyes off the path from whence she'd come—not unless she wanted the creatures to come groaning up behind her. She braced her back against the crates and locked her elbows, holding the gun out and facing the wood plank path.

The colonel demanded, "What are they?" and now his voice was cracking, losing the battle-hardened calm that had served him well so far. "What are those things?"

"They aren't real; they aren't real. *This isn't real,*" the lieutenant babbled.

A shot went wild and clipped the edge of the crate, casting splinters into Josephine's hair and up against her face—where one left a brief, hot sting.

"It isn't true!" Cardiff was shouting now, and firing again; she was almost certain the wilder shots were his. Another one, two, three blasts.

How many guns did the men have between them? How many shots?

Josephine cursed herself for not observing them better. She should've noticed, should've counted. Nothing to be done for it now.

"Pull yourself together, man!" the colonel ordered. Two more shots landed in something dense and wet. Then he tried a different tactic, addressing the incoming creatures directly. "Who are you? What do you want?" But it was a desperate, foolish thing, and the officer sensed it immediately.

"Cardiff," he called. "What are these things?"

Three more shots rang out, and Josephine wished to God she could cover her ears, shut them out, give herself a moment of quiet so she could listen again, and better pinpoint the things that were to come.

Not a chance. Two more shots, and then the fall of something heavy that clattered and rolled. A gun, discarded as empty. Texians always went armed, and surely two officers like these would have backup, or so she told herself as she stared with all her might— unblinking, lest she miss a crucial moment—and watched for more monsters, arriving up the back way.

They were coming right for her. She knew it, even though her whole head was buzzing from the percussion of the gunshots so nearby.

Two more uneven shapes, ambling up the walkway.

Tightening her grip, readying her aim, she gave up on hiding from the Texians, who had problems of their own. Several more shots—she'd lost count how many—and the firing ceased amid a hail of rapid-fire swearing and struggling.

"Goddammit! What are these—get away from me! Get it off me!"

"Oh God! Oh God!"

"What are they—what are they?" the colonel continued to shout.

A hail of muffled blows and the rending of fabric. A scream from the lieutenant. A bellow from the colonel. The pounding slugs of something heavy—a gun in someone's fist?—bludgeoning strikes in the midst of what sounded like a crowd but might be as few as three or four.

It didn't take many of them.

And here came two more.

Every shot had to count. Josephine took a deep breath. If the Texians were still alive behind her, it wouldn't matter if they heard her now. She rose to her feet in a leap that was made melodic by the lift and swish of her skirts and the cracking shift of her undergarment stays snapping back to attention, and as the first newcomer came over the slight rise and stepped onto the planks, she blew off its face with a single shot.

A second one was right behind it. She stopped that one, too— but her mark was off, a few inches too low, and the bullet tore a hole in the thing's throat. It tumbled to its knees but started to crawl. Josephine took a brief running start and then kicked its head with all her weight and strength—sending the bulbous, foul-smelling skull flying off into the river, where it landed with a splash.

Was that all of them?

She didn't *see* any more, but seeing wasn't easy, and she was all but shooting blind. Whirling around to check the state of the Texians, she saw there was nothing to be done for them, even if she'd been inclined to. She didn't mind two fewer Republicans in her city, not for a second, and if those two had known what she was up to, she'd have been thrown in jail or shot. She had no illusions about their shared humanity, or any fairy tales of cooperation to warm her.

The lieutenant was down and dying, writhing or perhaps only being tugged this way and that by the two monsters that jerked on his limbs, biting them, tearing off hunks of flesh—anything they could fit in their mouths.

The colonel was sitting upright, swinging with his gun, clapping

a third one in the face while he held a fourth at bay with his hand.
It wasn't working. Number four ducked its head and tried to bite
the colonel's neck. Colonel Betters was not a young man, and his
strength was failing. Any minute would be his last.

His eyes met Josephine's. He didn't say anything; he only looked
at her there, holding the gun. She aimed it at him. He nodded, understanding in some final flash of insight that this was the last favor
he was ever going to get—and it was coming from a woman who
ordinarily wouldn't spit on him if he was on fire. But this was not a
fire.

She pulled the trigger.

The colonel stopped fighting. His head slumped to his chest,
and now the two ragged creatures met no resistance. They dived
mouth-first into his carcass, moaning their enthusiasm even as one
raised its head and wailed a shaky, raspy sound . . . a call that was
returned from several sides.

"Shit," Josephine swore.

The howler scrambled to its knees and scuttled toward her and
she stopped it with a bullet between the eyes, its body snapping
backwards and falling across the colonel's knees. Its fellow monsters,
no longer content to chew on the remains of the Texians, also rose
from their gorging positions and reached out for the woman, who
might have the bullets to shoot her way past them, or then again, she
might not.

One, two.

She hit one in the temple and it spun away, rotating like a dancer
until it tripped and fell off the wharf. It thrashed in the water and
then it didn't, sinking or merely stopping—Josephine couldn't see
that far, and was distracted by the creature she'd missed with her
second shot. She fired another and caught it low in the neck. The
bullet was so powerful, it blew the thing back away from her—if it
didn't send it down for good.

Behind her, from the way she'd come as she'd followed the
Texians to their doom, she could hear more cries, more wheezing

moans, more uneven footsteps. More of the famished, snarling, semi-dead creatures.

Her heart in her throat, she squeezed off another round and took an ear and a huge chunk of brain from the skull of the next attacker.

But she couldn't stay there, hemmed in with the wharf stretching out over the water one way and a row of shipping crates to her left; higher than she could expect to climb in broad daylight and without the restrictions of her clothing. Back along the planked walkway two, maybe three more *things* were coming—and in front of her, the edge of the pier let out onto the manufacturing row, now mostly abandoned.

She heard the rumblings of more trouble from that way, but she chose it in an instant. It was the only direction where she might be able to find an open spot and run. If she could lose them in the row, or barricade herself inside one of the old factories, she might have a chance.

No going back.

No going out to the water—she could throw herself into the waves and hope the things chasing her couldn't swim, but she'd likely drown in what she was wearing, and the river's currents were riptide strong, killing hardier souls than her own every day.

A last resort, then.

She'd leave it for that—only if everything else failed.

Ducking down, she grabbed the lieutenant's lantern and ran, her felt-softened feet making barely the lightest hiss with each footfall. The lantern wasn't broken, and that was good. It hadn't even been turned down all the way—she wouldn't need a match to move it, she'd only have to raise the wick and pray there was oil enough to keep it bright.

But not yet.

Not while they were rallying, and homing in. Not until she had so much distance between them that she could afford the luxury of sight.

To her left and right reared cliffs of freight, or the wooden boxes that once contained it. In places, the passage narrowed to barely a doorway's width, but she shoved forward, thinking she might have a bullet or two remaining. She was too distracted to estimate, and estimating wouldn't do her any good. Either she had more ammunition or she didn't.

She zigzagged through the maze and into an open stretch with muddy floors or no floors at all. Tripping, then recovering, she saw three lumbering shadows approaching from behind and to her left—and one more closing in from directly ahead.

To her right, at the far end of a wide pier, squatted an old oyster-shucking facility that had long since moved to a brighter part of town. It was partially boarded and none too inviting, but any port in a storm, Josephine figured. She was on the verge of dashing toward it when some new presence caught her eye, and she hesitated.

A small, still silhouette stood near the wharf's edge, outlined against a sky-high stack of folded nets that no one had used in half a century.

"Settle down, child. Give me some light," the silhouette said.

Stunned, Josephine stood there. From two sides, then three sides, the creatures came closer.

"Child, you *heard* me. Raise the lamp."

She recognized the voice, which in no way made the speaker's appearance less stunning. Josephine said, "Ma'am?" and then hastily, as if she'd only just remembered she was holding the thing, lifted up the lantern and turned the crank to raise the wick. She did this in a rush, rolling the small metal knob and making the glass-cased lantern into a brilliant beacon in less than a second.

It was counter to all sense. The creatures could see her more clearly. They knew where she was and that she was virtually trapped, if indeed the mindless things could be said to truly "know" anything at all.

And now the monsters could see the speaker, her shape shrunken by tremendous age.

The woman was sturdily built and nearly squat, as if the years had melted a larger woman into something smaller and wider, but no less commanding. On her head she wore a feathered black turban fixed with a gem that couldn't possibly have been real, and across her shoulders hung a long red jacket in a faux mandarin style. It flowed neatly over her dove gray gown, and from the bottom hem of this gown peeked two small black points—the tips of her shoes.

In her left hand she held a cane made of knotted wood. Her ring-covered fingers curled around the top, her jewelry flashing like sparks off a flint.

Josephine would sooner have run right into the arms of the nearest monster than tell this woman no. She held the lamp up high, letting its light douse the scene, bringing whatever terrible clarity it was bound to show.

The ancient colored woman in front of the nets raised her cane until she held it by the center, in her long-fingered fist. She swung it back over her head for momentum, and brought it crashing down against the coal-black column of a broken gas lamp that hadn't been lit for years. The single resulting gong reverberated across the wharf, radiating in a wave that shook the boards beneath Josephine's feet and brought every flesh-eating beast to a sudden, total standstill.

They posed statuelike and utterly unmoving, staring into space or at the newcomer. Even their gnawing, slathering jaws ceased their eternal chewing.

"Ma'am Laveau," Josephine croaked. Then in French, "I don't understand."

In French the woman replied, "What's to understand? Come here, dear. Come to me." She beckoned with her free hand. "The zombis won't be so cooperative forever."

As if it'd heard and recognized the truth of this matter, the creature nearest to Mrs. Laveau shook its head. The old lady shook her head, too, and reached into a pocket—from which she withdrew a small bag filled with powder.

She blew a pinch of the powder into the monster's face and it flinched. In that flinch, even at a distance, Josephine could see a glimmer of what had once been human; but it was gone as quickly as it'd appeared.

Once again, the thing was immobile.

"Come, child. Let's go. We'll walk, and they'll stay."

"For how long?"

"Long enough. You trust me?"

"Yes, ma'am."

"Then walk with me." She pocketed her powder and beckoned again.

This time, Josephine obeyed immediately. The lantern shook as she ran toward the old woman, and the boards of the wharf creaked beneath her feet. Her fear was a shocking, unfamiliar thing, and her body was so prepared to fight or run or die that her hands quaked and her teeth chattered, but Mrs. Laveau patted her shoulder and smiled. "There, you see? The dead must be reminded of their place."

Four

Captain Cly closed the enormous door behind himself and kept his head low as he descended the stairs. Two floors deep, beneath the initial bank basement where the door was located, the "vaults" remained one of the safest corners of the city—the deepest, most secure, and most like a collection of ordinary homes. This bunker-within-a-bunker also served as storage for the most direly needed essentials: clean water, ammunition, gunpowder, gas masks and their accoutrements, and grocery supplies to keep the population fed.

Over in "Chinatown," nearer the wall's edge on the far side of King Street Station, the oriental workers kept stores of their own, as their food preferences did not strictly overlap with the doornails. But in the last year, some of the doornails had taken to wandering toward the Chinese kitchens in search of unfamiliar food—while likewise some of the Chinese had shown an interest in dried salmon, occasional fruit tarts, and intermittent baked sweets.

Food was a language all its own. And it was in no one's best interest for anyone to starve.

The halls were not particularly mazelike, and they were as well lit as anything else beneath the city's surface. The ceilings were lower than Cly might have preferred, but this set the vaults apart from few other places in the world; so he watched his forehead and made his way along the first corridor without complaint, silent or sworn aloud.

From the stairs at the other end he heard someone approach,

moving with an uneven gait. Before the other man's head could rise into view, Cly called out a greeting. "Swakhammer, is that you?"

Jeremiah Swakhammer appeared with a lopsided grin and a cane. "Yeah, it's me. You heard this thing tapping, did you?"

"You've never been too light on your feet," Cly said, extending a hand, which Swakhammer shook. "But now that you've got a third leg to bang around, sure enough. I know the sound of you."

"I won't have it much longer, maybe. That crackpot Chinaman doctor Wong says if I'm careful, my leg will be right as rain within another few weeks. I might not even have a limp to show for it."

"That crackpot Chinaman doctor saved your lousy ass, Jerry. Don't act like you don't know it."

"I do, I do," he said. The grin stayed put, even spreading. "But he puts the most god-awful muck on me—these salves and creams— and he makes me drink teas that taste like tobacco simmered in horse piss."

Cly was not altogether unfamiliar with Chinese medicine himself, having spent time in San Francisco and Portland with his first mate, Fang. "Do they work?"

"Mostly. I think."

"Then quit your bellyaching, eh?" The captain slapped Swakhammer on the back, just to make him wobble. Jeremiah was a big man in his own right, but built wide—whereas Cly was built tall. "You ought to buy him flowers, next time you see the topside!"

"Yeah, that's pretty much what my daughter said." The words came out of his mouth a little funny, like he wasn't accustomed to referring to anyone that way. "But she's a tyrant of a thing, just like that doctor. Must be common to medical folks."

"It'd shock me silly if any child of yours was a pushover. Speaking of her, how's she doing? Is she settling in here to stay, or thinking of heading home?"

Swakhammer shifted his shoulders and gave half a shrug. "She's doing good—she gets on great with Dr. Wong, and helps him out down in Chinatown, and around here, too." A note of pride crept into his voice when he added, "She's as tough as me and twice as smart—so she fits in all right with the other women we got down here."

"When am I going to meet this kid, anyway?"

"She's no kid, not anymore. But you can meet her right now, if you want. I think you're headed right for her. You're looking for Briar, aren't ya?"

Captain Cly's perennial flush bloomed around his collar. "I was . . . well, sure. Headed over to see her, I suppose. But I'm looking for Houjin, too. And he's usually clowning around with her boy." Suddenly it occurred to him to wonder, "But what's your girl got to do with it? Did somebody get hurt?"

"Briar's all right, since that's what you're really asking." Swakhammer said, "Come on, I'll walk with you, and introduce you to my tyrant offspring."

Cly fell into step beside Jeremiah, and together they strolled around the next corner, down to the next flight of stairs. "Is something wrong with one of the boys?"

"Zeke got himself scratched up. Those kids were out in the hill blocks—they'd gone through Chinatown and let themselves up near one of the pump rooms, poking around at the big houses up on the hill, or what's left of them."

"Scavenging?"

"Playing around, is my guess. Boys do dumb stuff. Anyhow, he fell on something—or fell *in* something. I'm not too clear on the particulars, but they can give you the story."

"Will he be okay?"

"Looks like it. He'll be walking around like me for a while, dragging one foot behind him. But he didn't break anything, so he'll wind up with a scar and not much more for his trouble. As long as it doesn't fester."

By way of announcing himself, Swakhammer leaned forward and knocked on a door that was halfway open. He poked his head around it. "Everybody decent?" he asked. It was a joke between him and his daughter, after she'd walked in on him while the doctor was helping him bathe. Ever after, he'd insisted that she knock and confirm decency before entering.

But she usually didn't.

"Decent as we'll ever be," Mercy Swakhammer Lynch called back her father's own favorite response. "Didn't you say you were headed topside?"

"I did," he confirmed as he stepped inside. "But then I ran into *this* guy, and I realized you hadn't met him yet—so I figured I'd show you off."

"Show me off?"

Andan Cly followed Jeremiah Swakhammer inside, doing his best to make himself look smaller. An exercise in futility, given that he could've reached up and placed both elbows flat on the ceiling, but he hunched anyway.

The room was large and quite bright, due to Mercy's insistence that she couldn't work in the dark, goddammit, and a place with so much potential for injury and illness ought to have some kind of clinic . . . or if nothing else, a room that could serve as one in a pinch. She'd picked the empty "apartment" next to her own sleeping quarters and stocked it with every gas lamp, oil lamp, candle contraption, and electric lantern at hand, and with the help of Dr. Wong, she'd gotten the place more or less serviceable.

Now she was staring intently at Zeke's leg as he lay flat on a table, grimacing for his life. She wore a set of lenses strapped to her face, helping the light show her what the trouble was. When she looked up at her father and his friend, her eyes were as big and strange as an owl's.

"Hi, there," Cly said to her. "It's . . . not *Miss* Swakhammer, is it? Jerry said you were married, once."

"Widowed," she said. "It's Mrs. Lynch if you like, or Mercy if you can't be bothered."

"Nice to meet you. I'm Cly. I have a ship, and I swing through every now and again. If you ever need anything, you can let me know, and I'll try to pick it up for you."

"Thank you for the offer. I'll likely take you up on it one of these days." She used the back of her hand to shove a stray bit of hair out of her face. Her locks were lighter than Jeremiah's, on the dark side of blond and worn in a braid that was knotted at the back of her neck. Even though she was seated, Cly could see that there was something of her father in her shape. She was too sturdy to be called slender, and her strong, straight shoulders were a direct inheritance.

Zeke made a muffled *umph* noise when she dived back in with the needle, stitching a long, jagged gash with swift, sure strokes. He said, "Sorry."

Mercy said, "You're doing just fine. I've seen bigger, older men be worse babies than you by a long shot." It was probably true. Before coming to Seattle at her father's behest, she'd worked in a Richmond hospital, patching up wounded veterans.

Zeke knew this, and he said between gasps, "I could be a soldier, you know."

"What are you now, sixteen or seventeen?"

"Sixteen."

She nodded, and squinted. "Old enough," she said, but something in her tone suggested she'd seen younger. "I don't recommend it, though."

"I ain't looking to join up," Zeke assured her, then bit back another yelp.

Cly noted that Zeke's mother was not present, but he assumed she'd return before long. He went over to a seat—in the form of an old church pew someone had hauled down to the underground—and made himself comfortable. Swakhammer joined him. Between the pair of them, they occupied almost half of it.

"It's just as well you're not interested in fighting," Cly told the boy. "You'd give your momma a fit."

Zeke gave a pained laugh that ended in a gulp. "Shit, Captain. You know *her*. She'd probably sign up and come to war after me."

"I do admit, there *is* a precedent," he said. He leaned back and made a halfhearted effort to get comfortable. "What happened to you, anyway? And where's your partner in crime?"

Mercy answered the second question before Zeke could unclench his jaw again to answer the first. "Houjin went back to Dr. Wong's to pick up some balm for the bruising that's going to come with this cut. Mostly I needed him out from underfoot. He was hovering like a hen."

"Feeling guilty," Zeke mumbled. "*He's* the one who dared me."

"Dared you to what?" asked Cly.

Zeke sighed, a ragged sound that was drawn in time to the needle threading through his skin. He craned his head around to look at the men on the pew, giving himself an excuse not to watch what was happening to his leg. "We went hiking up the hill, where there aren't so many rotters. Hardly any of them, really. But there are a lot of big houses, where the merchants and sawmill fellows used to live—and Houjin said some of them hadn't been bothered since the blight."

Swakhammer shook his head. "I find that unlikely."

"You never know," the boy replied, a hint of his opportunistic optimism shining through even now. "And even if someone had already gotten inside, people miss things. So we thought we'd go take a look."

Mercy murmured, "And how'd that work out for you?"

"We found a whole drawer full of viewing glass." He referred to glass that had been polarized, so even trace amounts of blight gas could be detected. This glass was helpful to have around for the sake of detecting leaks, but it was worthless aboveground—given that the gas was absolutely everywhere. "And we found some canvas, a whole bunch of it folded up inside a wagon."

"Would this be the same wagon you fell through?" Mercy asked.

"I thought it'd hold! It was one of the old covered kind, abandoned back behind a real tall house near the wall's east edge. Someone had been using it to store junk, but junk is sometimes useful. Houjin said he wouldn't climb inside it, and I said he was chicken.

So he dared me to do it instead, and I *did*. But the floor didn't hold, and—" He gestured at his leg without peeking at Mercy's activities.

The nurse paused and reached for a rag inside a bowl of water. She wrung it out with one hand and wiped at the wounds, which had mostly stopped bleeding. "And congratulations, fearless explorer. For your reward, you get thirty stitches." She lifted his leg by the ankle and turned it over to get a better look at his calf. "Maybe more than that."

He groaned. "My mother says she's going to kill me, but she'll wait until I can run again, so I can have a head start."

"Mighty generous of her," the captain said. "Considering all the times she's told you not to go exploring on the hill."

"Exploring on the hill by *myself*. I wasn't by *myself*. Momma said I was obeying the letter of the law, but not the spirit. Apparently that ain't good enough."

"Speaking of your mother, where's she at?" Cly said with all the nonchalance he could muster. "I thought she'd be here, pacing around you."

From the doorway, Briar Wilkes responded. "I went to hit up the bottommost storage room, looking for a pair of pants no one wanted so I could cut off one of the legs." She held up a pair of Levi's that had probably once belonged to a logger. "They'll swim on you, so you'll have to belt 'em. But I don't think anyone will miss these things, and if anybody does, he can take it up with me. Hello, Jeremiah."

Andan Cly stood up, but Swakhammer only nodded in her direction. He figured she wouldn't begrudge him the gesture, since his leg was still on the mend. But the captain couldn't stop himself, and didn't try.

"Weren't you down here just last week?"

"It's a slow season, and I felt like coming back."

"You must be the strangest man alive," she teased.

"Maybe that's it. Maybe I'm just looking for the company of my own kind." He smiled, and since he was up, wandered over to Zeke's leg to take a look at the damage. The boy's skin was snagged and torn, but his muscles were intact, and Mercy Lynch was a formidable seamstress.

Zeke winced as the curved needle dipped again, and shuddered as the thread slipped through his skin.

Cly said, "Before long, you'll have one hell of a scar to show off. Girls love scars."

"They do?"

"They're always a conversation-starter."

"I just bet they are." Briar only half stifled her smile as she added, "Except, come to think of it, I don't believe we've ever heard any stories about *your* scars. I assume you have some, somewhere."

Cly tried not to look at her and mostly failed, his gaze darting back and forth between the morbid sight of Zeke's mangled leg and the petite, curly-haired object of his truer interest. "None of mine are very interesting."

"I find that difficult to believe," she pressed. Her eyes followed him as he shuffled from foot to foot.

"Captain," Mercy Lynch said sharply. "You're standing in my light. Am I going to have to send you errand-running like your junior crew member?"

"Um—"

Before he could form a smarter reply, the nurse declared, "All of y'all, this is silly. I don't need an audience, and neither does my patient. Everybody *out,* except you, Miz Wilkes, if you'd care to stay and look after him."

"Funny thing is, I *don't* care to," she said. She brought the pants over to Zeke, who stretched out his hand and took them. "I'm glad he's all right, and I'm glad you're here to take care of him—but I'm still none too pleased with him, and anyway I don't think he needs the comforting."

"I could use a shot of whiskey," Zeke tried, because hope springs eternal.

"You could use a boot to the rear end, but you're not going to get that, either. *Yet.*"

Mercy said, "I'm sorry I don't have any ether or anything. I know this doesn't feel very good."

"It's not that bad," Zeke fibbed.

"You're a liar. Still, I wish I could give you something for the pain. I think I'll put that at number one on my wish list, Captain."

"I beg your pardon?"

"You offered to make a supply run, and I'm telling you about a supply I could use."

"Oh. Sure. Just put it down on paper, and I'll take it with me when I leave."

"You're leaving right *now,*" she reminded him. "But come back in an hour. I'll have him finished up by then, and I'll start considering my inventory. Now, what's everyone standing around for? Didn't I ask for peace and quiet?"

"Yes, ma'am!" Swakhammer said to his daughter with exaggerated deference. "I'll pick up my sorry old bones and be on my way."

Captain Cly stood aside to let Swakhammer pass, which also allowed Briar to slip out underneath his arm on her way back to the door. He stopped her by saying her name the way he always did. "Hey, Wilkes."

"Cly?"

"Suppose I could have a word with you? For a minute, if you can spare it."

"I was headed down to Chinatown to scare up some supper. You care to join me?"

"Yes," he said quickly. "I mean, sure. Fang's probably down there anyway, and Houjin will wander over once Mercy shoos him away again—or that's my guess. I'll be leaving for a long trip soon, and if he wants to come, he'll have to get himself ready."

"A long trip?" Briar repeated. "How long, and are you taking off soon?"

"Might be gone a few weeks, but I'll stick around until morning.

Everybody and his brother wants to add something to my shopping list."

"Have you been offering?"

"I suppose I might've been."

"Then it's nobody's fault but your own." She bumped her shoulder against him, and he pretended to recoil—as if she'd knocked him so hard, she'd sent him off balance.

They made a funny pair, walking together back up the way Andan had come. Him so tall, he had to duck at every doorway. Her so comparatively small that the top of her head barely reached his chest. The captain felt conspicuous beside Briar Wilkes; he felt his height more acutely than usual when he had to crane his neck to look down at her, and she had to twist herself to look up at him.

But he liked it when she did.

Once upon a time, she'd been a notorious girl—a pretty teenager who'd run away from home to marry a man twice her age. But sixteen years, widowhood, hard work, and raising a son alone had taken away the imperious tilt of her nose. (Cly remembered it from a drawing he'd seen, a wedding announcement he recalled from ages ago.) The intervening time had worn away her wealth, her softness, and her youth—but not the symmetry of her face. And for everything the years had claimed, they had given something in return.

At thirty-six, she was a patient and confident woman.

She was also the sheriff of Seattle, insomuch as the walled city had one. Her father had been a lawman who died a folk hero, obeying the spirit of the law if not the letter.

She'd never intended to replace him. She'd intended to live and die a rich man's wife in a house with expensive furnishings and silver cutlery, pampering a brood of well-dressed children who played the piano and learned to ride horses with perfect posture. But time had had other ideas, and now she wore her father's hat, his badge, and his belt buckle engraved with his initials, *MW*. And even the underground's newcomers knew who she must be, whether they recognized her as Maynard's daughter or not.

Cly lifted the big vault door and held it up while Briar climbed past it, into the subterranean underworld that passed for "outside." He followed her, asking, "What's the fastest way to get where we're going? I'm still learning my way around down here."

She paused with her hands on her hips, checking the signs and finding her bearings. "This way's fastest in the long run. The other two ways I know are roundabout, and I don't know the tunnels so well myself. Every time I think I've got my directions figured out, I turn around and wind up lost."

"You've been lost down here?"

"Sure. These days I carry one of Frank Creat's compasses and it helps me a lot, but sometimes I just have to find my way topside and look around to figure out where I am."

"I wish you wouldn't do that," Cly said. "All those rotters up there. All that gas."

"That's what the masks are for, and the rotters aren't so hard to avoid, once you know what lures them. As long as you stay off the streets, it's not so much trouble to stay out of their way. Nobody's seen any down here since Minnericht died. No coincidence, if you ask me." She started off down a wood-slat trail with a sign that said KING STREET on it. Chinatown was shortly beyond the train station. "You worry too much," she told him.

"Do you take Swakhammer's Daisy with you?" he asked, meaning the sonic weapon that could stun the rotters into submission, if only for a few minutes at a time.

"Lord, no. I can hardly lift that thing."

Falling into step beside her, Cly argued, "Then it sounds like I'm worrying just the right amount. I don't like it, you all alone up there."

"I could show you the topside way, if you want," she offered. "We could go left at the fork instead, and come up through the old Continental Hotel. From there, we could go rooftop to rooftop all the way to Chinatown, almost. You'd see it's not so bad."

"You're only trying to make me feel better."

"Is it working?" she asked, looking up at him with a gleam in her eye.

"No. And if it's all the same to you, I'd rather stick to the under-side. I don't like wearing gas masks, and I don't like rotters."

"Then you took a terrible wrong turn someplace, because you're sure as hell in the wrong city, Captain."

"Oh, I don't know about that. The surface here isn't much to look at, but the underground is a sight to see. And . . ." He stopped himself from saying more.

"And?"

"And I know plenty of great people down here," he finished weakly. Then, to change the subject while he still could, he said, "By the way, there's a shorter way to Chinatown."

"Why didn't you say something sooner?"

"I only just learned about it. Yaozu told me about it on the way from Maynard's."

Briar was silent for a moment. Their feet made conspicuous and uninterrupted stomping sounds on the hollow sidewalks, until she finally said, "Yaozu, eh? I didn't know you two were buddies."

"Not buddies," he was quick to counter. "I don't know him hardly at all, and I won't lie—it was plenty odd. He came up to me in the bar, and said he wanted a word."

"And what did he *really* want?"

"He wanted to hire me," he explained, and then he told her about Yaozu's plans for civic improvement.

By the time he was finished laying it out, carefully choosing his words and how he presented the situation, they'd hiked to the outer edge of Chinatown. "Where do you want to stop?" he asked. He knew of only three eateries in the Chinese district.

"How about Ruby's? She made me something last time I was there that filled me up all day. Back before I came *inside,*" she said with a gesture that suggested she meant the city, and not merely in-doors, "I never wondered what oriental people ate or how they made it. But Houjin got Lucy eating some of his uncle's meals, and she started spreading it around."

Cly nodded vigorously. "One day, I'll take you to San Francisco. They have a big Chinatown there, and there are dozens of places to stop for a bite. Hundreds, maybe. And all of it'll knock your socks off."

"Really? You'd take me to San Francisco? I always wanted to see it."

The captain cleared his throat. "Sure. I'd love to get you out of here, even if it's only for a few days. We could go flying if you like."

During their walk to Chinatown they hadn't seen or heard anyone coming or going; but now they detected the pump rooms roaring a few blocks away, drawing fresh air from over the wall down into the city and forcing it through the airways that laced through the entire underground. Chinatown had three of the biggest pumps, which between them provided the majority of the fresh air to the sealed spaces below. Three other rooms were scattered elsewhere, operating in shifts night and day to keep the bad air out, and the good air in.

Two men in work clothes, fresh from a shift at the pumps, came rushing down the walkway. They nodded at Andan and Briar, who nodded back—keeping the communication simple, for the language barrier was not insignificant. Many of the Chinatown residents and vault residents recognized one another on sight, but very few of them could share a conversation.

Ruby's place was not so much a restaurant as a storefront stand with benches and tables, and no counter separated the eating area from the kitchen, where there were several fires heating strange round pans, filled with vegetables and fish, and chicken or pork when they could be found. It took ten minutes of careful enunciation and gesturing, plus a moment with a pencil on a piece of paper, but eventually the proprietor understood what they wanted.

Cly paid for both meals, then he and the sheriff sat on a bench outside to wait for their food. Together they watched the men come and go, some of them in coal-stained leather aprons from stoking the furnaces. Around their necks hung the goggles that protected their eyes from the white-hot fires that powered the air-bringing bellows.

"Hey, Wilkes," he said, nudging her gently with his elbow. "I've been thinking." He gazed down at her and felt very big and very silly. He knew the flush was back; he could feel it curling up his neck and around his ears. "It's about these transports, and this . . . this next job, in particular."

"For Yaozu." She said the name quietly, lest it be heard over the sizzle of the cooking fires.

"I think he *does* want to improve the place. He's a criminal and a mystery, and I don't trust him. But at the end of the day, being crooked doesn't make him any different from the rest of us down here. Not in any way that matters."

Briar peered up at him. "*Us* down here?"

Cly cleared his throat again. "I was thinking maybe it'd be good to have a station out at Fort Decatur—an *official* station, not just a place where people drop by and park for an afternoon. With the kind of money he's offering, I could do it," he told her, leaving out the part about the extra money he'd pick up from the New Orleans summons. There was no reason for her to know about that. It'd only make her wonder about things that didn't matter, and hadn't mattered for years. "I could build a pipework dock without too much effort, and keep it as a home spot for the *Naamah Darling,* between supply runs and deliveries.

"Fang and Houjin spend plenty of time down here already, and my new engineer, Kirby Troost, probably won't mind it. He's a weird one—you haven't met him yet, but I think he'll work out fine, and maybe you'll even come to like him. Anyway, it's a lot of money, and all I have to do is head to New Orleans and pick up a few things."

"New Orleans?" She sounded worried. "That's where you're off to tomorrow?"

"Yep. And in New Orleans, I can hit up one of the Texian machine shops and get the *Naamah Darling* refitted—or unfitted—so it's better for moving real cargo instead of sap and gas." He made that part especially clear, because he knew how well she'd like the sound of it. "While I'm there, I can pick up everything everybody needs, and a few other things besides. In particular, I was thinking . . ." He finished the rest in a rush: "Once it's all sorted out, my ship and the Decatur dock, I could come back to Seattle and maybe I'd just . . . stay. And run the dock. Out at the fort. For good."

At first she said nothing, her face unreadable. It always unnerved him when she made herself so blank like that. He prided himself on his ability to read people, and he wanted to read her—he *needed* to read her—but he had no idea if she was about to endorse the idea or call him an idiot.

"How would you, do you think . . . I've got to ask, Wilkes. How would you feel about that?"

She stood up, and she stepped in front of him—facing him almost eye-to-eye, since he remained seated. Her inscrutable expression cracked into confusion, surprise, and something sweeter. "Captain," she said. "Would you be doing that for me?"

He swallowed hard, knowing that the uncontrollable blush was truly getting the best of him. "Yes, ma'am, I believe I would."

"Are you sure it's what you want? To make that kind of change? I didn't even ask you to. Shit, Cly. I'm old, and I work too much, and I can't remember the last time I wore a dress, and I run around in the dark with my daddy's gun all day, and I . . . Are you *sure*?"

Without thinking, he slipped his hands around her waist, drawing her closer until her knees knocked against the bench. "I don't care if you've never cooked a meal. I don't care if you never wear a dress, and I'd be proud as hell to have a woman who can shoot as good as you. And as for old, well, I'm older than *you*. And I'm too big to walk down the street without people staring and pointing—and even if I wasn't, I know I'm not much to look at. All I can tell you is, I've known ever since you stomped up to me on Bainbridge and demanded to hitch a ride. . . ." He did not know what to add. It was too hard, too dangerous to say out loud.

Gently, she took his face in her hands. She leaned forward until their foreheads touched, and he could feel the warmth of her breath against his cheek. She whispered, "You've known what, Captain Cly?"

"That I wanted a chance to prove I'm worth your trouble."

Even when he was standing at street level on Seattle's topside, Andan Cly still felt like he was underneath something. A long shadow covered much of the contained city, cast by the two-hundred-foot wall that surrounded it, and the sky above was gray like usual. Even at the very height of noon, any light that managed to make it past the shadow was filtered and dim. Direct sunlight, on those few days of the year when it appeared, was never quite brilliant within the wall, either. Every speck of illumination—from the sun, from the ever-present lanterns—was rendered thick and watery by years of accumulated blight gas, which filled the blocks with a thick, yellowish fog.

Watery, yes. That was it.

It felt like being underwater.

The gas mask he wore underscored this impression. The lenses rounded off the edges of his vision, creating a very slight fishbowl effect, and the charcoal filters through which he breathed made the air feel stuffy and taste strange. He didn't like to hear the sound of his lungs working, and even the faintest whisper of a stuffy nose reached his ears as a hearty whistle. The straps were rubbing a groove into the back of his head, and the rubber seals made his face itch.

But all in all, it was better than breathing the blight. A few thousand of the walking dead would have attested to it, if they could.

Most of the ships that came or went from the city did so over at King Street Station, half a mile away. Decatur was more often considered a pit stop of last resort or desperate straits.

But Andan Cly saw potential.

He saw a sturdy protective barricade thirty feet high around the main compound, and a large shelter that could serve as a depot for goods and airmen and had an entrance to the underground through its basement. Conveniently located—almost triangulated—between Chinatown, the train station, and the vaults, it was within easy reach for the three main populations. All it needed was a framework of lead pipe sunk into the ground, so hydrogen ships would have something to dock against, rather than the present method of hitching down to an enormous fallen totem pole that grew softer and more rotten by the month.

Well, it'd also need a set of tanks for hydrogen manufacture and fill-ups, and some tubing to pump everything up. Cly had a feeling the tanks would be best positioned underground, since untreated metal corroded so quickly in the blight, and there was no telling how, or if, that pervasive gas would interfere with hydrogen production.

But he was getting ahead of himself.

It was difficult not to, when he thought about the possibilities. The underground could have a real, honest-to-God dock inside— where people could reliably send and receive goods and messages . . . maybe even mail! It'd make Seattle something like a real city again, despite the rotters and the toxic air. It'd mean easier access to the outside for people who wanted it.

Cly put his hands on his hips and watched as the *Naamah Darling* prepared for takeoff. His ship was full of fuel and had hundreds of miles to go before it'd need a fill-up, but his crew members were checking the last-minute details, running down the list of things that needed attention before a cross-country excursion.

Hydrogen stores: check.

Thrusters and hydraulics in good repair: check.

Cargo hold emptied, cleaned, and ready for stocking: check— though in this case it was emptied, cleaned, and ready for the retrofitting in New Orleans. This meant all the gas bags had been dumped, and the bracing crates had been removed. The long ceiling rails with their ball-bearing rollers would be cut off at a machine shop, and the resulting seams would be soldered. Rubber seals needed to be restored and augmented if he was going to carry cargo that he didn't want tainted by the city air.

"Hey, boss, we're about ready to fly," reported Kirby Troost, the *Naamah Darling*'s new engineer. Troost was a little man, roughly the height of Briar Wilkes and maybe ten pounds heavier. But what he lacked in size, he made up for with a keen intelligence and a willingness to try anything once. He was fresh out of jail. What he'd done to land there, he wasn't fond of saying.

Cly knew, but he didn't spread it around. The secret protected them both.

The captain nodded down at the engineer and looked back at the log structure that led to the underground, courtesy of a pair of ladders. "Before we go, I want to make sure nobody has any 'one last things' to ask for."

Kirby Troost bobbed his head. The bob looked heavy, as if his gas mask threw off his balance.

"You doing all right in that thing?" Cly asked, indicating the mask.

"Yes, sir. No trouble at all."

"Really? Because mine itches like a son of a bitch."

"Didn't say it was pleasant, sir. Just said it wasn't any trouble."

"If it bugs you, they've got a bunch of different models you could try. On the return trip, I'll take you to the storage center in the vaults, and you can try 'em on one after another, like they're hats in a shop." Seeing Mercy Lynch coming toward him, he called out, "Mercy! You think of something else?"

She said, "Yep, and I'm glad you're still here. I was afraid you'd already left." She wiggled her hand in a *gimme* motion.

"Oh, your list. It's right here." He removed three of them from his pocket, selected hers, and gave it back to her.

"Thanks. I'll be right back. Since it doesn't look like I'm holding you up, or anything."

"No, ma'am. Take your time."

Kirby stood beside the captain, watching Mercy retreat to the station house—or the building that would become a station house if Cly had anything to say about it. The engineer said, "Fine figure of a woman, there."

"How can you tell? She's wearing a mask."

"Not talking about her face, sir. She looks strong. I like that."

"You like them taller than you?"

"If I stuck to the ones who were shorter than me, I'd never have any fun at all."

Cly shrugged. "She's young. But not so young that people would talk."

"Are you saying I should have a word with her?"

"I'm saying if you did, it wouldn't be a scandal. But there are two things you should know first."

"I'll start counting."

"First," said the captain. "She's been married before."

"Widowed?"

"Her husband died in the war."

"And what's number two?" Troost asked.

"Number two is her father. If you decide to have a word with her, you'd best do it while he's still on crutches."

"Is he a big man?"

"Yup."

Kirby Troost said, "Good. They're the easiest kind to outrun." And then, as Yaozu strolled into the compound area he added, "Men like that one, on the other hand . . ."

As was so often the case, the lord and master of King Street Station was dressed in white except for his shoes—making him easy to recognize, even in a mask that obscured his face. He moved ghost-like through the foggy gas, which thickened and thinned in clumps around him, parting for his passage.

"Captain Cly," he said. "I trust Houjin gave you my requests?"

"Got 'em right here," he said, patting the vest pocket where all his lists went. "Some of this will take some looking for, but I'll scare it up."

"Of that I have no doubt. But there's still the matter of how you'll pay for it. I'm certain your credit is good from coast to coast, but money speaks louder than reputation, and some of my requests are expensive." After reaching into the folds of his long pale jacket, he extracted a pouch. "This should cover everything, with some to spare. And you'll find the second half of your fee when you return. Now, at the risk of making a sudden shift in conversation, is this your new crewman? I understand that Rodimer died last year."

"That's right." Cly answered both questions at once. "This is my new engineer," he said, indicating Troost.

"You seem . . . very familiar to me," Yaozu said, squinting through his visor at the smaller man, who squinted back through his own.

Troost said, "Can't say we've ever met. It's hard to tell with these masks."

"You're right, of course. Still, there's something about you. Whatever it is, it reminds me of someone I met years ago, in a desert town called Reno."

"Never been there."

"Never once? Are you certain?"

"Well," the engineer said. His tone oozed contrived carelessness. "Since you've asked me to reconsider, I'll have to think on it. I've done a lot of traveling in my time."

Yaozu said, "It's possible I'm mistaken. At any rate—" He held out the pouch to the captain.

Cly took it and stuffed it into the pocket with his lists. It made a heavy bulge against his chest, but he was layered up against the blight, and it did not show through his clothes. "I appreciate the vote of confidence."

"And I'll appreciate receiving everything I've asked for. Make no mistake, this *is* a vote of confidence."

"I'll be back in one piece, with all your goodies."

"Oh, I know you'll be back," Yaozu said, glancing over his shoulder. "I can count on the fact that you're too smart to come back empty-handed."

"Thanks," Cly said, ignoring the unsavory implications—not because he doubted Yaozu's sincerity or capacity to be unpleasant, but because he had no intention of letting him down. He'd be back, and they both knew it.

Briar arrived, emerging from the station house with Mercy, who had finished making her revisions. The nurse gave her list to the captain, and she told him, "It's no small thing, you doing this. They trust you around here, don't they?"

"I hope so," he replied.

In his other vest pocket, he had an envelope of money from Lucy O'Gunning, gathered from the patrons at Maynard's, and to that envelope, he'd added Mercy's contribution—gleaned from Dr. Wong's patients, and those she'd helped to patch up in the months since she'd arrived.

Briar made a point to stand away from Yaozu. She couldn't ignore him, but she didn't have to like him, and she felt no compunction to be friendly. She told Mercy, "Cly's good for it. And you must be the new fellow, Kirby Troost."

"Yes, ma'am, and you're the lady sheriff I've heard so much about. I do hope you'll pardon me if I don't remove my mask."

"Why on earth would you remove your mask?"

"I'm not wearing a hat, and it only seems polite to remove something when meeting a lady."

She laughed and said, "At least you didn't offer to take off anything else. Where'd you find this one, Captain?"

"Tacoma. I've known him for ages, but don't believe everything he tells you. I like him better than I trust him." He said it as if it were a joke, carefully devoid of weight. Then he added, "Anyway, I was starting to wonder if you were going to make it."

"And let you leave without seeing you off? Not a chance. Is

everything ready? You've got everything you need, and everything's working all right? I hope you've tested everything, and double-checked everything, and—"

"All of it, and some of it twice," he assured her.

From within her mask her voice was muffled, but he could still hear the worry when she said, "I don't mean to nag you like you don't know what you're doing. It's just that New Orleans is an awful long way away."

"You gonna worry about me?"

She admitted, "More than I'd like to. Three weeks?"

"Three weeks," he promised. "And if I'm running any longer than that, I'll send word by telegram. Tell Princess Angeline to keep her eyes open at the Tacoma taps, or get a friend to check it. She's got friends all over the place, anyway. I swear to God, that woman knows half of everyone on the coast."

"Just about," Briar agreed. "I'll flag her down next time she passes through."

Underneath the *Naamah Darling,* the retracting steps quivered as Houjin descended. The seventeen-year-old Chinese boy was accompanied by fellow Mandarin Fang, who had served as Captain Cly's first mate for over a decade. Both were wearing long sleeves, long pants, duster coats, and gas masks, lest the blight cause itching rashes on whatever parts were exposed.

Houjin cried, "Hey! Are we going to hit the skies, or hang around here all day?"

Fang said nothing, because he had no tongue. But his posture echoed the question, feet apart, arms folded, head cocked to the side.

Cly took a deep breath. It was hard to do so inside the mask, where every intake was hauled through the filters that kept the air from killing him. He said, "I think this wraps up all the official talk, and there's no reason we can't be on our way. Everybody inside, and buckle up. I'm right behind you."

"Behind us?" Houjin asked from the foot of the steps.

"You heard me."

Andan Cly leaned down to Briar and said, "Hey, do me a favor."

Behind the lenses, her eyebrows knitted. "What?"

"Take a deep breath."

"What?"

"Just do it. For me."

"All right? . . ." Her chest inflated and she held the air, as requested.

The captain did likewise, and snapped one hand out to her mask, and one hand to his own. Faster than lightning, he lifted the filters on both contraptions and leaned in for a swift, sudden kiss. Seconds later, because there was no time to dare more—not on the surface, where the air was made of poison—he popped both masks back into place and exhaled as hard as he could.

While everyone stared and no one spoke, Briar did likewise, adjusting the fit over her face.

"Now what'd you go and do that for?" she stammered.

"For good luck," he beamed. "Besides, everybody knows by now, anyway." He wiggled his mask to tighten the fit and added, "Goodbye for now, Briar Wilkes. I'll be back in a few weeks, you just watch me."

 *Five*

Agatha Knotts turned another card over.

The Hanged Man was revealed, suspended by his foot over a grill. The weathered edges of the paper were fuzzy from humidity; a crack in the old stock split across the gallows. The whole pack was worn like this, from years of use by skillful fingers—decades of patterns, possibilities, and promises spread across a bright silk scarf beneath a parasol.

Josephine sighed. "I was hoping for something a little more auspicious."

Agatha shrugged and said, "It's not the worst you could've pulled. Think of it as balance, your world suspended between two tugging forces."

"It is helplessness."

"It is *not*."

"Give me the last one," Josephine urged. She was careful not to glance over her shoulder, or to peer from left to right. The Square in front of the Saint Louis cathedral was not so crowded now. Curfew would descend within minutes. The fortune-tellers with their stands, their small tables draped in bright colors, their battered and mystical tools . . . they were folding up shop and preparing to leave before the Texians made them go.

The statue in front of the church cast a horse-shaped shadow that stretched the beast into a monstrous mockery of four legs and a rider drawn spiderlike between the angled lines of the church's pointed spires. Josephine did not look at that, either, because she already knew the hour was late.

The fortune-teller said, "Temperance."

"Oh, for pity's sake."

"Again, you are thinking too narrowly, my friend." Agatha tapped the card with one long fingernail. "The lady does not stand for restraint—no more than you do. Consider how metal is forged. This is another card for balance, for the subtle power that comes after a trial."

"You're making this up."

With a flick of her wrist and a very fast sweep, Agatha scooped the cards into her palm. "You're the one who asked me to read. If you don't believe, I don't mind. But there's no need to be rude." She shuffled the stiff rectangles idly, jostling them in her hands, slipping cards in and out of the stack and massaging them back into the whole. She lowered her voice and was careful to keep her eyes on the orange silk before her. "It won't be long now."

"I know. Give me another spread. A short one."

"Another row for you to mock?" The colored woman in the pretty shawl lifted an eyebrow, mocking back. It was friendlier than it appeared. Agatha and Josephine had known each other since childhood, and their differences ran deep without coming between them.

Josephine dropped her voice as well, making a show of reaching into her bag for another warm coin to set upon the box that served as a table. "Another excuse to linger. I want to see how they clear the Square. I want to see if the new man comes and sweeps it himself."

"Three cards, then." She spread the pack in an arc and said. "Choose wisely, and concentrate on your question, so the cards can respond."

"I'll do no such thing," she mumbled. Even so, a query buzzed through her mind in a flash. *Will Cly come—or will I have to find someone else?* She shook her head, doing her best to empty it of the superstition. Then she randomly tapped three selections. "Those."

"Very well," Agatha said with a patient, practiced nod. As she removed the cards and retrieved the rest of the deck, she asked under her breath, without meeting her companion's eyes, "Hazel said you spoke with Madame Laveau?"

"Yes. Four nights ago. She saved me." She said it matter-of-factly. Regardless of her opinions on tarot or the stars, or God or the devil, or any other unseen thing alleged to walk the city . . . she believed in the elderly vodou queen.

Agatha remarked, "She has not spoken much about the Dead Who Walk. Some people think she made them herself. They say she's building an army of the damned to throw the Texians out of New Orleans."

"They can say whatever they want. I do not believe she made the zombis."

"Zombi? Is that what she calls them?"

Josephine nodded down at the cards, maintaining the fortune-seeking charade in case they were being watched. It was safest to assume, in the occupied city. They were always being watched. "Do you know the word?"

"I do." For a moment she paused, as if she censored herself. "It should not surprise me. It is an old word, an African word brought to the islands, and then to the delta."

"Is it like your cards? One meaning on the surface, and another below?"

"It implies that the dead have brought their state upon themselves, and that they are restless because of their own sins."

Josephine murmured, "Aren't we all?"

"It is a good word. Or an *appropriate* word, I should say." She turned her attention to the cards once more. Revealing the first, she said, "Here we find Justice. He suggests satisfaction and success, brought about by leadership and cooperation. Whatever question you asked the cards, this is an auspicious answer."

Josephine said, "I asked them nothing."

Agatha did not argue. She flipped the second card. "The ten of wands. You must beware of your own responsibilities, and keep your own house. Someone may try to deceive you, or play you for a fool."

"Meaningless. That's every day of my life."

"So skeptical, for someone who so badly wants guidance."

"Is that what you think I want?"

"Well"—Agatha reached for the third card—"you want *something*. Look, it is the six of swords."

"And what does that mean?"

"Change, and swiftly coming. It is a card that urges concentration and focus, lest your goal be lost. And I suppose that's meaningless, too."

"You know me so well."

The fortune-teller's hand hovered over the spread. Impulsively, she pulled another card.

"What are you doing?"

"Asking a question."

"I thought it was foolish to read one's own cards." Josephine repeated something Agatha had told her once before.

"Not a question for myself," she said, turning it over. "A question for you. Ah. The Magician."

"Now *that's* somebody I could use, right about now."

Agatha shook her head. "In this case, I think he stands for *you*."

"Why do you think that?"

"Because as you said, I know you so well." She smiled and leaned forward, pretending to explain some arcane bit of divination, but only leaning in so that even the closest observer might not overhear. "You believe Madame Laveau? You do not think she made the zombis, or controls them?"

"She says they Walk through no magic of hers. But she controlled them a bit. I saw her do it."

"Hm."

"I do not think she was lying, and I do not think her control is absolute. Nor," she added quickly, "do I think any *magic* is involved."

"How did she control them?"

Josephine hesitated. "I should say instead that she stopped them. She stunned them, with a very loud noise, and something about it . . . the timbre of it, or the tone. Something made them all stand still. But I don't know if I could repeat her success, and I would not dare to try."

"It's wise of you, to defer to her judgment."

"I don't believe in magic. I don't believe in cards, or curses. But I believe that Madame Marie has power, and I have no interest in offending her. Besides, she saved me."

"You believe that?"

"I *know* that," she confirmed. "I was trapped between the dead and the alligators, and she intervened."

"Then she wants something from you," Agatha said coolly.

"Whatever it is, she can have it."

The fortune-teller retrieved her cards again, and resumed her slow shuffling. "If I were you, I'd be careful what I promised to the little queen. I would not offend her myself, but beware of what you offer unbidden."

"Does that advice come from your cards?"

"No, it comes from my heart—one old friend to another: Be careful of her motives, and the favors she asks of you. I believe she means well for the city, but also that she leans quite hard on the ends justifying the means. At any rate, look: you've used up all your tarot time, which will come as a relief, I'm sure."

Josephine heard the rolling-crawlers before she saw them. She'd know them anywhere; she listened to them for the last three nights patrolling beneath the Garden Court windows every hour on the hour as the curfew that seized the city was forced into effect. Ostensibly, this new measure was meant to address the disappearance of Colonel Betters and Lieutenant Cardiff four days previously, and just this once, Josephine didn't doubt the Texians and their sincerity. They wanted to know what had happened to their officers, and they didn't understand anything about the Dead Who Walk, the "zombis" whose population had risen so much over the last year.

It was hard to blame them, except that they'd failed so thoroughly to listen. Anyone could've told them.

The people who worked the docks, who managed the piers, who loaded and unloaded cargo both virtuous and clandestine. The men who drove the ferries over the river, who worked the engines on the little flat boats that carried people across the bayous and into the islands in the bays; the women who separated shells from seafood in the old canneries, who mended the nets down by the shore under the heat of the sun reflected off the river, and off the ocean.

They could've asked the rich children who were warned by bedtime stories about the zombis, or the poor children who were threatened with zombi punishment when they misbehaved. They might have asked the old folks who knew to shutter their homes against the dead as if against a storm; or they could have inquired after the young folks, who were fast enough to run and knew all the ways of escape from the in-between world down by the water.

Anyone in the city could've said, "Yes, the men-shaped things Walk the shores and roam the abandoned spots where no one else dares to go. They moan and cough, and chase and bite. They kill, and you'd best be leaving them alone."

But the Texians had largely kept to their barracks and bases, and they did not ask about the occasional soldier or sailor who went missing . . . and later, perhaps, was seen again in a terribly transformed state. Desertions were not so very rare, after all.

Over the years, the occupation had become a stable and sedentary thing. The men on top of the command chain ignored the citizens' complaints, just as they ignored Marie Laveau and her church, and her graveyard pastimes.

Anything out of sight can be ignored, when knowing the whole story is too much trouble.

But Colonel Betters and Lieutenant Cardiff were gone, or worse than that—and if anyone but Josephine knew precisely what had become of them, no one was saying. If any bodies had been found, no one had honored them with a public burial. If anyone Walked, no one was speaking of it. Instead, the Texians went to ground like frightened animals, enforcing old rules and instituting new ones to keep people indoors at night.

And so the rolling-crawlers came puttering on their diesel engines, around the corners and through the alleys toward the Square in front of the Saint Louis cathedral. The last of the determined fortune-tellers and corner preachers and salesmen offering boiled crawdads or knuckles of sugarcane, everyone who'd insisted on staying until the final moment . . . they all admitted defeat, and grumbling, they put away their stalls, their makeshift stands, and their wares.

The rolling-crawlers were called such because they patrolled on hard-rubber wheels that bounded independently of one another on floating axles, allowing the carriage-sized craft to climb forward over curbs and navigate the narrow streets of the old Gulf city.

They were both better and worse than horse-drawn affairs. Better because they left no manure. Worse because they were louder, and the diesel stink of their exhalations polluted the damp, heavy air—which locked on to the best and worst of odors, keeping all smells close to the earth.

The fortune-teller said, "There's the new fellow. He came tonight, after all."

"I heard he only just arrived yesterday," Josephine replied, scanning the scene.

"Two days ago," Agatha corrected. "I'll say this for the Texians: They replace their own fast."

"I hope they don't replace Cardiff anytime soon." Josephine rose to her feet and stretched, then began to help her friend break down the little station from which she earned most of her living. "I won't be too brokenhearted if there's no one to focus on a certain lake project anymore."

"It wouldn't break my heart either, but I won't hold my breath. I hear Travis McCoy is more trouble than two Cardiffs and a mule. He'll be patrolling for your prize"—she used her preferred euphemism—"sooner rather than later."

Josephine asked, "Where is he? Do you know what he looks like?" She held a hand up over her eyes, shielding them from the last of the sun's setting glare as it bounced off the windows on the far side of the Square.

"Over there." Agatha tossed her head, indicating a large rolling-crawler, painted Texas dun. "Yellow-haired maniac atop the biggest brownie. That's him."

"How do you know, if he only got here the other night?"

"He's the only one I don't recognize. The rest of these lads"—she waved in the general direction of all four corners—"I've seen before. Not closing down for curfew, but around the Quarter. Besides, he's the only man being driven around, like the machine is his private cabriolet."

He was young for a man sent to marshal a city, probably the madam's own age—if not younger—and he was lean inside a uniform that fit him well, and was buttoned up to the top despite the early evening warmth. He had the ramrod posture of a lifelong military peg, and the lantern jaw of someone who ought to be twice his size, though the fluffy reddish-blonde beard made his exact lines hard to determine.

Given what could be seen of his face, Colonel Travis McCoy possessed the kind of bone structure that's considered "strong" on a man, and would be "unfortunate" on a woman.

While Josephine and Agatha closed up shop and sneaked glances at the rumbling machines as they puttered around the Square, the colonel lifted an amplifier to his mouth. He said something, but the words weren't loud enough and no one heard him. He fiddled with the electric coils and turned a dial, then tried it again.

This time his voice bellowed out—boosted by a handheld device shaped like a witch's hat.

"Ladies and gentlemen, I can see that most of you are in the process of wrapping up your daily business, and I thank you for your promptness." His accent leaned toward the higher-class end of the Texian spectrum. He sounded like he'd had an education someplace else, but exactly *where*, Josephine couldn't pinpoint. "I do apologize for the inconvenience, and would like to remind you that this is for your own safety."

"Like hell it is," she grumbled.

"Hush now," Agatha urged. "At least he's being polite."

"I don't care if he hands out five-dollar bills while he brushes my hair and calls me *sweetheart*, he's closing down the Square for no good reason."

"I'm trying to look on the bright side."

"There's a bright side?"

Agatha folded up her scarves, wrapped her cards, and gathered all the small things that were part of her trade. She then placed them inside the overturned box-table and picked it up. "There might be. Think about it this way: New Orleans has a zombi problem. It's also occupied by the most heavily armed military in the world, and now that military is on alert. It's a long way to go for a glimmer of light, but if nothing else good ever comes of Texas squatting here, I'd be glad if they can clear the dead out of the in-between, down by the river."

Josephine held out her hands, offering to help carry something. Agatha jutted her elbow out, pointing crookedly at the parasol, so her friend picked it up and closed it, then held it under her arm. "You give them too much credit. For all we know, they're the ones who brought the dead. We didn't have any zombis before they moved in, now, did we?"

"You've got me there. Hey, mind your mouth."

Josephine boosted an eyebrow, but didn't ask questions. A moment later, she heard the pounding footsteps of someone jogging up behind her. She pivoted on her heel and saw a man in his twenties sporting a brown uniform, homing in on her like a man with a purpose.

She bristled and gritted her teeth, but Agatha put on the sort of smile worn by a woman who earns her living dealing in pleasantries with unpleasant people. The fortune-teller exaggerated her accent when she called out, "*Bonsoir,* boy—and there's no need to rush us. We'll be on our way, you just give us half a minute."

Huffing and puffing, he drew up to a stop immediately before them and removed his hat. "Not trying to rush you, ladies. I'm—" He threw a fast, sharp look back at the rolling-crawlers, and toward Colonel McCoy. "—I'm looking for Miss Josephine Early, and that's you, ain't it, ma'am?"

Cautiously but coldly, she replied, "Yes, that's me."

He crushed the brown flop hat in one hand and punched it absently with the other. "Ma'am, I have a message from Fletcher Josty," he said.

Agatha was puzzled, but Josephine was careful not to reveal any hint of recognition. "I'm sorry, I can't say that I understand."

"This ain't my uniform, ma'am. I took it off a fellow I left back in the Rue Toulouse alley. Fletcher said to give you this." He reached into his pocket and produced a folded note. "And I'm begging you, read it fast. It's only a matter of time before some of these boys figure out none of 'em know me."

Josephine hesitated, but took the note. She recognized Fletcher Josty's handwriting immediately: *Barataria attacked. Rick injured. Holding on at the fort.* Her stomach clenched, but she had too many questions to lapse into outright panic.

"Wait, now—wait," she said, holding out one hand toward the man in the Texas uniform. "Someone's hit the pirate quarter?"

"*That* someone over there, on the lead brownie. His first rule of business when he got to town the other day was to plot it out, and yesterday he ordered the raid. Ma'am, we need to get off these streets. Hurry along, will you? I'll walk back with you to the Garden, all right?"

"All . . . all right? . . . ," she said, not moving, not taking her eyes off the note. "I just, I don't understand."

Agatha broke in. "You heard him, let's go. I'll come with you, we'll all of us walk." She put an arm on Josephine's hand and tugged.

"You're right. Let's go. Here, I have an idea."

With a swift knock of the parasol's handle, she struck Agatha's box out of her grasp. It toppled to the ground and landed on a corner, breaking in two. The fortune-teller said, "Hey!" but the pretend-Texian got the idea and said, "I've got it, ma'am. Let me help you carry these things." And in a whisper he added, "It'll give me an excuse to join you, see?"

Throughout the rest of Jackson Square, the last of the stragglers were being ushered on their way, and the Texian soldiers were assisting where it was necessary or helpful, or where they were impatient to have the streets cleared for the evening hour.

Josephine struggled to keep from shaking as the three of them abandoned the common area. The church doors closed as they walked past, and the darkness had fallen nearly enough to call it night—so that when they ducked into the alley to the right of the church, they were suddenly all but invisible. In those narrow minutes between the sun going down and the gas lamps being struck, they were indistinguishable from the shadows.

The cathedral loomed above them, its iron fencing and thick stone walls blocking them in like a fort. Josephine drew up short in the alley, unwilling to step into the Quarter beyond, not yet. She seized the young man by the shoulder and spoke quickly, quietly.

"Why would McCoy invade the bay? What was my brother doing there, and how did he get hurt? Where is he now?"

As fast as he could, the man rapid-fired his responses. "I don't know why McCoy took the bay, I only know he gave the order and it happened—but it took 'em all day. Pirates don't hand over easy, especially not when they've been dug in somewhere for so long. Your brother was there hitching a ride on a Cajun rig called the *Crawdaddy,* doing I'm-not-sure-what. Rick got caught in a firefight and he's taken two bullets. Neither of them killed him, but he needs a doctor, and that means he's got to get upriver. Nobody in the city will risk treating him right now, and with the curfew—well, he's still at Barataria, holed up with Fletcher and one of the Lafitte boys," he said. "But they'll move him out one way or the other, come morning. They'll get him someplace safe."

"How bad is it? And don't you lie to me, now."

"I didn't see him, I only agreed to run the message from Fletcher. Let's get back to the Garden Court, and we can talk about it. I'll tell you everything I know."

"I have to go to my brother."

Horrified, Agatha said, "You don't mean it, Josie! Let the men take care of their own. When he's out of town and all healed up, you can go meet him. You'll do nobody any good by throwing your-self in harm's way. Think what Rick would say if he knew you were coming."

"He'd tell me to get the hell back into my house and he'd see me on the other side. But he isn't here, and I never listened to him much, anyway." Her words cracked around the edges, and she was glad for the darkness. "*I'm* the elder. It's his job to listen to *me,* and mine is to . . ." She tore the note to tiny pieces and dropped it into a stream of manure and river runoff along the street's edge. "Mine is to take care of him. Just like I promised Momma I would."

A rolling-crawler went roaring past the alley, filling the slim space with diesel fumes and a rattling echo that rang around the walls. It dimmed, the brownie moved on, and Josephine continued. "I won't leave him out there, nursed by pirates who can't stitch a button. I'm going to him, and I'm going to take him to the bayou myself—so Edison Brewster can run him north and get him the help he needs, if he needs more of it than I can give him."

"Josie, you're *daft.*"

"You know it's true, both of you," she appealed to her compan-ions in turn. "If he stays there, under siege on the islands until morning . . . God knows what'll become of him. No." She shook her head, not clearing her thoughts but winding them up. "No, I'm go-ing after him. I'd rather die knowing than sit at home and wonder."

The young man sighed and caught her arm when she turned to run back the way she'd come. Before she could haul off and hit him, he said, "Fletcher told me you'd say as much. He said you wouldn't stay put and it was up to me to keep you from coming out there, but he also told me it was a lost cause from the get-go."

"Do you know where they are? Right now?" Josephine asked. She pried her arm out of his grasp.

"Just like the note said, they're at the fort—unless somebody's moved them. I'll take you there, if you won't have it any other way. But first, we have to get off the streets. The patrols will catch up to us any minute. Hurry up now, back to the Garden Court," he begged. "We can leave from there—it isn't far, is it?"

"Only a few blocks. And you're right, I have to go home first. Come on, let's go."

"Josie?"

"Aggie, you coming, too?"

"No, I'm heading back to my own place like a law-abiding citizen. But I want to say good luck, and I love you."

Josephine swallowed hard, then kissed Agatha on the cheek. "Don't say such things. It's like you don't think I'll be back."

"I hope you'll be back," she said. Josephine didn't answer.

Instead she fled the alley and rushed back down the warren of narrow blocks overhanging with balconies and lamps, streets wet just like always. Her feet slapped side by side with the young man's as together they darted through the Quarter. All along the way, doors were being closed and windows were being drawn; shutters were being pulled and lights inside were coming on, same as the lights in the streets—lit one by one as low-ranking Texian enlisted men complained their way up and down the ladders to spark the lights and brighten the gloom.

They slipped inside the Garden Court just ahead of the first patrol of rolling-crawlers, their dastardly engines churning and lumpy wheels rolling up and down over the curbs, splashing through puddles, and spewing ghost-gray clouds with every shove of every cylinder.

Josephine slammed the door shut behind them and nearly locked it, but changed her mind when she realized she was only frightened.

Curfew or no, this was an after-hours business. So long as customers stayed off the streets, no one had gone to the trouble of shutting them down. Business was off by about 30 percent, yes. But it could be worse. It could be off altogether, and locking the front door would be a start in that direction.

The madam's sudden and dramatic entrance stunned the lobby's occupants into silence.

Delphine Hoobler and Septima Hare had been talking together on the long dais, but their conversation drew up short and now they stared at their employer. Likewise, Olivia Tillman and her suitor had paused on their way upstairs, and the perennially present Fenn Calais had stopped in his tracks, Ruthie under one arm and Caroline under the other.

"Miss Josephine?" asked the old Texian with the deep pockets and large appetite.

She put one hand on her chest beneath her throat, and did a lady-like show of not gasping for breath. "I beg everyone's pardon, please," she said—directing the apology first to the unknown guest and Fenn Calais, then the rest of the ladies. "The curfew, you understand. This gentleman was trying to find his way here, and I only stepped out to lend him a hand. Please, everyone. Carry on, and let's enjoy the rest of the night."

But Ruthie slipped out from under Calais's arm, quickly replaced by Septima—with Fenn's blessing, or apathy. She came back to Josephine, who dropped herself onto the hard-padded couch beside Delphine. Still waiting for the coast to clear, she gave the men another half minute to retreat and then gave her orders quietly as the women gathered around and the man who'd accompanied her stood stiffly, nervously by the door. He looked out the window, watching through a slit in the curtains.

"I'm leaving tonight," Josephine said. "For a day or two—that's all. My brother's been hurt, and I need to see him."

"Deaderick?" gasped Ruthie. "What happened?"

"He's been shot, but he's alive—and he's going to be all right, I'm pretty confident of that. I have to go take care of him, though. I have to help Fletcher Josty move him safe back to the bayou. From there, Edison will take him up the river to a doctor, if we can't find one any closer."

Olivia's eyes welled up with tears. This was not an uncommon event, but just this once, Josephine didn't mind it. The young woman asked, "Is he in town? Why don't they bring him to town? We'd find a doctor for him here. Maybe Dr. Heuvelman—"

"Miss *Tillman,*" the madam said with less than her usual measure of patience. Olivia was lovely, kind, and well intentioned, but sometimes painfully slow. "Between the curfew and his face being on wanted posters from Metairie to the Gulf, that's possibly the worst idea in the world. I'll go to him and get him moved, and then I'll be back here by week's end."

Ruthie, on the other hand, was much sharper. "He's not in town and he's not in the bayou? Where is he?"

"Somewhere else. This fellow here—I'm sorry, darling, I didn't catch your name."

"Gifford," he provided. "I'm Gifford Crooks." Upon suddenly finding himself the most interesting person in the room, he blushed and kept talking. "I'm with Mr. Pinkerton's Secret Service—his Saint Louis office, working with the bayou boys as of last week. I'm . . . new. This is my first job."

"I'd have never guessed it," Josephine said dryly.

"He's a Pink?" Marylin's face hardened.

"The Union hires them sometimes. They sent Mr. Crooks here to give me the message. "Marylin, I'm leaving you in charge for now.

Swap off with Hazel if you need to take a customer, and Ruthie—
I know you stay busy, but you're third in command."

Ruthie said, "No."

"Excuse me?"

"No, ma'am. I'm coming with you."

"You're doing no such thing. You're staying here and working.
I know you have a soft spot for Rick, but there's nothing you can
do to help except get in the way."

Ruthie turned to Gifford Crooks and asked, "Did you tell her
the same thing, when she told you she was coming along?"

"Yes, ma'am."

"You leave him out of this!" Josephine commanded. "You're not
coming, and that's it." Ruthie could prove problematic, if they were
intercepted and searched.

"I *am* coming." Then, in French—because it was easier for her,
"You'll need me, if something goes wrong. You'll need someone to
come back and tell everyone what's happened."

"Nothing will go wrong. And any fool can run a message home."

"Well, I sure as all hell hope nothing goes wrong," Ruthie blasphemed in her native tongue. She strolled to the hall closet and
removed her best navy blue jacket, a jewel-toned silk confection
with more pockets than anyone would ever guess. "And I may be a
fool of an errand girl, but I will not be left behind. I'll be back in
two shakes. Don't leave without me, because I do not want to run
and catch up." With that, she climbed the stairs.

Josephine growled, "Fine! Since Ruthie can't be trusted to stay
put on her own, she's coming with me. If anyone shows up and asks
for her by special request, tell him she's down with a fever and they
can come back Friday night. I'll offer a discount for the wait."

Marylin listened to every word with great concentration, com-
mitting the whole of it to memory. "Ma'am?" she asked when Josephine stopped to take a breath. "You *will* come back, won't you?"

"Yes. By tomorrow, or the day after at the latest."

"But if this is dangerous, and I suppose it must be . . . what if you don't?"

Josephine looked around the room, meeting their eyes one by one. In every face, she saw fear. "I *will* be back, and Rick *will* be alive. You trust me?"

All the ladies nodded, some more slowly than others. Olivia sniffled and wiped at her nose with the back of her hand, even though she was holding a handkerchief.

"Good. Then keep trusting me, and I'll be back soon."

As if she'd been waiting for an entrance cue, Ruthie chose this moment to swan back down the stairs and into the lobby, looking no different at all from when she'd left it—apart from a sturdier pair of boots than strictly matched her dress, and a few inconspicuous lumps here and there in the long silk jacket.

"I am back," she declared. "I have a gun, and I am *ready.*"

Josephine stood and went to the hall closet. She retrieved a black hooded cloak that was really too warm for the occasion, but she liked having it all the same. "One moment," she declared. "I need to gather some things as well. Ruthie, since you're so damn determined to be useful, see if Mr. Crooks wants anything."

Ruthie turned the full, blinding force of her charm on Gifford, who appeared embarrassed yet again to have been noticed. Everyone in the room knew by now that he was not terribly accustomed to such houses, and there was literally nothing that anyone could do to put him at ease. This didn't stop Ruthie from giving it a go, as directed.

On her way upstairs, Josephine heard the woman offering water, whiskey, rum, or coffee, and she heard only mumbles from Gifford in return.

It took no time at all for her to grab Little Russia from its spot in her desk; a box of bullets that she dumped into a pouch, which she stashed in the cloak's inner pocket; a small derringer she sometimes carried as backup; and a wad of emergency cash and assorted coins.

Downstairs she went again. Ruthie was champing at the bit to hit the road—as was Gifford, who couldn't turn any pinker with a pot of paint. "Ladies," she said to bid them adieu. "Ruthie, Gifford. When was the last patrol?"

"Right after we got here," Gifford told her.

"Let's say five or ten minutes . . . all right. We'll go out the back. We'll have more time if we head toward Rue Barrack." She tossed her big ring of keys to Marylin and gave Ruthie one last look—on the off chance her resolve was weakening, and maybe she'd change her mind.

No such luck.

"All right, then. Let's go."

Out the back door they stepped, into the wet, dark smell of the river that clung to the walls and wafted off the street—held in place by a layer of fog that was forming before their very eyes.

"Ugh," Ruthie complained. "Just what we need."

Josephine corrected her, "It *is* just what we need. It'll give us cover as we get out of town."

"Not if it stays like this," her determined assistant argued. "It is too thin to hide us, and so thick, it could hide . . . other things."

"The zombis are down by the river and the Texians are being useful, just this once. Their patrols will keep the Quarter clear, you can count on that. The dead are too dumb to run and hide. They only want to feed."

Gifford gazed uncertainly at the wisping fog. "The dead? I've heard stories, but . . . they're not true, are they?"

"They're true, Mr. Crooks," Josephine informed him. "The dead Walk, and they are usually hungry. But they're no threat to us here, or where we're going."

"You said they're down by the river, and we have to cross it!"

"We'll cross west of here, away from the Quarter. We'll be fine."

Ruthie whispered, "And how do we get to the ferry? It's too far to walk unless we've got all night."

"The cabs, out on Rue Canal."

"They will be closed for the night," she noted, even as she fell in line behind Josephine, with Gifford behind her. To the alley's edge they went, looking both ways before darting out onto the street.

Over her shoulder, Josephine hissed, "Then we'll have to wake someone up."

Night had fully settled now, and the gas lamps made pockets of brightness that lit the corners and crossways. Sticking to the shadows, the three fugitives from the curfew ran on toward Rue Canal at the Quarter's edge. Upon hitting it, they went left—back toward the Mississippi, down to the river in exactly the way that Josephine had promised they would not. But that's where the carriages usually waited. They were now folded up for the evening, except for a few stragglers who were allowed to break curfew for the sake of emergency.

These late-night drivers were mostly bored and huddled against the mist, playing cards with one another or drinking surreptitiously from the bottles they kept by their seats. This far edge of the Quarter's boundary was not so strictly watched, for even the controlling, aggravating Texians understood that this was a commercial border, and strangers to the city might not know the limits. Sometimes, a way must be found inside or out.

Josephine suspected it had more to do with leaving loopholes for Texians to wander off during their leaves, but there was no time to stew about the injustice of it all, not when Rick was hurt and surrounded by pirates.

She dashed up to the first carriage, manifesting under the closest gas lamp like an apparition. The driver gasped. He was an older man, with dark skin as wrinkled as last month's apples. Pulling himself to his feet, he stepped off the curb and said, "Hey, now, ma'am. It's after curfew, and here you are sneaking about—"

She cut him off. "What do you care who sneaks where, so long as we can pay? We've left the Quarter with Texas's permission," she lied outright. "We need a ride, and we have money. Get on your seat and drive us."

"Now, that's no way to talk to—"

"If you're not interested, we'll just ask one of those other gentlemen over there."

"Nobody said I wasn't interested. But you fine . . . folks," he said as Gifford and Ruthie emerged from the shadows of the cross street. "You can get an old feller in trouble! We're not supposed to move nowhere, not without a note from the new man's office."

"We have no such note. If you won't drive us, we'll try the next man in line."

Ruthie stepped forward, positioning herself so that her very best angles were lit by the grimy, fog-smeared light. She pushed herself very close into the driver's space, and he recoiled, but only in a perfunctory manner that was quickly eased by the prostitute's pretty smile.

"You wear no ring," she observed.

"No, miss, I . . . my wife, she done passed on. She's a long time gone, God rest her soul."

"Then let me sweeten the deal for you, eh, sugar?" She placed one long-fingered, perfectly manicured hand up against the driver's head and whispered behind it into his ear. The whispering took longer than Josephine liked, but the look on the man's face told her that whatever Ruthie was promising, it was working.

"I'll drive you, I'll drive you!" he stammered. "That's a real generous offer, and, and, here." He hustled to the side of the carriage and opened the door. "Y'all just climb right up inside and I'll take you where you're going." He paused. "Where *are* you going?"

Josephine accepted Gifford's hand and climbed up onto the carriage's step, stopping only to say, "Get us to the ferry at Tchoupitoulas."

"Yes, ma'am. Right away, ma'am."

Gifford crawled in behind her, and both of them settled into an interior that was cramped and dark, but clean. Ruthie poked her head up to the window nearest Josephine and said, "I will ride up front."

"Good girl, Ruthie."

Gifford sat forward, asking very close to her ear, "Is she . . . Is she—?"

"Don't ask if you don't want to know, Mr. Crooks." The carriage took off with a lurch. Their heads nearly knocked together, but they dipped away from each other at the last moment. "We are what we are, and we use the tools at our disposal."

"But she shouldn't have to—"

"She *chooses* to." And almost brightly she concluded, "Look, we're moving—and like the wind, I'll note."

Gifford Crooks settled back against his seat, his face unreadable in the flickering shadows of the gas lamps in the city as it disappeared behind them. Queasily, he said, "I hope our driver can keep his eyes on the road. Not every man can pay attention to two things at once."

"True, but I know plenty of women who can—and Ruthie is an excellent horsewoman, should the situation call for it. Don't worry, Mr. Crooks. Not yet."

"So I'm allowed to worry later?"

"Allowed? I'll positively encourage it. We're headed to a pirate bay that's under siege. The night will get worse before it gets better."

They rode the rest of the way in silence, unable to hear anything from the driver's seat and unwilling to speak until the river, where the lights of the ferry and the sound of its steam-driven paddle wheel were a huge relief, though not huge enough to take away any of Josephine's simmering terror. At any time, her baby brother could die from his wounds—away from home, away from the bayou, with no family and only the rough ministrations of his fellow guerrillas and unwashed privateers to soothe the pain.

She wouldn't have it. She'd arrive in time, and she would save him.

She squeezed her gun like a talisman, as if it could help her, or help Deaderick—beyond commanding someone to assist him.

There might be someone else present—someone with needles, salves, and tinctures. Pirates came from all walks of life, she knew this from experience. A doctor, disgraced from some terrible malpractice. A field medic, having escaped the war. Some foreigner with the training of a different land.

Anything was possible.

She'd heard that North Africans had good medicine, that the worshippers of Muhammad were well trained in math and surgery. The Chinese, too, were known to be great healers, though their medicine was strange to the Western mind.

Pirates didn't much care about an officer or medic's race or God, so long as a fellow could patch a body back into a single piece.

For that matter, Josephine mused as she stumbled down from the cab's step, she'd settle for a woman. A nurse would do in a pinch, if she could find one. If one were so mad as to surround herself with men like those at Barataria.

At the river's edge, the glowing pier looked like matchsticks against the flowing expanse of the Mississippi, snaking through the night. The river was awesomely black and sparkling, so wide that the other side was not apparent; so powerful that it moved like the monstrous leviathan of legend, undulating south to join the Gulf. It rustled and rushed, making the usual music of water being pushed and churned by the tens of thousands of tons.

As soon as the carriage stopped, Josephine and Gifford could hear the Gulf, and tried to take comfort from it. "Almost there," Josephine lied to herself and to him—and though he knew better, he did not correct her.

She threw open the cab's door before the driver could see to it, and as she jumped down off the stair, she heard Ruthie climbing to the ground on the other side. Ruthie walked around the front, stopping to pat the horse's sweaty brown head. She rejoined her employer by the time Gifford could extricate himself.

Josephine handed off a few coins, one of which ought to be several days' wages for the old driver. He thanked her with a mumble, grasped the front of his pants, and tucked in his shirt. He tipped his rumpled cap and wished the lot of them a good night, and he was on his way immediately—leaving the three would-be rescuers standing at the edge of a milling group of other travelers, all of them waiting for the ferry.

The low, flat barge was sidling up to the pier even as they watched. Its engines rumbled with the same sound and the same fuel as the rolling-crawlers, forcing the side wheel to dig deep through the current and haul the thing along. Carriages, horses, and two or three stray messengers and merchants crowded eagerly forward. Sailors on board threw ropes to the workers on the pier, lining up the long, pale boat and cinching it against the launch. Then a wide double ramp was lowered drawbridge-style from a power-driven pulley, allowing the ferry's late-night guests to disembark.

There weren't many people on board—not at this hour, coming up close to nine thirty, and not with the curfew dealing a death blow to the nightlife.

Only a few tired-looking travelers led yawning horses off the boat, and behind them came half a dozen Texians. Three were in uniform, three were not; but anyone who'd seen a Texian official knew the posture anywhere. Josephine recognized it as easily as the smell of baking bread. They wore an insouciance and a swagger she found infuriating. They walked as if they had authority, and they did not expect to be asked any questions about it.

Still, she smiled tightly and with civility. Some of them ignored her; one said, "Ma'am," in passing; and the last one off the boat tipped his hat in her general direction. As this final passenger debarked, a Texian almost too young to wear the uniform went running up to him, saying, "Ranger Korman, there you are. It's so good to meet you, sir. I'm so glad you could make it."

Rangers. Hat tip or no, they were the worst of the bunch.

A dockhand made the call for travelers to board with fares in hand. Gifford Crooks led the way, still in his Texian uniform and looking like less trouble than his two companions. Then again,

considering that he was accompanied by two ladies of the evening, perhaps he looked like the most trouble anyone had seen all
week.

Josephine might have passed for a respectable spinster—
someone's governess or middle-class aunt, hidden under her cloak—
and she might have even passed for white, for Gifford's mother, in a
pinch. But Ruthie, in her flamboyant garb, darkened eyes, tea-colored
skin, and brightened lips, would fool no one on any count.

They scrambled aboard quickly and settled in for the trip, but no
one was very settled, except perhaps Ruthie, whose face had firmed
into a look of grim, ambitious concentration. Despite her initial
vows to the contrary, Josephine was glad Ruthie had insisted on
coming along. She even reached out and took the woman's gloved
hand in her own, just to have something to hold that wouldn't mind
being squeezed a bit too hard.

Across from the pair of them, seated on a bench and trying not
to slump there, Gifford Crooks worked hard to appear alert and
ready for action; but it was easy to see that he'd had a rough afternoon, and he hadn't intended to go back to Barataria tonight.

The ferry fought the river, foot by foot, and the paddle wheel
dragged the lightly laden barge to the west bank. The engines
strained and the diesel spewed out over the water, where fish occasionally slapped against the surface and floating logs rolled over as
lazy and large as the alligators that hung closer to the marshes—
outside the current's pull, where the water was stagnant and
smelly.

Behind them, the French Quarter drifted away. Its gas lamps
struggled against the darkness, signaling the stars and mimicking the
moon. But the fog had rolled in hard, and it blanketed the blocks
with its warm coverage and left the curfew-quieted neighborhood a
low, gray smear against the waterline.

Finally the ferry pulled up against the western pier, and another
crane lowered another drawbridge down against the deck. The passengers disembarked into near emptiness.

Josephine shivered despite herself, and despite her too-warm cloak. "Now comes the hard part," she breathed.

"Pourquoi?"

Gifford Crooks answered Ruthie as they walked away from the water, back toward the docks and the small shipping district that springs up around any ferry's destination. "Now we have to cross the marshes. Now we have to get to the island."

Ruthie nodded. "Then, *on y va*! Before it gets any later."

Josephine asked, "You've never been to Barataria before, have you?"

"How do you know?"

"If you'd ever been, you'd understand why the rest of the trip is a problem. Gifford?"

"Yes, ma'am?"

"Where's our boat?"

"A mile from here down the river road, on the edge of the canal," he said quietly.

She asked, "Are you sure?"

"No, but that's where we've been leaving the blowers for coming and going—and that's where I left mine, when I came to town to give you Fletcher's message. If it's not there, I don't know what we'll do."

"If it's not there, we'll come back and look for something else. Mr. Crooks, do you have a light?"

"I do," he promised, and he pulled an electric torch from his jacket. It was small, but it'd have to do. The roads up and down the marsh's edges were not uniformly lit, and they were dangerous.

Now Ruthie's concern showed through, only a little, leaking past her determined demeanor. "We will walk a mile, in the dark?"

"Mostly in the dark," Josephine confirmed. "But it shouldn't be too bad. The Texians are purging the bay, aren't they? We shouldn't run into any robbers or mercenaries."

"Unless they have been chased *out* of the bay," Ruthie mused. "Some of them are alive. Deaderick's still alive."

Check Out Receipt

Hagerstown
301-739-3250
www.washcolibrary.org

Wednesday, July 11, 2018 5:15:06 PM

Item: 32395011427198
Title: Arcanum unbounded : the Cosmere col
lection
Call no.: FIC San
Due: 08/01/2018

Item: 32395011685779
Title: The dread wyrm
Call no.: FIC Cam
Due: 08/01/2018

Total items: 2

Visit us online at www.washcolibrary.org
to manage your account and renew items.

Gifford tried to reassure them. "Most of the pirates went out to the Gulf, heading south if they could. There are ships at the coast to take them in—and those who didn't get that far went deeper into the swamps. There are dozens of islands between the pirate docks and . . . and anything else. The rest of Louisiana. The river. The ocean."

"And we have to wade past them."

"The blower has an engine," Gifford informed them. "We'll get through pretty quick, all things considered."

"I hope it has oars, too," Josephine said, setting off down the packed-earth stretch leading in the direction Gifford had indicated. "Because we can't risk the noise. Not once we get past Bay Sans-bois."

The Pinkerton man took a deep breath and said, "Sooner than that, to tell you the truth. We'll have to take the water straight down to the edge of the islands at Point à la Hache, and then cross our fingers, cut the motor, and slink over to the big shore."

Ruthie asked, "What about the siege?" and she darted to catch up as Gifford pumped a switch, then flicked it—sparking a filament to create a wobbly yellow beam. The small device hummed in his hands. He reached into his pocket and pulled out a glove, which he wrapped around the torch like an oven mitt. Within twenty minutes, the thing would be too hot to hold.

He took Ruthie's elbow with his free hand, guiding her to walk beside him. "The siege . . . I don't know. They'd done their worst by the time I left 'em, and mostly they were just sweeping the place, blowing up what airships they could reach, and wreaking havoc to wake the devil. If we're real lucky, they'll have gotten bored and gone home. They've done what they set out to do, haven't they?"

"It depends on what they were up to. I mean, what they were *really* up to," Josephine worried aloud. "If all they wanted to do was scare some pirates, or blow Lafitte's old docks to pieces, I guess they've done their duty. Texas can afford to waste the time and ammunition on a bunch of outlaws who've been camped there for a hundred years, but why now? Why would this new fellow make it a priority, first thing? The pirates didn't have anything to do with his predecessor getting eaten."

Gifford speculated, "Maybe they don't know that. Maybe they think the bay boys had something to do with it, and they don't know anything about these . . . about the dead, down by the river."

Josephine didn't respond right away. She walked on Gifford's left, with Ruthie on his right, and she scanned the narrow strip of road she could see by the light of the electric candle. Eventually she said, "Deaderick was there, and Fletcher Josty. I hate to wonder, but I can't help it."

"Wonder what?" he asked.

"Wonder if Texas didn't follow them down from Pontchartrain. Wonder if Texas is killing two birds with one stone, uprooting the Lafittes and going after the *Ganymede* in one big push. *Ganymede* isn't at Barataria, but Texas doesn't know that."

And then all of them were silent, all the way down to the canal.

Six

North Texas was as good a place to stop as any, and on the edge of Oneida was a temporary hydrogen dock—the kind that was scarcely temporary anymore, and had become a small town of its own, hanging on to the settlement's edge like a barnacle . . . a barnacle that might explode and take half the desert with it, given just the right sort of accident. Bigger cities had bigger, better regulated docks; but on the unincorporated frontier, these mobile constructions squatted wherever they found a place to do so. Dangerous, dirty, and marginally managed by whoever was richest and had the biggest guns, the docks were not popular with travelers or merchants, but they were necessary. And heaven knew the air pirates were happy to make use of them.

All across the Panhandle, the flat, brown earth was speckled with tufts of dark grass, cactus nubs, and tumbleweeds being kicked about by the occasional dust devil. It was a dry, dull, featureless place in Cly's opinion, but he didn't have to live there, so he didn't feel moved to complain about it.

As the *Naamah Darling* arrived, the whole settlement—hydrogen barnacle and all—was digging out from underneath a windstorm that had knocked down horses, sent water troughs rolling through the streets, and picked roofs off buildings only to fling them miles out into the empty, prickly nothing beyond the town's grid.

Pale yellow sand the color of sun-bleached leather drifted into piles in the corners of fences and up against the warped wood walls of the church, bar, saddle company, law office, laundry, jail, dry goods store, and clapboard train station with its lonely pair of tracks. Men were already setting upon the tracks and sweeping them, and from the drifts of bone-dry dirt, the occasional flap of canvas would disturb the seamless layer of brown.

Dirigibles large and small were tangled together on the dock's eastern edge, implying a western zephyr that had moved with the might of a bored god's fist. Riggers and engineers swarmed around these docks, shouting to cooperate and untangle the lobster claws and lines, and to dig out the pipes themselves to determine what had been uprooted, and what had only been bent out of place.

But the western line of the dock was nearly unoccupied, save for two small mail express dirigibles that had been battened down with better rigging. Cly set his own bird down beside them, and ten minutes later he was on his way to town.

Fang and Kirby Troost remained with the ship to see if the sulfuric acid vats were stable and could be hooked up to the hydrogen hoses, and if not, to assist with repairs. But Houjin accompanied the captain, ostensibly to get a gander at Oneida. Houjin was seventeen, and nothing short of brilliant. But he'd spent most of his life sheltered under the Seattle streets. Any chance to get out of the city was a chance for him to learn, observe, and drive people crazy.

"This place is a wreck!" the kid declared. "Is it always like this?"

"No, they've had a storm," the captain told him again. The subject had already come up while they were overhead, surveying the damage in advance of landing.

"But everything is so *dry*!"

"That's why they call them windstorms. Or . . . dust storms. But they're common out here. No trees, you see. No grass, no plants with roots to hold on to the soil. No mountains to break up the sky and give the weather something to work around."

"It's hot as hell."

A straggling gust of warm, dusty air smacked them in the face and dragged itself past them, tugging at their clothes and coiling off into tiny dust devils behind them. The captain pulled his goggles down off his head and fixed them over his eyes to keep out the next batch of blown debris, and he said, "You think this is hot? Wait until we get to the Gulf."

"It's even worse?"

"It's just as bad. It's wet, and the river runs through it—so there aren't just trees but swamps, and grasses that grow out of the water as tall as me. Moss hangs off every branch of every tree, and everything is green and overgrown. Everything lives there. Giant trees that look like they're melting. Animals like you've only heard about in books." An almost wistful look crossed his face, but he put it down quickly by recalling, "You'll sweat through everything you're wearing. It's like you never dry off, not really."

The boy's enthusiasm flagged, but quickly buoyed back up again. "Can we swim in the river? That'd be a good way to cool off."

"I wouldn't recommend it, not unless you want to get bitten by snakes, or eaten by alligators."

"Hm," Houjin said, chewing this over as they strolled past a dog crawling out from under a saloon's porch. The animal sneezed and shook itself, then wandered away. "And you used to live there?"

"I didn't . . . I didn't *live* there. Not exactly. I just spent a lot of time there."

"Why?"

"You sure are full of questions today."

"Kirby says I'm always full of questions."

"Kirby's right."

"Where are we going?"

"Over there. Train station."

"Why? We don't need a train."

"No," the captain agreed. "But we need a telegraph operator, and that's where towns usually keep them."

"Why?"

"Because the people who run the trains need to know who's

coming and going. And they need to know the weather and all," he said vaguely. "And passengers do, too. They like to send notes to their friends and families, if they're traveling a real long way. Remember how Nurse Lynch was sending dispatches from the road—when she was on her way from Virginia?"

"I remember."

"Well, there you go."

"Where are you sending a telegram?"

"To New Orleans—to the lady who wants us to take a job," Cly said, preemptively answering the next thing poised to fly out of Houjin's mouth. Speculating on the third thing the kid had on deck, he added, "I tried to drop a wire from Portland, but there was some kind of problem with the poles, they said. And I forgot in Boise, and the office had closed by the time we made it to Denver. Now we're only a thousand miles out, and I've dillydallied about letting the lady know we're coming. So I'm doing it now."

"Oh."

Andan Cly had bought himself a few yards of silence, enough to reach the wood plank walkway of the train station, and to hike the last few feet to the sign that announced WESTERN UNION. He ducked the sign but still managed to clip it with the edge of his head, sending it swinging on its chains. Upon entering the small office, he swiped his goggles off his face and let them hang around his neck.

"Hello," greeted a tiny, chipper woman with enough highly coiffed black hair to weave a blanket. It was difficult to escape the impression that she'd chosen the style with the specific intent of appearing larger. "What can I do for you, sir?"

Houjin slipped into the office behind the captain, and the woman gave him a puzzled look, but didn't address him.

"I need to send a telegram. To a . . . boarding house. In New Orleans."

"Very good, sir. Our rates are as posted." She pointed at a sign that noted the charge by the line.

He said, "That's fine." He withdrew a square of scratch paper

from his back pocket and unfolded it to reveal a message, addressed
to Josephine Early at the Garden Court Boarding House on the
Rue Dumaine. It had been distilled down to its essence, with all
the important parts preserved, but not a drop of sentiment to be
detected.

WILL TAKE THE JOB. INCOMING APPROX. APRIL 16.
STOPPING AT BB FIRST, THEN INTO TOWN TO TEXIAN
DOCK/MACHINE WORKS. SEE YOU THEN. AC.

The operator examined the message and flipped through her
listings of New Orleans connections, then hesitated. "Can I ask you
something—is 'BB' short for Barataria Bay?"

Cly replied, "Sure, that's where I'm going first. Got to pick up a
few things."

"Ooh," she exclaimed. And in a low, conspiratorial tone, she
added, "I suppose I ought to pass along a little warning to you,
then, in the spirit of friendliness." The operator leaned forward and
crossed her arms, the veritable picture of a woman who was thrilled
by the opportunity to gossip with a real live person, and not a face-
less set of dots and dashes over the taps. "You know how Texas oc-
cupies the city, don't you?"

Cly nodded. "Sure, I know."

She lowered her voice even further, as if anyone but Houjin were
within overhearing range. "All right, then. Something happened to
a couple of officers down there—something that no one wants to talk
about. They disappeared or died, that's my guess. Anyhow," she continued, "a *new* officer went in to replace the colonel a couple of days
ago. And the first thing he does when he takes post . . . oh, Lordy.
Just guess!"

"I'm a terrible guesser. Just tell me."

"Well!" she went on, downright breathless. "First thing he does
is, he comes down on the bay with a full brigade of soldiers, and
they wipe Barataria clean off the earth!"

Stunned, the captain exclaimed, "You can't be serious!"

She settled back and leaned in her chair. "I don't know how bad the damage is, 'cause I ain't seen it in person, you know. But it's all anyone's been talking about on the lines. And if you don't mind my bringing it up, a lot of the men like yourself who are passing through . . . they're the kind to stop by the bay, if they're headed that far south."

"I don't mind," he all but mumbled, but not because her observation bothered him. He pressed for more. "But surely the bay's not . . . I mean, it wasn't *destroyed*? It's been . . . what it is . . . for seventy years or more. It's practically an institution! And Texas hadn't bothered it yet, occupation or none." The great pirate Jean Lafitte had established the bay as his own personal kingdom, back in 1810 or thereabouts. It'd come and gone, changed hands, changed allegiances, and changed flags with the rest of Louisiana . . . but it'd always been held by pirates. Lafitte's sons, after he'd died. And after them, his grandchildren.

She sighed heavily and shook her head with great drama. "I'm sure I couldn't say, sir. All I know is that the new man made it his mission to stomp the place flat, and he got his plan under way just the other night. I don't know if there's anything left standing but the fort, and I'm none too sure about that."

"Captain?" Houjin started to ask something, but Cly waved him into silence.

"Now, how much of what you're telling me is gossip, and how much do you know for sure?" he asked the small woman with the big hair.

"I told you, I haven't seen it myself. But I've heard the story from more than one tapper along the lines, so there's *some* truth to it. You'd best be careful, if you're thinking of docking down that way. Or skip it altogether, that's my advice."

"Thank you," he said to her, and he reached for his money. "I might skip it, like you said. There's nothing over there that's so important I can't pick it up someplace else."

He paid for his telegram and ushered Houjin out of the office, back into the street, before the boy could unleash his insatiable questioning upon the woman. It worked, but that meant Cly had to answer all the questions himself.

"Do you think she's right? Do you think the docks are all gone? I wanted to see the pirate bay."

"I don't know if she's right. I don't know if the docks are all gone. And I wanted to see it, too, for the rum and absinthe moves cheaper over there—without the city, the state, and the Confederacy all taking their taxes on it. Now I'm not so sure."

"Are we going to stop there anyway?"

"Let me think about it."

Back at the docks, the excavation and return to order were under way, and Fang was helping someone beneath an overhang. His head and hands were buried under a tank, and two other men were bracing it up on a set of jacks. One of them turned to Cly and said, "Lines are all clogged up, but we're clearing them out now. We'll have these ready to start fueling again in a few minutes."

"Thanks, Fred," Cly told him.

"You know these guys?" Houjin pounced into the conversation.

"Sure. That's Fred Evans, and underneath with Fang—that's Dale Winter, isn't it?"

From under the tank, someone called, "Cly, that you?"

"Yeah, it's me."

"What are these tanks for? Is this where you make the hydrogen? How do you do it? How did the lines get clogged? Do sandstorms always do this? Do—"

"And who's this?" Fred Evans looked quizzically at the boy.

Cly sighed. "This is Houjin. Call him Huey if that's easier. He's learning to fly with us, and this is his first big trip away from home."

"You're a more patient man than I am."

"Not sure if that's true or not," the captain said. "Is there anything I can do to help? We need to hit the sky."

"Not much. I think they've got the bottom tubes just about cleaned, ain't that right, fellas?"

Dale Winter said, "Uh-huh," and Fang flashed a thumbs-up sign from under the crate.

"Then I suppose I'll get out of your way. And I'll take *him* with me," Cly said with a nod at Houjin.

"But I want to stay and watch—I've never seen the hydrogen generated before, and I might need to know someday. I especially might need to know if we're going to start a generator of our own, back home," he pointed out.

The captain didn't want to admit that the kid was right, but before he had to, Fred said, "Don't worry about it, Cly. He can stay, and he can ask questions. You thinking about setting up a dock for yourself?"

"Back in Seattle, one of these days. Maybe soon."

"Seattle? That backwater? I didn't know anybody lived there anymore."

"You'd be surprised. And I've been talking to the . . . uh . . . well, he's kind of like the mayor," Cly exaggerated. "We're thinking a hydrogen dock would be a good thing for the town."

"Would you be running it?"

"I think so, yes."

Fred nodded thoughtfully. "Not a bad way for a man to retire. The work's not so hard, and I guess out there up north, you don't have these god-awful dust storms to worry about."

"No, no dust storms."

Cly retreated to the *Naamah Darling,* leaving Houjin to learn about the system. Though the lad had never undergone any formal education, he was smarter than almost anyone the captain had ever known—a boy with an easy mastery of everything with gears, levers, valves, wires, or bolts . . . to say nothing of his flair for languages.

Fang understood Portuguese, English, and both Mandarin and Cantonese—but he couldn't speak any of them, and most of his communication with others came in the form of hand signs or written notes. Cly himself knew a smattering of French, left over from his days lurking about New Orleans, and he could not read or write Mandarin, but he spoke enough to make himself understood . . . if the other speaker were very, very patient. Otherwise, he was limited to the English he'd learned from the cradle onward, and it was sometimes insufficient.

But Huey had a brain like a sponge.

Born to speak Mandarin, he'd picked up Cantonese alongside it and learned English from Lucy O'Gunning and some of the older white men who lingered in the underground. As soon as he could read the English, he'd demanded books composed therein, and before long, he'd developed a better vocabulary than any of the native English speakers the captain knew. Now Fang was teaching him Portuguese out of a few novels, and lately Huey had shown some interest in Spanish.

In short, the Chinese boy could read, write, and speak almost everything useful. And he was busy learning what he didn't already have a handle on.

The captain himself had only a fourth-grade education, and he was occasionally intimidated by the well-read, the well-heeled, and the well-to-do. However, he was not at all stupid, and he was quietly thrilled by the idea of grooming someone like Houjin for his crew and company. Andan Cly had been a pirate so long, he didn't care that the boy wasn't educated, or of age, or even white. He'd learned the hard way that you take the best crew members for the job, regardless of the particulars, and if the best man for the job of engineer was a teenage boy with a ponytail, so be it.

Technically, Kirby Troost was the ship's engineer. And technically, Cly called Houjin his "communications officer." But realistically, everyone on board performed whatever task was needed, and the duties were fluid.

Kirby Troost was sitting outside the bobbing hull of the *Naamah Darling,* still clamped to its pipe dock and awaiting a Goodyear tube of gas. "Cap'n," he greeted him with a nod of his head.

"Kirby. You got any business that needs attending, while we're here?"

"Already attended to it. And I've got a bit of bad news. There's trouble at Barataria, sir. Texas stomped through it a couple nights ago."

"Oh, good," Cly said. Then, quickly, he adjusted the sentiment. "I mean, your bad news is the same as my bad news, so between the two of us, there's just one parcel of it."

"Ah. Right you are, sir. And it could be worse. We could've been there when the Texians put their boots on the ground."

"You're right about that. Say, how'd you hear about it?"

"Begging your pardon?"

The captain said, "I only learned it through the tapper girl. You got a source out here moves faster than the wires?"

"No, sir. Ran into some old acquaintances, that's all. They flew over Barataria the day before yesterday, and thought to tell me about it. What did the tapper girl tell you?"

Old acquaintances . . . that could mean anything, but the captain didn't press for more. "She said she'd heard lots of rumors, but nothing firm. What'd your acquaintances have to say about it?"

"Only that it happened, and the surviving bay boys are digging themselves out as best they can. Texas didn't get everybody—a bunch of the brighter fellows holed up in the old Spanish fort, and rode it out that way. But the place has been done a real blow. It's a shame." Kirby shook his head. "There ought to be some kind of exemption, for someplace with such a long and colorful history."

"You think they ought to leave it alone, just because it's been there awhile?"

"Something like that. Mostly I want to get liquor without paying taxes six ways from Sunday, but a man can't have everything like he wants it. But I won't lie to you, Captain. It smells funny to me. Word in the clouds has it, Texas was looking for someone in particular, or some*thing*. Nobody knows what. Or if anybody does, nobody's talking."

If no one was talking to Kirby Troost, it must be a secret piece of information *indeed*.

Andan Cly sat down on the ship's steps, which were unlatched and dangling down. His sudden weight made the stairs sway, until they settled against the ground beneath him.

Troost sat beside him. He pulled out a canteen and took a swig of something that wasn't water, and he asked, "Our business wasn't with the bay, though, was it?"

"Nope. We're running for the city, and I'm going to swing by the Vieux Carré to . . . help out an old friend."

"An old friend?"

"She wants me to make a short trip for her."

"She does, does she? I don't guess you have any more details than that."

Cly shook his head. "I'm sure it'll be fine. It should be real quick."

"We flying Miss *Naamah*?"

"I don't think so. But when I do know, I'll pass it on. Until then, don't worry about it."

Kirby took another swig. "All right, then. I won't."

And back into the sky they went, into the currents and clouds that would take them the rest of the way south, the rest of the way to the Gulf.

Seven

The blower was a flat-bottom boat that sat high on top of the water, like a very small barge. Barely big enough to hold all three passengers without dipping below the rippling waterline, the craft shuddered until everyone sat very still. Behind them, a large diesel-powered fan loomed like a tombstone.

No one said anything until Josephine stated the obvious. "We'll need something bigger to bring Deaderick out, won't we?"

Ruthie shivered and drew her jacket closer around her shoulders, but said, "To be sure, but we can find something bigger on the island, *non*?"

"Sure," Gifford agreed. "We'll find something."

"Something that still floats, or still flies," Josephine muttered. "They can't have grounded or sunk *everything*."

"Yes, ma'am, I think you're right," he said. But something in his voice said he was afraid they were all wrong, and this wasn't going to work at all. His small electric torch sputtered, and he turned it off, leaving them all in absolute darkness except for the moon overhead, halfway full and surrounded by a fogged-white halo.

Suddenly the crickets and frogs seemed very loud, and the buzzing drone of a million night bugs hummed against the background splashes of tiny wet things moving in and out of the water, up and down the currents, around the tree-tall blades of jutting grass.

"Does this thing have any lights of its own?" Josephine wanted to know.

Gifford Crooks leaned across her knees, saying, "Excuse me, ma'am—and yes, she does. Good ones, even."

"Better than your *flambeau*?"

"Much better. This is a rum-runner, you know." He lifted a panel and threw a small switch.

With the faint click and a fizz of electricity, a wash of low, gold light blossomed at the front of the boat.

At the fan's base, a rip cord dangled from a flywheel. He gave it a yank and the engine sputtered; a second fierce tug and it grumbled to life. The fluttering gargle was terrifyingly loud, and the rushing suck of the blades made their hair billow backwards. Gifford Crooks adjusted the throttle, lowering the speed and dampening the drone until it was a low, throaty putter.

"Hang on, ladies. It's going to get bumpy. And damp. Sorry."

Slowly the boat turned as he drew on the steering lever, its caged fan churning the air and the water, too, so low in the marsh did the blower sit. The spray blew into the air, and a mist of swamp water and algae settled into their hair, onto their shoulders, and across their laps.

Little craft like the blowers were built to navigate the difficult terrain between land and water—the wet, deep places clogged with vegetation and animal life, thick with mud and unpredictable depths. They were made to skim the surface, to flatten the tall, palm-width grasses and slide across them, powered by the enormous fan—and aided by a pair of wheel spokes mounted on either side. The spokes were lifted up like a gate around the passengers, until and unless the boat became stuck. If the fan became tangled or the passage was too thick with grass or muck, the spokes could be dropped, and the band moving the blades could be rehung to move them instead. It was a jerky, difficult, last-ditch way to get the craft through the sopping middle-lands, but it almost always worked.

Never quietly. Never smoothly. Never without soaking the occupants.

They puttered through the marsh in silence, for speaking

would've required louder voices and added more noise to the night than the diesel engine's drone. Gifford Crooks navigated by some manner he didn't feel compelled to share; he looked up at the sky from time to time, so Josephine assumed he went by the stars like the sailors, or perhaps his sense of dead reckoning was better than the average landlubber's.

As the evening ticked by, the moon rolled higher.

And all the while, as Gifford manned the steering lever and peered intently at the flush of light before the craft, Josephine and Ruthie huddled close together, thanking their lucky stars that the night wasn't any colder, and their destination wasn't any farther. The whipping slaps of saw grass whispered awful things against the craft's hull, and the loud sliding splashes off to either side warned of large animals with rows of sharp teeth and beady, slitted eyes.

Texian soldiers or Confederate spies were not the worst things in the marshes, a fact that the travelers knew, but tried to ignore.

And when the blower would muck across a particularly pungent patch of moldering black water that smelled like death, they all thought of alligators and how those terrible brutes preferred their meals drowned, sodden, and half rotted to pieces.

In time, the travel numbed them with its treachery. When every shadow could mean discovery and every splash might indicate the approach of a creature so big, it could tip the boat . . . even terror became mundane. As the hour came for the engine to be cut and the oars to be deployed along with the spokes,. it was a relief for everyone on board.

This was different, at least. In a struggle against the algae-thick water by hand, and they had some agency over their own progress and survival.

Now, as the growling mumble of the engine was choked off into quiet, they would move themselves the rest of the way. This small measure of control should not have satisfied any of them so much as it did, but Josephine gladly grabbed one paddle and Gifford Crooks took the other.

"Ruthie, you may have to crank the spokes if we get stuck. Can you do that?"

"*Oui, madame,* and if you are tired, you can trade places with me. *Moi aussi,* I can paddle."

"I know you can, dear. And I might take you up on that, but not quite yet."

So the churning gargle of the motor was replaced by the soft slip, strike, and dip of the long, flat paddles, moving in an arc on either side of the craft, drawing it farther and deeper south and west. Josephine didn't realize at first that she was holding her breath between strokes, but when she did, she used those quiet seconds to listen for any signs of humanity.

Within an hour, she was rewarded by the murmur of big engines rumbling in the distance, and as they came closer still, the engine noise was augmented by chattering shouts projected by amplifying cones. And, with gut-churning intermittence, the background drone was punctuated by explosions—fireballs from hydrogen tanks meeting stray weapon fire, burnishing the horizon's edge with bubbles of warm, yellow glow that flared, ballooned, and collapsed.

Josephine heard Texian accents, and the shifting gears of enormous ships, and the humming overhead purr of dirigibles. When she looked up, she could see them, mostly painted brown—some displaying the large lone star from the Republic's flag. A few searchlights were poking down, their diffuse beams casting tubes of light that turned vague in the low-lying fog over the marsh grasses; but those lights were far away.

Gifford Crooks cut the forward lights and pulled his oar into his lap. Josephine did the same, and Ruthie tried not to fidget. She wrestled with her gloves regardless and finally asked in a tired, hoarse whisper, "What do we do now? Where do we go? How do we move past them?"

"We'll have to take the long way around, and come at the big island from the west bank. It's another mile of paddling, but it's our only chance. Look at them up there—scanning the south and eastern shores, looking for folks who are running off, or trying to sneak out. They won't be watching for folks coming in."

"Why aren't they watching the west banks?" Josephine asked.

A large spray of antiaircraft fire blew through the sky, its tracer bullets drawing a seared yellow line from the island to the clouds. The fire winged the edge of a dirigible, which made a halfhearted attempt to fire back before its thrusters flared and it scooted out of artillery range.

Gifford replied, "West side's better fortified. That's where the Spanish fort is. It's mostly rubble, if you're just looking at it during the daytime. But the bunkers are solid, and the pirates—or merchants, or whoever—use it for storage. There's gunpowder and ammunition in the fort. It could fend off a siege for days."

Josephine squinted at the dirigibles, and over at the small warships that had successfully squeezed past the bottleneck at Grande Terre and Grande Isle. None of them were the huge battleships that Texas often kept out in the Gulf proper. Only the lighter, faster models had made it without wrecking against the sea bottom or knocking into any of the scores of small islands and promontories that clogged the entirety of the bay.

She said, "They aren't trying very hard."

"What?" Gifford asked.

"They aren't trying very hard—to take the west side, I mean. I guess they aren't as dumb as they look. These little ships, they might be able to gang up and take the place, but it'd cost them more than it'd gain them. And the airships—" She gestured at the sky. "—if the bay boys have antiaircraft, those big hydrogen beasts are nothing but enormous targets. None of them look armored. But it's hard to tell from here."

"You're right," Gifford agreed thoughtfully. "They're mostly transport ships. One or two armored carriers, but only the light variety. Maybe that's all they had on hand."

Ruthie asked, "What does that mean? I don't understand."

Josephine filled her in. "It means they're surveillance ships, not warships. And there are a *lot* of them. Texas didn't bring those ships to attack Barataria. They're looking for something, not shooting at anything. They're looking for *Ganymede*."

"Ma'am, we don't know that," Gifford cautioned.

She turned around on her hard wood seat, and only then realized that half her behind had fallen asleep, and her ribs felt bruised from all the paddling in her unforgiving undergarments. "What else could they be looking for?"

"Pirates?" Ruthie offered.

"They already know the pirates are here—it's the worst-kept secret in Louisiana. But Colonel Betters and Lieutenant Cardiff had the wrong idea. They thought we were smuggling the ship out in pieces, moving it down to the Gulf with pirate help."

Ruthie asked, "Moving it through Barataria?"

"It's a secluded spot with good docks, crawling with men who will do anything for a dollar—men who have been sneaking products in and out of the city for a hundred years. Goddamn," she swore. "Clear out the viper's nest with the government's blessing, and scrounge up the *Ganymede* while you're at it. Even if you fail at one, with money and planning, you've got a good chance of succeeding at the other."

Crooks shook his head. "Are even the Texians that arrogant? To think they could uproot the bay in one strike?"

Josephine returned her gaze to the gliding lights of the searching ships in the water and in the sky, and fixed it there as she said. "They've done it, haven't they? Temporarily, I'd wager. But they've beaten down the Lafittes in the short term, that's for damn sure."

"I wouldn't write them off yet," Gifford argued as another streak of antiaircraft fire broke the velvet blackness of the marshland midnight. "They were caught off guard, that's all. Texas will get bored. They'll eventually figure out *Ganymede* isn't there and wander off—or the Lafittes will safely abandon the place and restore it later."

Josephine said, "Probably. Pirates are lone wolves, as often as not. But if you call a number of lone wolves to your aid, you wind up with quite a pack."

And then Gifford asked, "Do you think they'd come? For the Lafittes? For Barataria?"

"They'll come from all over the world," she said softly. "This bay is the closest thing they have to a homeland—it is their nation, in a way—and I do not think they will let the insult stand. Not for long. Give them time."

"Deaderick doesn't have time," Ruthie reminded them.

"Then we won't wait for them. No cavalry coming but us, isn't that right, Mr. Crooks?"

"Yes, ma'am," he said without even the faintest note of enthusiasm.

"Then let's get paddling, shall we?" Her next questions came close on one another's heels, as if she might get answers she wouldn't like if she quit asking them. "He'll be fine there, won't he? He was fine when you left, wasn't he?"

She began to stroke with the oar, and Gifford followed her lead. He answered so far as he was able. "Yes, ma'am, he was hanging in there. I don't think—" He grunted as his oar stuck, and he pulled it out again. "—I don't think the shots he took were so bad."

Ruthie sneered. "Two bullets, not so bad."

"There's different kinds of being shot. Rick took his lumps, and they missed his heart. Missed his lungs, as far as we could tell. His worst trouble will be festering, if the wounds take a fever. And there's only so much we could do about that, under circumstances like these."

"We'll need a doctor. A nurse. Somebody." Josephine paddled grimly.

"We will find one. We will find somebody." Ruthie patted Josephine's shoulder, then wrapped her arms around herself as if the night were cold.

For two hours more they paddled, coasted, and hid between the tall clusters of waving fronds and bubbling holes where alligators hid and small fish slept. Eventually they'd circled the largest island and sneaked around to the far side where the fort was hunkered low near the narrow coastline, such as it was.

Even from the blower, with its fan long silenced, the three occupants could see that the fort's walls were worn down, their corners rubbed into softness by the years. It looked like nothing so much as an assortment of pale stone walls, and from so far away, those walls appeared so short, a woman could step across with a lifted skirt and a tippy toe. Their height was shortened from age, yes. They were dwarfed by the latticework of pipe docks and oversized ships drifting close, and drifting away again. But they were not as short as they seemed, and they were not so fragile that they hadn't stood a hundred years already.

"Not much of a fort," Ruthie complained, having never seen it from the inside. Her words were muttered as low as a bullfrog's hum.

Josephine replied in kind, keeping everything muted, lest they be discovered. "There's more to it than you'd think. Let's go around to the fort's southwest corner. There's a canal going under the wall, but you can't see it from here. For that matter, you can barely see it when you're right on top of it."

"Will there be a guard? A lookout?"

"I assume," Josephine acknowledged. "But leave him to me."

A Texian search ship eclipsed the moon, the clouds, and the faint sparkles of stars shining through them. It moved slowly, like an oversized balloon, or that was the impression it gave on the ground. Untrue, of course. The big thing's graceful sway belied a terrible speed, and it swung a brilliant yellow searchlight. Josephine, Ruthie, and Gifford could hear it all the way from down in the marsh—the sizzling pop and fizz of the electric filaments simmering against the mirrors that reflected and focused them.

"Hurry," Josephine gasped, leaning harder against her oar. She was exhausted. They were all exhausted. But the big white beam was sauntering nearer, sweeping and scanning, and they were pinned on most sides by the oversized grass.

Ruthie struggled for optimism. "We're almost there!" she whispered fiercely, spying the curved archway like a mouse hole in the fort's southwest wall.

"They're going to see us," Gifford fretted. His eyes stayed on the sky, on the too-big ship hovering just out of shooting range, combing the edges around the fort. "We can't dodge the light. We can't outrun it!"

"Maybe we don't have to."

"Ma'am?" Gifford asked, lifting his eyebrows at Josephine.

"It's not far. Another what—fifty yards? Start the engine."

"Ma'am!" Ruthie gasped.

"You heard me. Start the engines. This blower can outmaneuver that dirigible any day of the week. We'll make a dash for it, cross our fingers, and slide right under the wall before anyone up there has any idea what to make of it."

"But, ma'am—," Gifford began.

Firmly, she cut him off. "Every single moment you delay costs us time. The ship will swing around momentarily, and the light will come with it. The longer it takes them to see us, the less time they have to shoot us."

Ruthie looked faint, but Josephine clasped a hand down on her knee. "Buck up, darling. They aren't likely to hit us."

"How can you be so sure, eh?"

"Because if we're within striking range, so are *they*. Pull the cord, Mr. Crooks! Pull it now, or I'll do it myself."

He reached for the cord and gave it a yank. The engine sputtered, but did not catch. He pulled again. This time it burbled to life in a cough that rose to a roar. He threw the boat into gear as the two women simultaneously lifted the spokes up out of the water and drew their oars into their laps.

Lacking the forward momentum of a craft in motion, the little

blower struggled against the saw grass, forcing past it only with dif-
ficulty at first. But as the motor drove and the diesel chugged, it
pushed onward, stronger, faster, so that the grass slapped up against
the sides. The women ducked down and Gifford Crooks leaned
forward, one hand gripping the steering lever and the other man-
ning the gears. He dropped them lower when the turf choked their
progress, and urged them higher when the way was clearer.

The dirigible above swooned and spun, and its light swung
around to hunt them. It found them within moments, but it had a
hard time keeping them.

The blower dashed through the black-water muck, skimming the
top and leaving a terrific trail of fetid spray and shredded leaves,
grass, and cattails behind it. Every few moments, the light would
catch up to them, hold them, and slip away again. They were moving too swiftly, in too stark a zigzag pattern, for any lamp above to
track them for long.

Overhead, the sound of artillery came in a smattering line of
pops, but if anything landed close to the blower, there was too
much noise and motion for Josephine, Ruthie, or Gifford to hear it.
If bullets landed, they were fired from so far away that they merely
dropped into the water, and any larger shells that were incoming,
only stabbed at their wake.

Josephine wished to God she'd thought to bring a flag, not that
it would've mattered, necessarily. She had to trust that whoever was
watching from the fort was aware that this small blower speeding
toward the canal was not the transport of any Texians or other of-
ficials. She had to believe that the men on guard would assume they
were in search of shelter, or to provide reinforcements or information, or for some mission other than sabotage.

It was either assume this or turn back. If she was right, they'd be
allowed under the wall. If she wasn't, they'd be blown out of the
water before they reached it.

At night, with or without the light that beamed down from above
like the angry glare of an archangel, no one would recognize her on

the tiny boat. No one would know her, or hear her name even if she had time to shout it.

Soaked to the bone, she and Ruthie grasped the handholds, and each other, and kept their heads low, as if they could duck out from underneath the penetrating gaze of the light. Faster and faster their destination approached. They neared it at a breakneck speed, dodging left to right and back again, zipping around unnavigable clumps and clusters of foliage, tree stumps, and fallen masonry boulders from the old walls.

Their mouse hole destination wall grew bigger on the immediate horizon, illuminated by the swishing glances of lights from the air, and by the sometimes-flashes of tracer bullets flicking from ground to sky, sky to ground. Gifford Crooks aimed for the portal and squinted against the spray of swamp water misting into his eyes, flying off the grasses. He set his course, gunned the engine to the outside limit of what it could sustain, and gave it all the fuel the thing could manage.

Surging with a bounding leap, the blower nearly leaped off the surface of the clotted water, then slapped back against it and moaned, the swamp hissing against its undercarriage.

Ruthie prayed in French. Josephine held her breath.

And just before the craft slipped beneath the arch, Gifford cut the engine and let the blower glide forward—holding its course but slowing to jerk them all in their seats. Josephine toppled to the floor and took Ruthie with her. Gifford threw himself down on top of them, sheltering them with his own body.

The blower drifted from violent night to sudden midnight, emerging on the other side of the mouse hole into a ground-floor warren that was more mud than water. It heaved and skidded sideways up onto the closest bank, lodging itself in the mud and settling with a wet sucking sound.

The engine died.

The sudden silence left Josephine shaky; she lifted her head and pulled Ruthie close, just in time to hear the clicks of guns being made ready, and pointed in their direction. Gifford looked up, held out his hands, and said, "Fellas, kindly ignore the uniform. I'm with the bayou boys, and they'll vouch for me. This here is—," he started to say, gesturing at Josephine.

"Miss Early!" the nearest man gasped, and he lowered his gun. He was not a tall man, nor a particularly fearsome one in appearance, but the others deferred to him all the same, and all the guns present were soon pointing at the ground.

Though he was balding on top, around the sides and back, he had enough hair for a ponytail tied with a bit of leather. His clothes were smeared with gunpowder and soot, which had clearly become the operating uniform for everyone inside the fort. At a glance, they might have all been the same race, or the same army. The same group of burrowing resistance fighters, determined to dig in and raise hell.

"Mr. Boggs," she replied.

He extended a hand to help her out of the blower, and she took it. "Here about your brother, I assume?" Every word was pronounced with the oddly emphasized vowels of the Cajuns. His eyes protruded slightly and his stocky frame was approaching fat, but was comfortingly sturdy as he pulled Josephine onto the firmer surface of packed earth at the mud's edge, then drew Ruthie up as well.

"Deaderick, yes. He's here in the fort, isn't he?"

"Where else would we take him? He's here, and he's all right for now."

"Have you any doctors?" she asked.

He shook his head. "No doctors, no lawyers, no teachers, no judges—or anything else too civilized, I'm afraid. They've got us in a pickle, pinned down. But it could be worse." Mr. Boggs extended a hand to Gifford, too, and soon all three of the small blower's passengers were standing on something closer to terra firma than they'd known since leaving the riverbanks.

"How's that?" Gifford asked.

"We have fresh water, some food—and ready fishing, right outside the wall—and all the gunpowder and ammunition we can

carry." He returned his attention to Josephine and cocked a head at the other men who'd joined him as part of the welcoming committee. "Listen, ma'am, we didn't mean to alarm you. We had to check out the newcomers, you know how it goes."

"You'd be madmen if you didn't. You know me—and this is my girl Ruthie Doniker, and our escort, Gifford Crooks."

"I seen you before," said one of Boggs's men to Gifford.

"I was here before, out on the island—not in the fort. I fight with the bayou lads, been sent down from Saint Louis. And I got no complaint with Barataria, let me make that real clear up front."

"Don't worry about it, son," said Mr. Boggs. "You're with Miss Early, and that means you're all right. I'm Planter Boggs," he introduced himself, and then his men. "This is Arthur Tate, Mike Hardis, Frank Jones, and Tam Everly. They're all that's left from the crew of an airship called the *Coyote Black,* which is no longer with us."

The man introduced as Frank Jones was very thin, with ginger-colored hair and a pointed beard. He said, "It was one of the first to go, over there." He waved a hand to indicate something outside the fort.

And Mike Hardis added, "It went up like a Chinese New Year, though. Took half the dock out. Can't say she didn't leave us with a bang."

"Still, it's a shame," said Tam Everly. "I figured I'd run her 'til it was time to retire. Then pass her off to one of my nephews. Won't be happening now." Arthur Tate patted him on the shoulder.

"I'm sorry to hear about your ship," Josephine told the lot of them. "But can one of you, or all of you, I don't care—can *someone* take me to my brother? I'm so tired, I can hardly hold my head up. But I won't settle down for the night until I've set eyes on him."

"Right this way, Miss Early." Planter Boggs led the way. "And you there," he said to Gifford. "Get out of those browns before you get yourself shot. You know what the Good Book says about avoiding the appearance of evil, don't you?"

"Yes, sir, but the evil was a good disguise to get me in and out of town." He stripped off the jacket and tossed it into the empty blower, but despaired at the vest and pants.

"Everly, Tate. One of you fellows—can you get him something less . . . troubling?"

So Gifford Crooks took his leave, and Josephine and Ruthie followed Planter Boggs back into the depths of the old Spanish fort. "He'll catch up to us later," Boggs promised. "Come on now, and watch your step. It's none too bright back here. We're doing things the old-fashioned way, without any of those electric torches. Trying to conserve our power, you know how it goes."

He reached for a torch of the ancient variety, a wooden club with fuel-wrapped rags knotted around its head and set aflame. The stink of burning petroleum wafted along, carried and deposited in thick black smoke that stained the walls and the low stone ceiling.

Ruthie stuck close to Josephine, holding her mistress's elbow as if she was steadying her, and not just looking for an excuse to keep the comforting contact. She asked, "Are we underneath the fort? I do not understand. We went under the wall, but . . ."

Mike Hardis, a terribly young man with a potato-shaped body but sharp, smart eyes, answered her. "The canal used to be deeper. The Spaniards moved supplies in and out of the fort on flats, all the way from the center inside . . . out to the bay, and then to the Gulf. But the years have filled it in, as you saw. And now the basement chamber—which is only halfway underground," he noted as they began to climb a short flight of stairs, "is filled with a century's worth of tidal mud and backwash. Even so, I can't say it doesn't make for a convenient back door. How'd you know to come looking for it?"

Planter Boggs looked pointedly at Josephine. She answered for herself. "In my younger days, I spent a good deal of time at Barataria, and sometimes in the fort."

"I imagine you still have a number of friends here," Mr. Boggs said as he led the way up the narrow stairwell, torchlight bouncing off the walls around the rounded corners, up ahead of him.

"Friends and paying customers, if I cared to have them. Most of the men I knew back then are older now, and either wiser or dead. I hope you'll pardon me saying so, gentlemen."

On that somber note, they hiked up into a large common room that was so sealed up, it felt to Josephine as if they were still underground, or mostly so. More firelight burned from every corner, some of it chimneyed away by ventilation shafts and columns of brick—but some of it accumulated within the long, flat room with the ceiling so low that the tallest men were compelled to hunch. Some forty or fifty men eyed the newcomers warily, then opportunistically, upon seeing that two were women. And then a name was breathed, somewhere in a back corner.

"Miss Early."

The whisper carried back and forth throughout the closed, dark nightmare of that cramped and awful place, until the men who stood in their path parted and let them pass.

In French, Ruthie said into Josephine's ear, "You're a bit of a legend to them. I had no idea."

"It was a long time ago."

"And still they know of you? You must have been remarkable."

"Still am."

Cramped and crowded, the room's walls felt uncomfortably close and the air was stale with smoke, sweat, and the worry of men who knew exactly how much death could be dealt from above and outside. Somewhere off to the west the *rat-a-tat-tat* of antiaircraft fire shook the fort and was answered by the nearest armored dirigible. Tiny explosions smacked overhead, drilling into the roof and digging into the fortifications. Something heavier landed, and the roof shook. The ceiling quaked and rained mortar dust down on the already silent, already anxious collection of souls below.

"This way," Planter Boggs pushed. "Never mind the return fire.

They haven't breached us yet, and we're holding the worst of it at bay from the corners, and what's left of the other canals."

"And from the walls themselves," Mike Hardis added.

Ruthie's eyes widened. "There are men outside still?"

"Only the crazy ones," said Frank Jones. "But they're launching hand-bombs and taking potshots at the boats that slink up close. Somebody has to do it."

Josephine didn't want to think about it. "Just get us to my brother. Please. Hurry," she begged.

"Come through here. It's this way."

Another short set of stairs, half a flight down and then up again, and the small band arrived in what had once been a galley—if the leftover counters, racks for pans, and drawers for cutlery were any measure. It'd been converted to a makeshift clinic of sorts. No doctors, no lawyers, no teachers, no judges. No one in charge, but that was always the way of pirates, and no emergency could change it.

The galley was a room full of motion, and the only electric lights she'd seen so far blazed with comparative brilliance above old food-preparation tables, which were now occupied by moaning, groaning injured men. Half a dozen dead bodies were piled in a corner, a fact that was only feebly hid by the application of a filthy tablecloth as a shroud. Limp hands and feet jutted out from the pile, and warm, sticky bloodstains showed up where the wounds were not yet finished leaking. Ruthie put her hand over her mouth and tried not to gag. Josephine would've done the same—the smell of urine and burned flesh and gunpowder and blood was almost more than she could stand—but she'd spotted Fletcher Josty in the room's middle, beside a decrepit pump-water sink that, against all odds, was still working.

The bayou guerrilla yanked and shoved on the handle and water did veritably appear, though it wasn't as clean as one might hope. Many hands held out bowls, cups, and dirty rags, hoping to collect some of the liquid for refreshment or cleansing.

Josty pumped furiously, trying to force the men to take turns. "One at a time, you bastards! There's water to go around, but you have to wait your turn! I can't make it come out any quicker," he grumbled.

"Fletcher!" Josephine cried.

The room stopped for an instant, as even the eyes of the wounded turned at the sound of a woman's voice. But another jagged cry rang out and the chorus of aching voices rose behind it, and the sad scene carried on as before, except that Fletcher quit pumping. He grabbed the nearest able-bodied soul and shoved him at the pump, ordering, "Keep that arm moving. Keep that water flowing."

Then, as he abandoned that wretched post, he danced between the tables and the sprawled arms and legs. "Miss Early," he said, looking like he would've tipped his hat if he'd had one on. This free man of color was as filthy and smeared with soot as everyone Josephine had seen so far, but she was overjoyed by the sight of him, and it was all she could do to keep from hugging him.

Instead she grasped him by the shoulders and asked, "Deaderick?"

"In the cellar, ma'am."

"Oh . . . oh, God . . ."

"No, no. He's still alive, it's just cooler down there, that's all, so that's where I've stuck 'im. Some of the men who are stable, and needing to rest . . . it's all we could do to make them comfortable. It's more sheltered, too, I think. If Texas brings in anything bigger, or shoots anything worse, we might be digging for cover."

"Then to the cellar. Now."

Planter Boggs gave Josephine and Ruthie a little bow and said, "Ladies, if you'll excuse me."

"Of course," the madam said without looking. She was already trailing behind Josty, and Ruthie behind her.

And down into the cellar they followed—back to the level where the canals came and went. A large round of artillery connected with a thick mortar wall somewhere to the east. Josephine thrust out an arm to brace herself. The whole world shook, and it seemed like even an old fort built by Spaniards to survive the Second Coming couldn't stand beneath the onslaught.

But stand it did.

And in the cellar, on the old concrete docks that were barely raised above the mud, Deaderick Early lay between two other men in similar states of injury and consciousness.

She ran to his side, trying to keep from disturbing the others. Without stepping on them or kicking them, she knelt beside her brother and took one of his hands in hers—clasping it to her breast and examining the damage with as much cool reserve as she could muster. She tried to keep the panic out of her eyes when Deaderick opened his own.

"I knew it," he said unhappily.

"You knew what?" she asked. It was a relief to hear him talk, even to hear him complain. But the bubbling red across his chest was not a relief, and his face was blanched and pale beneath the burnish of his complexion. Every muscle from his forehead to his chin was stretched tight with pain.

"I knew you'd come. Whether or not anyone told you not to. That's why I told them not to tell you. Josty did it, didn't he? Damn fool."

Ruthie seized Deaderick's other hand and held it up to her cheek. "*Bien sûr* she came, you ridiculous oaf!"

"Christ Almighty, not you, too."

"*Oui, moi aussi.* Now, hush and let us take care of you."

"I don't need you to take care of me."

Josephine released his hand so she could explore the injuries with her fingers. Gently, thoroughly, and trembling, she unpicked his buttons and revealed the sad, masculine attempts at bandaging. An ash-colored rag that might once have dried dishes was balled up and compressed against the largest of two holes, or so she learned upon lifting it. It stuck, blood drying to chest hair, and Deaderick grimaced.

"Woman, let it alone! If you leave it be, it'll stop bleeding."

Fletcher Josty hovered into the scene and contradicted him. "It hasn't stopped yet, not for good. Not like the other one. Rick, I'm starting to worry."

"Save your worry for yourself, because when I'm up again, I'm going to tan your hide for getting Josie involved."

"Oh, shut your mouth. You've met your sister, haven't you? Like we could keep her away."

Just then, someone shouted from the far end of the cellarlike nook. "All right, you goddamn pirates have gotten your way. I'm here, and you won't do any better—not for trying. Who needs attention?"

"Are you a doctor?" Josephine asked like lightning.

"Used to be. I'm starting down here and working my way up like the free men of the air have demanded. So tell me," said the man. "who's in the most danger? Has no one sorted them out, grouped them by seriousness of condition?"

Fletcher rolled his eyes and said, "This ain't no hospital, mister. It's been all we could do to get 'em out from underfoot!"

Josephine stood and shoved Fletcher Josty aside. "Never mind him. Get yourself over here, Doctor, if that's what you are. My brother has two bullets in him, and he needs your assistance now."

"Only two? He's one of the better cases."

"I'll pay you. Whatever you think you're worth. I . . . I own a boarding house, in the Quarter. Get over here and fix my brother, and I'll see to it that you have a week you'll never forget, do you understand me?"

"No, but I'm open to the explaining," he said, coming toward her. He was an older man and, by the look of him, a lifelong alcoholic. The skin across his nose was the color of blisters and streaked with broken blood vessels; his eyes were likewise shot through with red, and his face hung off his skull with a droop like a hound dog's.

"Get over here, then. Fix this man."

"No," croaked Deaderick. "There's worse up there, men who need the attention more."

"Shut up, if your woman's willing to pay. I was dragged out of bed for this, and I'll help who I like—and who I'm paid to patch. I said I'd start in the cellar and work my way up, and you're as likely a patient as the next man, aren't you?"

"What kind of doctor are you?" Josephine thought to ask, feeling suddenly uncertain about this.

"A genius or a quack. Either way, I'm Leonidas Polk, and I'll patch this fellow up if I can, but you need to get out of my way. Good Lord, they've just been letting you bleed?"

Deaderick replied, "No. But the one bullet hole, it don't want to plug up right."

"You can stitch it, can't you?" Ruthie asked, still squeezing Deaderick's left hand as if she could lend him some of her own life force.

"Stitching won't do any good on something like this," he said, whipping out a pince-nez and examining the bloodiest spot on Deaderick's chest, where the blood had sensed an opening and was beginning to flush afresh. "Do you have any other conditions? You're not a dust sniffer or an absinthe drinker, are you?"

"No . . ."

"Is the bullet still inside?" he asked.

"No, I don't think," the patient replied. "Straight through, both shots. If the blood would stop coming, I think I'd be all right. I could stand up and see myself out," he swore, though no one believed him.

Ruthie kissed his hand and said, "Stop it, you silly man. You'll lie there and get better. The doctor will fix everything, won't he?"

"Son of a bitch, ma'am. Don't tell him *that,*" Dr. Polk swore.

"But you'll do what you can," Josephine told him more than asked him.

"I'm going to need some gunpowder and a match."

Deaderick swallowed hard, his Adam's apple bobbing in a nervous slide. "I was afraid of that."

"Afraid of what?" his sister demanded. "Afraid of *what*?"

Dr. Polk asked, "How long has it been since you were shot?" He looked again at the wound. "Five hours? Ten?"

"Thereabouts."

"We've got to cauterize it. I'd break it to you more gentle, but there isn't time. Ma'am, get me some gunpowder and a match."

"I don't understand."

"It's best that you don't."

Josephine hauled herself to her feet, confused and even dumbfounded by how difficult it was. She staggered toward the stairs that led to the galley, and within a few minutes she'd talked herself into a dead man's powder pouch and a box of matches. Horrible though it was, she had a feeling she knew where this was heading . . . and she couldn't stand it. But this was a doctor—maybe a quack, maybe a drunk, but the only one present, roused, bribed, and impatient—so she'd do as he asked, because heaven help her, she didn't know how else to proceed.

Dr. Polk reached for the gunpowder. "Ladies, avert your eyes. For that matter, you might want to do the same," he told Deaderick. Then he spilled a tiny trail around the wound and on it—a black sprinkle of glittering stuff, barely a dusting. "I mean it," he reiterated. "Look away. All of you."

He struck the match.

Deaderick screamed.

And Ruthie passed out cold.

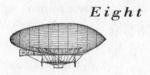

Eight

The captain said, "Goddamn, Kirby. Your acquaintances weren't half-kidding."

"Nor was the lady from the taps," the engineer graciously replied.

Everyone gazed out the thick glass windscreen in silence, even Houjin—whose incessant questions had drawn up short when confronted with the wreckage at Barataria Bay, where the great pirate Jean Lafitte had established his empire . . . an empire that had stood a hundred years and might have stood a hundred more, were it not for Texas.

The *Naamah Darling* drifted slowly past the big island's edge, steering clear of the thin, curling towers of black smoke that still coiled from the ground, and avoiding the other ships flying nearby, likewise creeping up to the edge of the destruction and gawking at what was left. Everyone gave everyone else a clear berth, since the details were still so few, and the devastation so very awful.

Below, the pipe docks were melted and twisted into a crumpled parody of their prior shape, and the burned-out hulls of dirigibles were flattened against the ground or in the water. Their stays jutted like the ribs of huge dead animals, like the big stone bones of long-extinct beasts from another time. Dozens of ships. Maybe fifty or more, charred and useless.

They dotted the landscape in lone craters and in clusters. What few buildings the island had boasted were burned or blasted into obsolescence, leaving the whole scene below a weird panorama of a place cleansed by fire.

Even from the *Naamah Darling*'s height, the captain and crew could see brown-uniformed Texians moving about below. Digging trenches. Toting corpses to burial—or here and there, moving a survivor on a stretcher. Cly wondered why they bothered. Surely anyone found on Barataria would be tried and jailed at best, hanged at worst, for being found on the island and firing back at the Lone Star's airships.

But there was much he did not know about the situation, and the uncertainty left an uncomfortable warm spot in his stomach, as if this impersonal attack on someone else meant more to him, personally, than it ought to. It would be an exaggeration to say that the sight of the blighted island churned his stomach. He hadn't visited it in years. But it'd been one hell of a bustling place once—a rough-and-tumble spot, to be sure, but one where a certain kind of man could find a certain kind of freedom.

When he pulled out his spyglass and aimed it at the mess below the ship, Captain Cly could see alligators, nearer to the island now than they tended to creep in daylight. Their long brown-black forms lounged as motionless as logs—and easily mistaken for the same—but their bulbous eyes and heavy tails twitched in the afternoon sun.

"Are those—" Houjin finally found his questions. He'd found a spyglass, too, and was likewise watching the water's edge. "—alligators? Down there, look—one just dove under the water, and it's swimming, you can see it. Right there, Captain."

"Yes, that's an alligator."

"It's very big, isn't it? It looks almost as long as that canoe."

"They're sometimes very big, yes."

"They aren't afraid of people, are they?"

He swallowed. "The smell of death is drawing them out—even more than usual." And before Houjin could demand to know what he meant by that, the captain changed the subject. "Anyway, look what else is going on—over there in the water, around the old island docks."

"Let me see," Kirby Troost said to Houjin, who handed over his spyglass. Upon getting a gander, the engineer said, "A handful of strange-looking flatboats, and something bigger. And nets. Looks like they're dredging for something. Maybe they sank something they didn't mean to."

"Maybe. People call those flatboats *blowers*. Some spots out in the bayous, and in the marshes, it's the only good way to travel. The boats are nice and light, see. And the fans just blow them along."

Houjin grasped the situation instantly. "And since the fans are up, out of the water, their blades don't get clogged by the grass!"

"Atta boy," Cly told him. "Any other propeller or engine you stick in the water is done for."

Things might have digressed into a conversation about transporting men and goods through inhospitable terrain, but a loudly shouted, "Ahoy, *Naamah Darling*!" jolted the chatter in another direction entirely.

All the men on board tore their attention away from the scene below and looked around, trying to spot the speaker. The captain pointed out to the west and nudged the steering levers to better point the dirigible toward another airship—one much closer than they'd realized.

Someone had snuck up on them.

The ships were near enough to each other that Cly, Troost, Houjin, and Fang could plainly see three men in the cockpit of the other dirigible. Houjin waved. One of the distant men waved back. The voice came again, and this time its source was obvious: a large electric speaker mounted to the exterior of the hull.

"You've entered airspace deemed restricted by the Republic of Texas. I have to ask you to accompany us to a landing dock a short ways east, at Port Sulphur. Do you agree to comply at this time?"

Cly and his crew members looked back and forth between one another.

Houjin, always the first with a query, asked, "Captain?"

Fang shrugged, and Troost did likewise. The engineer said, "We aren't carrying any contraband. We can play dumb."

Thoughtfully, Cly said, "We're from out of town. Nothing bad on board. No reason to put up a fight or make a stink." Out the windscreen he could see more Texian ships, approaching the other gawkers in the same way. "They haven't singled us out. They're just clearing the area. Sure, let's see what they want. I'm not familiar with Port Sulphur, but maybe they can point us at a good machine works."

He returned his attention to the Texian ship, waved, and nodded. He added a thumbs-up for good measure and held out one long arm as if to say, *After you!*

One by one, they buckled back into their seats and waited for the Texian ship to lead. When it did, they followed at a respectful distance—but close enough to make it plain that they meant no trouble, and were abiding by the Republic's orders.

Houjin said, "I don't like this, sir."

"I'm not highly keen on it either, but it might work out. Maybe we'll learn something. And we're headed in the right direction, anyway. There's nothing to worry about, you hear me? We haven't been up to any mischief, and they aren't shooting at us. Mostly, I think, they didn't want us watching what they're doing in the bay."

"That's my guess," Kirby Troost observed quietly. "And it backs up what my acquaintances and your tapper lady said."

"How's that?" asked Houjin.

"Texas took Barataria apart with a goal in mind. They're looking for something—something they thought the pirates were holding or hiding."

"Something in the water," Cly added.

The boy frowned. "Some kind of ship? But you were just saying how hard it is for ships to—"

The captain shook his head. "I know what I said. But I also know what I *saw*. This has the stink of a military operation all over it."

It was Troost's turn to frown. "Isn't *everything* Texas does in New Orleans a military operation?"

"Mostly they're here to keep the civil order. Police work, and the like. They occupy, they don't govern—that's still left to the Confederacy. And this wasn't police work. This was army work. I wonder how much we can get them to tell us about it."

Fifteen minutes later, they were setting down at a large industrial pipe dock on a promontory near a wide canal, at the edge of the marshy swamplands, like almost everything else between the city and the Gulf. Being careful to preserve every appearance of innocence, the captain disembarked and used the lobster-claw anchor to latch the *Naamah Darling* into the nearest slot.

As he did so, he was approached by a Texian who might've been tall by anyone else's standard, but was merely neck height to Andan Cly. The beefy blond was wearing the local version of the brown uniform—pants and boots as usual, but jacketless and with the sleeves of his white shirt rolled up past his elbows and unbuttoned halfway to his waist. It was the captain's opinion that telling any Texians anywhere to wear any uniform was an act of futility, but it wasn't his army and he didn't say anything except, "Hello, there," when the man stuck out his hand for a shake.

Handshakes accomplished, the Texian said, "Hello back at you," with a heavy Republican accent. "And I want to thank you for your cooperation. Not everyone has been so quick to leave when asked. I'm Wade Bullick, captain of the *Yellow Rose*," he said, waving a hand at the ship that had escorted the *Naamah Darling* out of Barataria's airspace.

"Andan Cly, captain of the *Naamah Darling*."

"Pleasure to meet you, and I do beg your pardon about all this. We had ourselves an incident at the pirate bay, and right now we're in the middle of getting it all cleaned up. You know how it goes."

"I suppose I do."

"And I don't suppose you had any business there yourself?" Bullick asked casually.

"None whatsoever, I assure you. We saw the smoke, is all. And I won't lie—we heard rumors, on our way east."

"On your way coming east? Most folks come here by flying west. Where do you all hail from?"

"The Washington Territory," Cly told him. He also took this opportunity to provide his ship's licensing papers, which he'd stuffed into his vest before leaving the ship. He knew they'd be asked after, and it was always better to offer such things when one was innocent of any wrongdoing. "We're registered out of Tacoma."

Wade Bullick examined the papers, and Cly noted that the man either read very quickly or made only a show of reading—and he couldn't tell which. "Everything does look to be in order here. Might I ask why you've come to the good land of Louisiana, Captain Cly?"

"Supply run, mostly. We serve the little frontier towns up and down the Pacific Coast, and I homestead in a tiny port town called Seattle," he exaggerated only slightly. He preferred to think of it as an optimistic prediction. "Also, this bird was built to move cargo I don't care to carry, so I was hoping to find one of your Texian machine shops and get her all fitted up for regular trade and supplies. You're welcome to climb inside and take a look."

"You got crew with you?"

"Three men—my first mate, but he's a mute Chinaman and can't tell you about it; an engineer; and a young fellow who's apprenticing to ride aboard more permanent-like. We don't have cargo right this moment, nothing but our own possessions. We flew down empty, with intent to load up before heading home."

Captain Bullick went to the stairwell and climbed halfway up, poking his head into the interior and looking around. Cly couldn't see if anyone waved at him, swore at him, or stuck out a tongue, but he trusted that nothing too out-of-the-ordinary took place outside his line of sight. He also trusted that Bullick had noticed the tracks running along the ceiling, and the empty sacks he'd once used to move the blight gas.

"I see what you mean," the other captain said as he retreated back down to ground level again. "Been moving things to make other things, have you?"

"Once upon a time," Cly confessed. "But I'm giving it to you straight—that's not what this is about, and not what we're here for. And I really am hoping you can make me a recommendation for a shop where I can get some of that unnecessary gear stripped out."

"All right, then, I'll take you at your word—since you've been so agreeable thus far, and all. And as for Barataria, I don't blame you for wanting to come take a look. It left a big ol' hole in the marsh, didn't it? Not that I expect the fun's been rooted out for good."

"Excuse me?"

"Aw, come on. Between you, me, and the entire Gulf coast, everybody knew what was going on out there."

Cly retrieved his papers and stuck them back in his vest. "I don't suppose there's any chance you could tell me what all the hoopla was about, is there? Gossip was all over the taps, but that's all we heard. Nothing but gossip."

"Honest to God, I don't have much more than that to share. A couple nights ago, the bay went up like firecrackers—and yesterday Colonel Travis McCoy called everybody out to help clean up what was left. I'm not a military man myself, except in the loose sense. I mean, I'll show up if they offer me Republican money to fly around like I was going to anyhow, that's for sure. But I'm no fighter, and no Dirigible Corpsman. McCoy told the fellas like me to act with Texas authority and keep the sky cleared. And now you know about as much as I do."

Cly assumed there was plenty Bullick was leaving out, but pressing for it would only look suspicious. "Well, then, I thank you for clearing that up for me. It's strange business all around, but I suppose it's none of mine."

With another minute or two of chitchat, Cly learned that Travis McCoy had taken over the city's management following the disappearance of the previous colonel, which Bullick was not prepared to divulge any extra information about—or perhaps Bullick himself wasn't sure what happened, and he was only parroting the official line. He also said that the nearest machine shop of the caliber Cly required was located in Metairie—and he offered this recommendation without hesitation, including the instructions to, "Tell Baxter Devitt I sent you, and he'll fix you right up!"

With this, they were free to go so long as they steered clear of the pirate bay. By evening the *Naamah Darling* was moored at the machine shop in Metairie, where Baxter Devitt had been tickled pink to hear Wade Bullick was sending him customers. Devitt was a small, dark man—almost the descriptive opposite of Bullick—but he possessed a similar savvy cheerfulness that Cly had come to recognize as a general trait of Texians, or at least one common enough to remark on.

Before long, Captain Cly had an estimate for the price—at the high end of reasonable—and time frame—within the week—for all the work he wanted accomplished on the *Naamah Darling,* and a general tour and inspection of the facilities had convinced him that this was an establishment capable of doing good work, and worthy of being trusted with his most valued possession. With a gentleman's agreement and another round of handshakes, Cly took his crew out to the street rail station near the great cemetery, and together they waited for the next available car to take them into the city proper.

The street rails were halfway between a streetcar and a proper train, running on standard rails but lighter than any long-distance freight or passenger movers, and without the creature comforts of a Pullman car. But they were quick by anyone's standards, able to take people between Metairie and New Orleans proper in twenty minutes on a good day, and thirty on a bad one.

A smallish station had been erected, again almost halfway between a streetcar stop and a train depot. Mostly it was open, with a tall roof overhead to shield the waiting passengers from sun and rain—and a set of enormous propellers set into the roof's underside to keep the airflow circulating. It didn't do much to cool the station, but it kept the diesel fumes and coal smoke from collecting, and that was something.

"Why do I smell both diesel and coal smoke? Are there street rails leading in and out of the city everywhere, or just here? Is that a cemetery across the street? How much longer until our streetcar comes?"

"Does he ever shut up?" asked Kirby Troost.

Cly defended him. "If he doesn't ask questions, he'll never learn."

"I never asked questions like that. And I didn't grow up to be no dummy."

The captain kept his eyes on the rails, watching Track 6 for any sign of an incoming transport. He picked Houjin's two easiest questions, and he answered them. "Huey, you smell coal and diesel because some of the streetcars are coal powered and some are diesel. I reckon one day they'll make them all one thing or the other, but it hasn't happened yet. And yes, that's a cemetery."

The boy whistled, drawing the attention of a small colored girl seated on a bench with her mother at Track 7. The child's eyes went wide, but her mother said, "Don't stare. It's not polite." She stared anyway, and Houjin gave her a wave that she sent back with a dubious flap.

"It's a cemetery? Must be about a million dead people. I don't think I've ever seen one so big."

"Not a million, but a lot," Cly told him. "They call it the city of the dead."

"A whole city full of dead people. Hey, we've got one of those back in—"

Cly whomped him on the arm and gave him a look that said to shut up.

"Ow," he complained. "Well, you know what I was going to say."

Fang rolled his eyes. Kirby Troost said, "We all know, yes. Maybe you could put a lid on it, eh, kid?"

Fang gave the captain an elbow jab and pointed at the tracks.

"Here comes our car," Cly said. "We'll be in the city soon. Save up a few questions for when we get to town."

"Can I ask just one before we do?"

"One. Just one."

"Where will we stay while the *Naamah Darling* gets her work done?"

Troost said, "Actually, that's not a half-bad thing to ask. Where *will* we stay, Captain? That lady friend of yours has a boarding house, doesn't she?"

Cly rose to his feet and stretched. "We won't be staying at the Garden Court. It's not that kind of boarding house."

Troost said, "Ah," and Fang looked relieved.

Houjin didn't get it. "Why not? If she's an old friend, and if she has rooms—"

"We'll find someplace else. I'd hate to impose. Let it go, Huey. The Vieux Carré is full of places we can stay. Hotels by the score. We'll pick one."

Soon Track 6 was host to a street rail car called *Bayou Bess*. Houjin rode the whole way to town up front, hanging over the rail and watching the scenery change. Cly, Troost, and Fang sat on a bench behind him, taking it easy since they didn't know when they'd next get the opportunity. The wind blew through their hair and clothes, and even though it was every bit as warm as Cly had promised, they were comfortable riding along beside the main road, past the swampy parts of earth that filled up the space between grasslands and forest.

Fang nudged the captain, and since no one was paying much attention to them, he signed. *Someone has to teach him, someday.*

He said under his breath. "Not me. Not now."

One of the women at the Garden Court?

"God Almighty. His uncle would never let me hear the end of it."

They arrived at the downtown station just past Canal Street late in the afternoon, and upon debarking they headed toward Jackson Square, a few blocks nearer the river. "That's strange," the captain observed, watching someone draw down the shutters and begin the work of closing a restaurant.

"What's strange?" asked Troost.

"I remember this as more of a round-the-clock town. Folks seem to be shutting up shop early."

From the stoop of a narrow, unmarked store that smelled of incense and coal, a stout black woman with a broom informed them, "It's the curfew, closing us up. Costing all kinds of business, too—not that the Texians give a sainted cuss about it."

Cly and his crew members stopped, and the captain asked, since she sounded happy to share—"What curfew?"

"The city goes home at sundown," she said, swooshing the broom back and forth, clearing a day's worth of dust from the two short steps. "Ever since those two Texians went missing. As if the world ought to stop for a pair of brownbacks without the sense to come up from the river at midnight." The woman spit fast and hard, leaving a damp spot on the cobbled walkway.

"I didn't know," Cly admitted. "And if that's the case, we need to find ourselves some rooms for the night. Could you recommend anything?"

She stopped her sweeping and appraised the group before saying, "Other side of the Square is the Widow Pickett's place. She puts up men, soldiers, sailors. Folks like yourselves—airmen, I'm guessing?"

The captain said, "That's right."

"And a couple of Chinamen like you got there—they shouldn't be a problem for her. She takes negroes and Creoles and everyone else, as long as you can pay. Or if she's all full up, I think the Rogers place on Esplanade could take you."

"Thanks for your time," Kirby Troost told her. He touched the front of his hat as they walked away, on toward the Square at a somewhat quicker pace. As they walked, he added to the captain, "Shame we can't just stay at the Garden Court. Can't cost *that* much more."

"Don't you start, now."

"Who's starting? He's what—sixteen, seventeen? I was younger than that when I got married for the first time."

"When you—?" Cly gave him a confused gaze, then shook his head. "Forget about schooling Houjin. Leave that up to his uncle."

"Back in Seattle, where there are about fifty men to every woman?"

"More men than that, if you count all the fellas in Chinatown—and there's no reason you shouldn't."

"And the women who're there, you could count 'em on one hand . . . most of them so old, they could be his mother. Not that there's anything wrong with learning from an older woman, mind you."

"Can we change the subject now?"

"Sure. Why can't we stay at the Garden Court?"

"How about we don't talk at all. I like the sound of that even better."

To the captain's left, Fang laughed, silent except for a series of soft snorts.

"Not you, too," Cly complained.

I didn't say anything.

"You didn't have to."

"What are you talking about?" Houjin had been walking ahead, eyes up on the brightly painted buildings with their brilliant white latticework balconies and tumbling planters full of gardenias, daisies, and flowers with bright pink petals like trumpets.

"Nothing," Cly said quickly. "Turn left up at the next street, will ya? We're almost there."

The Widow Pickett was not precisely what anyone had expected, but Kirby Troost in particular was quite charmed to meet her acquaintance. Said widow wasn't thirty unless she was practicing witchcraft. She had a figure to inspire envy in ladies and lust in gentlemen, with a tall pile of hair the color of wheat and strawberries. As the black woman on the storefront stairs had predicted, the widow had no problem whatsoever providing shelter to the oriental men or anyone else, and before long two rooms were arranged, paid for, and settled in.

Fang and Houjin shared one two-bedded room, for Houjin could ask all the questions he wanted and Fang never appeared to mind; the captain and Kirby shared the other—though the captain never did bother with the skinny, too-short bed. As a matter of habit, he pulled the mattress onto the floor and flipped the frame up against the wall. He'd hang off the padding one way or another, but there was no reason to let his feet dangle in midair.

"You may as well settle in for the night," he told Kirby Troost. "Go downstairs and see about some supper. The sun'll be down in another hour."

"You say that like you don't intend to do likewise."

"I figured I'd head over to the Garden and have a real quick business chat with my old friend."

"You're headed to the whorehouse without me?" he asked accusingly.

"Yes, but I can't stay long, not with the curfew, and—"

Troost nodded knowingly. "And that's why you want to go *now*. Shit, man. You must be scared to death of this woman."

"Am not."

"I'm coming with you. Maybe I've got the pocket cash to stay the night and you can have this whole room to your lonesome."

Cly threw up his hands and said, "Fine. Suit yourself. Let me go tell Fang and Huey we're headed out."

Fang agreed to stay behind, and Houjin was so excited about eating the big weird bugs called *crawdads* that he was prepared to miss almost anything for the adventurous culinary fare. They planned to meet again at sundown to discuss the next day's duties, and Fang signed, *I'll keep him out of trouble.*

"Thanks. I do appreciate it."

On their way out the door, Kirby Troost asked, "But who's going to keep *us* out of trouble?"

"I didn't know you understood his signing."

"I'm picking it up as we go. It's one-part Native, what they use between two tribes—and one part deaf-man's hands, and one part something that's just between you two. But it's not so hard to figure out, once you get a few of the phrases down."

Cly said, "It's worth your time to learn it, I suppose—if you plan to spend any time with us."

The walk to the Garden Court was only a few blocks, ten minutes of ducking beneath balconies, dodging the tickles of hanging plants, staying out of the path of the rolling-crawlers, and ignoring the insistent last calls of every tavern and pub house in the Quarter.

Troost hesitated in front of a sign advertising in no uncertain terms the availability of women and alcohol both, but Cly ushered him past it. The engineer complained, "It isn't right—imposing a curfew on a place like this. This is a town made to stay up all night and toast the sunrise."

"That's one of the things it's made for, but not the only thing."

"I'm still right."

"I didn't say you weren't," the captain said. "I don't know why Texas has done it, but I'm sure there was a good reason."

Troost's eyes didn't believe him.

Cly sighed. "Whatever their reasoning, it doesn't matter to why we're here. And I'm frankly glad for it right now, because I don't want to spend more time in the Garden than I have to."

"You're a madman."

"I'm . . . happily attached."

"So you agree with me."

Cly escaped answering with a pointing jab of his long index finger at a swinging sign. "Look, that's it."

"Just like you remember?"

"The paint's new." He hesitated, standing still on the sidewalk and making two small, dark-skinned boys walk around him. "Otherwise, it looks pretty much the same."

"You're stalling. But we came all this way, and here we are.

Let's get inside and take a look around." Troost set off down the walkway.

Cly surged forward and caught up to Troost with only a few long strides—just in time to open the door and propel himself inside it first. Kirby couldn't decide whether to be annoyed or amused, but settled for amused and followed the captain into the plush, pretty lobby.

The carpets were red and maroon, laced with a buttercream trim, and the curtains were thick but colored to match. All the visible wood was dark with polish, age, and imported glamour. A long couch with a back curved like a sea serpent was pressed against the far wall, and a matching love seat was propped for cuddling inside the door to the right. Two plush solitary chairs that should've held one body apiece were spaced between the larger pieces of furniture, but in the nearest chair were two lovely colored women on the lap of a white-haired Texian—identifiable as such by a fluffy mustache that might have been made of a dove's wings . . . and then by his accent, when he exclaimed, "Newcomers, girls." Then to Cly and Troost, he said, "Y'all come on inside and make yourselves comfortable. Hazel or Ruthie will be downstairs in a minute."

The women on the Texian's lap smiled in welcome, but he showed no interest in letting them leave, so they stayed.

"Thank you, sir, I do believe I'll do exactly that," Kirby Troost declared, taking off his hat and making himself comfortable on the love seat. Cly was less certain. Partly for the sake of comfort, given his size—and partly because he'd rather not be crushed up against the engineer in such an intimate setting—he retreated to the couch and folded himself awkwardly, looking and feeling like a grown man sitting inside a dollhouse.

The captain asked the Texian, "You said Hazel and Ruthie. Is . . . is Josephine still here?"

"Miss Early? Oh, sure. She's the woman in charge, but she's not around—not right this moment. I believe she's out with a family emergency of some sort," he said vaguely. "Ruthie went with her, but she came back last night. Anyway, for what it's worth to you, I don't think Miss Early takes customers too often anymore."

"No? I mean, no—that's not . . . that's not why I ask. She's invited me here, to hire me for a job."

"What sort of job?"

"I'm not too rightly sure yet. But I've finally made it to town, and I mean to ask her about it."

The fluffy-faced Texian nodded and said, "Perhaps Hazel or Ruthie can help you out. They're real competent girls themselves, and so's Marylin. They're the ones she usually leaves running the business while she's out."

"Good to know. Thank you, sir."

A slender mixed-race woman who was more white than anything else chose this moment to descend the staircase and enter the lobby, a vision in pink taffeta and ivory lace, with her hair tufted up and fastened with elaborate combs. "Mr. Calais," she said to the Texian, "you surely do look comfortable, sir."

"Couldn't be happier, Miss Quantrill!" he assured her, though when he reached for his scotch, it was barely beyond his fingertips. The girl upon his right knee retrieved it for him and leaned so that he could squeeze her close and take a swallow at the same time. "And these men here, they're looking for Josephine."

Kirby and Cly both came to their feet, and Troost announced, "*He's* looking for Josephine. I'm just looking."

She gave them both a demure smile that showed no teeth. To Troost, she said, "You'll be the easiest to assist. My name is Marylin, and I'll be happy to make any arrangements you require. But as for you, sir," she told the captain, "Miss Early isn't here right now."

"That's what your friend said. Any chance you know when she'll be back?"

Before Marylin could answer, a second woman slipped up behind her. The dark-haired beauty was wearing maroon that bordered on brown, and every inch of her shimmered. Kirby Troost's eyes went wide, and he opened his mouth. Then he closed it.

She swished forward, taking in Troost's gaze and discarding it in favor of catching Cly's. Unabashedly she appraised him from head to foot, and when she felt she'd seen everything she needed, she declared, "*Je suis* Ruthie Doniker, and I manage the house for Miss Early while she is out. Are you Captain Cly?"

"Yes . . . yes, ma'am. I am. Josephine sent for me."

"*Oui,* I know. For a while, she thought you would not come."

He hunkered, even though the ceiling accommodated his height. "I do apologize—I tried to reply to her telegram sooner, but I had a hard time getting hold of the taps until a few days ago."

"Your message reached us, but she was called away suddenly. She has left instructions. Could you come upstairs with me, *monsieur*?"

Marylin gave Ruthie a look Cly couldn't decipher, but he thought it might mean, *Trust me.* And she turned with more swishing to ascend the stairs.

"You won't be needing me, will you?" Troost asked with optimism dripping from every word.

"I don't guess so."

So the captain left him there, in the company of Marylin Quantrill, the Texian Mr. Calais, and the two women on his lap who were spoken for; Cly followed the stunning, slim-bodied woman up the stairs while trying to neither knock his head nor stare too hard at the swaying bustle that covered her backside.

By way of making conversation he asked, "Does she—does Josephine, I mean—still keep an office up here?"

"She does, *oui, monsieur.* And that is where we are going." Ruthie paused on the stairs and looked back at him, appraising him afresh, though the captain didn't know why. She turned and continued upward, added, "Madame said that she knew you, a long time ago."

"That's right."

"She said you are a very good pilot."

"I don't get any complaints."

"She said you were the tall man, and I should know you that way."

"Many men are tall."

"She said that in any room, filled with any group of men, *you* were the tall one."

As she said this, he swung his head to avoid an old wall sconce that had not yet been fitted for gas, but still held a candle that had melted down to a thumb-sized nub.

On the third floor, the stairs emptied into a walkway, just as Cly remembered, and he followed Ruthie to Josephine's office. The office was not quite the same as the last time he'd seen it, but he would've recognized her touch anywhere. New curtains, in burgundy instead of green. Two new chairs—no, two *old* chairs with new striped upholstery. And the desk she'd inherited from someplace or another, half as big as a bed and ornately carved at the corners—where cherubs held harps and the wings of angels curved gently downward to the lion's-paw feet.

Gaudy, she'd called it once. But she'd never replaced it.

Behind this desk sat an attractive colored woman with a curvy body and kind eyes. She wore a beautiful blue dress in some high style that hadn't yet made it to the West Coast, and when she gracefully rose to meet Andan Cly, the tiny bells sewn into her sleeves made a delicate tinkling sound. Ruthie introduced them by declaring, "Captain Cly, Hazel Bushrod." And in French she said, "Hazel, this is the airman Josephine sent for."

Hazel ducked her head in a discreet bow, and said, "It's a pleasure to meet you, sir. I'm sorry Miss Early isn't here right now, but I hope I can help you all the same."

"Miss . . . Bushrod? Is that right?"

"Yes, and no, I didn't make it up or acquire it on the job," she said, the kindness in her eyes hardening briefly into something else. "It was my father's name, and now it's mine. And if you have anything further you'd like to say—"

"No, no, ma'am. It's an unusual name, that's all. I've never heard it before."

"Well, now you have. And if we're finished with the subject, I'd like to invite you to pull up a seat." She sat back down, her skirts and those tiny silver bells conspiring to make music. She crossed her legs beneath the desk, unleashing a new round of rustling, and the rubbing together of fabrics and thighs.

Ruthie pulled up one of the striped chairs and offered it to Cly, who sat gingerly upon it. Then she drew up the second one and positioned it beside Hazel's, so that the captain could not escape the feeling he was about to be interrogated, quizzed, or possibly sentenced.

He didn't recognize either of these women. They hadn't been with Josephine back in the old days, which stood to reason, given that neither of them appeared to be older than her mid-twenties. A decade before, they would've been young for such a life, by Josephine's business standards.

Cly shifted in his seat, attempting to get comfortable without damaging the furniture, which looked delicate on the surface but bore his weight without creaking. "I suppose Josephine told you, she called me here about a job."

Hazel said, "How much did she tell you about it?"

"Almost nothing. She wants me to fly something from the lake to the Gulf."

"Did she say what she wanted you to fly?"

"No."

"And did you think it was strange?" she asked, reaching into a drawer and withdrawing a collection of papers without taking her eyes off the captain.

"I did," he admitted. "But I needed to make a big supply run for my town anyway. And say what you will about Texians—I'm sure they're none too popular in this house—but they know their way around a machine shop. And I need one, because I'm having some work done on my own bird."

Ruthie and Hazel considered this response and exchanged the kind of gaze that old friends can sometimes share—squeezing a whole conversation into an instant's worth of facial tics, blinks, and small frowns. When the moment had passed, Ruthie rose from her seat and went to shut the door. Then she returned to her position beside Hazel, and the pair of them turned their full and absolute attention upon Cly, who could scarcely recall having felt so uncomfortable in his life.

"I get the feeling this is trickier than I thought. Stranger than I thought."

Hazel said, "Miss Early told us you weren't stupid, and so far, so good. Yes, what we have to tell you—what we have to *ask* you—is tricky and strange, and I want you to understand how much danger you could put us in, simply with one wrong word."

"Danger? For you?"

"For us," Ruthie said. "For the Garden Court. For Josephine."

Hazel folded her hands on the desk and said, "Dangerous for you, too, once we tell you everything. So first I must ask, and I expect you to answer me truthfully: Have you now, or have you ever, owed any loyalty to the Republic of Texas or to the Confederate States of America?"

Easily, he responded, "No. Nor the Union, either, if you want to get precise about it. I was born on the Oregon Trail, somewhere east of Portland. I've been a merchant by trade most of my life, and it's been worth my time to keep from making enemies."

Ruthie snorted, and Hazel said, "A merchant? Josephine said you were a pirate."

"Same thing, in a way. I've run plenty of goods that weren't good for anyone. But I'm trying to leave that life behind me now. That's one reason I'm here in the city, getting my bird refitted up in Metairie."

Hazel asked, "Why would you leave pirating? The only money anybody has anymore comes from working while the law isn't looking. We know that better than anyone, don't we, Ruthie?"

"Mm-*hmm*."

"Ladies," he said, opening his hands as if to entreat them. "Josephine and me, we have birthdays only a week apart—and I want to settle down while I've still got the life in me to enjoy retirement. But whatever Josie wants, I'm prepared to help her out—even if it's something that we don't want the law looking at, since that's what you're implying. I told her I'd fly for her, and I will. But you have to tell me what's really going on, and what Texas and the Rebs have to do with it. Is this a military thing? You want me to sneak something out past the forts?"

"Yes," Hazel said bluntly. "That's precisely what we want. We have a craft out at Lake Pontchartrain, and we need to bring it out to the Gulf of Mexico—*into* it, past the edge of the delta and then some—and deliver it to Admiral Herman Partridge aboard the Union airship carrier *Valiant.*"

"An airship carrier? I've heard of those, but never seen one. Fairly new to the war, ain't they?"

"Fairly new. Very big ships," Hazel said in a rush. "But if you chose to accept Josephine's mission, you won't be flying an *air*ship."

A hush descended on the room as Andan Cly struggled to figure out what on earth these women could possibly mean, and the women teetered on the brink of spilling everything, unsure whether they could trust him. Ruthie cracked first. She blurted to Hazel, "Just tell him! Or ask him, and then we will know whether to shoot him or pay him, eh?"

"Shoot me?" he asked.

Hazel took a deep breath, closed her eyes, and opened them again. "Captain, please understand—we are asking you to participate in smuggling something the likes of which you've never smuggled before. And the entirety of the Confederacy and the Republic of Texas will be stacked against you."

"Must be important."

"Very," she told him gravely. "We are not talking about an airship. We are talking about a war machine with the power to enforce the broken naval blockade. A machine that can choke off the ocean supplies, and perhaps the river supplies . . . and in time, the whole South. Do you understand what I'm telling you?"

"You're telling me you want me to spy for the Union, here inside a Southern city controlled by the South's number one ally. You're telling me I'll be risking my neck to take the case, and you're risking your own necks to describe it."

"Sums it up rather nicely," Hazel agreed. "So what do you say?"

After half a dozen seconds of silence, he told her, "I suppose the war's got to end one day, one way or another. And all things being equal, I'd rather it gets won by the Federals. I can't much rally for any government that'll call a man a piece of property. So if you're asking if I can keep my mouth shut and do the job, I'm telling you I can."

"Are you sure?" Ruthie asked, hope in her lovely face, but also fear.

"Yeah, I'm sure. If Josephine thought it was important enough to bring me here, then it must be a job worth doing. But I do want to know, before we come to any formal arrangement: What do you mean, it's a war machine, but not an airship? I've never flown anything but an airship. Is this some special kind of warbird? I've seen a few armored crafts, including a big one a buddy of mine stole from a base in Macon . . . but you're going to have to be more specific."

Hazel smiled. It was a worried smile, and it trembled around the edges—but it was a smile that had come to a decision and was prepared to dive on in. "Captain Cly, if it's specifics you want, it's specifics you'll get." She sorted through the loose papers on Josephine's desk and selected a few she wanted, then pushed them toward Andan Cly—who scooted his chair closer for a better look. "These are . . . schematics," he observed. "For something I'm not sure I understand."

Ruthie nodded, encouraged by his initial grasp of the matter, if not the depth of his knowledge. "They are old designs. For a machine."

Hazel picked up a newspaper clipping and turned it around so that it faced the captain right side up. "Horace Lawson Hunley," he read from the caption beneath a line drawing of a mustachioed man striking a dashing pose.

Hazel said, "Hunley was a Tennessean by birth, but his family brought him to New Orleans as a child, and this is where he did most of his work. He was a marine engineer, and those schematics you're holding are engineer's drawings for his first successful machine."

"If you could call it *successful,*" Ruthie mumbled.

"It *did* drown a few people," Hazel confirmed. "But ultimately, it worked."

"Worked at what?" he asked.

"It sailed underwater."

"I beg your pardon?"

Hazel said, "You heard me. The *Pioneer* was a tube designed to hold men and move them underwater, by the use of these hand-cranks and whatnot, as if they were in the belly of a shark. It was a flawed design, put together with the help of these two men—James McClintock and Baxter Watson." She pushed forward another clipping with a pair of portraits. "The first sailors drowned, or nearly drowned, when the *Pioneer* sank in Mobile Bay. The folks who tried to pilot the next version of the craft, the *Bayou St. John,* didn't fare too much better."

Ruthie spelled it out. "They drowned, too."

"You'd think this Hunley fellow would've had a hard time finding crew members after a while."

"He did, but there are always eager young men who want to be in a history book. Besides, the Confederacy was willing to pay big money to fellows who'd try it out. Imagine it, would you? A boat that sails underwater, loaded up with explosive charges and contact fuses, sneaking up on ships and blowing them to pieces without ever being seen . . . then slipping away and doing it again."

Cly stared down at the papers. "I can imagine it."

"A few years and a few more dollars later, Hunley made himself a new model—which he named for himself. The *Hunley* did better than his earlier boats, which is to say that it drowned only five men on its first run, and eight on its next—including Hunley himself, who was riding on board. But his old partners, McClintock and Watson, they kept on working, kept on designing. Kept on building," she added quietly.

Ruthie selected a folded sheet of paper. She unfolded it and handed it to Andan Cly.

It depicted the interior workings of a ship, but not one like anything he'd ever seen before. It looked like fiction, there in his hands.

These lines showing gears, and valves, and portals; these careful engineering sketches showing bolts, and curved walls, and compartments for flooding or pumping; these enormous rooms that seated six to eight, with side and bottom holds for ammunition— and tubular sleeves for explosives and fuses.

He did not look up from the schematics when Hazel began talking again, but he listened to her as he perused the pictures with wonder.

"Then McClintock caught Watson red-handed, with telegrams and instructions from the Union army. Whether Watson was a double agent all along, or he simply wanted the bigger payday from the bigger army, no one knows. But he was all set to sell their research to the North, and McClintock wouldn't have it. They fought, and Watson shot McClintock through the heart before trying to flee inside the vessel he'd helped create.

"But Watson was a designer, not a skipper. He understood the mechanics of the beast, but not the nuance of making it sail—even if that *were* a task a single man could accomplish. The ship sank halfway across Pontchartrain. Watson drowned.

"But his message had already gone back to the Union engineers, who knew the craft existed. They came to investigate—only to be caught by the Texians, who were also looking for the ship."

"How did Texas know about it?"

Hazel nodded approvingly, as if this was a good question. "It had been made with Texian technology, and Texian machinists, so they knew it was out there somewhere. They didn't find, it, though."

"And your people did?"

Both of the women smiled, identically and in perfect time with each other. Hazel continued. "It took three weeks of looking, but the ship was found and lifted by a group of guerrillas in the bayou . . . the free men of color who fight Texas and the Confederacy from the shadows. They hauled it to a different shore and hid it there, where it remains now—waiting for the right man or men to take it all the way to the ocean, where it was always meant to go. And *that,* Captain Cly, is the story of the *Ganymede*."

Cly finally looked up from the intricate engineering sketches. He looked each woman in the eye and said, "You want me to fly a ship underwater."

"Once we can man-haul it to the river, yes. The Mississippi is deep enough to take it, and once you're in the river, you'll have slip past Fort Jackson and Fort Saint Philip. From there, it'll be smooth sailing straight out into the Gulf of Mexico."

"In a ship that's drowned . . . how many men?"

"*Ganymede*? Oh, hardly any," Hazel dismissed his concern hastily, and with a wave of her hand. "Only Mr. McClintock, so far as we know. As you can see from those plans, *Ganymede* is a much stronger design—a much better ship than the ones that came before. Learning how to create a ship like her . . . it was costly, yes. But the end result is *this* majestic creation. And it will end a war, Captain."

Ruthie rose and left her chair, approaching Cly and crouching beside him. With her elegantly gloved hands, she called his attention to various highlights on the schematics that sat across his lap.

"Right here, you see? This is the steering mechanism, and the power system for the propellers. They were designed like thrusters on an airship."

"I see that, sure. But there's no hydrogen to keep steady. No gas to maintain, or to power the thrust."

"But of course there is gas, *monsieur*! The gas is the air you breathe. It is pumped and cycled, through these vents here, by this tube. If the men breathe the same air too long, it makes them sick. They faint, and they die."

Hazel confirmed, "That's one of the hard lessons learned from the *Bayou St. John* and the *Hunley*. The men inside must have fresh air, drawn down regularly. The air within the cabin cannot support them forever."

"So this—" He jabbed a finger at one long set of pipes, and drew it along the lines. "—these pipes don't stay above water, not all the time? So you don't have to keep this breathing tube up above the surface?" It reminded him of Seattle, of the system that likewise drew fresh breathing air down underneath an inhospitable surface. They did it the same way, essentially. Tubes bringing in the fresh air for four to eight hours a day, always keeping it moving, never giving it time to grow stale.

Ruthie nodded. "The tubes do not stay up. You can close them from within, like this." She indicated a rubber-sealed flap that was manipulated by a hydraulic pulley. "There is one main breathing tube, with fans to draw down the air—and an emergency tube in case the one should fail. But they can both be shut so that the ship can sink and hide."

"For how long?" he asked.

The ladies paused, but Hazel replied. "We're not certain. Twenty or thirty minutes, at least."

"So really, it's a ship that can hold its breath for half an hour at a time."

"Yes!" Ruthie rose to her feet and clapped. "You see? Josephine said he would understand. She said we needed an airman, and she was right!"

"But what about the original crew? You said it's been tested, out on the lake. Where are the guys who know how to pilot this thing already?"

Hazel handed him another sheet with a different angle on the *Ganymede*'s inner workings and said, "Most of them were captured. Two men were sent off to a prisoner-of-war camp in Georgia, and three were sent to the barracks here, but escaped and went back to New England. And the man in charge was shot for treason."

"Treason?"

"He was from Baton Rouge—a Confederate deserter who'd come to work with the bayou boys. Name was Roger Lisk, may he rest in peace." Hazel leaned forward, restlessly arranging and rearranging the remaining documents. "Without the crew, and without the men who created it, the *Ganymede* is a big hunk of metal full of potential . . . but precious little more than that. The bayou boys have all the information—all these schematics, and instructions. But they're soldiers and sailors by trade, and sailors haven't performed well so far, when it comes to keeping the ship afloat and running. And the Union is not so convinced of its value that it'll risk its own engineers and officers on the project—not unless we can get it to the admiral."

But Ruthie appeared more hopeful, now that the ball was rolling. "Josephine said no one could work the *Ganymede* because only the sailors were willing to try. But *Ganymede* is not built like a boat. She is built like an airship, one made to fly in the water, not in the clouds. Josephine said we needed a crew of airmen. Airmen would know how to make her go."

"Now, let's not get ahead of ourselves," Andan Cly cautioned. "I can see that you're right—partway right, at any rate. Whoever built this bird," he said, then corrected himself. "Whoever built this *fish* drew a lot of inspiration from an airship, that's true. The controls are similar, or so I gather from looking at this. And the shape is more or less the same, with fins instead of small steering sails, and the propeller screws instead of the left and right thrusters. Hmm."

"Hmm?" Hazel prompted.

"Hmm," he repeated. "I don't know anything on earth about

sailing, but I understand it's pretty different from flying. The principle is easy to sort out, but the principle and the practice are two different things."

Ruthie leaned on the edge of the desk, halfway sitting upon it and halfway resting her bustle there. "It's true. It's all true—and we know you are an airman, and not a sailor. But can you make it swim?"

"I . . . I don't know what to say."

"You told Josephine you'd take the job," Hazel reminded him.

"I didn't know I was agreeing to a job that might get me and my crew drowned at the bottom of a river, and that's part of my trouble. If it were just me, that'd be one thing. But a boat like this . . . it'd take at least two or three men to control her. Maybe more. I'd have to ask my crew members how they felt about it. We'd need to see it in person."

"That can be arranged!" Ruthie exclaimed. It was clear she'd made up her mind already: this was going to work, all would go smoothly, and the problem was all but resolved.

Hazel was not so confident, but she was willing to risk a shred of hope. She told Cly, "We can take you to it, tonight if you like. Josephine is there, out at the lake with her brother."

"Wait a minute, wait a minute. Hold your horses, ma'am. Let me go back to my rooms and have a chat with my men, all right? I'll tell them what you've told me, and they can decide whether or not they want to take the chance."

"But, Captain!" Hazel objected. "You can't go running around willy-nilly, spreading the story around the Quarter!"

"And I *won't*. But I won't ask my men to risk their lives spying and smuggling against two governments at once, not without knowing what they're risking. For what it's worth, I expect they'll be willing to help. Two of my crewmen are Chinamen, without any more political allegiance than I've got, and the other is Kirby Troost, who you met downstairs, He's always game for anything—the more unlikely and dangerous, the better—and if the prospect of friendly women is involved, you may as well call him sold. So they can make up their own minds, and even if they decide they *don't* want in, you can sleep well knowing they won't have any interest in handing you over to Texas, either."

Hazel chewed at her lip and tapped Josephine's silver letter opener up and down on the desk's edge. "We were hoping for a definite commitment."

"I'm sorry, but that's the best you're going to get right now." He glanced out the window. "It's almost sundown, and the curfew will be settling soon. I know you're not too worried about it—and honestly, neither am I—but if we want to hang around without drawing extra Texian attention, we need to follow the rules. Until we break the ever-living hell out of them, anyway."

Much as they didn't like it, the women had to admit that this was reasonable. Ruthie said, "In the morning, then. Tell me where you are staying, and I will come for you. I will take you out to Pontchartrain, and you will see *Ganymede* up close, and crawl inside, and show the bayou boys how to make her swim."

"That sounds fine to me," he told her. "We've got a couple of rooms over at the Widow Pickett's on the other side of the Square. You can come collect us there in the morning. So if you'll excuse me, I'll go round up my engineer and . . . On second thought, you know what? Keep him. Or send him along when he's ready to come back."

With that he climbed to his feet, returned the papers he'd collected, and excused himself.

But Hazel said, "No, you keep those. And this one, as well." She handed him another sheet, detailing the propulsion screw and the diesel engine, as well as its exhaust system. "Look them over. Make yourself familiar with them. And for the love of all that's holy, don't let the Texians see them."

Nine

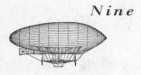

Ruthie Doniker knocked on Andan Cly's door brighter and earlier than he truly cared to see her, but he'd told her "morning," and so it was morning when she came calling. When he opened the door, she stood there swathed in a green cotton dress too formfitting to be called plain, with a very light jacket that had a high cream-colored collar cinched around her neck. Before the captain had a chance to greet her, she said, "It is time to leave for your day at the lake, Captain Cly."

"No kidding." He blinked blearily. He was awake, but he hadn't been for long. Not long enough to shave or wash his face, and only barely long enough to realize that Kirby Troost hadn't come back to the room. "Well, I guess you can come on in while I get myself together."

"Merci," she said, and sidled past him.

"Have a seat wherever. Give me a minute, would you?"

He pulled out his razor and tried to forget that Ruthie was present and looking at him. It was easier said than done. Every time his eyes slipped away from his own face in the mirror, he caught her reflection and felt strange about it.

At some point, he paused with the razor braced under one cheek and asked, "So, Kirby. I guess he stayed at the Garden Court last night?"

"I guess he did. Marylin took care of him. He came here with me."

"Oh. He did? Where is he?"

"Awakening your other crewmen."

As he drew the razor across his skin, Cly realized that she'd never asked him if they'd agreed to take the job or not. Ruthie was assuming they would take it, as if she could bend reality to meet her whims.

He was glad he wouldn't need to disappoint her.

The night before, he'd sat with Fang and Houjin after supper, showing them the schematics in the privacy of their room, where no Texians, Confederates, or other unwelcome eyes might take a look. Houjin had responded with enthusiastic glee—he would've risked a coin-flip's chance of drowning for the mere opportunity to get a look at the *Ganymede,* much less crawl around inside it. His passion for all things mechanical would draw him to the lake even if they told him it'd cost a dollar and he'd get a beating when he arrived.

Fang had been his usual unflappable self, nodding his agreement to investigate the craft and, later, when Houjin could not see his hands, signing to the captain, *Very dangerous?* To which Cly had shrugged a *maybe.* Then, while the boy's nose was still stuck in the diagrams and drawings, Fang had added, *I will do this, for the Union.*

Cly signed back, *Didn't know you cared one way or the other.*

I care for the West. If the South wins, and claims new states, they will be states where men can be owned as slaves. If the North wins, maybe the new states will be . . . He paused. *Not much better. But where freedom is declared, it can be negotiated. Besides, I liked Josephine. Smart woman. Easy to agree with.*

"Easier to agree with her than to argue with her, that's for damn sure."

As Cly finished up his shaving, wiping down his face and neck, a knock on the door was followed shortly by the entrance of Fang, Houjin, and Kirby Troost, who touched the edge of his hat in Ruthie's general direction.

Ruthie stood to her full height—three inches taller than Troost, though that was emphasized by the boots she wore—and announced, "If everyone is ready, we should go catch a carriage."

"Shouldn't we just grab the street rails, instead?" Cly asked. "Surely that'd be faster than a cabriolet."

"A carriage to the edge of the Quarter, and then we can take the rails to the far side of Metairie, but no farther. Where we go beyond the City of the Dead . . . only trusted eyes may lead us."

Together they followed Ruthie's lead down to the street, where she nabbed a carriage in the blink of an eye, even though she needed a larger transport than was usually running. Before long, they were back at the street rail station where they'd first entered the city, and then on the car to Metairie, to Houjin's continued joy.

On the way, Kirby Troost sat beside the captain. When Ruthie stood at the protective guardrail, likely out of hearing distance, the engineer asked quietly, "Are you sure about this?"

"No."

"Me either. Did they tell you about what happened to Betters and Cardiff?"

"Who are Betters and Cardiff?" Cly asked.

"The Texians who went missing. They're the reason New Orleans has a curfew."

"No, the ladies didn't mention it."

"Josephine knows," Troost said softly. "The girls at the house say she was there when they died. Do you know they've got a rotter problem, here in New Orleans?"

Taken aback, Cly gave Troost a hard stare of uncertainty. "That's impossible. No gas, no rotters."

"Impossible or not, that's what they sound like to *me*. Except they don't call 'em rotters here. They call 'em zombis. And I don't think they're made by the gas. I think they're made by the sap."

Cly considered this and said, "We've known for a while that the drug makes people sick, if they use it too long."

"I think it does worse than make them sick. I think it kills them, and keeps them upright, just like the dead in Seattle. All I'm saying is, when you meet back up with this lady friend of yours, you should ask her about it. The girls say she saw the whole thing. Her and some voudou queen, but I don't rightly know what to make of that part."

The captain stayed hung up on the undead particulars. "I'm not saying there aren't any rotters outside the city, Troost. Ten minutes talking to Mercy Lynch'll tell you that much. But those rotters happened because a dirigible crashed, and the gas got loose—poisoning the air where all those people were. That was a mess of an accident, but I don't think that could happen around here, not without people noticing it."

"I'm not arguing with you. A big load of hungry dead folks didn't just appear one night down by the river. They weren't here ten years ago, were they?"

"If they were, I never heard about it."

"That's what I mean," the engineer said. He was wheedling now; he had an idea and he was determined to share it—by verbal force if necessary. "They didn't spring up overnight, but they've been happening gradual-like. One or two sap-heads, here and there, going so deep into the drugs that they didn't ever come back. Then what happens if another one or two, here and there, does the same thing? And another few?"

"It's a stretch, Troost."

"I know it is. But it's not a *big* stretch, and I don't think I'm wrong. The streets aren't crawling with them, not like in Seattle, but they're a problem down by the river, and the Texians are on a rampage, trying to wipe them out and make the place safe again."

"How do you know that?" the captain asked.

"You saw that Texian in the lobby, the fellow who practically lives there? His name's Fenn Calais, and as long as you're buying, he's talking. You know what else he told me?"

"Go on."

"He said that the raid on Barataria was an official operation, and Texas was looking for a ship—something they thought the pirates might be hiding, or in the process of smuggling out to sea. And when we saw them from the sky, watching over the bay, they were poking around in the water, weren't they doing just that?"

"Doesn't mean they were looking for—" He chose not to say the name aloud. Just in case. "—the ship we're looking at."

"All I'm saying is, I hope we're not biting off more than we can chew."

Cly grinned. "You don't hope that. Not for a second. You hope it gets so messy, you can make your own fortune."

"Goddamn, sir. You know me entirely too well." Troost rolled a cigarette and stuck it between his lips, then lit it and puffed on it the rest of the way to Metairie.

At the Metairie station, they all disembarked and were met by a handsome, heavyset black man named Norman Somers. He greeted them wearing denim pants, a linen button-up shirt with a vest, and a big smile that did not appear practiced or false. If he was a spy or a man with a covert mission to attend, he was a very fine actor—or so Cly thought.

Ruthie gave Norman a kiss on the cheek, which he returned. "You must be the captain and crew," he said to the rest of those assembled. "I hear your ship is out here at the Texian yards, over yonder."

"Just on the other side of the station, that's right," said Cly. "Having a little work done while we're in town."

"You've picked a good shop. Mostly it's run by Texians and a group of colored fellows from the Chattanooga schools. They'll do good work for you. But I understand you're here to take a gander at another fine piece of machinery, isn't that right?" He did not lower his voice or treat the subject with any specific gravity, and this was no doubt for the best—given that they conversed in public, with dozens of passengers fresh off the street rails milling to and fro.

Cly replied in kind, "That's the plan." And then he made the rounds of introductions, following which, Normal Somers urged them to follow him to a service lot beyond the edge of the cemetery.

"Lots of folks park their buggies and carriages and whatnot, then ride the street rail into town. This here lot," he said with a sweep of his arm, "is watched by Charlie over there." His sweeping gesture ended in a wave at a tiny old negro with at least half a dozen firearms in his immediately visible possession, probably more. "Charlie keeps an eye on things, and if you come back to your ride and it's in one piece, you tip him whatever you've got handy. That's our buggy—if you want to pile inside, I'll go settle up."

The buggy in question did not come attached to a horse. It had a front-mounted motor that drew a big wheeled contraption that looked cobbled together from a rolling-crawler, a cabriolet, a street rail car, and perhaps a two-man flier. It was a hodgepodge piece of machinery, but it was big enough to take everyone wherever they felt like going, and the stretched-wool surrey top kept the worst of the sun off their heads.

Kirby Troost again sat beside the captain, and leaned over to mumble, "I was going to complain that this was a conspicuous sort of ride, but looking around at the lot, I am forced to revise my opinion."

It was true. All the vehicles in Charlie's lot were similarly patch-worked and rigged together. It could not be said that they were all of a single type, except that none of them had started out looking like they did at present. The captain detected the occasional small dirigible chassis, boat motor, carriage frame, and dual V-twin engine protruding from a hood . . . but most of what he spied was made of unidentifiable bits.

The captain said, "I suppose people out here like to improvise."

Ruthie replied, "They do it because they must. Many of these—" She cocked a thumb at the next row of buggies. "—are made with things the machine shops throw away."

"I believe it," Troost said. "The whole yard looks like a big science experiment."

Shortly, Norman Somers returned and climbed up onto the driver's seat. He pulled a lever, which produced a large black umbrella, and with a popping sound it opened to shade him from the sun so that he was protected as well as his passengers. "All right!" he declared. "Now we can get on our way. And how was your trip from the city?" he asked over his shoulder.

"Just fine," said Cly, who was still a bit surprised by how unstealthy this whole production felt. "And might I ask, where exactly will the rest of our trip see us heading?"

"The rest of your trip?" He gave a narrow chain a hearty yank, and the engine burbled to life, spewing fumes and soft puffy smoke clouds in every direction. Over the diesel rumble he said, "We're going to take a stroll around a lake, that's all we're goin' do. Maybe we swing by the bayou's edge and visit with some of the fellas we find there, huh? This your first time in New Orleans?"

Cly said, "Mine and Fang's? No. Huey, yes. Troost?"

"I never been here before," the engineer informed them. "Been around the Gulf a bit. Visited Galveston once, and Houston. Spent some time in Mobile. Somehow, never managed to land myself right here on the delta. Not till now."

"Then, let me welcome you to my home city, and I hope you enjoy your stay."

The rest of the way was filled with jovial chitchat of a similar nature, and gradually the tall grasses, half-paved roads, and spotty marshes gave way to more fully untamed wet, thick grasslands and roads that were not paved at all. The rumbling buggy drove them bumpily along the rutted dirt paths and beneath gigantic trees that oozed lacy gray curls of Spanish moss and peeling spirals of bark and vines. Though the day was young, the world became darker as they moved farther from the city's hub; before long, the paths were so overgrown that the long elbows of cypress trees met above them, and the whole road was cast in shadow. Whereas before, they could hear the guttural hums of other buggies and the clattering buzz of the street rail cars moving back and forth between their stops, now the passengers heard nothing but the rollicking grumble of their own engine. And behind it, in shrieks and whispers, they picked up the calls of birds and the croaks of a million frogs, plus the zipping drone of clear-winged insects the size of bats.

Off to the side of the road, among the trees, the land grew less landlike and more swamplike.

"Where the hell are we?" wondered Kirby Troost aloud.

Norman Somers somehow overheard him, and he replied, "Over there, to the right, see? That's the Bayou Piquant."

"Where's the lake?" Troost asked, louder than he needed to, given the superior quality of Mr. Somers's hearing.

"On the other side of the bayou. No worries, my friends! I get you to Pontchartrain just fine, okay? We'll be there soon."

True to his word, Norman pulled off to the side of the road on the far side of what could reasonably be proclaimed a swamp. He dismounted from his seat and said, "One moment, fellas." And Ruthie did her best not to look put out at being lumped in with the lads.

Somers disappeared behind a buttonbush slightly taller than himself. Sounds of rustling, heaving, shoving, scraping, and finally the steady *tick-tick* noise of a chain cranking clattered out from the spot where he'd vanished. He did not immediately emerge again, but a definite shift occurred—some strange motion that at first made so little sense that Cly and his crew members couldn't be sure what they were seeing.

But as the seconds clicked by and the chain pattered on, seams appeared in the landscape.

What had seemed at first to be a pair of colossal bald cypress trees were lifted, and as if mounted on a track, they slid to the left, taking a significant chunk of the landscape with them. The buttonbush and two smaller members of the same species went jerkily scooting away as well, and the whole scene slipped as easily and thoroughly as the dropcloth background of a play—revealing a pair of large mirrors that served as the juncture of three unnatural lines. Their angles made the trunks, mosses, twigs, and vines repeat indefinitely, creating the perfect illusion of infinite swamp-space as long as they were touching.

Fang let out a low, impressed whistle.

Houjin's mouth hung open.

Kirby Troost adjusted his hat and sniffed as if he encountered this kind of thing every day.

Ruthie gave a small, smug smile.

And Captain Cly said, "I'll be damned."

Ruthie asked in French, "You've never seen anything like it, have you?"

"Non," replied Cly. *"Jamais."*

If she was surprised to hear him reply in kind, she did not give him the satisfaction of showing it. Instead she said, in English this time, "Anderson Worth designed it. He grinds glass lenses for spectacles, and he says that mirrors are not so different, the way they change the light—and the things we see."

Houjin found his voice and asked, "Where's Mr. Worth now?" "Is he still here? I'd like to talk to him. I want to know how he made this!"

"You will meet him at the camp."

Before any more questions could be generated, Norman emerged from behind a water oak with a mile-wide smile on his face and said, "This is something else, *bien sûr?*"

"It surely is, Mr. Somers!" Houjin exclaimed. "Can I come down there and look at it?"

"Right now? No, but maybe later if you want, okay? For now, we got to get out of the road and close this gate back up again." With that, he climbed back onto the buggy's driving seat and restarted the engine with a yank of its chain. "We can't go leaving the way open for anyone to come inside. It keeps out the riffraff, because this is one of only two ways through the swamp to the camp."

"What's the other way?" Cly asked.

Ruthie answered. "You'll find out later."

Norman drove the machine past a certain line, deeper into the swamp than it felt the wheels could possibly turn, given the terrain . . .

and he dismounted again, landing with a splash in a soupy mess that was not half so deep as it looked. He skipped back to a set of controls, large cranks and a locking lever, and as he moved, he walked on water.

"Another illusion?" Cly asked Ruthie.

She said, *"Oui."*

And when Somers returned, still smiling that toothsome grin, he said, "What we do, you see—is we drop down stones into the bayou, and then we build a road on top of them."

"What do you use to make it?" Houjin asked.

"Oak boards, mostly. We paint them black, and just like that—" He snapped his fingers. "—they disappear, and for all anyone can tell, the bayou is as deep as the ocean. 'Cept for the cypress knees. Those don't lie, but they fib."

Another mile through what looked like open swamp—without any roads, without any signs, and without any hint of a path—and the way opened to something like a clearing, though it was not very well cleared.

It might have been better described as a settlement, for such it was, and a well-considered settlement at that.

Tree houses were lifted up above the soft, easily flooding ground. They were mounted six to eight feet up the trunks, and accessible with ladders; they were roofed with native flora and insulated with thick bundles of dried moss, so that when viewed from above, they would not rouse suspicion. Let the dirigibles scope and soar. Nothing at the bayou camp would give any scout a cause for alarm.

Large canopies, woven from palmetto leaves and carefully camouflaged, were strung up on willow poles in order to hide two rolling-crawlers either bought or stolen from the Texians. Another canopy covered boxes of munitions and supplies, which were stashed upon a platform that was raised off the bayou floor much like the houses—and yet a third canopy clearly functioned as a meeting place, and possibly a dining hall.

There beneath the verdant overhangs both natural and man-made, the swamp was a green-black place of beauty and shadow. It was a place of precision and caution, activity and consultation.

At a quick, casual count, Cly estimated perhaps two dozen men in the camp, the majority of them dark skinned and wearing Union uniform pieces in much the same way that the Texians wore their own garb—without any attention paid to the official lines of the garments. Everything was adapted to the thick, wet warmth that was trapped there in the swamp. Everything bowed to the dense heat and close-pressing smell of vegetation being soaked in its own rot—of new plants and freshly broken branches, of stringy grass filaments and gray-felt moss, and the leftover whiffs of catfish fried at an earlier meal but long since eaten.

Shirts were left open, and sleeves were rolled to elbows. But pants were worn down long, sometimes cinched at the ankles or tucked into boots. Cly understood. There were places where a man didn't dare walk with his ankles unprotected, regardless of the temperature, for fear of stinging insects, snakes, and thorns.

From the corner of his eye, he watched Houjin stick a finger into the mandarin collar of his shirt and wipe away the dampness that collected there. Then the boy swiped at the back of his neck, at the place where his ponytail hung over the collar, and his hand came away wet with perspiration there, too.

The buggy was lured up beneath yet another canopy, which was not otherwise covering anything. It was guided into place by a thickly muscled man with skin that gleamed with humidity and sweat, and hair that grew into a soft black halo. Using both hands, he helped Norman Somers park the machine in the perfect position, where every edge, bumper, corner, and cranny would be covered by the net of manipulated foliage.

"Welcome to camp!" Somers announced. "Everybody be careful getting down, you hear? And stay to the walkways when you can. The earth is half made of mud, my friends. Ruthie, love—you especially. Shall I help you down?"

"Mr. Somers, I am always happy for your assistance," she said, with a bat of her eyelashes.

When everyone had left the buggy and no one was standing in the mud, the man who'd guided them into the shelter said, "Folks, I'm Rucker Little, and I'm second in command here after Deaderick Early. You," he said to Cly, "must be the captain Josephine's been telling me about."

"Yes, yes, I am," he said, extending a hand and receiving a shake. "I'd ask how you knew, but Ruthie's already said that my description is going around."

"Tall son of a bitch, that's what Josie told us," he said. "And this must be the rest of your crew?"

His question called for introductions, and these were made.

By the time the captain had finished, two more men had approached, and these were identified as Chester Fishwick and Honeyfolk Rathburn. Like Rucker Little, they had served in the Union's colored troops, and they carried themselves like men who'd seen the inside of a military operation.

Once everyone was formally acquainted, Chester Fishwick said, "I can take you to Josephine, if you like. She's with her brother, in his place. There's not much room for the whole gang in there, but I expect Rucker would be happy to give the rest of you folks a tour of the camp. When you're finished speaking with Miss Early, we'll take you out to the *Ganymede* so you can see it for yourself."

"I'd appreciate that," Cly said, and seeing that everyone agreed to this arrangement, he followed after Chester, who led him up to one of the tree houses closest to the lake's edge—though he did not realize how close it was until he'd scaled the ladder. From halfway up it, he could tell that they were in fact quite near to Pontchartrain, no more than fifty yards away from one of its banks.

The ladder creaked beneath Cly's weight, the willow wood flexing and springing as he climbed from rung to rung behind Chester Fishwick, who scaled the thing swiftly, like a man who did so every day and no longer needed to think about the particulars of hanging on, stepping precisely, or watching his head. At the top, the captain hauled himself over the edge and into a cabin that seemed larger on the inside than the outside would have led him to expect.

Again contrary to its outer appearance, the cabin was not remotely rustic. If anything, it looked like the headquarters of an advanced operation. Texian manuals and tools were shelved and mounted on the walls; a large chalkboard was covered with mathematical formulas and maps; and high-grade military guns were racked beside the door, their ammunition boxed beside them in crates with precise stencils detailing the contents. Mosquito curtains hung from the ceiling, but were tidily bundled above a row of three cots, or draped across the open windows to function as screens.

On the edge of one cot sat a man with wide, strong cheekbones and skin the color of coffee. His hair was long and braided tightly into rows, and his chest and shoulder were swaddled in a bandage fashioned from clean cotton strips.

Beside him on a small camp stool sat Josephine Early, looking not remarkably different from the last time Cly had set eyes upon her. She rose from the camp stool and her brother—for the resemblance was not overwhelming, but decidedly present—shifted his weight as if he'd like to do the same. But she stalled him with a hand upon his unbound shoulder.

Ten years had left her body fuller by perhaps that same number of pounds, as if she'd grown into her age. It looked good on her, Cly thought. And he tried not to think any harder about other things that had looked good on her, in other times.

Now she wore a dress that was out of place among the camp full of men; it was too fancy by at least five dollars, and its fabric was meant to shimmer in a ballroom rather than perch upon a stool. It was easy to see that she still wore whatever she'd arrived in. She'd tucked up the lace on her sleeves and traded her pretty boots for a brown set of workman's footwear—though the boots, as well as a beaded bag and a light brocade jacket were folded as carefully as if they were in a shop-front window. They rested underneath the next cot.

Before the captain could summon any words, Josephine said to him, "Cly, I can't believe you came."

"Well, you asked me to."

"I guess this isn't exactly what you expected."

"Not exactly."

"But, you're here."

"Yeah, I am."

The man on the cot said, "I'm Deaderick Early—and I don't believe we met, last time you were passing through New Orleans."

"I don't believe we did. You were off in the war, weren't you?"

"Sounds about right. It's good to meet you now," he said, and since Josephine had stood, he stood as well—with effort and some pain, but also with dignity. He extended a hand and Cly shook it. "And it's good of you to come."

"Rick, sit yourself back down," his sister told him, more gently than crossly. "You're supposed to be resting."

Cly saw a chance to be helpful, so he went to pull up a stool and said, "We should all sit. We've got some talking to do." But upon getting his hands on one of the stools, he changed his mind and said, "I suppose I'll just go cross-legged," for he didn't think the chair would hold his weight.

Chester Fishwick took the seat instead, and when they were all settled again—Deaderick wincing and Josephine working hard to keep from babying him in front of the other men—the captain said, "So I hear you've got a big boat, only it's not exactly a boat. And you want me to fly it."

"That's the sum of it," Deaderick said.

While Cly figured out what else to add, and how to add it, Houjin's excited voice carried through the windows, spouting a list of questions a mile long. Cly said, "The kid must've found Mr. Worth."

"The lens-maker?" Josephine asked. "Yes, he's here. Who's the kid?"

"He's apprenticing with me. Smart boy. Wants to know how everything works, and he's real excited about that gate you folks have set up—the one with the mirrors. Norman Somers said a guy named Worth designed it, and now Huey needs to hear the details. But I'm not here to tell you about my crew. I'm here to hear about your ship."

Deaderick took a deep breath that appeared to sting. He said, "I'm not sure how much the ladies have told you already."

"The history of it, mostly. And I've seen the engineer's drawings, the ones that show most of the workings. But I'm still trying to wrap my head around how to operate it, or get it to the ocean. I mean, I can tell from what little I've seen of your camp that you fellows have plenty of good machines and good mechanics to keep them running. Surely *someone* here can pilot your bird. Your fish," he corrected himself.

Chester declared, "We have four mechanics from the schools at Fort Chattanooga, and a couple of men who trained in the machine shops in Houston. So yes, we're all set for men to make and maintain what we've got, that's a fact. But the men we have . . . they're drivers and sailors. They're engineers who've worked on rolling-crawlers and the big diesel walkers the Rebs are using on the northern fronts. They aren't men who know much about airships, or this kind of . . . watership."

Deaderick added, "I think they could be forgiven for not knowing much about the *Ganymede*. Everyone who ever understood it is dead or in prison, miles and miles away from here. The *Ganymede* is a tribe of one. Wallace Mumler wants to call it an undermariner, but that's a mouthful, isn't it? Hunley called these things submarines, so that's what I'm sticking to."

Josephine smiled, every bit as cool and measured as he remembered she was capable of being. "Chester and Rucker, and Deaderick here, and Edison Brewster, and Honeyfolk—they all know *how* it works. They can tell you what every lever means and what every button does, but not a one of them knows how to turn the thing in a full circle without so much shouting, arguing, and complicated finesse that you can't imagine them ever moving it down the river.

These men have all the paper know-how, and none of the hands-on experience to pilot the thing correctly."

Chester added, "But like Rick just said: Nobody does. There's no one within five hundred miles who's been inside a submarine and hasn't drowned."

Deaderick looked to Josephine, whose smile had not melted. She said, "It was my idea to go hunting for an airman instead of a seaman. The sailors all know how to sail, but this isn't sailing. The drivers all know how to drive, but this isn't driving. It's flying under the waves, and I think you'll have an easier time of it. *Your* instincts will be the right ones."

Andan Cly thought about it hard. Slowly he said, "Maybe. Maybe not. I've had a word with my crew, and everybody's interested in giving your job a chance, but I'm not interested in getting any of them killed. Myself either, for that matter. So I think I'd better take a look at this submarine."

Deaderick once again hefted himself to his feet. "Rick, baby. You should stay here," Josephine insisted.

"The hell I should. I know that thing better than anybody, and I'll show him around it."

Appealing now to Cly, and to Chester, too, she said, "But it's been only a couple of days since he was shot. He should stay."

Chester wasn't about to overrule Deaderick Early, and Cly didn't know any of them well enough to intervene. So he said, "Josie, if the man says he's fit to leave, you'd better let him. He's kin of yours, so I won't stand in his way."

She relented unhappily. "Fine. But Chester, do me a favor and get Dr. Polk and have him join us, will you?"

"That achy old drunk?" Deaderick sighed. "I don't need him watching over me like I'm a baby in a bathtub."

"I want him here in case you start bleeding again," she pushed. "I didn't go through all the trouble to drag you back to the bayou just to have you drop dead because you think you're too much of a man to take a week and recuperate." Then she turned to Cly and said, "He was at Barataria when the Texians raided. He took two bullets, and only by the grace of God is he still here living and breathing. He's a lucky bastard, is what he is."

"Lucky to have such a devoted sister," he said, and gave her a penitent kiss on the cheek.

One by one they descended the ladder, and Chester Fishwick went in search of the doctor. Josephine called after him, "Tell him to meet us at the dock!"

When everyone was back on the ground, Cly asked, "You have a doctor out here?"

"Technically. He's a drunk Federal who was drummed off the field four years ago for killing a man on the operating table," Deaderick replied. "That's a hard call to make—a man on an operating table isn't in the best shape in the first place, but if the doctor's been drinking, I don't guess that improves his odds any. Regardless, he patched me up out at Barataria, and Josephine brought him along."

"I promised him some of Wallace's grain alcohol," she said.

Deaderick pointed at a path, a winding trail contrived from dirt ruts and planks that had been jammed into the mud for better footing. "We're heading that way, down to the river." He pressed one hand against his injured chest, and for a moment he went pale beneath the hue of his skin.

"Rick?" Josephine asked.

"Don't, now. I'm all right. Come on. Let's go."

"Hold on." Cly stopped him. "See that oriental boy, badgering that old guy in the spectacles? That's Houjin. Let me grab him. He'll want to see this." The captain rather wanted Houjin to see it, too. It wasn't that he doubted the knowledge of the men who were guarding the *Ganymede* so jealously, but he wanted to get the fledgling engineer's take on the matter as well. Sometimes the advantage of being young and bright is not knowing what's impossible. "Huey, get over here a minute, will you? Get Fang and Troost if they're handy."

Houjin looked left and right, and didn't spot his comrades. So he shrugged and trotted up to the group alone. Cly introduced him.

"Josephine and Deaderick Early, this is Houjin. He's going to be an engineer."

"Good to meet you," said Deaderick, and Josephine said something similar, though she looked at him with open curiosity.

"A bit young, isn't he?" she asked.

"He's young, but he does all right. Anyway, Huey—we're headed to see the *Ganymede.* I thought you'd like a look."

"Yes, sir!" he said excitedly, and almost headed off down the trail without them.

"Chester will tell your other men where we've gone, and likely bring them along with Dr. Polk," Josephine assured Cly, falling into step beside him.

He wasn't entirely certain how he felt about being so close to her again, having been so far away for so very long. But this was business, wasn't it? And they were friends now, weren't they? Or couldn't they be? It'd been long enough since the fighting, the arguing, the battling of wills. It'd been enough years that the good times seemed warmer, and the bad ones were weaker, more fuzzy. Harder to recall, somehow. Surely it was like that for her, too; otherwise, she wouldn't have called him out.

Maybe she hadn't left their relationship as mad as he'd thought.

He resolved to have a word with the crew on the way home to Seattle, and during this word, he intended to give them all a firm understanding of why there was no earthly good reason for Briar Wilkes to know anything at all about Josephine Early.

By way of making conversation, or maybe only for the sake of business, Josephine said, "We call its resting place 'the dock,' but it's no dock to speak of. We have to keep it submerged. Texas watches from the clouds, and if they spot it, they'll claim it in a heartbeat."

"They'll *try,*" Deaderick said.

His sister chided, "Don't talk that way. Especially not now. Texas took the island, and they could take the lake, too. I feel like a goddamn coward about it, but right now, all we can do is hide. It's the only way to finish this operation."

"It's not cowardly; it's *strategy*," her brother corrected her. "I don't want to have to defend it. We might have the firepower, but we sure as shit don't have the manpower. And it's hard smuggling diesel back here in decent quantities. The rolling-crawlers are ready to ride, but they can't go more than fifty miles without refueling, so we can't waste it."

Houjin dived into the conversation with a question, as he was so often inclined to do. "Does the *Ganymede* run on diesel?"

Josephine answered. "It can, and does. But Wallace Mumler—he's one of the Fort Chattanooga lads—thinks he can run almost anything on alcohol, if you make it pure and strong. So he's experimenting. He keeps a still out in the trees, away from the main camp."

"Why?" the boy asked.

"Because the still requires fire, and fire makes smoke. We keep it to a minimum, and he's working on a converter that would process most of the smoke out of the air before anyone ever sees it—but that's not ready yet, so for now he does it all the old-fashioned way."

Deaderick said with a smile, "He'll distill *anything*. Or by God, he'll give it a shot. Corn works best, but from a scientific standpoint, there's no good reason he can't distill all kinds of things. And by God, he's giving it a shot."

"I bet he's a popular fellow."

"And *how*. Even the alcohol that won't work to power anything . . . usually it's drinkable."

Josephine shuddered. "After a fashion."

"I didn't say it was fine wine," Deaderick joshed her. "But after hours, when things are quiet and we're all settled down for the night, most anyone in the camp is happy to give his latest batch of . . . whatever he's brewed . . . a taste."

Hiking the rest of the way down to the water was a warm, sticky experience fraught with a hundred slaps against mosquitoes and a general wish from Captain Cly that it would rain or dry up already.

The heavy, humid lingering of the damp air so close against the earth, so moist on his skin . . . it felt like inhaling through a wet bath sponge. He'd all but forgotten the weight of it, in his ten years of absence, and though he'd been in town not even two days, he'd already forgotten the season. Springtime in the Gulf was hardly any different from its summer, though the nights were still cool enough to breathe, and the days were not yet hot enough to fry bacon on the side of a ship. It was still too warm to be comfortable, and too moist to breathe deeply.

Conversely, the springtime chill of the Pacific Northwest was not terribly different from its fall, or its winter either, for that matter. With all his heart, he missed it—even though he'd left it not so long before, and could expect to find himself once again cool as the tides within the month.

Even now it blew his mind that Josephine had preferred this sunken swamp to the cooler, clearer Northwest. Then again, back when they'd first started fighting about who should live where, she'd said it blew her mind that anyone would want to live in the rain by an ocean that was never warm enough to swim in, and didn't even have a beach.

Then they'd fought about the differences between a beach and a coastline, and fought furthermore about what on earth she'd wear to stay warm all year if she left—and what he'd wear to stay cool all year if he stayed.

In reality, they weren't arguments about the weather. They were always about other things. Other issues. Other matters of control, and autonomy, and money. It was the same fight again and again, regardless of the details, and it took them months to figure out that they were bickering over who was being asked to give up the most . . . and who would do so, for the sake of being together.

So she'd felt abandoned. So he'd felt rejected.

So neither one of them compromised, and both got what they wanted most. Or least. Sometimes it was hard to recall.

The smell of dead fish swelling in the sun invaded the usual

odors of the bayou, and soon the hum of mosquitoes was matched
and drowned out by the fiercer buzz of larger insects. Stagnant
pools and puddles rippled with the small slaps of long-legged water
birds stepping carefully among the tufts of grass, fishing with their
javelin-sharp beaks; somewhere not too far away, a heavy-bodied
pelican with shimmering brown feathers launched itself off the
surface of the lake and into the air, its powerful wings spreading
wider than Captain Cly's arms and pumping hard to lift the big
bird into the sky.

The pathway opened against a sodden, silt-thickened bank, and
Lake Pontchartrain sprawled before them.

The water was quiet, save for the softly broken rushes of short
waves pushed by wind, alligators, muskrats, or more pelicans with
their pendulous torsos. Mostly it spread out flat and dark, its water
the same shade of murk that made up the sopping bayous and the
bubbling swamps. The tall, stiff grasses sagged as small white birds
with spindly feet clutched at and bounced atop the vegetation.
Turtles as slick and black as oil clustered on logs and rocks, sometimes ignoring the intruders and sometimes slipping away with a
quiet plop. Glistening spiderwebs wider than curtains were strung
between plants, trees, and the occasional piece of man-made pier
blocking.

Everything, everywhere, was alive.

"This is the dock," Deaderick said, and he leaned up against a
rough-hewn banister that led to a wood-slat walkway over the water's body. He looked as if he'd very much like to sit or lie down, but
had no intention of doing so.

Houjin asked, "Where's the ship? I don't see it."

Josephine flashed her brother a look that told him to stay right
the hell where he was, and led the way out onto the planks. "Over
here," she told them, as she stopped to kneel at the walkway's edge.
Leaning over, she reached underneath and pulled a lever or a switch
that no one could see. With a loud clank and rattling of chains
much like what they'd heard at the gate, the pier began to shake. Its

pilings cast ringed waves in tiny loops as the whole structure shuddered.

"Look!" cried the boy.

He pointed at a separate set of pilings hidden in the grass. These, too, were wobbling, straining to heft something enormous—lifting it up between the two structures on a platform that must have been resting on the lake floor. The pulley chains twisted and tightened, and the clattering was raspy with rust, but the underwater lift did its work.

Up from the silted basin of Lake Pontchartrain rose the hull of a grim metal leviathan.

The whole of its steel cranium sloughed off swamp water and grass, clumps of runny mud and slippery tangles of fallen moss. It reared up out of the water, its bulbous and misshapen skull hammered into a shape influenced by the airships. But even with two-thirds of its bulk yet submerged, Cly could see the design elements that made this machine ready for water, and unworthy for air.

At water level, a pair of fixed fins were mounted on either side, left and right; larger fins were barely visible beneath the murky lake. The front was remarkable for what could not be called a windscreen, but a rounded glass window split down the middle and reaching up like a forehead.

This window gave the overall impression of a nearsighted mechanical whale wearing an oversized pair of spectacles.

Through it, Captain Cly could spy seating in the ordinary configuration: one spot for the captain, two chairs on either side for a first mate and engineer. All the fixtures were bolted to the floor or the wall, in case of . . . not turbulence, but waves, and tides, and currents.

Cly walked to the end of the pier in order to see the back end of the *Ganymede,* or what was visible of it above the water.

From the rear, the ship more closely resembled an actual sea creature. The back was snubbed, and then fitted with a fin that clearly moved not side to side, but up and down; below this fin—which

must serve for stability more than for propulsion—a set of flaps
were mounted, maybe for steering. Below these flaps, a pair of propulsion screws jabbed, dripping with river-bottom muck.

The large round portal to the left was likely matched by one on
the far side, and if Cly recalled the schematics correctly, these were
vents for taking on or ejecting water in order to let the craft rise or
sink more easily.

Around front, Houjin was leaning so far off the pier that a spar-
row's wing could've knocked him flat into the water, bouncing him
off the front windows of the *Ganymede*. Probably, he wouldn't have
minded.

"Watch out, Huey. I don't know if we could fish you out of there
before the alligators get you."

Houjin jerked back upright and peered anxiously into the water.
"Are there alligators? I didn't see any? . . ."

Deaderick said, "There are *always* alligators. The damn things
are a fact of life around here. But," he added as an afterthought,
"they *do* tend to keep unwanted visitors away."

"Can we take a look inside?" Houjin asked.

"I'll just open the hatch," the guerrilla replied.

Josephine said, "No, I'll do it. You hold tight."

"I'm *fine*."

"If Dr. Polk says so, then all right. And here he comes."

"Now I need a permission note?" he argued.

"No, *I* need one. You don't want me to worry, do you?" Without
waiting for an answer, she stepped to *Ganymede*'s side. She anchored herself by holding on to a piling with one arm, and then she
leaned out with the other to grasp a lever embedded on the craft's
upper left side. When she gave the lever a yank, a panel jerked open
with a sucking pop, revealing a bright red wheel.

Josephine turned the wheel with one hand, still holding tight to
the dock with the other one. Going was slow until Cly joined her,
saying, "Let me."

"I can do it."

"I know you can, but I'm the one with the ape arms, so let me help."

He could reach the wheel without leaning and without bracing himself, so Josephine sighed and let him at it. Cly gave it a couple of twists, and then a second, much *louder* sucking pop was accompanied by the sudden appearance of a round seam. It was a door, its edges announced by rivets the size of plums, but otherwise indistinguishable from the various nodules and lumps that made up the *Ganymede*'s exterior.

The captain glanced at Josephine, who gave him a quick nod of encouragement.

He tugged and the door squeaked open, pivoting on a thick round hinge as wide around as a woman's wrist. A puff of air escaped the interior. It smelled like rubber, lubricant, and industrial sealant, with a hint of diesel.

"Captain?" Houjin asked.

Cly jumped. The kid had moved so quietly, so quickly to come stand at his side—right under his lifted elbow. "What?"

"Let's go inside!"

"I'm going, kid. I'm going."

Behind them, Dr. Polk emerged from the path, mumbling something about how he ought to be in Ohio right now, but not sounding much like he meant it. Chester Fishwick was behind him, and Cly heard other voices bringing up the rear from the camp. Fang and Kirby Troost were on their way as well.

"We're about to have a regular crowd," he told Huey, bracing himself on the pier with one foot, and on the ship with his other. The craft felt firm underneath him, and when he left the pier completely to straddle the door, it bobbed only gently.

Inside the round door—which admitted him, but only if he crouched—a vertical row of slats functioned as a ladder. He didn't need it. It took only one long step and half a hop to drop himself into the interior. From this vantage point he spied a smaller, more flexible ladder rolled up and stuffed to the right. He picked it up and tossed it out the door, letting it unfurl against the exterior.

While he listened to the scrambling patter of Houjin's hands and feet against the wood dowel rungs, he surveyed the bridge. All things being equal, it was only a little smaller than the *Naamah Darling*'s seating area, though the ceiling was lower, and of course the captain's chair wasn't tailored to his height.

Inside the craft, the architectural details were more prominent and less delicately concealed than they would've been in an airship, for few people would be subject to seeing them in a war machine such as this. Every exposed edge, every low beam, and every unfinished surface declared that this was a workhorse, not a passenger ship.

"Work *sea* horse," he said aloud to himself.

Houjin answered him anyway, dropping down off the ladder with a thud that gave the vessel a slight quiver. "Sea horse? Maybe that's what they should've called it. Why'd they call it *Ganymede,* anyway?"

"I don't know. I doubt the fellows outside know either—they didn't name it. I don't even know what a *Ganymede* is," the captain confessed.

"Who."

"Beg your pardon?"

"*Ganymede* was a who. He was a prince of Greece—kidnapped by Zeus, and brought to Olympus on the back of an eagle. He became the cup-bearer of the gods," the boy said off the top of his head.

"Oh."

"But I don't know what that has to do with this ship."

"I don't either," the captain admitted. "But look at this thing, will you?"

"I'm looking, sir. I'm looking. This, over here—," he said, waving his arms at a central column that disappeared up into the ceiling. "What's this part?"

Cly consulted his memory of the diagram. "I think it's a viewing device. It cranks up and down, see that wheel over there? Try that, and see if it does anything."

"Why does it crank up and down?"

"There are mirrors inside. It lets you look out on the surface without bringing the ship all the way up out of the water. Or that's the theory."

"Brilliant!" Houjin declared. He inspected the column, poked at the wheel, ran his fingers across some of the buttons and knobs . . . and with a deft, instinctive tug, he deployed the mirrored scope.

Cly almost stopped him—almost reached out and cried, *No!* But he withdrew, letting the boy inspect the scope, and turned his own attention to the bridge.

Over his head, the curved window sloped. He dropped his shoulders and leaned forward to cut his height by half a foot, and nudged the swiveling chair to the right so he could step sideways past it. He examined the console, touching its buttons. He tapped at one label, screwed onto the surface above one of the nearer, more prominent levers. DEPTH was all it read. And a series of marks scratched below it notched off feet, or yards, or fathoms. The captain had no idea exactly what they designated, for they were not marked with any corresponding numbers.

A ratcheting noise drew his attention.

He looked over his shoulder and saw Houjin walking in a circle, his face smashed up against a visor. "I can see it, sir!"

"See what?"

"The pier! The woods—or, the what-did-they-call-it?"

"Bayou."

"The bayou! And . . . *oh* . . ." He paused with near reverence. "Sir, I think I see alligators—real ones, up close this time. Are they real dark, almost black? And do they look like they're made of old leather? And do they have eyes on top of their heads, that stick out of the water?"

"Sounds to me like you're answering your own question." Cly smiled, returning his attention to the console—but only for a moment. More footsteps and the climbing crawl of hands announced a newcomer, Troost. And behind him, Fang.

"Get a look at this, will you?" Troost said. He jabbed a thumb at the exposed metal beams, curved like ribs—like they were really within a whale, and could call themselves Jonah. "Not a lot of creature comforts went into this thing."

"It's not meant to be comfortable," Cly told him. He pushed at the captain's chair, which had been furnished with a leather pad in the shape of a cushion. It looked approximately as soft as an old book.

Fang joined Cly at the console, investigating the controls and the seats as Cly had before him, occasionally pausing over a set of lights or buttons, or a handwritten note stuck beside a switch with a daub of glue. He indicated one, scrawled on rough pulp paper. It read, *forward charges—top two/aft charges—bottom two.*

Cly scanned it and said, "Charges. Must have something to do with the weapons system. I'm sure it'll all make sense in time."

Fang showed him another note, mounted on another glob of adhesive.

"Diesel-electric transmission/propeller," he read. "That's almost self-explanatory, ain't it?"

The first mate nodded, but swept his hand across the controls.

"Yeah, more notes. These fellows, they've been figuring it out as they go along."

"You've got that right," said Deaderick Early from the doorway. He lifted up his knees and climbed onto the round rim of the opening. He did not descend to join them, but spoke from where he was perched. "After McClintock died, and Watson was gone . . . we had to sort it out from scratch. We've messed up a lot, and we even scuttled her once by accident."

"Ah," said Cly. "That's the extra smell. It's old water."

"We pumped her out as best we could, and left her open to dry—but there's only so much to be done about it. She doesn't leak," he added quickly. "She's just hard to clean. Inside, there's not anything much that'll rot. The designers got that part right. Everything you see can be swabbed down, and shouldn't get too nasty. I'd worry about rust, but the special paint they used in here protects it pretty well. The electric system is built into the walls, sealed off tight, and the diesel engine—and the propulsion mechanics—are also cordoned off. You'd need a fuse and a keg of powder to soak it down."

Houjin was still facefirst in the mirrorscope mechanism. He swiveled it toward Deaderick and announced, "The top of your head is *huge*! I mean, it looks huge. From here."

Early laughed. "You got that working right quick, didn't you?" He stretched up out of the doorway and waved with one hand.

Houjin waved back. "It's amazing! And it's all done with mirrors?" Before Deaderick could answer, he asked, "Did Mr. Worth set this up, too? Did he just make the mirrors, or did he design the scope, or did someone else do all that?"

"Mr. Worth didn't make it, but he's the man who told us how it works. He also improved it a bit, adjusting the angle of the mirrors and changing a few of the searching gears. What you see now, when you see *Ganymede*," he said, blinking back some deep internal pain, and talking past it, "is dozens of men, working together, building on the knowledge of the men who came before us. The ship was working when McClintock died, and it was working when we first dredged it up from the bottom of the lake. But in the last six months, as we've been forced to figure out *how* it works . . . we've also figured out how to make it better."

Cly waved at the console and asked, "Are these notes yours?"

"Mine and Mumler's, mostly. A few might've been written by Chester, or one of the other lads. We've been meaning to draw up plates like McCormick started, and get 'em engraved. But for right now, all we have is pencil and paper, and a nail to scratch marks into the metal when we feel like we need them."

The captain said, "Whatever works. Hey, when is it safe to fire this thing up and take it around the lake? Or is it a crapshoot, given how Texas is watching from above?"

"Safest time is always night, of course. But as far as we can tell, it's not honestly that much different from swimming around during the day."

Kirby Troost looked up from the control panel he was examining. "How's that?"

"The water's pretty dark, and even when the sun's up, you can't really spot the ship from the air—not unless you know exactly what you're looking for, and even then, sometimes you can stare right at it without seeing it."

"Spoken like a man who's given it a try," the captain observed.

"Absolutely. I went up in one of the Barataria ships and took a look for myself. In fact, that's what I was doing at the bay when Texas attacked—returning with the crew of the *Crawdaddy* from doing a little reconnaissance. It was miserable timing on my part, but it was a good exercise and I don't regret doing it. We brought that little flier over here and scanned from all altitudes, high and low, making double sure she wouldn't draw any extra attention if we tested her out and ran her around the pond."

"It's a shame it cost you a couple extra holes."

Deaderick said, "Every day's a risk. I was bound to take a scratch eventually, and this one didn't kill me—so there's something to be thankful for."

"True, true."

The guerrilla continued. "*Ganymede*'s outside surface isn't black, but it's such a dark brown, it might as well be. It matches the lake bottom just about perfect, especially if there's been a storm of any kind. Then all the dead grass and moss, all that swampy stuff, it gets stirred up and pools on the surface. It's damn near perfect camouflage."

"Like the tents you've got, out in the camp," Troost noted. "You could look down from the sky and never notice a thing on the ground. It's nicely done."

"Thanks. And it *has* to be nicely done, otherwise we'd be dead by now. That's the first thing I learned when I joined the bayou boys a couple years ago. Our technology isn't everything, but it's second only to our wits when it comes to keeping us alive. Sometimes it's hell to maintain. Wet as it is out here, we have to paint everything over and over again, to keep it from rusting."

Houjin finally withdrew his face from the mask at the mirror-scope. "But paint won't keep rust away. Not forever."

Deaderick said, "We use what Texas puts on its naval skimmers and the like. It's made with a few extra ingredients, and it keeps things more waterproof than not. Still, we have to keep layering up the coats to keep things straight."

The boy gave this a moment of consideration, and then said, "It's a good thing Texas uses so much brown."

Early laughed. "You're right about that! We steal most of what we use, but they don't ever notice it's missing."

"So when do we get to try and—" Houjin hunted for a word. "—drive it?"

"We should wait until later in the afternoon, at least. Let the shadows get good and long, and take some time to sit around with our operators. We can teach you everything we know about making this fish swim, and then I'll hand you over to Wallace Mumler," Deaderick said to the captain in particular.

"What can he tell us?"

"Wally's been busy making maps—but not maps of the land. Maps of the water, of the lake out at this end, and of the Mississippi."

Cly settled gingerly into the captain's chair, spinning it with his knees so that he could face Deaderick, sitting up in the entrance portal. "Getting *Ganymede* through water won't be as simple as flying at night."

"The currents won't be very different—air and water, they move in a similar way. And you can actually *see* the water gusting around, and sometimes you can tell which way it's pushing just by looking. But it's true, the sky doesn't have much in the way of obstacles, I wouldn't think . . . except maybe other ships, sometimes. Hidden in the clouds."

"That hardly ever happens, but I've heard of it—once in a while.

And I've sailed right into a flock of birds once or twice, but I bet that's not half as bad as the shipwrecks, charges, and other boats waiting at the bottom of a river."

"You're betting right. You'll be piloting more blind than not. They don't call it the Muddy Mississippi for nothing. Everything is a danger, something to be run aground on. Uneven spots on the bottom, sunken trees, boulders, roots, and worse. And out on the river, you won't just be hiding from the forts, you'll be hiding from commercial vessels. Mostly they're flat-bottomed things, riverboats and barges, which you'll need to dive beneath, or dodge. We'll have men on the river who'll help out as much as they can, guiding you from the topside.

"But you have to understand, once you're sealed up inside this thing, there's no good way to communicate with the rest of us. You'll be on your own—no speaking amplifiers like the Texians use, or anything like that. And if you run into trouble, we might not be able to help."

Cly squeezed the arms of the captain's chair and looked at each of his crewmen in turn. Fang, first mate. Sitting in the next seat over already, as if he'd assumed it'd play this way all along. Kirby Troost, standing by the bay doors that led to the engines, to the blast charges, and the rest, looking like he wasn't 100 percent certain of this after all, but was unwilling to say so. And then there was Houjin, one hand resting on the pivot handle for the mirror-scope, his face beaming with excitement because the risks meant little to him. Even if he understood them as well as he thought he did, obliviousness to death was the privilege of the young.

"Well?" Deaderick asked. "What do you say?"

Captain Cly replied, "I say it's time for supper almost. Let's have a bite to eat, then spend the rest of the afternoon getting to know this thing."

 *Ten*

Josephine waited on the bayou dock between Wallace Mumler and Chester Fishwick, with Anderson Worth, Honeyfolk Rathburn, Dr. Polk, and Deaderick Early standing by. Much as Deaderick had wanted to ride along, his sister and his doctor had given him such grief about it that eventually he'd decided it'd be easier to do as they said.

Josephine didn't enjoy treating him like a child, but men were childlike when they were sick or injured—she knew that for a fact, and sometimes it was simply easier to insist, so long as it was for his own good. She would have done anything to keep him safe, and she suspected he would do whatever he wanted the moment her back was turned.

She watched him out of the corner of her eye. His arms were folded across his chest, one of them held a bit awkwardly because of the bandage. His injuries could have been much worse, and so far, nothing had begun to fester. His strength was returning with his appetite, and though he shouldn't have been up and around so much—he should've been resting, damn him—she had to admit that for a man who'd taken two bits of lead, he looked very well.

Still, she eyed him constantly, looking for signs of weakness or a worsening state. Every breath that came with less than perfect ease, every small stumble, every wince and cringe . . . she cataloged them in her head and played them over and over again, constantly trying to assure herself that all was well, and he was fine.

He was a cat with eight lives left. Or seven: one lopped off the total for each bullet.

Together the small group watched the water where *Ganymede* was once again fully submerged. Sealed inside it were Captain Cly, Fang, Houjin, Kirby Troost, and Rucker Little—who had volunteered, knowing the risks. If anything, he knew them better than the *Naamah Darling*'s crew.

Josephine had wanted to call Rucker aside before he got on board; she wanted to have a private word with him, explaining that Cly and his men didn't know the whole truth. She hadn't been straightforward with them, because she was afraid that if she'd given them the numbers, they would've balked. She'd told Hazel and Ruthie to lie, and lie they had. Ruthie'd quietly confirmed it for her while the men inspected the vessel.

"What did you tell them?" Josephine had whispered.

Ruthie had whispered back, "That it was safe. That it worked just fine."

"And no one died?"

"Hardly anyone. I think that's how Hazel put it. Just Mc-Clintock."

"Jesus," Josephine had blasphemed under her breath. "I hope nobody tells them the truth."

"I hope they do not die," Ruthie had added.

Josephine hoped they survived, too. She wanted nothing more than a living, breathing, successful crew to emerge from *Ganymede* out in the Gulf of Mexico, at the airship carrier *Valiant*. But deep down, in a hard, dark little corner of her heart she did not care to confront . . . she was glad it was Cly taking the risk, and not her brother.

Bubbles sputtered to the surface and stopped. A wide ripple cut concentric circles across the lake and then, with an almost silent click of gears and the slip of lubricated metal, the mirrorscope's small round lens poked up through the low ripples—like an alligator's eyeball on a thick steel stalk.

The mechanical eye dipped once, and resumed its position.

"That's the signal," said Chester. "They're doing okay."

But Josephine noted, "They haven't left the dock yet. I'll hold my cheers until after I've seen them take it out for a lap."

"Show a little optimism," her brother urged. "This was your idea, wasn't it?"

"It was. And Cly is good, but I guess we'll see *how* good."

Honeyfolk said, "I'm not sure that's fair. He might be the greatest pilot who ever flew, but *Ganymede* might still be more than he can handle."

Josephine wanted tell Mr. Rathburn that she was sure he'd be fine, but she kept silent and watched, because it was easier than making proclamations she was too nervous to believe in. She wrung her hands together without even noticing, squeezing her fingernails into her palms and staring down hard at the lake. "They don't know the risk. They don't know how bad it's really been—how many men have died in that thing."

Deaderick didn't look at her. "Yeah, well. That was your idea, too."

The ripples lurched, then shifted, and began to move.

The mirrorscope eye swiveled and aimed forward. It cut through the water's surface cleanly, leaving only a tiny wake to mark its passage. Then it gave another quick dip and retracted again, leaving nothing to indicate that the craft had passed except for the squawk and parting of a group of ducks, bending reeds, and the peculiar sense that something heavy was just out of sight.

"They're doing it," she breathed.

"I'll take the small engine rower and see about guiding them," said Wallace Mumler, reaching for a rope that hung off the pier's side. He drew the rope with several long, hard pulls of his arms, looping it between his hand and his elbow, until a little craft was drawn out from its hiding spot under the gray slats. Two long poles were crossed atop it, and cradled in the boat's bottom was a trumpet-shaped device approximately the size of a tuba.

Mumler jumped down inside the small boat and used the poles to leverage himself across the water in the direction *Ganymede* had gone. Upon locating it, he used one of the poles to pound two whacks against the hull. Then he dropped the horn into the water, holding it by a rubberized tube that ended in an ear-pad shaped like a bun. He held this pad up to the side of his head and hit the ship again.

Then, hearing something he liked, he flashed a thumbs-up signal at the observers on the pier. "They're good!" he said.

It wasn't the world's most sophisticated system, and it wouldn't work very well when the water was deeper, but the short system of knocks and replies served for training purposes. In case of emergency or more complex communication requirements, Morse code would be the signal—performed with a hammer inside the *Ganymede,* and with one of Mumler's poles from the surface.

While Josephine watched, there was a moment of concern when the ship dug itself into a submerged bank of silt and mud, but with Wallace's guidance and some crafty maneuvering within the ship itself, *Ganymede* was extracted and continued its explorations.

After an hour of tense examination, the sun was going low and gold in the sky, and Josephine started to relax.

Ruthie had joined the party sometime before, arriving late because she'd paused to brew herself a cup of coffee before strolling to the scene. She'd watched the proceedings in silence, since there was little to say and, frankly, little to see. But now she raised the question, "Ma'am, should we head back to the Garden Court tonight?"

"I don't know. I shouldn't leave Hazel for too long. She handles herself all right when it comes to being in charge, but she doesn't like doing it. Besides, if anyone notices we're both gone, it might not look good—and I don't want anyone looking too close at the house." She then asked Chester, "Do you think . . . it'll be tomorrow night? Or the night after? We have to move this while the admiral is still within range. Last I heard from Edison Brewster, the

Valiant will be in the Gulf only until the end of the week. Texas is eyeing it too closely for them to risk staying any longer."

"Is Texas dumb enough to attack something that big?"

"They attacked Barataria and were successful. That can only make them cockier than they already are. The airship carrier isn't a sitting duck, but the longer it leaves its anchors down, the more time Texas has to round up trouble."

Chester nodded unhappily. "I know you're right, but I don't like it. We can't rush this, Josie."

"We can't take our own sweet time about it, either," she warned.

"It can't be tonight," he told her. "You've got to be patient."

"Why not tonight?"

"Because tonight we have to take her overland. We need to get her into position, to dump her into the river. Then, the night after, we can launch her. There won't be time to do both, not before sunrise. And moving something that big, it's dangerous as hell under the best of circumstances. If the sun comes up and catches us, we'll be found out for sure."

"Damn it all, I hate it when you're right. How far is it to the river from here?"

"If we can get the ship a tad north and west of here, it'll be maybe five miles. But it won't be five fast miles, and we'll be mighty conspicuous as we go. The plan is to haul it over to New Sarpy and stash it in one of the warehouses on Clement Street."

"And it'll be almost dawn by the time you're done."

"If we're lucky," he said. "Assuming Rick didn't use up all the luck we're owed in one lifetime, eh?"

Deaderick said, "Nah. I'm sure I left some for this week. We might have to scrape the barrel's bottom for it, but we'll make it work."

"Ma'am?" Ruthie asked.

Josephine patted at her hand to reassure her. Then, to the men, she said, "Things are under control here, aren't they?"

"As controlled as they're going to get," said Honeyfolk. "Now it's up to that crew to figure out what they're doing. There's nothing we can do to help from here, so you might as well head back, if that's what you need to do. We'll send someone ahead to let you know when we're coming downriver, and you can catch up to the assist-boats in the Quarter. Someone'll pick you up."

"Ruthie, looks like you get your wish—and we're heading home."

"*Mais non, madame.* You do not understand. I wish to stay *here.*" She shot Deaderick a protective, almost possessive glance. "I will watch out for the men, eh? Someone has to keep them out of trouble. I will ride with the assist-boats, when they help lead the ship down the river, *d'accord*?"

Under different circumstances, Josephine might've put her foot down, but in truth, she didn't want to leave the men either—and at least Ruthie could send messages, report back, and watch to make sure Deaderick didn't overexert himself. If Josephine couldn't remain, Ruthie was the next best thing.

"Fine, Ruthie. That's fine. And you'll keep me posted, won't you? If anything changes, or, or . . . happens?"

"You know I will."

An hour later, Norman Somers had deposited Josephine back at the Metairie lot near the street rail station, and shortly after dark, she was back in the Quarter.

Two Texians stopped her about the curfew, but all they did was demand that she find her way indoors. She assured them that she was on a mission to accomplish that very thing, at which point, one of them recognized her and escorted her back to the Garden Court.

She thought about inviting him inside, in gratitude for delivering her back to the house without further stops or inquiries. It was always good to play nice with the men who could shut off her customer base. But not tonight. Instead, she gave him a round of thanks and shut the front door behind herself. Until it was fully closed, her escort struggled to peer past her, then gave up and left when the front room curtains were drawn.

In the lobby, Hazel Bushrod was lurking near the large desk by the stairs, keeping watch for customers. When Josephine walked in, Hazel leaped up from her seat and seized her with a hug. "Oh, ma'am, I'm so glad you're back!"

"Thank you, Hazel. I'm . . . I'm glad to be back, too."

"Liar."

"No," said Josephine. "I'm mostly telling the truth. It's good to be back in a place where it's not just me and Ruthie in a skirt. The company of men is one thing. The company of men and *only* men . . . that's another."

"How's Deaderick? Is he—?"

"He's fine. Or he *will* be fine. He's up and around too much, that's for damn sure. If I had my way, he'd be lashed to a bed and forced to rest like a civilized man who's recovering from a pair of bullet holes . . . not running the show as a member of the walking wounded."

Hazel raised an eyebrow and asked, "You left Ruthie at the camp?"

"She insisted."

"Then he might get lashed to a bed yet."

"Oh, you stop it," Josephine said, but she smiled. And she added, "But I want to thank you for sending Cly out, like you did. He was as well prepared as anyone could expect, and I appreciate it. But now that I'm back, I don't suppose you could cover things for me just a few minutes longer, could you? I'm absolutely filthy from that camp, and if I don't get a bath soon, I'll chase away whatever customers we have left, now that this damn curfew is taking hold and sticking."

An hour later she was back, freshly dressed and feeling fully human once more. Her hair was pinned and free of leaf litter or moss scraps, and there was no more peat beneath her fingernails.

Hazel was no longer alone in the lobby.

On the love seat under the frontmost window, much to Josephine's surprise, Fenn Calais was happily chattering with Marie Laveau.

At first impression, they nattered as if they'd known each other for a lifetime already, but as Josephine descended the stairs and overheard more of the conversation, she realized that impression was misleading. It was a "getting to know you" chat of the strangest sort—the elderly voudou queen and the somewhat less elderly Texian, who was testing out his precious few words of French and getting a friendly, giggling reaction from the woman. She corrected him gently.

"*Non,* Mr. Calais. You *spell* the *t* on the end, but you do not *say* it. You let the word end a few letters from its conclusion. Say it again: *vraiment.* Say it, and don't close your mouth at the end to make the *t* sound. It's not so hard, *vraiment,*" she added with a wink.

"Ma'am, I just can*not* do it to save my life. I think the French are the only folks on earth who are harder on their vowels than us Southerners. And if I never master it, *c'est la vie!*"

She laughed and said, "Now I *know* you've only been teasing!" Then, upon seeing Josephine, stalled and perplexed on the bottom stair, she said, "Ah, my dear. There you are. Hazel told me you were in the bath."

"Madame Laveau, yes. Hello. Welcome to the Garden Court. Can I . . . can I get you anything?"

"*Non,* sweet dear. Only your time, if I might impose."

"At any time. Ever."

Fenn took this as his cue to relocate, saying, "I suppose Delphine is starting to wonder where I've gone off to. Perhaps I'll just rejoin her."

"Have a good evening, Mr. Calais," Josephine told him, never taking her eyes off the woman ensconced on the firmly padded seat. When Fenn was gone, she took his place. She did not bother to ask how her visitor made it past the curfew. Instead she asked, "What can I do for you, ma'am?"

Mrs. Laveau took her hand and squeezed it. "I'm here because you'll be receiving a visitor, any minute now. A gentleman."

"This *is* a certain kind of business," she murmured, half joking but half nervous, too.

"Not a customer, a *visitor*. And I'm not telling your fortune, dear one. I'm here to prepare you for the introduction. He's a man you're likely to treat with hostility, insofar as you're able. But I'm here to tell you, you *must not* do that."

"I don't understand." Josephine frowned over at Hazel, who looked back anxiously.

"He's a Texian. But he's no part of your . . . present interests. He wishes to consult you, about the Dead Who Walk."

"Ma'am Laveau, I try hard to be a hostess, and in this city that means I am compelled to be civil to many Texians, whether I like it or not. I'm sure I can find it in my heart to be polite to this one. Why is he coming here? Why would he think I know anything about the zombis?"

"He's a Ranger, dearest. An investigating man, for a matter requiring careful investigation. And he's coming here because I suggested it," she said, lowering her voice and leaning close. She held Josephine's hand tighter, and Hazel drew in her breath with a tiny gasp—reminding them both that she was in the room.

The hands that clasped Josephine's were as thin as twigs, despite the woman's otherwise stout appearance. Gas lamplight twinkled on the silver of her rings, and on the red, blue, and green of the gems or colored glass found therein. The queen smelled like sandalwood and sage, feathers and dust. And in her eyes, sunken with age, there smoldered a deep, grim light.

"Child, do you know how long I've walked this world?"

"No, ma'am."

"Eighty years, give or take, as the Lord gives—and the Lord takes. I do not think I shall live to enjoy another one."

"Ma'am, don't talk that way."

She released Josephine's fingers and gave them a loving pat. "Why not? Such is the way of things, isn't it? Time turns us all, and I've danced longer than many. I do not regret a single tune." Her smile slipped, only a little. She restored it and continued. "But that's why you must speak to this Ranger. He will help you, when I'm gone."

"Ma'am, I am very confused. A Ranger?"

"Speak with him," she pleaded. "New Orleans is home these days to worse than Texians, dearest. The zombis grow in numbers every day, and soon even the most determined nonbeliever *will* be forced to face them. They must be managed now, before they become unmanageable. And I will not be able to help. These Texians who you hate so much, they are only men—only living men, and most of them would leave as happily as you'd have them gone. While they are here, you must work with them. We do not always get to choose our allies."

Josephine sat back, staring hard at Mrs. Laveau. Was the woman dying? She looked healthy, given her advanced age. But there was something . . . less about her. Something missing, or lacking—something that had been stronger in their previous encounter, not even a week ago. "People have . . . I've heard that you were controlling them. Has it been true, all this time?"

"Yes. And no. I can urge them, and guide them. As you saw, I can often stop them. But bend them to my will? Command them to do my bidding?" She fluttered one elaborately jeweled hand in a gesture of bemused contempt. "Not at all. Though if it comforts people to feel that they are controlled, so let them be comforted."

"I think I understand."

"I knew you would. We're two of a kind, you and me."

"You flatter me to say so."

"You and I both understand, as women of color and women of power . . . that power is too often in the eyes of the beholders." Her right hand drew up into a closed fist, a pointed finger. The finger aimed between Josephine's eyes. "And let me give you some advice, eh? One devilish old crone to a devilish *young* one: Never, never, *never* diminish yourself by correcting the beholders out of modesty. When your beauty is gone, when your money is spent, and when your time in this world runs low . . . the one thing you'll take with you into the next world is your reputation."

Footsteps outside on the stoop came uncommonly loud, or so

Josephine thought. She started at hearing them, the scrape of hard heels on the stones, and then on the steps.

Marie Laveau brightened. "Ah. Here he is now." She rose to her feet and Josephine rose with her, in perfect time to the door opening.

It let in a gust of air that smelled sharp and softly sour, like the river before a storm. And it let in a Texian.

He was approximately Josephine's age, perhaps as young as forty, with a truly outstanding mustache occupying most of the acreage below his nose and above his mouth. It spread like a pair of wings, as if at any time his face might need to take flight. Despite the warmth of the evening, he wore a duster and, instead of the military leather boots of the enlisted boys, proper snakeskin cowboy boots.

Josephine thought he looked familiar.

If he knew what kind of business Josephine operated, it didn't inhibit his manners. A shapely suede hat the color of old bones rested atop his head until he removed it, revealing a pressed-down swirl of dark hair that was beginning to go light at the temples.

He said, "Ladies?" And he shut the door behind himself.

"Yes, please come in," Josephine said, too late for it to mean anything.

Marie Laveau added, "Nice to see you again, Ranger. I'd stay and chat, but it's time I went on my way. My daughter is expecting me, and now that I'm so old, she worries if I'm gone too late."

He held his hat in his hands and opened the door to let her pass, then closed it again behind her, shutting the old woman out into the night, where she preferred to be—and where she met no resistance. She was gone as quietly as she'd arrived, without even footsteps to remind them that she'd ever been there in the first place.

The Texian frowned, looked back and forth between Josephine and Hazel, and shook his head as if to clear it. "Pardon me, I was just wondering how she'd navigate the curfew home. And then I realized that she's got her ways, and I shouldn't worry about it."

Hazel actually smiled, and Josephine's mouth tightened involuntarily into something similar. "She got here on her own, she'll get home on her own—I have no doubt of it. I'm sorry, but she didn't tell me much and I'm not sure why you're here."

He came forward, seeming uncertain of how to proceed politely. Settling for a small bow in her general direction, and then one to Hazel, he told them both, "I'm Horatio Korman, a Ranger of the Republic. Are you Miss Josephine Early?"

"Yes, that's me. Mrs. Laveau said that you and I should have a talk."

"That was her recommendation, yes." He glanced back at the door, as if not quite believing she'd really gone. "I get the feeling people tend to follow her recommendations."

"Perhaps we could step into my office, upstairs. Hazel, I hate to ask you for yet another favor, but do you mind watching the parlor a little longer?"

"Not at all, ma'am," she said, but her eyes were wide with curiosity, and a silent demand that she should be told all about it later. "I've been here this long, a little longer won't matter. Besides, it's been slow tonight, what with the curfew and all."

Horatio Korman said, "Yeah, I'm real sorry about that. I mean, I didn't do it. But. You know what I mean. I wish it weren't the case."

Upstairs she guided him to the wood seat with the shoulder-height back and padded arms that faced her desk, which she then sat behind. The show of authority might not have been called for, but it was as Laveau had said about power in the eyes of the beholder. She wanted the Texian to behold that he was on her business, her property, in her city.

The Ranger was not particularly ill at ease, not as far as Josephine could see. He was composed and confident, bordering on arrogant even just sitting there, but he'd shown a small sign of respect to both Josephine and Hazel on her premises, which was not something every Southern man did. She'd give him that much credit, but if he wanted more, he'd have to earn it.

She opened the conversation by saying, "You aren't stationed here in New Orleans, are you? Rangers aren't military, are they?"

She wasn't absolutely clear on the distinctions between the designations.

"No, we're not part of the military, and no, I'm not stationed here. Not precisely." He rested his hat on the chair arm and crossed one leg over the other, his ankle upon his knee. "I was sent here to look into a situation y'all been having, down by the river. Sent as punishment," he mused, nearly to himself.

Josephine's tone was icy. "I beg your pardon?"

Realizing her displeasure, he clarified. "The Republic wants me out of its hair, so to speak. My superiors wanted to get me out of Austin for a while, and I suppose someone figured the river was far enough away that I couldn't bother them too much."

"Are you a difficult man, Ranger Korman?"

He didn't exactly answer. "Boy, if they think *I'm* difficult . . ." His voice trailed off, then returned. "There's worse trouble than me weighing against Texas. Maybe not yet, but soon. And bad."

Josephine went straight to the meat of it. "Zombis. That's what Madame Laveau calls them."

"The walking dead men? Same thing?"

"Same thing." She nodded. "And it surprises me to have a Ranger under my roof, wanting to talk about it."

"Why's that?"

"Up until Betters and Cardiff went missing, you couldn't convince Texas anything was wrong down by the river. Not for love or money, and believe me, I tried both."

"Pardon me for putting it this way, but nobody *would* believe you. I know, because I've been trying to warn them for months— and I'm one of their own. Nobody wants to hear it."

Josephine looked him up and down, reaffirming her initial impression that this was a dyed-in-the-wool, run-of-the-mill, straight-out-of-the-mold upstanding Republican, at least by all appearances. Why would he meet resistance from his own men?

Horatio Korman eyed her back, likewise weighing something as he assessed her. Coming to a decision, he said bluntly, "Mrs. Laveau said you were there the night Colonel Betters and Lieutenant Cardiff were killed. She said you saw what happened. I'm not accusing you of anything, Miss Early, but right now we've got Texians down on the riverbanks hunting something they don't understand—trying to defend *this city* from it—" He tapped his finger on the armrest to emphasize the point. "And they're having the shit scared out of them. I was directed here on the basis of other people's reports, soldiers and merchants who've worked down there, people with friends who've gone missing. My boss sent me to New Orleans to get me out of their way, yes—but they might've done us all a favor."

"And how's that?" she asked cautiously, giving away nothing.

"Because no matter what you tell me, I'm likely to believe it and likely to help you. These . . . *zombis,* or whatever Mrs. Laveau wants to call them. I've seen them myself, and I know what they're capable of."

"You've been down to the river?"

"No, and that's the bad part. It's a national secret at the moment, but those things, those zombis, they're *not* just down by your river. They aren't just in New Orleans. They're in north Texas, and the turf west of that, too—all the way to the Utah territories and maybe farther west than *that.* Texas is getting positively lousy with them."

A shiver went tickling down Josephine's neck. "Are you . . . are you *sure?*"

"I've seen them myself, at the Provo pass. Seen them by the hundreds. And I almost didn't escape to sit here now and tell you about it."

"But how could they possibly be anywhere else? Lots of folks think they're a voudou thing—spell-blind or ritual-maddened men, maybe even created by Marie Laveau herself! Lord knows half the city thinks she's in charge of them."

"Count me in the other half," Korman said dryly, his mustache bobbing. "And you, too, I bet."

Slowly, she bobbed her head in the affirmative. "Yes—me, too.

Tonight she said we had to learn to manage them now, before they become unmanageable." The thought made her head hurt. Then her exhausted brain caught up to something else he'd said a moment before. "I'm sorry, did you just now say you'd seen *hundreds* of them?"

"That's right. Mexicans, and other assorted folks they'd picked up along the way. They'd been migrating, if you could call it that. Maybe wandering is more like it, but they roamed from a spot southwest of Oneida all the way up to the Rockies."

"Dead men?"

"Women, too."

"Dear God," she breathed. "If only we knew what was making them—what was causing them, I mean."

His mustache bounced upward at the corners. He was smiling. "Ah, that's where me and you might have some useful things to tell each other. Nobody believes what I tell 'em, same as nobody believes you when you say that the dead are walking. That's why you didn't report what happened to those men, isn't it? You thought McCoy—or whoever was in charge until he got here—would've thrown you in the clink, figuring you had something to do with their deaths."

"Of course that's why," she lied. She'd kept the information to herself because if she'd shared it, she would've had to explain what she was doing following the men. And *that's* what would've gotten her thrown in jail. "They were swarmed, Ranger Korman. Absolutely overwhelmed. Two Texians, armed to the teeth, and there were too many of the things for it to matter. What's doing this? You have to tell me!"

"I'd be happy to tell you. Goddamn, I've been telling the world, but the world isn't listening. Zombis happen one of a couple of ways, all of it going back to a very strange gas that's being toted down from the Pacific Northwest."

Stunned full of questions, Josephine had no idea what to ask first. She stammered, "Gas? A gas? From where?"

"Gas, you heard me. Like hydrogen, only not like hydrogen at all. This gas comes out of the ground, and it has something to do with volcanoes—that's all I know."

"They have volcanoes in the Northwest?" she asked, mystified. "I had no idea."

"At least a couple of 'em. Best I can figure, from talking to a whole bunch of folks between here and there, this gas is mostly collected in a little podunk backwater of a place—some port city in the Washington Territory called Seattle."

Seattle? Where Cly was living?

She sat there openmouthed, struggling for words and not finding them.

The Ranger continued. "This gas is sometimes called *blight,* and it's not hard to figure out why. By the sound of things, it basically killed that little city. The locals had to wall it off and abandon it."

"I . . . I didn't know."

"Hardly anybody does. No one wants to talk about it, not anymore. Thirteen years ago, the city's former residents petitioned the Union to see if they'd accept Washington as a state. They thought if they were part of a country, and not just a distant territory, maybe they'd see some tax money or some military help. As far as I can tell, they gave up a few years later. With the war going on, the Federals weren't looking to take on any new responsibility—least of all, responsibility thousands of miles away."

"So . . . what happened to the people who lived in the city? The ones who abandoned it?"

"Couldn't tell you. Either they moved back East, or maybe they stayed out there. Might've gone to Tacoma, or Portland. Might've gone up north to Canada."

"All of this . . . ," she began, trying to arrange her thoughts into words. "I'm not saying I don't believe you, but I will say that it sounds far-fetched."

"Dead men walking around a riverbank sounds far-fetched, too."

"I'll be the first to admit it, and both of us know it's true. But this gas . . . why would anyone store it, or transport it? And what would anyone do with it?"

His smile swelled. "You're asking the right questions. The gas is processed through some method or other. Distilled, or something like that. Then it's dried down to a yellow residue, which can be cooked up and smoked, or snorted, or even swallowed."

"But why on earth would anyone—?"

"Miss Early, have you ever heard of a substance called *sap*?"

"Like . . . like tree sap?"

"No, ma'am, like *yellow sap*. That's the most common term I've heard for it, though I've also seen it called *cracker piss, sick sand,* and a few other things. It's a drug, something like opium but a whole lot stronger and a whole lot cheaper. Soldiers are taking to it left and right, looking to escape the war, as you do. As anyone does."

"And it's made from a poisonous gas?"

"Deadly poisonous. So deadly, it kills you without stopping you. I'd heard tell that this sap has been finding a place among sailors, and with the young Texians, too—the ones sent far from home, especially. The lonely men, or bored men. Men without the sense to know any better, or men who've lost so much already that they don't care."

"It starts with a gas."

"Yes. The gas itself turns people into zombis faster, more directly. Breathing it will kill you deader than a stone before you know what's happened. But the drug does it slow. It takes time— time to build up in a man's body, time to work into his blood. And gradually: not all at once, but in time . . ."

"In time, the men who use the sap become zombis?"

"Men who've used too much of it, for too long."

"But you said a group of Mexicans in Texas . . . they weren't all using the sap, were they?"

He shook his head. "No, no. A dirigible from Seattle was carry-ing a big load of gas, and it crashed out in the desert—right on top of them. It's a long story," he added fast, as if he wished to cut off commentary. "But that's what happened to them, and it could happen here, too. Out at the airyard, or at the pirate docks—anyplace where dirigibles come and go, moving the gas around. Any leak or failure of their equipment could unleash it."

The shivers on Josephine's neck went down to her knees, which were beginning to tremble against her will. "How much gas are we talking about, Ranger? How much will a dirigible hold? How many people could one load of gas—?"

He held up his hands, and thereby his hat, which dangled from his left one. "How much gas depends on how big the dirigible is, and what kind of equipment's on board. The one that turned some seven hundred Mexicans and their kin was pretty big. One of the biggest, I'd say."

"Seven hundred!" she exclaimed. "And out in the desert? Here in the city, we have that many people on a given block at the right time of day or night. More than that down at the market on a Saturday, to be sure! And the market isn't terribly far from the—"

"Ma'am, let's not panic yet. I don't know all the factors that make up a tragedy with this sap; I'm still learning, myself. All I'm suggesting is that maybe it's one reason you're getting such a population of the things here, collecting at the riverbank. It's possible someone wrecked a craft and it's leaking, or it happened once before. Or maybe with all the servicemen, and sailors, and pirates, and airmen . . . maybe you've got a whole lot of men here who are looking to escape their problems. Now I'm asking you, Miss Early, can you tell me anything at all that might help me out, given what I've just told you? I'm aware that I'm in a house of . . . that I'm in a ladies' boarding house, and it sees a great number of visitors from the kinds of men I'm talking about. So I'm asking you, and praying to God that you'll cooperate with me even though I'm sure you've got no great love for the Republic . . . do you know of your clients abusing any substance that might fit this bill?"

She took a deep breath and said quietly, "Yes, I do know. They don't call it sap here—they call it *devil dust*—but that's what you're looking for, Ranger Korman. You're looking for the men who make and sell devil dust."

He snapped the fingers of his free hand and said, "I knew it! And I don't suppose you could point me toward anyone involved in the manufacture or distribution of this devil dust, could you? Obviously I'd never mention it was you who sent me."

"I can't," she admitted. "None of my ladies are allowed to touch it, or anything like it. This isn't that kind of place, and these aren't those kinds of women, no matter what you might think."

"I never said—"

"I know what you did and didn't say. But I can't help you find it, unless . . ." She rose from her seat, pushing it aside. "I know someone who might have an idea."

"A customer or two?"

"He's more like a resident, these days," she muttered. "A Texian. I wouldn't accuse him of using the dust, but if anyone could point you toward it, it'd be Mr. Calais. Let me see if he's indisposed."

Horatio Korman rose from his seat and waited for her to lead the way again. "He lives here?"

"He might as well. Wait here. I'll knock, and bring him up."

Down on the second floor, she stood outside Delphine's room and rapped in her most businesslike fashion. Momentarily it was opened by the girl in question, mostly dressed.

Behind her, Fenn Calais was seated in a pair of pants and nothing else. He looked up from a chessboard. "Miss Early?"

"Mr. Calais, you're up. Excellent. And I'm glad I'm not interrupting anything."

"Only the whipping this girl is giving me." He scooted off the bed, which he was using as a seat, with the board on an end table. "You never do give room and board to the dumb ones, do you, Miss Early?"

"Not if I can help it. Could I possibly have a word with you? In my office? Momentarily?"

"Should I dress?"

"It's up to you. There's a Ranger present, if that makes a difference."

He nodded solemnly. "It does." Rather than reaching for his shoes or shirt, he grabbed his hat, jammed it onto his head, and said, "Let's go."

Eleven

Captain Cly and his crew members had spent as long as possible getting further acquainted with the intricacies, quirks, and foibles of the strange machine. By the onset of nightfall, they knew it well enough to usher it around even in the dark—not speedily, not perfectly, but effectively.

Could they shuttle it around the lake? Absolutely.

Would they be able to navigate the river in it? Debatable. But no longer negotiable.

Word had come from the *Valiant,* by taps and spies and eventually Norman Somers, that the ship wouldn't wait much longer. Texas was homing in, hovering and sweeping, gathering enough forces to chase the airship carrier farther out into the Gulf. It wouldn't be safe for the Union to hang around any closer, any longer.

They had forty-eight hours to bring *Ganymede* out to the Gulf to dock with *Valiant.* After that, the window would close and the opportunity would be lost . . . perhaps indefinitely.

As the sun set on that afternoon, the shadows all stretched out until they lost their shape, and the lake was dropped into the golden-edged dimness of twilight.

And then, these tense, frightened, brilliant men set their plan irrevocably into motion.

It was a precision operation, planned to the very smallest detail and—as Cly learned from Chester Fishwick—it had been dry-rehearsed at quiet, sneaky length. Not with the actual *Ganymede* in tow, of course. That would be too risky. They'd get only one shot at moving the enormous contraption from Lake Pontchar-train to the Mississippi River, and it had to count.

Eleven men worked as a unit, setting up an enormous cagelike contraption—a custom-made crane bracing a winch with the power to do what a thousand men would be hard-pressed to accomplish.

Lights flared to life throughout the bayou, dimmed by shades and covered with blue or red glass. They burned in lanterns, on poles, marking the pier's edges as the hoist began to crank. The craft began to rise.

On the lake's banks, just at the spot where it could be described as land instead of muddy water, a set of braced reinforcements had been sunk into the soggy earth to shore it up against the *Ganymede*'s unseemly weight. Backed up to these reinforcements, the two rolling-crawlers were hitched to the largest wheeled platform Cly had ever seen. The pilfered Texian machines were set up like a pair of draft horses, ready to pull.

Houjin whispered the captain's own concerns. "Will those ma-chines be able to tow it? And will they fit through the road leading out of the bayou?"

Before Cly could tell him that he didn't know, Anderson Worth replied, "Those things can pull it, no problem. But they can't cut through the bayou, not the same way you folks came inside it. There's a secondary road—one we've been building up for the last few months. We've cut it as wide as we can, given it all the beams, braces, and support possible, and we've covered it up with the net-tings, like the ones we use in the camp."

"An entire road?" Houjin gaped.

Worth patted him on the shoulder. "Not a very long one. Less than a mile of it, even. It only has to reach from the swamp to the streets outside Metairie. From Metairie, we'll have to haul tail to make it to New Sarpy without anyone seeing us."

"How do you plan to do *that*?" Troost asked, watching as the winch worked hard against the dead, dangling bulk of the *Gany-*

mede's hull. It was halfway out of the water, and still rising—and the pier was sagging where one leg of the enormous hoist contraption was braced. One of the other legs was pushing a clump of railroad ties deeper into the mud with every clicking rotation.

Mr. Worth smiled without any mirth. "We've got lots of friends between here and New Sarpy, and we'll have to rely on them to look the other way while we're working. There's a warehouse on Clement Street where we've made room to dry-dock *Ganymede* over the next day. And then, tomorrow night, we throw her into the river and you boys will take her out to sea."

"Easy as that," Troost observed, but whether or not he was being funny, it was hard to say.

Cly said, "Simple as that, anyway. I think we'll be all right. She handles like a big, drunk salmon—but she *does* handle, and that's something. With your boats topside, guiding us with the poles . . . it should be fine. We'll be counting on you, though," he said, bobbing his head at Wallace Mumler and Honeyfolk Rathburn, who had done most of the poling so far. "I don't like moving blind. You'll have to keep us out of trouble."

"And we will," vowed Mumler, who'd come to stand beside them as the big ship rose.

There were only so many positions where a man could observe and still stay out of the way. The winching contraption was a marvel of pulleys, foldable spiderlike legs, and a diesel engine determinedly chugging against the series of cranks that hauled *Ganymede* not merely to the surface, but up out of the water entirely.

The craft was watertight, and there was no longer any immediate risk of drowning within it—not so far as Cly could tell during his earlier inspections. If there were structural problems left undiscovered, well, they'd have to deal with that when the moment came. Two escape hatches were built into the thing, after all. He tried not to worry about the fact that Houjin could not swim.

After a full twenty minutes of too-loud jangle from the slowly spinning winch, *Ganymede* rose fully from the swamp. It emerged

covered in mud, roots, plants, and primordial slime, dripping like
something newly born, yet somehow ancient. Its hull shimmered in
the red lights, giving the whole craft an unearthly appearance, as if
it'd landed from some other planet—or been fired out of a volcano,
and now hung suspended, dripping with cooling lava.

From the structurally buttressed bank, Rucker Little used the
whole of his body to draw down a lever. The timbre of the ratcheting changed as a new set of gears engaged, and with a slowness that
was painful to watch, *Ganymede* swung in a semicircle toward the
wheeled flatbeds that awaited her.

The crane groaned and the gears strained, their teeth clacking
in agonized chomps; the legs of the makeshift device quivered and
sank into the still-unstable turf, shuddering with every bite. But the
structure held, and when Rucker leaned on another lever, the craft
dropped, an inch or two at a time. It settled with a creak and a
bong, with the scrape of a dozen seams and a hundred rivets grinding against the waiting pair of mated flatbeds.

The wheels compressed and the crawlers sank on their axles,
but nothing broke.

Not a single cheer went up. There'd been too much noise already.

One by one, the lights were snuffed until only the bare minimum
remained. Norman Somers removed the dimming lens from his own
light, mounted on the front of the rambling vehicle he drove that
night. It was smaller than the machine he'd used to bring Cly and his
crew into the bayou, but still so large, it could hold Norman in the
driver's seat and Ruthie Doniker beside him.

It was their job to lead the way out.

The rolling-crawlers revved to life, and plumes of billowing diesel
smoke choked the low, dark places between the bayou canopy and
the soupy ground. Wallace Mumler drove one, with Captain Cly and
Fang inside it. Honeyfolk Rathburn drove the other, with Kirby
Troost and Houjin as passengers. The machines were joined together
by a pair of bars on floating hinges. These bars kept the vehicles from

separating and causing the flatbeds to split, which would drop *Gany-mede* into the middle of the swamp, or the middle of the road. The coordination made driving difficult, a constant fight for navigational control, but like everything else about the operation, this had been practiced. Wallace and Honeyfolk knew what they were doing.

Cly clenched his jaw. It was excruciating, all this tedious cau-tion, but he knew as well as anyone how necessary it all was. The bayou boys had a million and one things to worry about, and this kind of care was the only surefire way to remove as many of those variables as possible. It was wise. It was important. And it was driv-ing Cly insane, because it gave him time to think of all the horrible things that could go wrong.

They could hit a bump and open a crack in *Ganymede*'s hull. A fuel line could be jostled out of place. The exhaust system could be unsettled, dumping bad air and fumes into the cabin when it came time to navigate the river, poisoning everyone where they stood.

How many men had died in these things, again? Had Josephine and Deaderick even told him the truth? Would they have lied, if they thought it would get them to their goal? Cly decided that in the name of fairness, he couldn't speculate on Deaderick's capacity for falsehood, but once upon a time he'd known Josephine very, very well, and he wouldn't put constructive fibbing past her for one short second.

And this time he wasn't just risking his own neck.

He looked over at Fang, sitting impassively in the central seat, since he was the smallest of the three men. Fang caught Cly's stare from the corner of his eye, gave it back, and then winked, but made no signs to say anything else that might have been reassuring—or discouraging, for that matter.

Cly thought of Kirby Troost, who had made enough trouble of his own for a dozen lifetimes. For Troost, this was nothing more than another adventure, one more job to augment a bizarre résumé, and he was entering it freely. But did he truly understand the stakes? Would it matter if he did?

And what of Houjin, insatiable curiosity and all, game for any-thing? What if something happened to him? It was a risk every airman ran, at some point. Everyone knew that the sky was not al-ways a hospitable place, and that not every pirate or pilot came to ground of his own volition. Huey was still just a boy.

Cly was seized with uncertainty. What would he say to Houjin's uncle if the worst should occur? For that matter, should the worst occur to the lot of them, who would tell *anyone*?

Back in Seattle, Yaozu would wait and wonder with increasingly sour impatience, watching the tower and Fort Decatur for a ship-ment that would never come. And Briar Wilkes, who'd lost so much already. Would she wait weeks? Months? How long would she hold out hope before assuming the worst?

He swallowed, or he tried. His mouth was dry. His nerves were frazzled, not that he would've admitted it. He'd been in tight scrapes before, hadn't he? Plenty of them.

None of them had ever involved spying, though. None of them had ever come with two governments—the Republic and the Confederacy—willing to shoot any and all comers. He found himself longing for the companionable violence of pirates, which only led him to think of Barataria Bay, and whatever was left of it . . . and his mood darkened further.

In front of the rolling-crawlers, Norman Somers and Ruthie Doniker left their light on bravely, no doubt nervously, knowing that they'd draw the most immediate attention if any attention were to be drawn.

The moment when the double-wide load turned out of the bayou and onto the main street was one accomplished with white knuckles, gritted teeth, and the grinding of wheels, accompanied by the surge and struggle of the diesel engines that powered the whole operation.

And now they were out in the open. No cover, no canopy.

It was late, but not so late that they were alone on the road. The way was not crowded, and it was trafficked mostly by men in riding crafts like the one Norman Somers drove at the head of the weird caravan. Norman waved at a few of them, even called out greetings, which were called back.

The other drivers gazed curiously, or made a pointed effort to look away—as if by seeing nothing they could know nothing, and be forced to recall nothing later on. People averted their eyes and shuttered their lanterns, holding away what light they could in order to let the strange procession pass as if unseen.

Onward they rolled, every yard a dreadful grind.

New Sarpy was not a large place. Not quite a town, not quite a stop. It was more like a cluster of warehouses, shrimp docks, liveries, cargo bays, and old piers half-turned to mush by the soaking churn of the river. But the largest of these was a depot built a decade earlier for a street rail stop that never came. Boarded and disused, and within mere feet of the water's ever-eroding edge, it was the perfect place to leave something large and not quite invisible.

As the procession drew to a stop outside, Wallace Mumler and Rucker Little leaped out of their vehicles and ran to the giant doubled doors at the building's north wall. Surely it had been meant to receive the cars themselves, shipped upriver, or maybe it had only been made that way for other incoming cargo of unknown size but conspicuous bulk. In seconds, the door—which looked firmly barricaded—was pressed open on hinges so silent, they must've been recently oiled and cleverly fixed to only appear so abandoned and impenetrable.

As the men went back to their seats, Ruthie Doniker leaped down out of the vehicle and ran inside. She reappeared almost instantly, bearing a torch so brightly lit that it made the old depot seem fully illuminated. She waved it and retreated, guiding the joined craft forward—around the sharp corner that had them on the verge of overhanging the banks, but never quite slipping over the side. Backwards she walked, and the drivers followed her at a snail's pace, creeping and creaking toward her, scraping the flatbed edges against the wide plank frames that held the massive doors. The whole structure shuddered but stood firm, and in a round of harrowing heartbeats, the *Ganymede* was finally inside.

 *Twelve*

Josephine waited on pins and needles all day.

She fretted, pacing back and forth between her upstairs office in the Garden Court and the desk in the parlor where either Hazel Bushrod or Marylin Quantrill held down the business end of things during the quieter daylight hours. Contrary to popular belief, not all of their business was conducted in the evening. There were a thousand other small beliefs to which brothels ran contrary, but only the regular patrons of such a place had any idea what really went on.

Fenn Calais knew many secrets, but he kept them to himself, a fact for which even Josephine Early, a woman who detested most Texians—though fewer of them than before, it seemed—could give him a grudging ounce of credit.

"Miss Josephine, I was wondering if you could tell me when Miss Ruthie will be back on duty." The Texian broached the question delicately. "I haven't seen her around much, these last few days. And I miss her lovely face."

"I'm quite sure that's not all you miss," Josephine said tartly. Her back was to the desk, and to Marylin and Fenn. She was holding the front curtain aside, peering out into the street, certain that any moment would bring word from the bayou boys that *Ganymede* was on the move—or that it'd be on the move momentarily.

Rather than taking offense, as he might've been within his rights, Fenn Calais chuckled and said, "Truer words were never spoken.

I was just hoping she wasn't sick, or nothing like that. Is she even . . . is she here?"

Josephine released the curtain, vaguely concerned by his query. He was openly fishing for information. It might be innocent, or it might not.

She forced a smile that was cool but not unkind. "I do apologize, Mr. Calais. I didn't mean to be short with you. We're all a bit on edge these days, with all the troops moving outside." As she said this, another row of brown-clad marching Texians went by on the street outside, and a rolling-crawler brought up the rear—its puffing, churning, fume-spilling body making the whole house shake with its passing. "Ruthie has been busy with some personal business these last few days. She'll be back before long."

When the vehicle had finally gone, and the last of its rumbles gone with it, Calais said, "These are trying times, and don't I know it."

Perhaps he saw the involuntary flinch Josephine made to hear him say such a thing. As if any Texian knew anything about the trouble in this, her city, her home. The occupation had changed the city forever—altering the trade, the population, the economy. It had made her city unwilling host to a few thousand houseguests who never cleaned up after themselves, bolstered a government that stood against everything Josephine believed in, and behaved abominably with impunity. Her home had become a prison, one she loved too much to leave and hated too much to tolerate—not without fighting back.

Fenn noticed her silence. He continued. "I don't mean to say it's the same for me as it is for you. I'm only sad to see the state of the place, those stupid crawlers tearing up the curbs and rolling over the plants. Did you know," he changed his tone, asking almost lightly, "that I've lived here since before the occupation?"

"I did not know that, Mr. Calais."

"It's true. When I was a younger fellow, and less of a fat one, I suppose . . . I landed the hand of a Garden District girl. And before you say it, if not before you think it—yes, that was very lucky for me." He settled into the love seat's corner, filling it up as if his body were made of liquid. He sighed. "I was an oilman's boy, or that's how it looked on paper. My daddy went bust after his well dried up."

"But a Texas oilman's son would be a good match for a Garden District lady," Josephine said politely. The Garden District was a universe away from the Garden Court. The District was a neighborhood of lawns the size of city blocks, and houses as big as churches. It was home to the richest of the white people and virtually nobody else.

"It was rather like being a bastard of nobility. Not a penny to my name, but property in Texas I stood to inherit. Her family let me in, though if they'd looked at us more closely, I don't think they'd have done so. Within a year of us being married, her daddy died in his sleep one night—God knows what from—and a year after that, her momma drank herself to death, leaving no one but the pair of us and all that stupid money."

Something like venom made it into his voice. Josephine said, "Strange that you'd put it like that."

"Money can't buy happiness, isn't that what they tell us? Money can't save a woman when she's taken in childbirth, or the baby either. No matter how much more you promise a doctor, if he can only save the child."

"I'm very sorry to hear that, Mr. Calais. I didn't know you'd ever had a family, much less that you'd lost one."

"It was a long time ago. Nearly thirty years, can you believe it?" he asked, but the question was aimed inward, and he appeared to expect no response. "Left me alone with all that money, for all the good it's done me. Except, I've found a comfortable place here—and thanks to all that stupid money, it's a place I can afford to frequent with great . . . frequency."

Marylin piped up from behind the desk. "Mr. Calais! We *do* enjoy having you, you know," she said, embarrassing her employer but pleasing the Texian on the love seat. "I'm so sorry to hear about your family, and I'm glad you're happy when you're here."

"When I'm here, and when I'm drinking."

"The two states are not mutually incompatible," Josephine murmured, gesturing with a look at the cabinet where the "public" alcohol was kept, for distribution to customers. Marylin took the hint, dabbed at her eyes, and rose to pour Calais another beverage. He held a glass in his hand, but it'd run dry.

Another round of Texian foot soldiers went stamping by, and Josephine moved the curtain again to look.

Fenn Calais grunted appreciatively as his glass was refilled, and after a swig, he informed them, "They're leaving, or that's how I heard it."

She turned around quickly, the curtain edge still hanging from her hand. "What? Leaving? Leaving New Orleans?"

"Not all of them. Didn't mean to get anybody's hopes up. Most of those fellows, though—they're the ones who came out when Texas went after the pirate bay. Now that they've taken it, they're heading home."

"Really?" Josephine asked. "They're just . . . leaving it?"

"They're sticking a small garrison there, just to hold the place down. But whatever they were looking for, I don't suppose they found it."

"I thought there was no such thing as *small* as far as Texians are concerned. Least of all when it comes to garrisons."

"So take the word *small* with a grain of salt. I know *I* did. I'm only repeating what I heard, that's all. Some of the soldiers are heading out, leaving the bay."

Josephine closed the curtain again. "Do you think the pirates will take it back?"

"Eventually? I'm damn near sure of it," said the old Texian. "If you want my opinion on the matter, I'd guess it'll happen sooner rather than later."

"Why is that?" she asked.

"Because the pirates want it more than Texas does. But like I said, that's just my opinion." He reached into his vest pocket and pulled out a cigar, which he proceeded to cut and clean. Running it under his nose, he took a deep whiff of the rolled tobacco and smiled before pulling out a box of matches and striking one up.

Marylin smiled, too. That silly girl loved the smell of pipe or cigar tobacco. It made Josephine's eyes itch, but considering how much money Fenn Calais had spent in the Garden Court over the years, it'd be daft to tell him to put it away, so she didn't. Instead she resisted the urge to peek through the curtains any longer, for it would be suspicious—even to someone like Calais, who probably didn't care.

Shortly after noon—perhaps half an hour later—Marylin announced herself with a delicate knock on the open office door.

Josephine jumped, for she'd once more been looking out a window—at the side street, this time. Watching the soldiers come and go. Watching the rolling-crawlers make their rounds, escorting the military men on their way through the too-narrow streets.

"Yes?" she asked eagerly. "What news?"

Marylin entered and shut the door softly behind herself. "No news, really."

"Have you a message?"

"Nothing written, ma'am. The boy who did the running thought it'd be safer just to whisper."

"Did Fenn Calais hear a word of it?"

"No, ma'am. He's on the second floor with Delphine."

"Then what's this news, or this non-news?" Josephine demanded quietly.

"The Texians leaving town are making the scene too crowded, that's the word from your brother. The bayou boys are holing up and lying low, with *Ganymede* inside the New Sarpy storage spot where they put it last night."

"God*damn*."

"It's not so bad, ma'am. They got it there in one piece, and everybody's safe, and nobody bothered them on the way. Everything is fine. They're just going to wait for one night before they drop her into the river."

"That's cutting it awful close. The *Valiant* . . . it won't give them another night to try."

"I know, and they know it, too. But Deaderick said the Texians have been marching along the main road out of Metairie ever since dawn. Maybe they'll be finished passing through by sundown, and maybe they won't. Either way, the boys are staying put. It'll be all right."

"It might." She sat down and squeezed at the arms of her chair, knotting and unknotting her fingers around the padded rests.

"What's wrong, ma'am?"

"I was hoping for a word with Cly before the boys went all the way to water. When they stop by the wharf, and I join the poling crew for surveillance, I'd hoped they'd pause so I could speak with him."

"Any special reason, ma'am?" Marylin asked with great and false innocence.

"Not the one you're thinking. Cly's a good man and our time together was fine, but that was a long time ago," she inadvertently echoed Fenn Calais. "I want a word with him because he's been in Seattle."

"What's Seattle got to do with anything?"

"It might have a whole lot to do with the zombis."

"I don't understand? . . ."

"Neither do I, dear. But I'm working on it, and it's coming together. Cly knows something important, something he hasn't told me. I don't know if he's keeping a secret, or if it just hasn't come up yet. But I need to ask him some questions."

"Does this have something to do with that Ranger who came by here last night?"

"Ranger Korman, yes. And Madame Laveau, too, because she's the one who put the pair of us in touch."

"It's funny, ma'am, you working with a Ranger."

"I'm not *working* with him. We have a thing in common, that's all. We both want the zombis gone. It'd be madness to ignore him if he knows anything useful—and if he's in a position to be help-ful."

"And you think he *can* help?" Marylin asked.

"Maybe. Texas isn't real thrilled with him right now, and Austin might not listen to anything he has to say, but I guess we'll find out. And Captain Cly might hold a piece to the puzzle, though I don't think he knows it. It might be worth our time—once *Ganymede* is safely in Union hands—to put those two men's heads together and see if they don't crack some sparks."

"That's a violent way of putting it, ma'am. I suppose for now we'll hope for the best."

"No, we won't," Josephine said, rising from the seat, although she'd only just taken it.

"We won't?"

"Well. *I* won't. There's plenty of daylight left. I'll take the street rail out and have a word with the good captain before the sun sets. Maybe this delay is a good thing for all of us. I'm determined to find a bright side, goddammit."

"It'll let you spend a little extra time together."

"That's not the kind of bright side I meant."

"Didn't mean to suggest it, ma'am."

"Oh, hush."

Josephine gathered everything she thought she might need for the trip, filling her favorite silk-lined leather bag—the only expen-sive one she owned, not that it looked half so fancy as the ones she wore with her best dresses. She wouldn't need a cloak, but it felt like a shawl might be in order, so she threw a light gray one over a similarly colored dress and grabbed a parasol.

With a few parting instructions to Marylin, she set out for Rue Canal to pick up the street rail line that would take her back out to Metairie.

Norman Somers wasn't hanging around the big lot where the transports parked, but Charlie pointed her in the direction of Norman's brother, Swinton, who was more than happy to drive her the rest of the way to New Sarpy without asking any questions. Likely as not, Swinton knew the answers regardless, but Josephine didn't feel like talking and the man didn't feel like making her, so they rode together in silence to the small riverside settlement.

She descended from the rattling, shuddering transport vehicle and thanked Swinton with a few coins from her bag. He made a polite show of refusal, and she made a polite show of insistence. In the end, he took the money and left her there, standing beside an unpaved road at the edge of a collection of squat, square buildings.

Narrow lines of dirt and mud ran between them, not roads, but walkways and driveways. The grass grew up tall among the spaces where wheels and feet came and went. New Sarpy wasn't an abandoned place. It simply wasn't much used.

The coughing of an engine announced the impending appearance of a rolling-crawler, giving Josephine plenty of time to get off the street.

She stepped out of the way and stood, watching as yet more Texians made their leisurely retreat from New Orleans. Not many of them this time, only a few dozen, with the rolling-crawler slowly rolling and crawling to keep their pace—its metal accompaniment serving to tote supplies and offer general marching encouragement, since the machines weren't big enough to hold more than a handful of men.

Texas had larger devices for transporting personnel and equipment, but Josephine didn't see any of them on the road. She assumed they were being used elsewhere, or perhaps whoever had recalled these forces figured that they were so tough, they could walk awhile. She didn't know, and cared only because the swiftness and completeness of their departure would mean the difference between success and a miserable near-miss when it came to her plans for *Ganymede*.

When they were gone, leaving a cloud of dust and the last echoes of their accompanying machine behind them, she was more alone than not. A pair of ancient colored men with fishing poles chatted on their way to the river. Two dark-skinned children chased a puppy across the road and into a ditch, then ran into the field and toward the forest on the other side. One woman sat reading a newspaper on the stoop of a laundry, while behind her the wet, swishing clank of the clothes-washing devices rumbled and roared indoors.

Josephine knew where the warehouse was, the one where *Ganymede* would be parked and stored. But it felt ill-advised to go stampeding toward it, so she didn't. She opened her parasol and held it up, covering herself in a thin black shadow as she strolled in the general direction of the river.

It wasn't far, barely two blocks before she could smell it in earnest when the breeze kicked air across the wide, muddy expanse of the thing, bringing it up to rattle her parasol and infiltrate her nose. Another block, and she could see the corner of the building in question.

She hesitated.

Should she simply approach it and knock? If the men were inside, they'd surely look first and not merely open fire on anyone who dared give a tap at the door. Anything else would topple past caution into counterproductive paranoia. But what if someone saw her? Most of the bayou knew about the mystery ship, if not its precise location or purpose. Almost everyone was aware that this was an operation against Texas, and therefore, almost everyone agreed to cooperate in a display of blanket ignorance.

Almost.

She made up her mind and assumed her best, most confident posture. Avoiding the huge double doors, she instead approached a person-sized door and gave it a series of raps that said in no uncertain terms that she was here on business, and she had every right to be.

From inside came the sound of absolutely nothing.

She listened, leaning her right ear toward the door. Maybe she caught the distant susurrus whistle of muffled whispers. Maybe she noted the scrape of a boot heel as someone tiptoed carefully. Or maybe she heard only rats and seagulls bickering within. Maybe there was nothing to hear.

No.

With a pop, the door unstuck itself from its humidity-swollen frame, revealing only a narrow slot of the darkened interior, and a fraction of a white man's face.

Only one eye greeted her, a hazel-colored orb offset by a darkly arched awning of an eyebrow. The eye showed neither surprise nor recognition. But it did not show concern or alarm either, and momentarily the door opened a few inches farther to reveal Cly's engineer.

He was wearing a floppy brown hat and chewing on the wooden end of a matchstick. He was half a head shorter than Josephine, and he looked at her with his chin angled slightly upward—still fixing her in that cool, dead gaze that told her nothing.

He said, "Hello, there, Miss Josephine."

"Hello, there, Mr. . . ." She wanted to say *Trout,* but she knew it wasn't correct. *Troost,* she remembered.

"Is everything all right?"

"Yes, everything's fine. I was hoping I could speak to Captain Cly."

Kirby Troost's teeth worked around the fraying match. "Well, then. I guess you'd better come inside." He opened the door to admit her, then shut it fast behind her.

Inside, the warehouse was not as large as she'd remembered it, from the one time she'd been there a few months previously. Then again, last time she saw it, the place hadn't been stuffed with two large flatbeds and the *Ganymede*—which had been covered with an assortment of tarps roped down over the sides and concealing most of its details.

The interior was shadowed. Most of the light came from a row of small windows up near the ceiling. The rest came from two strands of electric lanterns, hanging from the ropes somebody had strung from two sets of rafters, fizzing and popping.

"You covered it up," she observed.

"*They* did." Kirby cocked his head toward a back door, leading to an alley near the river. Then he said, "I mean, your bayou fellas did it. I didn't much see the point, myself. Anybody who looks in here will get a gander at that thing, wonder what the hell it is, and take a look underneath the wrappings, regardless."

She peered up at the loosely swaddled craft, wondering where they'd found so many big scraps of tarp. "Still, I suppose it feels safer this way, rather than leaving it exposed."

"It's not exposed. It's got a whole building over it."

"At any rate, Mr. Troost, could you tell me where the captain has run off to? I don't see him." For that matter, she didn't see anyone. Troost was the only warm body present. That didn't precisely worry her, but she wasn't particularly comfortable with his presence, either. Something about the little man bothered her. He reminded her of someone or something unpleasant, or perhaps it was only the impertinent way he spoke and moved. He was entirely too comfortable everywhere. No one should feel so immediately at home at the drop of a hat.

"Could I tell you where he's at for certain? No. I could make a guess or two, or you could wait until he gets back. I believe he's gone down the road to that little bar, the one three or four blocks east. We've been coming and going in shifts, and hanging around the one hotel New Sarpy sees fit to maintain. It wouldn't do anybody any good to see a bunch of men coming and going from this warehouse. I don't care if your brother says everyone in town is a friend of ours."

"Almost everyone," she murmured.

"Yeah. *Almost.* Almost means room for error, and I don't like it. So we're taking turns, just hanging around. One or two of us at a time. But Cly isn't much of a drinker, and he's keeping an eye on

Houjin, so I predict he'll get bored and swing this way within the hour."

Josephine said, "Hm," surveying the scenery with a critical eye. Then she asked, "Are you from Seattle?"

"Seattle?" he repeated, neither confirming nor denying anything.

"You heard me. Seattle. What can you tell me about it?"

He shrugged and leaned against *Ganymede*'s shrouded bulk, pulling a tobacco pouch out of his vest pocket. As he delivered a pinch into a white square of rolling paper, he told her, "Not sure what you're looking to hear. It's an old port town, up in the Washington Territory. Not much to it anymore."

"That's not what I've heard."

"What *have* you heard?"

She crossed her arms. "There's gas in Seattle, isn't there? Turns men into the walking dead, isn't that right?"

He didn't bother to deny it. "Something like that." He scrunched the paper into a cigarette and pulled the match out of his mouth. Lifting a corner of the cloth that covered *Ganymede,* he struck the match on the craft's rough-edged side. It sparked to life, and he used it to light the cigarette.

"How does anyone live there, if it's full of this poisonous gas?"

"So *this* is what you want with Cly."

"He's been living there in Seattle, hasn't he?"

Troost's eyes did not exactly narrow, since they had never been open all the way, but now Josephine felt as if she were being squinted at. "No. He's got a flat in Tacoma, about thirty miles to the south."

"But he comes and goes from Seattle a lot, doesn't he?"

"You'll have to ask him. I haven't been with his crew terribly long."

"You're lying."

"I'm not."

They stared each other down, him smoking carelessly and her braced for a fight that he wasn't prepared to give her.

Kirby Troost repeated, "I'm not lying. I don't know how much time he spends in Seattle, but I know he visits regularly. There's a woman there, and he's sweet on her. I think he'd like to settle down, if she'll have him."

"Inside a poisoned, abandoned city?"

"People still live there, underground. It's . . . complicated. They've got this wall around it, and a crazy system of air tubes and vents, and filters, and whatnot."

"And this woman of his, she lives there?" she asked without really meaning to. She didn't care. She wasn't even curious. She wasn't sure why she'd pressed the issue.

"Her, and her son. She's a widow."

"Is she—" Josephine wasn't sure what she wanted to ask. "—good for him?" she finished weakly.

"I don't know, I've barely met her. He sure likes her a lot, and that's what's important, as far as I'm concerned. He's got this plan to set up an airyard dock inside the city wall. The people who live there are willing to pay him to maintain it."

"Why?" she asked. It was a why that applied to any number of questions she couldn't yet formulate more specifically.

"It's hard for them to keep contact with the outside world. It's practically a secret, them living there. They like to be left alone; to their own devices, if you know what I mean. They don't bother nobody, and they don't want anybody bothering them. But sometimes they need supplies. They need to send letters or messages. Things like that."

"And if Cly does this, if he starts a business there—he'll live there, too, and marry this woman?"

"Yeah, I'd say he'll marry her if she'll have him." Then he turned the conversation just a notch to the right, in exactly the direction Josephine didn't want him to go. "You and him—the captain, I mean. There's history there, ain't that right?"

"He told you?"

"He mentioned it. Didn't say much, except that it was years ago, and it didn't work out."

She only just noticed that he almost never blinked. "That's about right."

Kirby Troost, still mostly unblinking, said, "I can see it."

"See what? Andan and me?"

The shadow of a smile tugged at the corner of his lip. "Yeah. I can see it. Not exactly two of a kind, but I suppose—given what I've heard—he's got a certain type he prefers."

"And you think I fit that type?"

"Smart and tough. You're taller, though. Taller than Miss Wilkes."

"I thought you said she was a widow."

"I did, but it's complicated."

"So complicated, you call her *miss*?"

"Complicated enough. We mostly call her *ma'am*. She's a yitty-bitty thing. A little smaller than me, even. But I don't know too many men who'd argue with her, push come to shove. That's what I mean, about him having a type. Not many men argue with you, either."

The back door squeaked open, and before Josephine even noticed him reaching for it, Kirby Troost was holding a six-shooter primed and ready. Upon seeing Cly and Houjin, he lowered it and tucked it back into his belt.

"Cap'n," he said. "You've got a visitor."

"Josephine," he greeted her with a nod. "Something I can do for you?"

"A word in private, if you please."

The oriental boy's face constricted into a sneaky grin, as if he looked forward to embarrassing the captain with this moment later on—but it would wait. He opened his mouth to say something, but Cly didn't give him time.

"Huey, you and Kirby stay close."

Kirby Troost said, "Great."

To which the captain said, "You can teach him to play cards if you want. Just keep each other out of trouble, will you? Josie, how about we go out back and walk along the river."

"That sounds fine," she told him stiffly, and she followed him as he went back out the way he'd come in, holding the door for her and—like his engineer—shutting it firmly and quickly as soon as they were through it.

Down along the river, there was a path built on old railroad ties and bleached-bone boards pounded into the mud. They walked slowly along this, going nowhere in particular, unwilling to look at each other.

After a minute or two of unhurried shuffling, he finally asked, "What do you want, Josie? Or what do you need? Why'd you come all the way back out here from the Quarter?" His words were tense, like he was afraid to hear the answer.

"It's about the zombis, Andan."

That caught him off guard. Whatever he'd been expecting or fearing, this wasn't it. "The what now?"

"Zombis. That's what we call them here, though you must have a different word for them in Seattle."

"In Seattle?"

"The walking dead, Andan."

"Yeah." He scratched at the back of his neck, feeling the sweat already gathering there, from the warm wet air by the river and from the company, as well. "We've got some of those. We call them *rotters.* I don't think there's any real word for them. They aren't like animals, or bugs—we don't have scientists falling all over themselves to catalog 'em."

"Madame Laveau calls them zombis, and she's the only woman on earth who seems able to control them at all."

"Laveau? The Queen? Hot damn, is she still alive?"

"Yes, dear," Josephine said without thinking; the phrase simply fell out of her mouth. "She's still alive, and she's brought me a Texas Ranger who thinks he knows what's making them. She wants me to work with him." She sighed.

"What's the Queen got to do with the dead things? You said she controls them? Maybe they aren't the same problem we've got.

Ours don't answer to anybody," he replied, but he didn't sound certain. Suddenly he added, "Come to think of it, I've seen them answer to a machine. My buddy Jerry, he has this gun he calls Daisy— and it shoots a big gong of sound. It stuns them into holding still, but only for a few minutes."

Josephine remembered watching Marie Laveau clang her cane against the lamppost. That was the same thing in its way, wasn't it? A *big gong of sound*? She did not believe in coincidences, so she filed this information away. "I need you to tell me about them, Andan. Tell me everything you know."

He did.

It came out haltingly, as he fumbled around the conversation— trying to spare her the things she already knew, and pass along only what was helpful. Much of what he told her was truly revolutionary, particularly one important point confirming what the Ranger had told her: One way or another, the zombis, or rotters, or whatever they were . . . they originated in the walled-up, poisoned city.

Seattle was the source. Seattle was the problem.

"No," he corrected her when she said as much aloud. "People like *me,* we're the problem. We moved the gas out, so the chemists could turn it into sap. We spread the poison around because we've been paid well to do so, but that shouldn't have mattered. We shouldn't have done it."

"You're being too hard on yourself. All of us, everywhere, everything we do . . . it hurts someone, someplace. I'm convinced of it."

"That's a god-awful philosophy, Josie."

"It's not a philosophy; it's an observation."

But privately she could only agree. She also understood that his desire to settle down and do something else had as much to do with someone named Briar up in the Washington Territories as it did with his own guilt.

She briefly considered bringing up this Briar person, then felt silly for the impulse. It didn't matter. When this was over, and *Ganymede* was in the appropriate hands, she and Cly would go their separate ways on the same grand scale as before, and that would be the end of it.

Sentimentality would do neither of them any good. She fought it hard, and turned it off, and walked beside him without thinking about how much she'd once enjoyed doing so.

She did not think about how much it'd warmed her, and been an odd source of pride, to roam with the giant pirate whom no one ever stopped or bothered, or assaulted or robbed, or even questioned—no matter how softly he spoke or how friendly his words. She did not recall how she'd appreciated his strength, even seeing it used against others when he'd fight for money in the ring, and she refused to consider for even a moment how she'd lengthened the bed they'd so often shared in order to make him more comfortable.

She worked hard to keep from considering the way things could have been, and might have been, but were not. Things had gone another way, and this other way had been best for them both. Or so she was forced to assume, not knowing what might have happened if she'd bundled up and headed north, and west . . . or if he'd taken off his coat and parked his dirigible in the delta.

Before he could mention that she'd grown uncharacteristically silent, she made some excuse to be done. "Tell your engineer I said thank you, and that it was a pleasure to meet him. And it's been . . . it's been good to talk to you again. I'm glad to see you're still doing well, and thinking of ways to do better."

Then she left him there, still standing by the river, his hands in his pockets, wondering whatever things he was wondering, but not following her.

She hitched a ride back to the Metairie station, sitting beside a sharecropping woman and her oversized, dull-faced son with sloping shoulders and enormous hands. At the station she waited for the correct street rail car and took it to Rue Canal, opting to walk from the final stop rather than hail a cab. It was only a few blocks back to the Garden Court, and she felt restless for reasons she could not explain—or chose not to.

She looked up from her reverie to note that the sky was going gray. At first she thought it was because the hour was swiftly growing late and the curfew coming soon, then realized that the sky must be shuttered with clouds, and not quite so far toward evening as it felt at first. The river smelled like summer coming in, and dead fish and waterlogged vegetation, and the air that carried those scents from bank to bank and beyond was dragged along the ground by those same dark clouds that blackened like spilling ink up from the south. She regarded the sky and said, to no one but herself, "A storm's coming."

Her parasol wouldn't help her if the bottom dropped out. But she'd been wet before, and she'd be wet again before she died, and it'd never been a catastrophe yet. So onward she went, deeper into the Vieux Carré.

She walked briskly past people who were opening windows to catch the breeze that would billow through before the rain came up behind it. They were tying back curtains and inviting the air to sweep on through, push out the odors of cayenne and Tabasco, crawfish and rum, red beans and rice, and cigars and cheap tobacco. The Quarter exhaled paraffin and charcoal, incense and manure. It breathed diesel and industrial lubricant, barbecue and salt.

It whispered.

Josephine stopped, unsure of what that sound had been—uncertain if it meant anything, or if it'd only been her imagination. A tumbleweed of newspaper went skipping across her path, rolling into the street and stopping in a puddle, where it unfurled to reveal the headline. The first words were blurred, but the remainder of them read, AT THE ST. LOUIS CATHEDRAL. As she stared, dirty water soaked through, obscuring even that scant message, but somehow revealing another, farther down the page—before the whole thing disappeared into soaked, illegible pulp.

GARDEN

She looked away from the sopping paper. It meant nothing, after all. She found herself casually surprised that she'd bothered to stop for it, and wondered why it'd seemed—even for a moment—like something worth examining.

She resumed her pace. Her feet clapped against the hollow side-walks with their planed slats, and her skirts skimmed the splinters. Still, she felt odd, as if she'd heard something but failed to understand it. As if she should've listened harder. Like she was being chastised at a distance, by a mother or grandmother whose voice she couldn't quite pick out of a crowd.

The creak of a sign hanging on a chain tickled at her ears. She spied it up ahead, and, catching its text from the corner of her eye, she drew up short again. She could've sworn—would've sworn, and at great length—that it'd said, TOO LATE TO WAIT. But it read only, TULANE WAITMAN, advertising a minister's office.

She stared intently at the sign as she passed beneath it. It performed no further tricks; it only swung squeakily in the shifting air ahead of the incoming storm.

Where was she again? Oh, yes. Rue Galvez, just past Esplanade. Funny how she felt so turned around.

She took the next turn and proceeded via dead reckoning, the kind that was engraved in her blood. She'd lived in the Quarter all her life, and she knew it like the corridors of the Garden Court. She could have navigated it blindfolded, in the fog, at midnight. Even so, her heart pounded, and she did not know why. She knew only that she had to keep moving. "Because of the curfew," she muttered to herself, but did not believe a word of it.

The streets were nearly empty, and this, too, was strange. True, the businesses were closing up shop against the storm, against the limits imposed by the Texians, but there was also . . . something else? It was a ridiculous thing to think, but Josephine thought it anyway, and she kept walking, and faster. Just short of a run.

Running would draw attention. She did not want attention, did she?

Well, why not? She was doing nothing wrong. It mattered little if anyone stopped her.

A seagull squawked loudly and flapped far too close to her head, startling her into flinging her hands defensively upward. The bird chattered its displeasure and dropped with a soft slapping of its splayed, webbed feet onto the planks immediately in her path. It stretched its wings, opening and closing them as if in warning, or summons, or some other gesture the woman couldn't decipher.

"What?" she asked it, feeling ridiculous. "What do you want? Get out of the way," she said, and prepared to aim a kick in its general direction. She knew from long experience that she'd never hit the thing; it'd be out of her way well in time, which was just as well. She didn't care to hurt it, but she would not be bullied by a creature the size of a cat.

It cawed once more and stared at something behind her, so she looked over her shoulder and spied—at a brief, outrageous glance—a storefront window that made her gasp. A large white skull filled the entire pane, but only for a split second . . . before it was replaced with a dress stitched for a bride, advertising the stock at Miss Delia's Dresses and Wares.

Josephine's throat went dry, and a warm flush began creeping up her chest. Her hands tingled and went numb. "What's going on?" she asked no one in particular. "What's happening?"

The gull answered with a scrap of stationery in its mouth. It hadn't been there at first, but it was present when she turned around. The bird dropped the shred of paper printed-side up, declaring in someone's overelaborate handwriting, *Join us for* something garbled and runny, dampened into meaninglessness. Then, *at Jackson Square, the north corner gardens!*

Jackson Square. The Cathedral.

A message, but from whom? From what? And who would communicate in such a fashion?

It would be better to go find out than to always wonder—or that's the conclusion she came to as the bird flew off, taking the paper with it. She adjusted her trajectory and increased her pace. At first she merely hustled, walking too fast for decorum, but soon she was all but skipping, then dashing outright.

She wasn't sure why she was running, or what she was running from, though she could take a guess.

"Not yet, not yet, not yet," she said under her breath as she tore along, ducking down alleys and cutting across intersections.

The whole Quarter ushered her along, clearing the way.

The doors moved and the sweepers stepped aside. Horses drew carriages out of her path, and rolling-crawlers lurched off as she darted toward them. Wisps of fog frayed and split at her approach, and Jackson Square was closer, closer, and closer.

Her chest ached against the bones of her corset, straining against the stays as she panted her way closer to the river. Her skirts tangled around her ankles, twisting around her knees and trying to slow her, but failing. She kicked herself free and pushed onward.

The texture of the streets beneath her changed. They shifted from the wood slats of lifted walkways as those side paths ended, then became the slick cobbles of humidity-damp stones that slipped beneath her feet despite her rubber-bottomed boots. She stumbled and recovered, ran out of steam, and leaned against a large, cool, stone square that turned out to be the foundation of the equestrian statue directly in front of the church.

Gazing up at it, she wondered if it, too, might have some arcane message to pass along. But the rider and horse both kept their silence.

Back behind the church, or somewhere past it, she heard a dull mumble punctuated with gasps and small cries. Catching her breath, she pulled herself together and continued onward, toward the ornate, dark church doors illuminated by fizzing electric torches on either side. She turned to pass them, still tracking the sounds and pushing toward their source.

A tall black fence cordoned off the church's back yards.

It walled off the gardens.

A crowd was gathering. Josephine joined it at full speed, stopping herself hands-first against the rails, leaving bruises on her palms that she wouldn't notice for days. She thrust her face between the bars and gazed openmouthed at the scene framed in the vivid green grass of the shadowed yard behind the city's holy Christian center.

There on the ground, faceup in a state of peaceful repose with arms at her sides, Marie Laveau lay unbreathing, unmoving.

On the lawn around her, items were accumulating. As Josephine watched, three gold coins were pitched through the gate with a prayer, shortly to be joined by hastily improvised bags as small as her thumb. One gris-gris after another went sailing over the fence or through it, to land in a gentle plunk near the serene, still body.

Josephine wrapped her fingers around the chilly bars and struggled to breathe. She watched the small things fly—the ribbons, the coins, the buttons. The bags and beads, the twine-twisted bracelets and bootlaces, the flowers, pebbles, and nails. They accumulated around the queen's corpse, yet none landed upon her. They gathered like a full-body halo, drifts of clutter, a fog of tiny gifts dredged from pockets and purses.

"No," she said in half a breath, and with the other half she said, "Not yet. It's too soon," she added. "There's too much I don't know!"

More mourners gathered, brought to the spot by whatever means had brought Josephine, or by word of mouth filtering from churchyard gardens throughout the Quarter. They joined her at the fence, gawkers who stood with eyes wet and heads bowed, whispering prayers or moaning.

No one heeded the curfew, and as the sun set more fully, the Texians came out to see the fuss. The first who came started with commands to disperse, then saw the uncanny tableau spread out within the fence. They recognized the body lying there and stopped yelling their orders. They, too, joined the lookers at the fence, drawn up close and made quiet by awe, or shock, or some other odd familiarity that told them this was not the time to insist upon anything.

Someone at the back cried, "What's going on? What's the meaning of this?" Josephine knew that whoever this was, he'd find his silence, too. But she recognized the voice and turned to spot the speaker. At the nearest corner where the gas lamps were sputtering to light under a colored child's expert spark, she saw Horatio Korman.

She watched understanding dawn on him and, closely following that, a nervous kind of horror. Their eyes met across the now-crowded side street.

They shared the moment, the fear of knowing—alone, together.

Thirteen

Andan Cly ran his finger over the map as slowly as a man learning to read. He traced the curve of the Mississippi River gently, lifting his hand to see a detail here, a notation there. The map was an older one and it had been abridged, amended, and scrawled across to make it more pertinent to the present situation. This sheet included not only the serpentine bends and miniature ports that dotted the way between the city and the ocean; it also included the canals, both commercial and semiprivate—and the docks that Texas likely didn't know about.

The electric lamps had been dimmed down to nothing, leaving only the oil lamps and rickety wire-frame lanterns to give them any light.

Outside, there were no sounds of soldiers or rolling-crawlers. No marching feet or passing patrols. The Texians had left—at least, those who were leaving were long gone, and no more were on the verge of exiting, so the time had come to put the finishing touches on the plan before putting it into action.

Night had not yet fallen, but it was coming, and it would be there within the hour—black and thick, a perfect shield from the eyes of anyone too interested in knowing about the giant machine hidden inside the nondescript storehouse.

"These are the forts, ain't that right?" Cly asked, poking at a spot in the river just past a bend that kinked sharply north and to the east.

"Fort Saint Philip on the north bank, and Fort Jackson on the southern one," Deaderick told him. "Fully manned, mostly by Confederates."

"Not Texians?"

"Naw. Texas lets them keep their forts as a matter of show. Makes it look more like a group effort, rather than an occupation. It's bullshit, and everybody knows it."

"So the Rebs keep the forts in order to keep their pride. Got it. Are they dangerous?"

"Dangerous enough to steer clear of them, as much as we're able. They don't have anything much in the water that we'll have to bypass—no charges or anything like that. They can't clog up the waterway with bombs. There are too many merchant ships coming and going to make it worth their trouble. But they do have lookouts aplenty keeping an eye on everyone who passes by—and anyone who goes steaming upriver."

Fang made a sign. Cly saw it out of the corner of his eye.

Gatekeepers.

"Gatekeepers," the captain said aloud, since he doubted anyone else but Houjin could understand the message. "That's all they are."

"Heavily armed gatekeepers. They've got cannon all over the place, and antiaircraft, too."

Rucker Little noted, "There's nothing keeping the antiaircraft from becoming antiwatercraft. All they have to do is tip the things on their fulcrum, brace them, and aim them at the waves. A buddy of mine used to work for them, doing maintenance on machine parts and the like. He says they have a pair of antiaircraft shooters mounted on each of the fort's two river-facing towers, and both of them have been modified so they can shoot up or down."

"Good to know," Kirby Troost said.

"We'll stay out of their way. Out of their sight, anyway. Let me ask you something," Cly said to Deaderick. "Is there any good reason we have to go right past them? They're guarding the way to the ocean, but only if we stay in the river."

"This thing won't grow legs and crawl, Captain."

"No, that's not what I mean. These canals, here and here." He tapped at them. "Are they deep enough to hold us?"

Deaderick rubbed at his chin. "*Maybe*. Not that one," he indicated a sketched-in line at Empire. "But this one might—the one just past Port Sulphur."

Houjin perked up. "Isn't that where we landed? When we first came into town? Those Texians made us set down there instead of landing at Barataria."

"That's right," Cly told him.

Rucker sniffed. "Doesn't surprise me. Texians trying to chase off perfectly nice pirates."

"They thought the Lafittes were hiding this thing." Deaderick cocked a thumb at *Ganymede*. "We'd actually asked for their help, a few months ago, and they were interested in assisting us, but for a fee we couldn't afford—and we couldn't get the Union to spring for it. I suppose someone passed our request along. Some spies, somewhere."

"The bayou's chock-full of 'em," Rucker agreed. "Just as well we couldn't take them up on it."

Kirby Troost stared at the map, baffled. "I don't mind telling you, it blows my mind how little help you're getting from the Federals. Here you are, trying to hand them a piece of hardware like this, and they just leave you hanging for the details."

Deaderick made a small grimace and said, "Eh, you know how it goes. They aren't sure *Ganymede*'s worth the investment, and we can't prove it until we show it to them. Funny thing is, the Rebs believe it. We wouldn't have any trouble convincing them that the ship is valuable—they're scared to death of it."

Rucker said, "And they know what it could do, in theory. They were the ones who commissioned the first ones, the *Hunley*, the

Pioneer, and the rest. They know what a difference a craft like this could make in the war, and God knows they're barely hanging in there these days. They can't afford to let the Yankees to get this thing, take it apart, and figure out how to make more of them."

"You think they could do that?" Cly asked.

"Sure. Within a few months, if they hire a few of us," he replied, indicating himself, Mumler, and Anderson Worth. "For that matter, if it comes to it . . . we might just head back North and make a case ourselves. The three of us, plus a couple of others—we might be able to sit down and draw up our own plans. We know it better than anybody else."

Deaderick Early agreed, but with reservations. "Of course, if you boys did that . . . it'd be another year or two at soonest before you had something working. No, this is our best bet for ending things fast." He glared down at the map as if he'd rather be looking at something else. "We've had trouble enough convincing those damn fools we know our heads from a hole in the ground. But we'll show them. Once they get a look at the firepower on this thing, and they watch it in action . . . once they see what it can do . . ." His voice trailed off, then returned again, stronger. "At any rate, Port Sulphur. That's the closest dock to Barataria, so it stands to reason that that's where they diverted traffic. Do you think they're still doing it? Guiding people away from the big island?"

Deaderick said, "Probably not. They didn't find the ship and they've sent their extra men home, so my guess is that they've mostly lost interest in what goes on over there."

"I don't like to work on guesses." Cly frowned. "But it looks like we're stuck between a number of uncertainties. The forts will be dangerous to sneak past. The canal at Port Sulphur might be safer, but it might be crawling with Texians."

Deaderick folded his arms, wincing as his shoulder shifted. "Might be, but I doubt it. Last word in from the city has it that there's just a residual force on staff at the bay, cleaning up and sorting out what's worth keeping and what's not."

"You think they'll set up a post there? A fort or something, where the pirates used to camp?" Troost asked.

"Maybe. Or maybe they'll scavenge for anything they can make use of, and let the place fall to ruin."

Cly shook his head. "It won't fall to ruin. The pirates will take it back. That's their hometown, their home nation. The only place they have with any history to it. They'll be back for it."

"You say that like you've given it some thought yourself," said Norman Somers, who was back to assist with the big trucks and the winch that would send the *Ganymede* swinging over into the river. "I'd be pleased to help you, if it means one less square of Louisiana that Texas gets to keep."

"Can't say it didn't occur to me. Can't say I wouldn't like to see it happen."

Kirby Troost stuck a match in his mouth and chewed it thoughtfully. "There's no time like the present, if you want it back. Or that's the word in the sky."

"How would you know?" asked Rucker.

"I got ears all over the place, that's how. Pirates are going to grab for it, pretty soon."

"Who?" Cly asked, interested against his better judgment. "Somebody arranging an operation?"

"Supposedly Henry Shanks is leading point, or that's how it's falling into place. He's got One-Eye Chuck Waverly coming in from the Atlantic coast, and Jimmy Garcia swinging up from the Yucatán. Rumor has it even Sweet Bang Lee is interested in raising some hell. He's on his way from California with Brigadier Betty and their son."

The captain breathed, "Jesus Christ Almighty. That's one hell of a crowd. Ol' Hank Shanks is in the lead, is he?"

"That's what they're saying."

"I can't imagine anyone else so big that others would follow him. Nobody but Lafitte, and he's dead—and so are half his grandchildren, or rotting in jail."

Deaderick uncrossed his arms and scratched at a sore spot where a bullet wound was healing, and itching. "I'd like to see the pirates reestablish themselves, myself. They took better care of me than they had to, when I was tore up during the raid. But fellows, I believe the conversation has gotten off course again."

Cly said, "You're right, you're right." Then he rattled off the coordinates they'd agreed to—the ones about twenty miles into the Gulf, where Admiral Herman Partridge was waiting on the warship *Valiant* . . . until morning, and no longer.

"How long do you think this will take?" Houjin asked. "It's a long way, isn't it? How far are we going?"

"All told? Sixty, maybe seventy miles. And you'll be right behind us with more fuel, won't you?" he asked Deaderick and Rucker.

"Right on top of you," Rucker confirmed. "Literally, sometimes. We're sneaking the diesel in sealed tubs covered in shrimping nets. And we've got a hose all strapped up and ready to deploy."

"But we can't do it while you're underwater. You'll have to break surface for us to refuel you. That'll be the most dangerous part," Deaderick said with deepening seriousness. "One of the things we're hoping to change on future models of this thing—is we'd like to see it take on more fuel without breaching."

"I sure as hell hope they *do* keep us around, so we can make some suggestions on those future models," piped up Wallace Mumler, who'd been leaning against a wall and smoking quietly as the conversation carried on.

Chester Fishwick, who'd come in late but now stood beside Wallace, agreed. "I'd like the chance to work on the ships they'll build after this one. I'm all full up on ideas—ways they could make it better. Ways it could run cleaner, and longer."

Cly lifted his head to direct his next question at the pair of them. "Speaking of running longer, how far can we expect to get on one full tank?"

No one answered right away, but Chester took a stab at a reply. "Twenty-five or thirty miles, or that's our best guess. It's hard to say, once you're out in the current. It'll help you, but we don't know how much. Maybe the river will take you an extra mile; maybe she'll take you an extra ten. Keep your eye on the fuel gauge, that's my advice. And give us a signal before you're ready for more—when you're down to a couple miles' worth of juice, we'll find a spot for you to pull aside real quiet and give you another dose."

"Got it."

Once more they went over the plan, working in the new particulars—a decided-upon detour at Port Sulphur, establishing estimated stopping points where refueling might be easiest, and alternative possibilities in case of Texians or Rebs. And when it all was pinned down at last, the smallest detail confirmed, all the men took deep breaths and stood up straight. They cracked their backs and their necks, stiff from having leaned over too long, staring at the assortment of maps.

They stretched their legs and gazed anxiously at the canvas-covered lump of the *Ganymede*.

Then Norman Somers and Rucker Little climbed into the big driving machines and started the engines. Deaderick Early and Wallace Mumler opened the double doors at the back side of the warehouse, while the remaining members of the party, except for Cly and his crew, went to stations outside to look out for the trouble that everyone secretly expected.

But none came.

Intermittent whistles like birdcalls—prearranged for meaning—chirped through the now-full night, declaring that all was clear and the time was now.

Hurry. Move it. Out of the warehouse.

Down to the water, where the big winch waited, having been moved from the bayou to the edge of the river. . . . There, it had been concealed with saw grass and reeds, and a tuft of false tree canopy that disguised it at a distance.

Such a disguise was the best they could do. If anyone got close, the illusion would not hold. It could never hide something so large, and so strange. The whole assortment of nervous men prayed that anyone who took more than a second look would assume it was be overgrown dock equipment, left over from the days when people more regularly fished, and fixed boats, and moved cargo from the small bend called New Sarpy.

First gear was always the hardest when towing something so huge and heavy. The trucks strained against their load, and strained to pull together in perfect time like a pair of mechanical oxen. They moved, crawling inches at a time, but gaining traction and turf; and the conjoined platforms that moved the craft hauled it forward.

Now the watchers kept their eyes peeled even harder. They scanned using spyglasses that could tell them only so much in the darkness—but alerted them to lanterns, lights, and pedestrians out on the main road. They peered and squinted in every direction, calling soft hoots and the croaks of frogs that all was clear.

Do it now. Get it out of sight. Get it to the winch.

Only a few yards separated the warehouse exit from the camouflaged winch, so it took only minutes to move *Ganymede* from one stopping point to the next. It took only a few terrified clicks of Wallace Mumler's watch for the craft to be affixed to the hooks at the top of the winch, and a few more for the dark-clothed men to move like shadows performing a dance, hitching the craft and swinging it over the water on a long, straining arm that could scarcely hold its weight.

Its bottom hit the water with a splash that sloshed a wave onto shore, soaking the legs of the men who stood nearby. They'd picked this place partly because there, the river was deeper than it looked, and would be an easy spot to launch from.

While the winch adjusted its position, the men who weren't directly operating it went scampering along the banks, removing vegetation to reveal small engine-powered boats. They were the boats of poor people, half-cobbled things held together with pitch and elbow grease, and a dab of spit. They were boats no one would look at twice, for the river was crowded with them—mostly run by older men who took to the water in search of night-blind food, or lazy companionship, toting their nets, poles, and shellfish traps.

The men in the dinghies got bored enough that they served as a network of sorts, passing gossip and news back and forth across the water almost as swiftly as the taps could carry it. They were spies of another sort, watching the world for signs of change or progress. For a few pence in the palm, they'd help the rum-runners or the blight smugglers, the cargo handlers and the crawdad scrapers.

But not the Texians.

Not one of the boatmen would've lifted a finger to share gossip with the occupiers, and the handful of men who knew what was passing downriver kept the knowledge to themselves—or spread it to others like themselves, so that the *Ganymede* and its attendants wouldn't be bothered.

Which was for the best, because there was no muffling the chains as they clanked and grinded, lowering *Ganymede* into the water. Everyone listened, terrified and tense, ears alert for warnings called from the watchmen beyond the warehouse. But nothing came, except the hoots and grunts that said all was well, and to continue.

So they did.

And when the ship was more in the water than out of it, the chains were released and it dunked itself, throwing up another sloppy wave. It bobbed, its entry hatch remaining above the waterline, but ducking and leaning, then stabilizing.

Norman Somers and Andan Cly used a pair of hooked poles to latch the craft to a set of pier posts, which had been driven deeply into the mud. These two men, the largest and strongest present, wrestled with the weight of the craft and nearly—for one horrifying cycle of waves slapping and watchers calling "still safe" in their bird cries—let it slip away from them. But they caught it, and hooked it into place as if they were tying an enormous horse to a pair of hitching posts.

Now the ship was more hidden than visible, the bulk of its shape concealed by the shimmering black water.

"The winch," Deaderick whispered fiercely. "Put it up. Get it away."

Again the men moved like clockwork, each one to a task, each one knowing exactly where to place each foot, twist each knob, unfasten each support. Soon the winch was teetering, and then it fell into the water, as planned.

Deaderick instructed them in his stern, low voice, "Cover it up. Sink it. Leave it in the mud."

This happened wordlessly, promptly. Completely. Their success would not be assured until the sun rose again, but it would suffice for now. The lanterns showed nothing beneath the surface but a roiling bubble of silt washed up by the heavy winch settling on the bottom.

It would do.

"Inside," Deaderick told them. "Hurry."

Hurry was the word of the hour, and they all obeyed it.

Cly stepped into the river on a small raft that'd been pushed into his path to use as a floating stepping-stone. He straddled the raft and the shore, the remarkable span of his legs stretching the distance. "Fang," he said.

Fang took Cly's hand, and, with barely a step upon the captain's knee, reached the *Ganymede*'s hatch and opened it—so gently that it did not make even the quietest clank when he set it aside. Immediately behind him came Houjin, moving almost as fast, almost as easily. Fang took the boy's elbow and tipped him inside, then followed him.

"Troost, your turn."

"Son of a bitch," Troost grumbled, adjusting the match in his mouth, taking a deep breath, and lunging for the captain's outstretched hand. He stumbled, caught himself—and Cly held him up, too, keeping him mostly out of the water—and then he was against the craft, clinging to it. He swung his leg over and crawled down the hatch.

"Early," Cly called.

When Deaderick walked over, Wallace Mumler objected, saying, "Wait. No. You're not healed up. Not yet."

"No one else knows that thing as well as I do. No one else knows it in and out, all the weapons systems and all the bailing systems."

"I do, almost," Mumler argued. "And I know the electrics even better than you, I bet."

"Then you come, too, if you're willing. The pair of us, me and you—and these fellows. We'll get it down the river. Norman can take over your pole boat, can't he? Norman?"

"I can take it, Rick."

"Good. Take Wally's pole-craft, and you," he said to Mumler, "get inside. Come on, if you're coming."

Wallace looked at *Ganymede,* and looked at his leader. "All right, then. Me and you."

"Go in, get in. You'll need less help than I will, with me in this shape. Not that it's as bad as you think," he added before Mumler could protest any further.

Cly came last. He leaned, stepped off the raft, and stuck to the side of *Ganymede,* hanging there. Before he climbed in, he looked over at the few assembled men who weren't on lookout duty, and said, "We're counting on you fellows, you know that, right? We can't make this work without you. We'll drown down here, if you don't keep us moving."

Rucker Little, now essentially in charge along with Chester Fishwick, nodded from the bank. "We're coming. We won't let you scuttle her by accident, we can promise you that. You do your job; we'll do ours."

Cly gave them a nod and a small parting salute as he flipped his leg over the hatch's round entrance and disappeared down inside it.

He drew the lid shut behind him, settling it as tightly as he could against the seal, then drawing the wheel hard to the right to compress that seal, and lock them all dry inside. As he did so, he felt a strange vacuum settle and he recognized it—he knew it from years of gas masks sucking themselves into position against his face, and from the layers of filters and seals that preserved Seattle's underground. He knew the feel of it, but here, somehow, it felt more sinister.

In the underground, up above there was only a street—only a city filled with poison air. But that poison air could be cleaned. No one would drown in the street. All it took was a mask to make the city navigable, never mind the rotters and the blinding clots of fog.

But not here.

Not in the water, where once the ship had been lowered, there was nothing above, nothing outside, nothing touching it but the suffocating weight of liquid.

In the previous days, it'd only been practice—only puttering around the lake and learning the controls. This was different. This was the Great Muddy, Old Man River. This was bigger, or at least longer. And maybe deeper, for all Cly knew. Definitely stronger, moving with its unrelenting current from somewhere up North to somewhere beyond the delta, meeting the ocean west of Florida.

He ducked down into the main body of the interior, where red, orange, and small gold lights flickered, brightening the interior, but not much. The dimness was necessary, for two reasons.

First, no one wanted any other craft to take notice of an odd glowing presence beneath the murky waves. And second, if the interior was too bright, the windows would be useless. It was very dark beyond the six-inch-thick glass, but with a small row of encouraging sunset-colored lights mounted externally beneath the watershield—beaming like a tentative smile—it was possible to spy the largest obstacles without being spotted from above.

They hoped.

They'd tested it out after dark on Pontchartrain, but the results had been inconclusive. The ship's visibility depended on too many things—how many other craft were present, what other lights were bouncing, reflecting, shimmering on the surface. They all quietly prayed, or wished, or crossed their fingers inside their pockets . . . taking it on fervent faith that the small fleet of pontoons, airboats, and skiffs above could hide them.

"How's it looking?" Cly asked, taking a sweeping assessment of the room.

Fang signed with one hand: *All ready.*

Deaderick Early was standing by the window, looking out into the swirling mud and dark, dirty water. Without turning around, he said, "We're as ready as we'll ever be."

Cly said, "Then everyone needs to buckle down, if you can. We're pushing out into the water, and we don't know how hard the current's going to take us. Early? I might recommend that you take a seat there at the window, so you can still serve as underwater lookout. We're running low on chairs at the moment, but you've got handholds there."

Wallace Mumler sighed. "Just one more thing we'd like to improve in future models. We don't need for it to be a luxury steamship in here, or anything like that. But it'd be nice to have extra sitting room for the occasional passenger."

Deaderick said, "Agreed, but for now, we'll work with what we've got. Wally, make yourself at home by the low right port, will you?"

"Already on it, sir."

A series of taps on *Ganymede*'s dome sent the message that the folks up top were ready to serve as guides, this crew of Charon's helpmates, paddling, pulling, tapping, and running small diesel motors that sounded awfully loud, but weren't, in the grand scheme of the river's mumblings. Up above, Cly could hear them starting, one by one. The low putter of the motors and the screw propellers from the two or three antique steam engines designed in miniature . . . these noises filtered inside, and in the submarine's belly it all echoed, muted and muffled.

"Turn down the lights as far as you can—but not so far that they

won't do us any good," the captain ordered. Houjin went to one con-
cave wall and threw one set of switches; Wallace Mumler reached up
and grabbed the other set. With the flickering fizz of electrics dimming, the interior dropped to a low, golden glow.

The men in their chairs were shapes and shadows, man-sized
cutouts of utter black in the charcoal gray of this scene, offset against
the wide, bulbous windows that gazed out into the darkness of the
river's underside. But from under the window, the smiling lights
glowed, struggling hard against the silt to provide some guide, some
illumination.

Morse code taps bounced down from above.

"They can see the lights," Deaderick said.

"Yeah, I heard it," Cly acknowledged. "But we're not all the way
under yet. We'll shove off and get some depth, and maybe they
won't be quite so clear. That's what I'm hoping, anyway."

More taps. A quickly sent word of readiness.

Cly took his own seat and strapped himself down. "Engines up,
Fang—don't burn the bottom propeller; we're still right up against
the shore and I don't want to screw us into the bank. Use the side
thrusters above the charge bays. All we need is a nudge."

Fang nodded, and his fingers flew across the levers with their
knobs and buttons so faintly alight that they could barely be
described as such. A hum rose up, accompanied by a curtain of
bubbles that brushed by the edges of the huge forward windows.

"They aren't synched," Cly reminded him. The side thrusters
were made to steer, not propel. There was no mechanism to make
them fire in time with one another.

Fang didn't nod this time. He didn't need to. He needed only to
lean his wrists forward, perfectly in tandem, and with a tiny lurch,
Ganymede pulled itself away from the bank, away from the sunken
winch, and away from the improvised dock at New Sarpy.

Slowly at first, the ship crawled forward. Then, as soon as the
riverbed had dropped away before them, Cly positioned his feet
on the depth pump pedals and began the nerve-racking work of

letting the craft drop, inch by inch, deeper into the river. At the top of the wide forward windows, a small seam of water sloshed outside, at the level where the craft's crown hit surface. This jiggling seam of inky water crept higher and higher, until it was gone.

And at last *Ganymede* dropped below the waves with one gigantic slurp.

They were in the river. There was no air except what they had in the compartment, and what would be pumped down every so often to cycle what they breathed.

It made Cly's skin crawl, and Kirby Troost's, too—the captain could see it when he glanced over at the engineer. Troost looked queasy. One arm over his stomach. One hand over the weakly illuminated dial that showed how far down they'd come, and how much farther they could reasonably go.

Houjin, on the other hand, was vibrating with excitement. They'd stationed him at the mirrorscope he'd liked so much upon first encounter; now it was his job to stay there and report what was coming and going whenever it was safe to leave the tube up in the open air. He turned it side to side, a voyeur to adventure, and the metal tube's joints squeaked despite their fresh greasing.

"What do you see?" Troost asked the boy.

"The other boats—the little ones, the rafts and skimmers. They're moving into place and coming up behind us. Ooh! Norman sees me looking at him! He's waving us forward. . . . He wants us to pull ahead."

"Is there anything or anyone in front of us?"

"No, sir, and I'll say so, if I see something."

"Then here goes," he breathed, and he engaged the back propeller screws. Slowly he toggled their controls. The hum of the engines was not quite loud in their ears, but it felt very close all the same. "Everyone hang on. We're headed into the current."

He gritted his teeth, not knowing what to expect. It might be easy as a cloudless day, or it might be bad as a hailstorm.

The ensuing jolt was a little of both.

Ganymede bobbed forward and was caught very quickly in a full-surface tug as the Mississippi River got a grip on the craft and hurled it forward. The ship swayed, forcing everyone to take hold of whatever handles they could find; Houjin's feet slid out from under him, leaving him hanging by the crook of his elbows from the scope.

But Fang's expert handling of the thrusters soon had the ship aimed steadily downriver, resisting the left and right yanks of the underwater pathways surging beneath the surface, so that it only twitched back and forth instead of swinging out of control.

"This isn't like the lake," Cly complained, wrestling with the foot pedals. "And it ain't like flying."

Kirby Troost, now fully green around the gills, said, "Bullshit, sir. It's the same thing as flying; you just have to find a current and ride it."

"But the currents are all over the place!" he declared. "And I can't see a goddamn thing. . . ."

"Can't up in the sky, either. Find the flow and hold it."

"I'm trying, all right?"

Ganymede dropped precipitously, and bounced up again. Troost said, "Goddamn," and clutched at his mouth.

"Hang in there, Kirby. Hang in there, everybody. I'll find it." He fought with the controls, watching out the forward windows that told him almost nothing about where they were going, or even what direction he was headed. He could feel the river shoving at his back, so he could assume they were headed east and south, since that was the curve and flow of the Mississippi from where they started. "Troost?"

Ominously, he burped. "East-southeast, sir."

"Fang, you're doing great. Keep us from spinning, and I'll get us level," he vowed.

Houjin was once more standing upright, and now he was braced that way with his legs locked. "The bayou boys are catching up to us, sir. They lost us for a minute. We caught a drag," he said, using the slang he'd picked up overnight. "Can you slow down any?"

"Nope."

"Can you . . . I keep losing the view," he warned. "Every time we dip under. I can't adjust this thing in time to keep it steady."

"Not your fault. I'm the one making trouble over here."

"No," Deaderick corrected. "It's the river. She's fighting you. Fight her back, and hold her off."

"I'm *working on it*."

Andan Cly closed his eyes. Looking out through the window into the swirling, sediment-packed void wasn't doing him any good, and the dim red lights of the ship's interior told him only where to put his hands and feet—which he knew already. His hands were primed on the levers. His feet were propped against the pedals that would expel water or draw it into the tanks, changing the underwater "altitude."

Or whatever it was called, there below the waves.

For half a minute he was breathless, considering and reconsidering how absurd this situation was—how impossible, and how bizarre it had become. But in the next half minute, he calmed as he sat there, holding fast to the instruments and feeling the water moving around *Ganymede*—pulling and pushing, urging and demanding, crushing and jostling—and some deep instinct told him not to worry.

It's only water, he told himself. *Only a storm. As above, so below.*

He let instinct move his arms and guide his feet, and he told himself it was only the thrusting power of a hurricane—water below, moving no differently from the air above. It wasn't quite true: the tug was different; the force was different. The weight of the craft was different, too, and it handled more slowly, more heavily.

But it handled. It worked. And soon the craft was stable.

Cly opened his eyes and gazed out through that near-useless window, and saw that Deaderick was standing now, blocking part of the view by looking out into the shimmering, brown-black panorama. In silence, the whole crew stared as the whirling waters went streaking ahead in curls and coils. Fish pirouetted past, their gleaming silver and gray bodies standing out like a flicker of gas lamps as seen from above a city. River-borne driftwood crashed along, smacking the metal exterior, cracking against the window, and spiraling away.

They were within the abyss, and it carried them.

But it did not dash them to bits like the driftwood, or hurl them beyond their abilities.

Houjin whispered, as the moment called for whispering. "Captain, Norman Somers and Rucker Little are caught up, and the other craft are fanning out. They're giving us the signal. They're telling us to go forward."

"Forward. Sure. Here we go. Hey, Mumler, refresh my memory—what's our first refueling stop?"

"We're stopping at Jackson Avenue, near the Quarter, but not right on top of it. There's a ferry stop where we've got enough friends to be left alone and we can still dock without any problems. We'd pick up Josephine closer to home, except we don't want to run into any of the zombis."

"Zombis?" Houjin asked, peeking his head around the side of the visor.

"I'll fill you in later," Cly promised him. "All right, let's go. We know the general course, but not the particulars. Mumler, you're on point. Stick with Kirby; he's got the instruments to tell us where we are, and you've got the know-how to tell us where to go. Me and Fang will keep this thing as steady as we can. Huey, you're our eyes above the water. Tell me if we get out of range, or if we outpace our escorts. And someone's gotta listen for their taps. Kirby?"

"I'll keep my ears peeled for 'em," he said. Troost was the fastest and best at understanding Morse, so it became his job to listen—in addition to the rest of his duties. If indeed he could listen as he wrestled with his digestive situation.

"Good man, Troost. And good on you, keeping everything inside. You'll get your sea legs soon enough. Mumler, what about our air supply? How are we looking?"

"Fine for now," Wallace told him. "We won't need to worry about circulating it for another half hour."

"Somebody keep an eye on a clock."

Mumler said, "That'll be me. I've got my dad's watch. It's as precise as any nautical piece."

"It'd better be. By the time we know we have a problem, it'll be too late—that's what Rucker said."

"And he's right. But we could go closer to an hour without having to worry about it."

"Glad to hear it," the captain said. He flinched as a submerged tree trunk careened toward the window, hit it, and ricocheted away. *"Jesus."*

"The window will hold," promised Mumler. "Don't worry about that. Just keep us moving."

Cly urged the pedals in accordance with the flow, his hands on the levers to manage their rise and fall; Fang worked the other set of controls, the ones that moved the ship from side to side. Between them, *Ganymede*'s trip downriver was not smooth or even graceful, but it was steady, and they neither sank too far nor rose too high.

Out of the corner of Cly's eye, he watched his engineer go green around the gills, and prayed the man wouldn't vomit . . . even as he was forced to admit that the submarine was giving them one hell of a wild ride. "Troost?" he called.

"Yes . . . Captain?"

"You still with us over there?"

"Still here, sir. Hey, Mumler, Early—I've got an idea for an improvement, for the next model."

Deaderick asked, "What would that be?"

"Buckets."

"Huey," said the captain. "How's our escort?"

"Sticking with us, sir. Some of them better than others. The little boats with the little motors are doing best, them and the ones with the big fans."

"Those guys have poles, don't they?"

"They do, Captain. But in this current, with all this movement . . . I don't know. I hope they can keep up."

Cly said, "When we stop at—what was that, Jackson Street?—to pick up Josephine and whoever she brings along, we can have a quick conference with the topside men and see how they're doing."

The *Ganymede* continued half-carried, half-piloted farther down the wide, muddy ribbon of river. Mostly she stayed away from debris, and mostly they stayed satisfactorily submerged, bobbing above the surface only once, and then diving again immediately. No one saw them, though, or if anyone did, no one knew what it was, and no one was alarmed.

Before long—and much sooner than Cly had expected—a loud series of taps on *Ganymede*'s top announced that the time had come to begin angling for the shore, for the hidden dock at Fort Jackson.

"Make for the north bank," Mumler said, and he called out some directional specifics.

"I'm on it," Cly told him. "Fang?"

Fang nodded.

"All right. Here we go. Let's see how well this thing steers when we're not quite running with the current, eh?"

As it turned out, *Ganymede* steered with no great ease—but she responded sufficiently to allow Cly to bring the craft up against the dock with a lot of swearing, a few faltering attempts, and finally, success that broke only one pier piling and splintered a second one. The whole crew considered it a victory that no one had died and no one onshore had been knocked into the river.

As the men outside tethered the vehicle into position, everyone within exhaled deep breaths and stood. An all-clear sounded above, and Houjin scrambled up the ladder to open the hatch. "Hi!" he announced.

"Hi!" responded Rucker Little. "Everyone all right down there?"

"Everybody's fine," Deaderick said in a voice just louder than the one he usually used for speaking. This was not the time to shout.

"How'd it go?" Rucker asked, leaning his head inside past Houjin to take a look around.

Kirby Troost said, "It went. And I've got to go, too, just for a minute. Pardon me," he added, leaving his seat and heading up the ladder. Houjin hopped out of the way, and Rucker retreated to let the engineer exit.

The sounds of retching barely penetrated *Ganymede*'s hull. The gags and heaves were followed by splashes, and no one complained, because Troost throwing up in the river was better than Troost throwing up while they were all trapped inside a sealed compartment with him.

Deaderick went to the ladder and said up the hatch, "While we're stopped, we'll deploy the hose and circulate the air."

"Damn right we will," Cly mumbled. "Fang, get on that, will you?"

Fang stepped to the panel console and released a latch to drop the hose. When a lever was cranked, the hose was pushed through a channel in the hull until it breached the surface.

"I see it," Rucker Little announced. "We'll get it and stick it up firm. Start the generator, and we'll let it run."

"How long will it take?" Cly asked.

"Not long," Deaderick vowed. "We can process everything inside in about two or three minutes, if everything's up to full power."

"Andan?" asked a new voice.

"Josie, that you?"

"It's me, yes." Her face appeared in the open hatch hole. "There you are. Is everything running all right? Everyone . . . everyone doing all right? Other than Troost, I mean. I saw him already."

"Everyone's fine. Everything's fine. What about you, up there?"

"Things have gotten messy out at Barataria, but I think it'll be good for us. Texas will be distracted, and maybe the Confederacy, too."

"Barataria?" he seized on the word, without yet mentioning that they'd agreed to cut toward the canals in order to dodge the Confederate forts. He also did not mention that the canals would take them close to the bay, and close to any messiness that might be going on.

"You heard me," she said. Then she ordered, "Make way."

"What?"

"Get out of my way, Andan. I'm coming down, and I won't have you looking up while I'm doing it."

He almost mumbled something to the effect of, *Nothing I ain't seen before,* but he came to his senses before anything escaped his mouth. Instead he got out of the way as commanded, and stood aside while she descended into the cabin.

"My goodness. Rather warm in here, isn't it?"

"Rather," he agreed, even though he hadn't noticed until she'd pointed it out. "What are you doing in here, huh?"

"Riding along. I'm no good to the men up top; they have enough polers and boatmen. I'll only attract attention that no one wants, so I'm riding down here with you fellows."

"What I mean is why are you riding along at all? I don't get it, Josie. Why don't you stay home where it's warm and dry and . . . safe?"

She lifted an eyebrow. "Practically answered your own question, there, didn't you?" Then she sighed, and said, "I've worked entirely too hard these last few months, planning and plotting, and buying every favor I can scare up to get this damn thing out to the admiral. I'm not going to sit someplace warm and dry and safe while the last of the work gets done. I intend to hand this craft over myself, and shake the admiral's hand when I do so. This was *my* operation, Andan. *Mine.* And I'll see it through to the finish."

A million arguments rose in Cly's mind, but he knew better than to voice any of them. Ignoring all the obvious reasons she ought to stay where she belonged, he said, "All right, then. But you'll have to fight Rick and Wally for a seat. Seats are few and far between on this bird. I mean, this fish."

"I know, and I don't mind."

"Suit yourself."

"I always do."

"I know," he said almost crossly. "Just stay out of the way. And don't forget, *I'm* in charge. If you're in my ship, you follow orders."

"I gave you this ship. Or I got you into it, at any rate."

"But you hired me to pilot it, and if I'm the pilot, I'm in command."

"No one's arguing with you, dear."

Houjin was back at the hatch, delivering a blow-by-blow of what was going on up top. "The hose is sticking out next to the scope. It's pretty quiet, but it's sucking down the air. Can you feel it over there?" he asked in the general direction of the vehicle's far right end.

Wallace Mumler wasn't standing there anymore, so he shrugged. Josephine approached it and waved her hand around the vents beside the unlatched hiding spot where the tube was unspooled. She declared, "I can feel it. It's blowing just fine. Plenty of air's coming in, and since the hatch is open, I can assume we don't need to vent anything."

Mumler told her, "No, ma'am. The level's holding fine—and we aren't moving up or down, so all's well from that end. Give it another minute or two, and we'll head back out."

"Josie, you said something about Barataria. What's going on over there?" he asked. He had an idea, but he wanted to hear something certain. Had it already begun? Had Hank Shanks launched an offensive so quickly—taken it from rumor to action in the span of a few hours?

"Pirates," she confirmed his hopes. "A bunch of them, swarming like bees who've had a rock thrown at their hive. They've mounted a rally, and they're raising hell. Maybe they can't take back the whole bay, but they're bound and determined to reclaim the big island."

"Glad to hear it!" he said with more enthusiasm than he'd meant to.

"Don't get too excited on their behalf just yet. Word out in the Quarter says they've bitten off more than they can chew."

He frowned. "Really? You don't think they can take it back?"

"I don't have any idea. I know precious little about the bay these days, or the people who inhabit it. Besides, there's a curfew—hadn't you heard? The chain of gossip would run a little smoother if the goddamn Texians hadn't been shutting down the Quarter." As she said the part about the *goddamn Texians,* a strange look crossed her face. Like she was reconsidering something, or reevaluating it. But she continued, "The important thing is, it's good news for us."

"You think?"

"The Rebs at the forts will almost certainly head out to help Texas, so the way downriver will be clearer than it might have been otherwise. Fewer eyes watching, and even if anyone sees us, it'll take them half of forever to recall their forces. We'll be in the middle of the Gulf by the time they can rally any response."

Cly turned away from her, revisiting his seat at the captain's chair. "This is all worth knowing, but there's been a change of plans. We're stopping at one of the canals. We're cutting through it down to the . . ." He trailed off.

Fang shot Cly a look that no one on earth but the captain could've read. The look was fleshed out by a smattering of signing. *You'd better lie to her.*

And until that moment, Cly hadn't even realized that this had been his plan all along. It was as if he'd been deluding himself so successfully that the truth hadn't dawned on him until he was confronted with adjusting it. But this *had* been the plan, hadn't it? Ever since he'd first heard that the bay had been taken, and that his fellow unlicensed tradesmen were planning to take it back.

Fang didn't blink, and didn't look away.

Cly returned his attention to Josephine and said, a bit too brightly, "Anyway, plans are made to be adjusted, aren't they? We'll work it out as we get farther downriver. We'll have to stop in the canal's general vicinity to top off our air and fuel supply, anyway. From there, we'll see how it goes."

"Andan, I don't like—"

He interrupted before she could go on fretting about protocol. "We're sitting inside an advanced military machine like nothing the world has ever known. This thing is armored from top to bottom, and it's armed to start a war, or stop one. This is just a detour. Nothing's going to slow us down."

She frowned and gently bit her lower lip, an old habit of hers that Cly had forgotten until he watched her do it again. It made her look younger, or maybe it only reminded him of when they both were young. "If you understood exactly what I'd risked, what I'd compromised to bring this about—"

"It wouldn't change a thing," he assured her. "You did such a great job that the rest of this will be smooth sailing. The hard part's already out of the way." He approached her and put his hands on her shoulders, forcing her to look up at him.

She did, and she told him, "Maybe you're right, but we won't know until it's over and we're on board the *Valiant*. But I hope we get to stand on that deck, so I can turn to you and tell you that you were right all along. Just get us there, Andan. Get this craft to the Gulf. I don't care what it takes, and we are *not* taking the canal."

"Stop worrying." He might've said more, but Troost came back down the hatch. Shortly behind him came Deaderick Early, moving slowly but resolutely.

Josephine extricated herself from the almost-embrace and went to her brother, about whom she was still allowed to worry. "Rick, you're not looking well."

"I'm getting stiff as I heal up, that's all. You worry too much."

Cly let out a laugh that sounded like a cough, and changed the subject before she could accuse them of ganging up on her. "Everyone get back to your places. Josephine, find someplace where you can hold on—this thing jumps and dives like an otter. Someone turn off that generator, if we have the air to keep us alert and alive for the next run?"

"All right," Troost said. He looked less ill, but still not altogether well. He went to the generator switch and turned it off, then pulled the lever to retract the air circulation hose. "Where's Mumler?" he asked.

"Right here," Mumler announced himself as he came down the ladder. "Is this everyone?"

"Looks like it," Cly confirmed.

"Then I'll close up the hatch and call us ready to set sail. Or set screws, or start charges, or whatever this thing does. Goddamn," he grunted, as he turned the wheel to seal them all inside. "They'll need to invent a whole new lingo for boats like this."

Josephine stood in front of the window beside her brother. She appeared to be transfixed by the scenery, dark, swirling, and largely undecipherable though it was. "I'm sure sailors the world over will be up to the task. Or airmen," she amended the sentiment, flashing Cly a look of honest gratitude that gave him a pang of guilt.

He already knew that this wasn't about to go as smoothly as she'd hoped. He didn't have any intention of telling her while there was still some trouble she could make about it, and he didn't yet know how Deaderick or Mumler would handle the news that their detour at the canal would be more extensive than expected, so he didn't say anything about it yet.

For the moment, though, he didn't have to. He only had to get *Ganymede* back into the river and as far as the canal. What he'd told Josephine off the top of his head was correct: It couldn't go much farther than the canal without needing its air circulated anyway, so it was a good excuse to pull over when the right place was located.

When all was in order once more, the craft shoved off, its propulsion screws churning at the rear, and the ballasting fins and pumps all working in accordance with the hands and feet of Cly and Fang. Troost called out degrees and directions, helping to adjust their course. Mumler kept an eye on his watch, Houjin kept his eyes plastered to the visor scope, and Josephine kept an eye on her brother—who watched his own reflection in the window, since there was little to be seen on the other side of it except for the black vortex of the river at night.

This time the launch was easier, and better controlled. *Ganymede* dipped hard only once, and swung left to right like a dog shaking its head for only a few seconds before Fang was able to steady it.

Josephine gasped and clutched at the wall, then sat down along it, only to stand again when the peril was past.

"It was worse the first time," Troost assured her. A small burp escaped his lips, but whatever else was tempted to come up stayed down.

"You've got it under control now, though, don't you?" Anxiously she regarded Cly, who nodded and cocked his head toward Fang, who did the same.

"Don't worry about it, Miss Josephine!" Houjin chirped. "They're getting the hang of it!"

In approximately half an hour, much to Cly's relief on several levels, the offshoot to the canal came within spotting distance on Houjin's scope. He announced, "Port Sulphur is dead ahead, up on the right."

"Veer eight degrees south," Troost called.

As if she already suspected something was amiss, Josephine said, "Wait. But we decided we weren't taking the canal. There's too much trouble out at the bay. We'd already decided."

Cly almost fell into a very old pattern of explaining that *we* had not decided anything; *she* had decided something, and that was not the same as a consensus. But he didn't. Instead he said, "We have to run the air tube up, Josie. May as well pull over where it's safe, or safer than any old spot along the river."

A series of taps up topside announced that their escorts either hadn't gotten the message about Josephine's decision, or they were prepared to ignore it in favor of a good docking spot. Either way, the tapping against the hull by the poling boaters backed up Cly's assertion that they were, in fact, stopping.

"I don't like this," she said.

"Sorry. But I like having fresh air to breathe, and the rest of these fellows do, too. We're stopping, Josie. We're putting up the air hose, and we're freshening up, and then we're headed back out again. I'll get you to the Gulf, I swear to God. But you're going to have to trust me, just this once."

Fourteen

Josephine fumed to herself about the stopping point, but there was little to be done about it. The captain had made his decision, and the crew was willing to go along with it; so nothing she could add or argue would mean anything to any of them.

Never mind that this was *her* operation to start with. She was the one who'd arranged it, top to bottom. He had no right to overrule her.

It wasn't that Cly was wrong. He was absolutely correct, and the air should be circulated on the half hour, as prescribed by the engineers. It was his insistence on being in charge, and the infuriating way that *this* stop—this one hidden docking spot, of all the hidden docking spots on the full expanse of the Mississippi—was the one closest to the greatest threat.

Josephine hated few things more than changing a set plan, and her plan had changed all over the place. No one had asked *her* if she thought a stop at the canal was a good idea. And now no one would listen when she told them there were better places, safer places, and that their change of plan must absolutely be reversed for the sake of the entire operation.

But what would she know, anyway? She was only the one who ought to be in charge.

While the men behind her unhitched the air hose and sent it chattering on the reel up through the water and into the open air, she climbed the ladder in order to take her foul mood outside, rather than risk being accused of being difficult, or in the way. The first man to broach either of those ideas would find himself missing teeth.

She wrenched the hatch's wheel, and her ears popped when the seal did. She poked her head out and immediately spotted Rucker Little, who had scrambled over to *Ganymede* first. He stood knee-deep in the water, hanging off the rotted and disused pier while preparing to knock upon the hull to get the attention of those inside.

"Everything still good in there?"

"Sure," she said. "They're running the air tubes up now, and starting the generator."

Behind her, something loud but far away cracked—and a warm yellow light bloomed in the distance. When she turned to get a better look, the glow of the far-off explosion revealed a small fleet of airships above the bay.

Even from this far away, Josephine could see that it was a motley, unofficial crew of ne'er-do-wells and pirates who occupied much of the sky. Their ships were not the uniform, predictable shapes of the Texian air brigades. The pirate craft were hodge-podged pieces of foreign ships and augmented weaponry. They were black and red, and trimmed with silver paints or flying their respective flags—not national flags, for there was no such thing among men who worked outside the law.

They flew the flags of the defiant.

They lifted their colors emblazoned with skeletons, skulls, and old-fashioned sabers, and they moved not in tidy ranks and rows, or with military discipline. They swarmed like hornets instead, menacing and independent of one another—yet everyone knew who was an ally, and who was a target.

Antiaircraft missiles blazed up from around the big island in the bay. They rose in a smattering of rockets that streaked from land to clouds, crashing and exploding against anything they hit. One illicit ship took a direct blow to its underside and began to spin—

slowly at first, and then faster as it toppled out of the sky, exploding into a vivid white nova long before it hit the ground. The fire from its demise set several flags ablaze, Texian and pirate alike, and forced the ships that were fighting too close to withdraw, and regroup, and reconsider.

Josephine didn't realize that her mouth had been hanging open as she watched, and she didn't notice that she'd forgotten Rucker was behind her, until he spoke. "They're losing, Josephine. Barataria's just one more piece of Louisiana that Texas will hold."

"How do you know that?" she asked without taking her eyes off the sky.

"The air pirates can only fly, and Texas has men on the air, on the ground, and in the water, too."

"In the water?"

He told her, "They've taken patrol boats and moved them around the blocking islands at the mouth of the bay. Their other boats were too big to make it through. But those patrols—they're small and sturdy enough to hold the antiaircraft guns. Texas can shoot from a dozen places at once, in every direction. Airships can't compete with that. They move too slowly, in quarters as close as that airspace."

Finally she faced him. "You're telling me all this like you think we should do something about it."

Rucker didn't answer. He only watched over her shoulder as the bay caught fire in fits and starts, and was extinguished, and was fired upon once more. "I don't think Texas deserves the bay any more than it deserves any other part of New Orleans. And the pirates . . . they saved your brother, took him into the fort when they could've left him out to die."

"We can't risk the detour."

"I didn't say we could."

"But you're thinking about it," she accused.

"Sure, I'm thinking about it. And if you think those men piloting this crazy craft haven't thought about it, then you're so focused on your goal that you can't see what's going on around you. They're pirates, too, Josephine. And before you curse them and their breed, just remember: *you're* the one who picked them."

"We're going on to the Gulf from here. Down the river, while Texas and the Rebs are distracted by the bay."

"I wouldn't be too sure of that, if I were you."

"What's that supposed to mean?"

From below, Cly called, "Josephine? You can see it up there, can't you? The rockets' red glare? We can hear it, down here."

She could, yes. And it stunned her, both the beauty and the violence of it. She had no great love for the bay or the pirates, but they were better than the Texians, weren't they? At least, they'd never occupied her Quarter, or closed down the streets she walked upon, or forced her to pay the taxes that kept them squatting on her city like a juicy, venomous toad.

"Rucker?" Cly saw the man's face in the hatch opening.

"Captain?"

"We can help them, can't we?"

"In this thing?" Rucker cleared his throat and spit over the side, into the river. "You could knock down the patrol boats one-two-three. Fish in a barrel, and they'd never see you coming. They'd never know what hit 'em."

"It's the right thing to do," Cly said, to Josephine more than to Rucker.

He already knew what the man up top was thinking. He could hear it in the tone of Little's voice, in the odd longing to see an old enemy routed—if not from the whole of the delta, then maybe from just this one small place. Maybe this one bay, this one island, which no one deserved to hold or keep, except the men who'd made it what it was.

From within, behind Cly, Josephine heard her brother—that traitorous devil. "Josephine, we could knock around the bay and cut past it to the south, right out into the Gulf. It's a shortcut, really."

Josephine growled and clenched her hands around the ladder's rungs, then gave up and dropped herself down inside to face the two men who now were directly allied against her. A brother and an old lover—aligned in opposition to the woman who'd made this whole venture possible. If only they understood the depths of their treachery . . . .

Then again, the looks on their faces said they understood just fine, and were willing to risk it.

Cly had made her angry once or twice before, and he thought he remembered how best to engage her. "Once the air finishes circulating, we'll have time to hit the bay and run reconnaissance around the island. We'll take down the patrol boats, and—"

"How did you know about the patrols?" she demanded, looking back and forth between the two men.

Kirby Troost, behind her and seated, and still looking none too healthy . . . cleared his throat. He told her, "Ma'am, I know some people, that's all. They told me it was coming, and what to expect. The pirates have been working on it for the last couple of days, sorting out the details. It wasn't so hard to learn."

When Josephine looked to Cly for an explanation, he shrugged. "I don't know how Troost does it. He just *does*. He always knows first, like he's got a set of taps between his ears. But he's never wrong, and he hasn't swindled me yet, so I follow his lead when he says he knows something. That's not the point, Josie. The point is, we can take the canal and save ourselves a few miles to the Gulf. And while we're at it, we can help keep one small parcel of Louisiana free of Texas rule. That's something, isn't it?"

She was on the verge of arguing, perhaps violently, when Deaderick chimed in. "More importantly, it'll give us a chance to test the weapons systems," he said quickly, understanding that Cly's cajoling would not work, and that perhaps the captain had never known her as well as he'd thought. "We didn't have the space or the privacy to fire off charges in Pontchartrain, and we didn't have anything to shoot at except the alligators, anyway. The admiral wants a full write-up of *Ganymede*'s capabilities, don't he? How are you going to give him that full report, when you don't even know if she can shoot worth a damn?"

She paused, uncertain of how to grant the point, yet still insist that it shouldn't delay them. "But the weapons systems have never been called into question. It's just the . . . the propulsion and steering, and the air circulation we've been asked to prove."

Her brother shook his head. "The Union doesn't need an underwater cruiser, Josie. It needs a war machine. And unless you can vouch for this bucket's ability to blow things out of the water, you're only handing over a curiosity. If we can show up at the *Valiant* with firsthand accounts of how well it thwarted Texas from the water, then you'll have something to lift their eyebrows."

"I fail to see how *merely* delivering a working, war-ready submarine can fail to lift eyebrows!"

"But you don't want to just lift them, do you?" Cly asked. "You want to shock the hell out of them, and inspire them to make more of these things. You're asking the North to make an investment, to speculate—and they may not believe it if we don't have the chance to prove it."

Josephine paused, closed her eyes, and thought hard. Finally, she said, "I don't like this."

"No one's asking you to like it," Cly told her. "We're only asking you to ride along with us and keep score."

"You're not asking my permission, either."

It was Cly's turn to hesitate. "If Deaderick and you, and all these other fellows up top . . . if everyone said no, then I wouldn't force the matter. But these men see it just as clear as I do. I don't give a damn if this thing lifts any Union eyebrows or not; I just want to head over to that bay and blow up some Texian boats."

He did not add that "forcing the matter" was hardly the point, given that he wasn't certain he could pilot the thing without help from up above—at least until they reached the Gulf, where he could break the surface to navigate by good old-fashioned reckoning and the stars. Of course, he might have been able to strong-arm

Deaderick and Mumler, especially with Fang and Troost behind him. But he'd seen the look in Deaderick's eyes as the hatch opened and the sounds of battle from the bay pinged and echoed down into the *Ganymede*'s belly. Cly knew that look. It was the look of a man who hears a fight and wants to join it. After all, the pirates had helped the guerrillas when Texas attacked; and after Deaderick's injury, they'd taken him down to the fort and hidden him, and summoned the drunken doctor. It hadn't been world-class service, but the rogues and rebels of Lafitte's last command had done as right by Deaderick as they'd been able.

So it might've been just that simple; Cly didn't know, and he didn't ask. All he cared about was having an ally against Josephine, who could be harder to move than an old stone church.

Josephine's hands were closing into fists and releasing again, in time with her breathing. She was hovering between agreeing and disagreeing—knowing she was outnumbered and could be over-powered. She would've fought Cly alone, absolutely. She would've fought her brother alone, without a second thought. She might even have taken on the pair of them if she were truly confident that she was correct.

But it wasn't just them.

It was them, and Wallace Mumler—who'd been suspiciously silent this whole time; and Rucker Little up above, who'd broached the subject first; and here came Ruthie Doniker, all but leaping down the hatch in a swishing, rustling tornado of skirts and hair-pins and fury.

In her way, Ruthie was the final straw.

Breathless, she came to Josephine and said, "Ma'am, you should see it outside!"

"I *did* see it, Ruthie."

"The rockets, the antiaircraft! Texas wants to wipe the bay off the maps! Wash it into the ocean!"

"I've seen it, Ruthie."

"Well?" The younger woman stood, nearly panting with rage,

excitement, and something else. Anticipation? "Are you going to let them? When you have these men, and this machine, right here? So close, you could practically shoot them from where we're docked? You're going to let Texas keep the bay?"

Josephine opened her hands and used them to smooth the pockets on her skirts. She sighed and said, "It sounds like you've made up your mind, too. You've already decided how you want to see this go."

As if she'd only now noticed Josephine's ambivalence, Ruthie's jaw dropped. In French this time, she asked, "And you *haven't*? You would let the pirates burn, though they saved your brother, when you could help? My God, what would Lafitte say?"

"From his grave? Not much," Josephine replied. Then, in English, to everyone present, "So the decision has been made. There's nothing I can say to change anyone's mind, is there? I want to get to the Gulf. You want to rescue the pirates."

Deaderick said, "No, we want to rescue the *bay,* if we can."

"We'll still need someone up top. Someone to help us squeeze past the islands at the mouth of the bay, when it's time to leave it," Mumler told them. "We can't have the whole caravan accompanying us, not into the middle of a battle. But two or three of the small motored boats . . . Houjin, you said those were keeping up the best, isn't that right?"

"That's right, sir." Houjin nodded vigorously. "But they'll be wide open. Exposed. They might get shot."

Mumler shifted his shoulders and said, "Any one of us might get shot at any time. Rick, if you stay down here with these folks, I'll join Rucker or Chester up topside. We can take the two lightest of the diesel motors and guide you around. Ruthie? Can you take my place here? Between me and Rick, we've showed you the ropes enough so you can fire and reload all the charges."

"*Oui,* my dear. I will stay."

Kirby Troost sniffed. "Used to be, folks considered it bad luck to have a lady on board a boat."

"To hell with what used to be," Ruthie spit. "Josephine and I will ride with you, and I will show you what luck we'll turn out to be, you hear me?"

"Everybody stop fighting, all right?" Cly demanded. "How's that air circulation going?"

Houjin responded. "Ready to retract and seal up. We can go again as soon as we spool the hose back inside."

Cly took a deep breath. "You heard the kid. Rucker, you hear me up there?"

"Sure do, Captain."

"Mumler's coming up. He'll explain the situation."

"Are we headed for the bay or the Gulf?"

"Both," Cly told him, and turned to reclaim the captain's seat without looking at Josephine. "We're going to do both."

Rucker said, "All right, then. Listen, if for some reason you lose us: Once you get to the bay, head due south and you'll hit the bottleneck between Grande Terre and Grande Isle. We'll catch up to you there if we lose you in the fray—or if we have to run for cover."

"Got it."

"I don't like this," Josephine murmured.

Ruthie took her arm. In French, she said, "Like it, don't like it. This is the right thing, *madame*. We will be in the Gulf within an hour or two, but first, we will save this one piece of New Orleans. We will save it, and the men who saved your brother. He owes them a debt, and so he wishes to lend them aid. And *you* owe them a debt, because you love Deaderick."

"And what of you, then, darling?" Josephine asked, allowing herself to be led back to the spot where she'd waited out the trip so far, beneath the great windows and holding on to a seam that served as a handrail. "What do you owe them, that you're so eager to rush into trouble?"

"It's obvious, isn't it?"

"Yes, I suppose it is."

"Nothing may ever come of it," she said sadly. "I am not his kind, but that makes my debt to the pirates no less true."

Cly was giving orders, and the men were buckling down where they could, and settling in where they couldn't. Deaderick came to sit beside his sister, at least for this beginning part—the moments when the air hose was retracted and the craft was sealed, when the propulsion screws churned to life and the craft shoved itself into the canal. Those first seconds had been the worst so far, and they were bad again this time, too—worse, perhaps, due to a brief and violent clip against a sunken stone piling that marked the old entrance to the canal.

Ganymede scraped against it and squeaked around it, pivoting and righting itself. Cly followed the frantic taps from Rucker and Wally above, though the men had not been able to warn the captain in time to let him avoid the obstacle altogether.

"It's mostly sunken," Cly griped. "They ought to clean out this damn canal once in a while."

"Left over from some other construction project, I'm sure," Deaderick observed, his voice only slightly shaky. The impact and the unexpected turn had unnerved him as much as anyone, and the truth was that no one knew for certain how much damage *Ganymede* could take before springing a leak or becoming stuck.

"We'll have to be more careful on the way down this ridiculous creek, won't we, Houjin?"

"I couldn't see whatever we hit, captain!"

"I know you couldn't, and I'm not accusing you of messing up. I'm just saying, keep your eyes open. Let us know what you're spying up on the banks. Help me keep us moving in a straight line."

"This canal . . . I don't even know if it's wide enough to take us," Josephine breathed.

"It's wide enough, all right," her brother said. "It'll take us, but it's like Cly said. Got to be careful."

Everyone fell silent as the captain and first mate navigated the dark, warm waters of the narrow canal; and in the midst of this silence, when all the conversation had dried up out of anxiousness or concentration, all the other small sounds were amplified. The pinging of sticks, rocks, and the shoving feet of canal creatures sounded like stomping soldiers. The twist and squeak of the mirror-scope under Houjin's direction seemed to scream, and the pops of levers at Cly's feet were as hearty as gunshots in the confined space, with its rounded walls and nervous passengers.

The water wasn't so rough, there in the sheltered space between the two man-made walls that kept the waters moving but kept them contained as well. The ride was smoother going—and the darkness beyond the windows was even more complete, now that the shadows of the canal conspired with the late-night sky to shroud the whole scene in terrible blindness.

The tiny lights that lit the front windows like a weak little smile did virtually nothing to show the way. They showed only sediment and trash, wagon wheels and the bones of dead things tossed into the canal and forgotten. Some of the bones were large, and Cly thought maybe they'd once belonged to horses. But some of the carcasses looked more like fish—with spiny, needly ribs and flattened skulls that jutted out from the canal bed like tombstones.

"Like tombstones." The words slipped out of his mouth.

"Those bones?" Kirby asked. "They do look it, don't they? It feels like swimming through a graveyard. What the hell once had a head like that, anyway?"

Deaderick answered, "Catfish. They grow as long as they eat, and they eat until they die. Sometimes they get bigger than you'd believe."

Cly breathed, "Jesus," and steered them up a few feet more, so that the bottom was not quite so near, but they were still below the surface.

Houjin adjusted the height of the scope and called out directions whenever they were appropriate. "You're veering left, sir." Or sometimes, "You're veering right, too close to the sides. Keep us in the middle."

"I'm working on it," the captain said. He might've said more, except that they all heard a wide, muffled *pop* that made them look up out of pure habit, despite the fact that none of them could see a thing except for the dull gray rivets that ran along the ceiling.

Ruthie's eyes blazed out the front windows, though she could only see a reflection of herself, and of the rest of the cabin area with its dull gold lights. "We must be getting close," she whispered.

"Sounds like it," Deaderick agreed, taking her hand and squeezing it.

She squeezed back. "I should get to the charges, to the side bays."

"Ruthie." Josephine climbed to her feet and extended a hand to her friend. "I'll come with you. Teach me whatever I don't know, and can't figure out."

"Yes, ma'am. This way. The charges must be prepared before we can fire them. I can show you how to load them."

Deaderick also rose, saying, "I can man the top guns, if we have to launch them."

Houjin frowned around the side of the scope's visor. "We have top guns?"

"There's a mount behind your scope and to the left. You enter it from the room at the rear, just aft of the ballasting tanks. But we don't want to get too trigger-happy with them, not until we're up close and personal. Or until they've already seen us anyway, and there's no more use in keeping a low profile."

"All right. Troost, once we get out into the bay, you might be better served to help the women hoist the charges."

"Josephine's bigger than I am, sir. I doubt I can lift too much more than she can."

"But they'll need to reload quickly—and a pair of extra hands will be helpful, given how heavy those damn things are." Cly knew from his afternoon of training at Pontchartrain, because he'd helped load them onto the *Ganymede* in preparation for moving it out of the lake.

Before the craft had been sealed up and dropped onto the platforms that carried it to New Sarpy, the bayou boys had packed *Ganymede* chock-full of every bit of ammunition that had ever been created for it. Mostly it used a modified charge stuffed inside a bullet-shaped casing about the size of a picnic basket. These casings were slotted into a chute, their powders packed and fuses lit, their back ends sealed off with a hammering slam from the chute door . . . and then they were closed into an exterior compartment and fired straight out of the submarine's lower right hull. If all went as planned, one of two things would happen: either the charge would explode upon connecting with its target, or it would lodge within the target and explode shortly thereafter.

"Sir, how do we know these charges are any good?" Troost asked. "How long have they been sitting around? And will the damn things explode underwater?"

"I don't know."

Deaderick filled him in. "We didn't test many of them. They're too valuable to waste."

Cly said, "I bet the Union won't feel like we're wasting them, if we're using them to shoot down Texians."

"I daresay they'll consider it ammunition well spent," Deaderick said. "Assuming it works."

"Let's go ahead and assume the best for now. If what we've got won't burn or blow, we can reconsider our high-and-mighty plans to rush in and save the day," the captain informed them.

Another blast occurred somewhere overhead, out of the water, up in the sky. This one was particularly loud, and so bright it made Houjin cry out and yank his eyes away from the scope.

"Sir!" he said. "Take us a lower, and do it now!"

"You want me to swamp your scope?"

"Now!"

"All right, kid," he said, and he worked his foot to change their depth until everything—including the oscillating scope—was withdrawn back under the waves. "What's going on up there? Talk to me, Huey."

"Dirigible, incoming. Coming down fast, hard, and on fire," he announced.

"Coming down on top of us?"

"Close enough as makes no difference!"

Deaderick stiffened in alarm. "What about Rucker and Wally?"

"Last I saw, they pulled a hard reverse and they're getting out of the way. I don't think they'll be cut off from us, but we might have to lose them for a few minutes."

A splashing crash shook the liquid volume of the canal, throwing *Ganymede* to the right and shoving it upward. The top of the window briefly breached the surface again, before diving back below in a sudden sinking that Cly struggled to control.

"Goddamn!" Deaderick Early cursed, pointing out the window where the wreckage of something huge was coming down in pieces, still burning and bubbling, and giving the whole canal the brilliant flickering glow of a fishbowl in front of a candle.

"Troost?"

"Rev it up and gun it, sir. That's my advice!"

"I like the way you think," Cly said gruffly, and pushed hard on the lever that powered the propulsion screws. "I just wish we could see where the damn thing above us was crashing, exactly."

The engineer clutched the sides of his console as *Ganymede* surged and wobbled forward, quivering in its path. Eventually Fang got a handle on the new speed and could keep it steady once more.

Troost was not quite shrill when he barked a sudden complaint, "It's right on top of us!"

"Settle down, Kirby. We're almost past it, I think."

Something huge squashed down on top of *Ganymede*'s hull. The resulting ruckus threw Deaderick to the floor, cast Troost out of his seat and sent him careening into the wall, and elicited a pained shout from the bays where the charges were being prepared and loaded.

Houjin fell off his seat and spun around, holding the scope for support, then clamored back into position.

"Huey, get a grip on something! Hang on!"

"Sir, we need to see outside!" he shouted, and turned the crank to raise it. "I can help, if I can see!"

Cly's knuckles were white and going numb from his death grip on the levers, but he hadn't lost his seat yet. "Everyone all right?" he cried. "Everyone?" he said again when no one responded fast enough.

"I'll live," Troost groused as he crawled back over to his chair. Cly gave him a quick look and saw no blood, and no broken bones.

Houjin announced, "I'm fine, sir—and I can see it. Part of it hit us."

"Are we high enough for you to get that scope out of the water? How can you see a damn thing?"

"No, sir, it's underwater, but I can see the hull of something big—it landed halfway on us, and halfway on the canal's edge. We scooted out from under it. We're fine. Just get us up and moving."

"I'll take you at your word, kid."

"I'm not saying there isn't more debris, because there is."

"I'll take that under advisement. Hey, ladies? You all right in there? I heard a scream?"

Josephine replied, "We'll be fine, I'm sure—you just get us to the Gulf."

Cly didn't like the sound of that. Deaderick didn't either, but Cly barked, "Early, you know how to keep this in a straight line, for a few minutes?"

"I can if I have to. I think—?"

"Get over here and take my seat," he said. As Deaderick approached, Cly cut the thrust to the screws and *Ganymede*'s progress slowed to the proverbial crawl. "Hold her steady, will you? We'll give your men up top a chance to catch up."

"I'll give it a shot."

"I have every faith . . . ," he said, abandoning his position to Early as soon as the other man was able to take it. "Josephine? Ruthie?" he called as he approached them, ducking low and swinging himself through the portal-shaped doorway that separated the main control deck from the side bay where the charges were kept and readied.

"Cly, give us a minute—we'll be fine," Jo said with caution and control in her voice, not yet realizing that he was already there, in the room with her. She was bent over Ruthie, who was moaning unhappily on the ground, holding on to her head. "Andan! Get back to your seat! She knocked her head, that's all. She's not hurt bad, and she'll be up again shortly."

"Thank you . . . for your worry, Captain," Ruthie told him, giving him a look that dared him to come and assist her. But Cly was the sort to take a dare, so he went to her other side—the one Josephine didn't occupy—and slipped an arm underneath her to lift her up.

"Andan, don't!" Josephine was firm now, commanding. "Let her be!"

He ignored her. "Ruthie, you all right? What happened?"

"No, don't—," she begged. "I've torn my dress. It caught on the charge launch door. . . ."

Too late. He used his long arms and considerable strength to sweep her gently onto her feet and place her in a seated position on the edge of the chute.

At this point, he realized that she was right—her dress *was* torn.

The outer skirt was ripped away like an apron pulled off a doll, leaving only light cotton undergarments between her and the world. She did not quite swoon, though she was clearly in some pain from a lump rising on her forehead; nonetheless, she struggled to collect the torn fabric and cover herself.

But in the instant between Ruthie being covered and uncovered, the undergarments had been her only shield, and they had not covered nearly enough. And in that brief occasion, many things occurred to Cly at once, chief among them being precisely why Ruthie Doniker, popular whore, had such a fierce desire to keep herself covered—there inside the *Ganymede,* where at least half her companions were unaware of a secret that surely couldn't have been much of a secret.

It blindsided Cly all the same.

Astonished, he turned to Josephine as if seeking some

explanation—but all he found was the barrel of a gun pointed at his face.

Over the barrel he saw Josephine's eyes, and they were harder and colder than an iceberg. Quietly she told him. "Do not say a word."

"But . . ."

"That's a word, Andan."

He whispered, lest he alert anyone in the other room. "You're not going to shoot me, Josie."

"I might."

"For . . . for . . . ?" He bobbed his chin toward Ruthie, who would've rendered him dead on the spot if looks could do such things.

"For Ruthie, yes. And for the Garden Court, where she is adored by a good number of people, all of whom would prefer to have their privacy protected. I guarantee that privacy, Andan. And I won't let anyone ruin it."

"You're not going to shoot me, Josie," he said again, still so softly that no one could've heard it over the rumble of the engines and the clatter of debris still raining slowly down upon the hull from the burning crafts above them and, increasingly, behind them.

"You're right." She lowered the gun and uncocked it. "Because you're probably not the type to go running off at the mouth about things that are no business of yours. Unless something's changed since we last knew each other well."

Slowly he said, "No, no. That hasn't changed." He looked away from his old lover and down at Ruthie again, who was still glaring at him. But somewhere under her glare he saw the source of her anger, and it wasn't an impinged-upon sense of propriety.

It was fear.

Still speaking in increments, every word that emerged cloaked in quiet, and confusion, he said, "But she's . . . she's not . . . she's not a *she.*"

Josephine brought the gun up again. Maybe not to shoot. Maybe to make a point. She lifted it and aimed it at Cly as if holding it gave her some power she otherwise lacked—and maybe it did. "*She is one of my ladies,* Andan. And if I ever hear you say a word to the contrary, even *implying* anything to the contrary, I swear to God, you will regret it to the end of your days."

Then she turned the gun away from his face and stuck it back under her skirt, in the leg holster he'd all but forgotten she sometimes wore.

Still pondering a hundred different questions raised by the contents of Ruthie Doniker's undergarments, Cly stood there stupidly, gazing back and forth between them. Finally he mustered the gumption to ask, "So . . . people. Men, I mean. They know?"

"Of course they know!" Josephine whispered. "And if you think she's the only woman in the world with a secret like hers, you're an idiot. But not *every* man, *every*where knows. It's not the kind of thing everyone understands."

"*I* don't understand."

"I know you don't. But I don't believe you're the kind of man to go on a holy rampage about it, either. You've always lived and let live, Andan, and I hope that's still the case. I'd hate to have to shoot you in order to shut you up."

"No one has to shoot me. I'm shocked silent, anyhow."

"Good," she told him. "And you damn well better stay that way. Nothing you've just now learned, seen, or figured out means a damn thing to what we're trying to do here. Now, get back to your seat and get this ship back up in the water. Who'd you leave in charge?"

"Your brother."

"Go relieve him. We'll sort out this ammunition over here, like I said we would."

"Sure," he said. Then, with one more look at Ruthie, he asked, "Are you . . . are you going to be all right?"

"All I need is a safety pin or two, *et c'est tout,*" Ruthie said through her teeth.

"Josie, do you have one?"

"Of course I do. Get back out there," Josephine said in her normal speaking voice, not wanting to draw any further attention. Surely the men in the other room were wondering by now, why it had gone so quiet in the charge bays.

"All right, then, I *will*."

Fifteen

The remainder of the trip down the canal occurred without incident. According to Houjin, both Rucker Little and Wallace Mumler were gaining ground. Neither man had been injured or otherwise dispatched when the dirigible fell from the sky—whether Texian or pirate, no one knew—and though their escorts had fallen behind, they'd signaled that they'd catch up.

Cly had fallen utterly quiet upon retaking his seat from a grateful Deaderick Early, who was finding the navigation more than he knew how to accomplish, except in a theoretical way.

The women in the charge bay resumed their work. The clanks and heavy thuds of crates and shells echoed from time to time, punctuated intermittently by swearing in French and English. Troost temporarily left his post to lend a hand, but he was told that no extra hands were needed, so he resumed his seat and kept watch on the coordinates.

Everyone listened, and everyone heard how much louder the atmosphere outside was steadily becoming. Occasional artillery booms escalated to near-constant racket and there were regular hearty bangs of airship pieces raining down from the sky. Some of them splashed and sank, drifting back and forth and downward in front of the big window; some clattered against the hull, none of them hitting very hard.

Not yet. Not while several feet of water still separated that hull from the open air above.

Houjin whistled at something only he could see, sounding impressed and antsy. "It's a good thing we're swimming at night," he mused. "All those ships up there, wow. During the day, someone would be bound to see us."

"How many ships, Huey?" Troost asked.

"Hard to say, exactly."

"Guess," Cly urged him.

"Guessing?" The boy chewed on his lower lip and concentrated, spinning the visor scope this way and that, adjusting its cranks for a better range of vision. "At least four big Texas ships. The real big kind, like warships up in the sky. They're armored up good, and that's a relief. Anything that big carries enough hydrogen to blow a bay sky-high."

The captain said, "That's a start. Four big Texas ships, at least. What else do you see?"

"Pirates. Lots of them. I see two Chinese fliers, and maybe a third. A couple of French ships, it looks like—maybe more than that. A few Spanish ships, or things that started out Spanish. And is that . . . is that . . . ?"

"Is it *what,* kid?" Troost asked crossly.

"Indian ships. Three of them—two Comanche, if I read the flags right."

"I'll be damned," Cly said.

Deaderick laughed, utterly unsurprised. "The Comanche beef with Texas is as fair as anybody else's."

"I just don't know too many Indian pirates, that's all," he replied. "But I'm glad to see them. Huey, what else is up there?"

"A couple of Union cruisers, I think." He made small, pensive noises while he adjusted the scope. "And on top of all that, maybe six or seven others I can't place. They could be from anywhere, but they're pretty clearly ours. Unfortunately, most of the ones in the water are, too."

"How many are down?"

"Can't tell, sir. But there's fire on the water, and burning trash floating between here and there. A lot of it. I'd guess half a dozen ships still floating, and more that have sunk already. Can't guess about those, since I can't see them from up here."

Cly nodded, even though Huey wasn't looking at him. "That's a good point. We'll need to keep our eyes open for debris right in front of us. Won't do anyone any good if we crash against it all the way down here. I'm not even sure how we'd get out if we got stuck," he said. The last sentence died in his mouth, and he swallowed away the bad taste it left behind. "Deaderick, do those forward lights get any brighter?"

"Not so far as I know. And if they did, they'd only mark us for the big ships to aim at."

"Damn. You're right, but damn."

"Sir?"

"Yes, Huey?"

"We're almost out of the canal. Maybe ten or twenty yards, that's all."

"Thank you, Huey. Everybody hang tight. I don't know how hard the current in the bay runs, but the canal's kept us sheltered. The starting jolt may throw us off our feet. Won't be as bad as the river, but it'll be a change, all the same. Ladies?" he called out. "You hear that?"

"We heard you!" Josephine snapped back. "And we're ready."

"Good. Because here we go—here comes the bay."

The bay didn't take them in a surge of rushing water, not like the river had done. It was more of a lower, cooler pull. The sudden openness and size of it gave everyone within the *Ganymede* the peculiar sense of stepping off a cliff while underwater, only to float instead of falling.

"I didn't think . . ." Early said.

"Didn't think what?" Troost asked.

"That there'd be any current in the bay. I only expected the tide." The captain was glad for the peaceable nature of it, since nothing else about the situation was half so quiet. He said, "Houjin, me and Fang are going to bring this thing down low. Keep your scope close to the surface; don't let it ride too high. We don't want to get ourselves spotted right out of the canal."

"Yes, Captain."

"Now, tell me what you can see about the boats in the bay. Any of them belong to our side, or do they all belong to Texas and the Rebs?"

The boy frowned hard into the scope, adjusting it to comply with the captain's command. "I see four, but there might be more. I can't see all the way around the bay, or past the fort at the island."

"That's fine," Cly told him. "Just tell me what you see, and we'll worry about what you can't see later on."

"Mumler and Little are still up there. They're taking turns sticking with us—falling back and taking cover where they can, along the edges where the grass is high. There's a lot of firepower up there, sir."

"Understood. But who do the *boats* belong to? That's what we need to know, so we don't go off shooting any of our own kind."

Houjin paused, still frowning, still staring into the visor like it was a crystal ball that might be able to tell him more than his mortal eyes would allow. "Two are definitely Texian. I see the Lone Star painted on the side. I'm pretty sure the third one is, too, but I can't say about the fourth. It's too far out. We'll have to get closer."

"We'll start with the ones we know for sure. What's the position of the nearest Texian ship?"

"Dead ahead, sir. Maybe a hundred yards. There's an antiaircraft mount on the deck, and it's kicking up a storm."

He didn't need to add the last part. Everyone could hear it, the too-near *rat-a-tat-tat* of the guns shooting and recoiling against the surface. As they drew closer, they could feel it, too—the shuddering of the waves as the water was bucking against the bottom of the Texian boat. Even below the waterline as they were, the motion of the other craft made the bay feel like a bathtub full of children learning to swim.

"Josephine and . . . uh . . . Ruthie?" Cly called into the charge bay. "How are you two doing in there?"

Ruthie came to the curved doorway. The bump on her head was darkening from the red of fresh injury to the blue of impending bruise, but she looked otherwise unharmed. Her dress was pinned back into position, and though it hung oddly, it covered everything important.

She announced, "First two charges are ready to fire. We can light the fuse and shoot them whenever you tell us to do it." She disappeared back inside.

"Deaderick? You know how to aim and guide these things?"

"I think so. I've never done it myself, but I know what the motions look like. The controls are there at Troost's console."

"Shit," said Kirby Troost. "Maybe you'd better take my chair."

"Fine with me," Deaderick said. He took Troost's spot and lowered the seat to accommodate his height.

Troost declared, "I'll head over there and help those ladies, whether they want me or not."

"Wait," Cly told him. Then he asked Deaderick, "That topside gun—is it anything special?"

"Naw. It's just a pod fitted with the same thing you've got on an airship. Repeating fire, bandolier bullets on a threaded stream. Troost can probably work it, no problem—but let's leave that for later. The ball turret has to rise up to fire."

"Not much range when you shoot it underwater, I guess."

"Yeah, the bullets aren't so keen when they're swamped."

"All right, then—Troost, do whatever you like. But keep your ears open. We'll need you in a bit."

"Aye, aye," he said with a small salute, ducking back into the charge bay and immediately getting an earful from Josephine, who did not feel that she or Ruthie required any help.

"Troost makes new friends easy as pie, everywhere he goes," Cly murmured. "He has such a God-given knack for getting on with people."

Huey piped up. "If you could call it that."

"I can hear you, you know," the engineer said from the bay.

"Yeah, I know. Early, how are you doing with those weapons adjustments?"

"Doing all right. I think I've got it—but I'll know better once we get one fired off. We may have to waste one for the sake of calibrating the equipment."

"Then we'll waste it at their underside." The captain pointed out the window and up to the surface—where a broad, low boat bottom was rising into view. "Is that it, Huey?"

"Yes, that's it. Right in front of us, sir."

The patrol ship didn't sit too heavy in the water, a fact that worried Cly. How could the charges shoot up so sharply? But he figured out from listening to Deaderick mutter under his breath that the charge bays were manipulated by having their angles changed through a series of dials and buttons on the left side of the console.

The captain thought to himself, *It's just as well Troost isn't left-handed. We might've blasted apart the canal by now.* But he did not say it, and he did not interrupt Deaderick's reverie as he talked himself through the calculations.

Finally Early said, "I think I've got it."

"You *think* you've got it?" cried Troost from the charge bay.

"That's the best you'll get from me right now. The weapons systems are the most untested, because they don't have to work in order to keep the crew from drowning, or suffocating. So you'll have to bear with me."

Before anyone else could pipe up from the other room, Cly said, "Take your time. We've got a minute or two."

"No more than that," Houjin said nervously. "We'll have to circulate the air again soon, won't we? Especially since we've got more people on board now than we did before?"

"We're all right for now, and we can pull off toward the marshes if we have to. Early?"

"I've got it—as far as I'm likely to get it, based on book-learning and guessing. The charges should be calibrated toward that big-bottomed boat right in front of us. If you and Fang can hold us in position, then the ladies—and Troost—can light the fuse and fire on your command. And then . . . then we'll see what happens."

"Cross your fingers, everybody. Josephine, Ruthie, Troost—one of you, do it now!"

"Fuse alight!" cried Josephine. A door slammed, and in a count of three or four seconds, *Ganymede* rocked as the first of her charges went zipping out into the bay, a mighty bullet fired underwater.

Everyone could see it, following a slight delay as the angle of water refracted and lied. They watched it violently deploy, appearing to wibble in its flight from *Ganymede* to the undercarriage of the ship that awaited it. But mostly it went true—propelled by the charge and driven to cut a weird, wavering tunnel through the dense, dark bay.

It did not quite miss. It grazed the bow of the Texian ship, knocking it so hard that it threw stray Texians into the water. They splashed down through the surface tension and struggled to get back to the air, kicking and flailing, learning to swim on the fly—or only just remembering the skill of it, having been surprised to find it was required of them.

Then the charge, which had come to rest inside the fractured bow . . . exploded.

The whole boat shuddered, and then the front third jerked away from the back. It started to sink in a pair of ragged pieces. Some fragments tried to float and failed; others were light enough to rise once they'd been cast free. Doors, flooring planks, shutters, and boxes bobbed below and then shot to the top again as their natural buoyancy overrode the unwelcome plunge.

Cly, Deaderick, and Fang watched as a man, halfway to the bottom, ripped himself free of the sinking hull and began to take himself to the surface with scissoring kicks. Whoever he was, the man was a strong swimmer and had every chance of making it, but on his way he opened his eyes and happened to see . . . what? *Gany-*

mede lurking between the bay floor and the surface? A curve of small lights, smiling in the darkness? What could he have seen, in that bleak twilight under the surface?

Maybe he'd go on to tell others what he'd spied lurking in the bay—but it would be too late to stop anything. Even if he didn't get eaten by one of the crawling, carnivorous reptiles that occupied Barataria, and even if he made it past the saw grass, water moccasins, and the copperheads and the tangling roots that could tie his feet and draw him down . . . he'd never make it to a sympathetic ear in time to stop the *Ganymede*.

"Goddamn!" shouted Deaderick. "It worked! And we barely even hit them!"

"We hit them hard," Cly insisted. He exchanged a manic grin with Fang, who flashed it right back at him. "Assuming the rest of the charges work half so well, we'll be in good shape."

From the doorway, Josephine fought to manage their expectations. "Half of these charges have been in boxes for years. We've already burned though a third of them, trying to pick out pieces that aren't so damaged by damp and mold that they're liable to shoot."

Undaunted, the captain triumphantly declared, "Josie's right, but when they work, they work like crazy! Troost, whatever you're doing back there—"

"I'm smoking."

"I can smell it. Put down your cigarette and start sorting out those shells. Pick the good ones, and line them up for the ladies to fire. Houjin!"

"Yes, sir?"

"Where's the next target? Who's closest?"

"Ninety degrees to the north, another hundred yards that way. Maybe more. Hard to tell from here, sir."

"Deaderick, can you set a course?"

"I'll figure it out."

"Great. Fang, take us to the right, would you?"

Fang nodded.

"Ladies, load up another one. Hell, load up two or three!"

Ruthie said back, "It doesn't work like that!" But Josephine shushed her, saying, "We'll get them ready. Give the order, Andan, and we'll load and lock them down."

"Great. Here we go," he added under his breath, and engaged the lift thruster. "Huey, work your scope. I'm taking us down a notch. Has anyone spotted you yet?"

"No, sir, I don't think so."

"Just the swimmer, then. I think we're still secure."

"You *think* we're still secure?" cried Troost, out by the charges.

He did not clarify or reassure. "Let's see how many of these fish we can shoot out of the barrel before they're on to us."

"And then what?" asked Deaderick.

"Then we kick up the top ball turret and Troost can cut loose on anybody who's still afloat. All right, men, let's line 'em up and knock 'em down."

"Men?" called Josephine from the other room.

"You know what I mean!" he shouted back. The other boat was within sight, and moving toward them. "Huey, is it just me, or is that boat coming our direction?"

"I think they're moving toward the ship we just shot. Looking to pick up survivors, or see what happened."

"I'd rather they didn't get that far in their rescue efforts," Cly declared.

Deaderick said, "Agreed. Don't let them."

"Can you adjust for their movement, incoming?"

"If I have to, Captain. Give me a second. . . . All right—bay charges set, aimed, ready to shoot."

"Ladies, you hear that?"

"Why do I get lumped in with the ladies?" asked Troost.

Josephine shouted at him, "Why do we always get lumped in with the men?" And then over him, she loudly confirmed to the captain, "We hear you!"

"Fire!"

The bay door slammed. "Fire in the charge bay!" Ruthie announced with wicked, exuberant glee.

And a second enormous bullet blew free of *Ganymede,* propelled toward the bottom of a Texian boat that was swiftly incoming. Everyone on board knew the approaching craft was moving fast, despite the way it appeared to crawl across the bay. From their strange position near the shallow seafloor, everything on the surface appeared to creep.

The charge in its hydrodynamic shell left a billowing trail of bubbles and a roiling, curling tail of disturbed liquid in its wake. It crashed against the bottom of the boat and lodged there briefly, while the ship bumbled back and forth, shuddering and shaking in response to the hole smashed in its underside. It did its best to settle again to a stable position on the rippling water of the enclosed bay, even as it began to take on water.

Everyone waited. Josephine ran out of the charge bay.

She searched the window for the target, and spying it, she hollered, "Explode, Goddamn you! Explode!"

But nothing exploded, and given another half a minute, the shell toppled out of the hole it'd made, sinking down to the silt of the bay floor and settling there, where it did nothing more interesting than stick halfway into the muck.

Cly stood up, and Josephine turned around. Their eyes met.

He didn't need to say it, but he did anyway—partly to Josephine's back as she dashed back into the charge bay. "Get another one! Fire another one before they realize what's happened! Launch another shell while we still have the advantage!"

She dived headlong into the bay and gestured to Troost and Ruthie. "The next one. Set it up! Load it!"

Troost was on it. The small man was stronger than he looked; he lifted the next shell in line and dropped it onto the track, then stepped out of the way. Ruthie was right behind him. She shoved the shell along the track and tried to slam the round door behind it, locking it into the firing chute. It stuck, and she swore at it.

Josephine pushed her out of the way and threw her weight against it, bruising her elbow badly in the process but shutting the door all the same. It smacked closed with a pop of the seals and a click of the latch. Josephine pulled the lever to spark the fuse. When it didn't take, she yanked it again to light the thing.

"Ruthie, I need another fuse. . . ."

"*Oui, madame!* It is ready to go!"

Indeed, the new fuse caught and lit and burned, and Josephine called out, "Fire in the charge bay!"

"Deaderick?" Cly asked, wondering about the angles and direction, but Early had already corrected for the boat's continued trajectory, and he announced, "All set, sir!"

The charge fired, and a third big bullet went billowing toward the boat, almost too close, almost so close that Cly had second thoughts. He turned to Fang, who shrugged—then he turned to Deaderick and asked, "Are we too—?"

But before he had time to finish the question, the charge connected and blew into a thousand shards, propelled by gunpowder and fire. It shattered and split, right in the middle, and the boat began to sink—this one faster than the first.

A huge—and hugely heavy—gun slid downward. The shell had come up right underneath it, and now the gun was falling, its weight pulling the craft apart. The antiaircraft piece had been bolted to the deck, and it took a slab of this same deck with it as it tumbled down through the serene, thick water. Pieces of wood shattered, and splintered planking came raining down through the swamp, then up again as it left the weight of the gun and its fixings.

Everything that could float, did. Everything that could not, drifted to the bottom.

Josephine came running out again, with Ruthie on her heels. "Did we hit it? Did we take it?"

"We took it!" Houjin shouted. "It's gone down! I can't see it anymore!"

"Look around that visor, kid!" Cly pointed at the window.

Houjin peeled his face away from the scope, revealing a red groove around his eyes and down his cheeks, where he'd pressed himself so hard against the seam that it'd left an imprint.

"There it is!" he all but shrieked.

"Yeah, kid. There it is . . . ," the captain said with a bit of wonder taking the edge off his voice. "How many more?"

"Um? . . ." Houjin crushed his face back against the visor. "Four more. I can see four. We should be down to two, but the other two—and they're all Texian—must have come from around the island. They're coming out to help. They're not shooting at the airships anymore, so that's something, isn't it?"

"It sure is. Now, where's the nearest boat?"

"About sixty . . . maybe eighty yards north-northeast. Turn us, and I'll tell you when we're lined up with them."

"Where are Mumler and Little?"

"I don't see them, sir. Wait—one of them is right behind us, and he says . . . he says . . . he's telling us to head deeper, to the north."

"Why?"

"I don't know!" the boy said, exasperated. "Maybe we're running into shallow territory. Can you see the bottom?"

"Not well," Cly admitted.

"Not at all," Deaderick amended.

"Fine. Follow the lead of . . . whichever one of them it is. You can't tell?"

"It's dark, sir. They're keeping low. People are shooting—everyone up there, everyone is shooting."

The captain grunted and said, "Good thing for us we're down here. I hope those fellows stay out of trouble."

Deaderick turned around and said, "Houjin—do you see the other one? Anywhere? Did he get shot out, or is he just holding back?"

"I can't tell, sir. It's too dark. It's just too damn dark."

At that moment, a shudder shook *Ganymede,* and its lower portion dragged. Cly and Deaderick leaned forward, and Houjin clutched at the scope to keep from falling—and from the other room came the rustle and tumble of knees and elbows clattering and rolling.

"What was that?" Houjin asked frantically. "What's going on? I didn't see anything!"

Deaderick took a stab at an answer. "Sandbar? Are we stuck? Captain—are we still—?"

"Not stuck, no," he said, and shoved harder on the propulsion levers, and on the depth setters. "But caught. That's what our friend up top was trying to tell us. Shit, all right. Hang on—and Huey, drop the scope back down, just for now. I've got to raise us to keep us going. We're snagged on the sand, and if we don't get some lift, we'll have a hell of a time pulling ourselves loose."

"Yes, sir!"

"Everyone good in the charge bay?" Deaderick shouted the question.

"All good over here!" Josephine replied. "Just get us moving again!"

"We never *stopped*," Cly swore, but he worked the levers with the passion of someone who was terrified he might be wrong.

Finally, with a lurch and a thrust, *Ganymede* came free and rose with a bound, breaking the surface—much to the captain's discomfort. The waterline sloshed at the top of the window, briefly revealing the fire in the sky above, and a flash of red and gold, flickering tracer bullets, and small explosions as ammunition collided with armor.

"Huey, get your scope back up!" the captain ordered.

"Yes, sir!" the boy answered, and turned the crank to raise it again, even as he smushed his face against the visor and tried to look through it, though there was nothing yet to see. "Got it, sir. Hold us steady, sir—the water keeps washing over, and I can't . . . All right, it's good. I can see again."

"Great. Now tell me this—did the two nearest boats see us, when we breached just now?"

He hesitated. "They're coming our way, or it might be they're coming toward the sunk-down boats."

"But either way, they're headed for us?"

"Looks like it."

"To blazes with the lot of them, then. Troost!" Cly yelled. "Get in here! Deaderick, can you show him around the top ball turret and get him situated?"

"If he makes it fast!"

"Fast is our only speed right now. We don't have time for anything else," he noted, swinging the chair around and seeing Troost come tearing through the rounded charge bay door.

"Right here, Captain. Early, set me up and I'll start shooting. We'll hit 'em from above and below, both."

The captain said, "Good man," and then flashed Fang a worried look. Those Texian ships . . . he could see the underside of one approaching, and before he had time to ask where the rest of them were, Houjin cleared it up for them.

"Captain, I see three Texas boats, all incoming. The fourth has headed back around the far side of the island. It looks like one of them doesn't have an antiaircraft gun and it's moving a lot faster. It'll be on us before the others."

"Ladies, get us another charge loaded and ready!"

It wouldn't be shootable until Deaderick returned, because God knew nobody else on board had the faintest idea how to calibrate the weaponry, but better to have it ready for firing than add to the delay of setup. In the back of the craft, Cly could hear footsteps and scrambling, and then the squeal of metal being drawn down a track unwillingly—followed by a ratcheting sound that meant something was either going up or coming down, with gritty, forced precision.

Muffled conversation occurred, and then, without warning, a spray of bullets bucked from the top of *Ganymede*'s hull, giving the whole vehicle an excuse to shake—and nearly giving the occupants their death of fright, even though everyone knew it was coming.

The suddenness of it, and the volume of it . . . and then the quivering of the compartment . . . it was too much, too fast. Bullets strafed across the water and clomped against hulls or battered guns and sank through the torsos and limbs of men on deck.

All these things hit the water, and some of them sank. Some of them floated.

Deaderick hustled back into the main cabin, and into the engineer's seat. "He's got it," he announced, and immediately began to configure the charge bays for firing. "What's our next target— what's . . . what's closest? Which one?" he amended, realizing that there were now two more boats within their immediate view. Never mind the darkness; the small suns of burning hydrogen, rockets, and artillery fire gave the sky a peculiar glow that offset the bottoms of the Texian boats, making them easier to see from down below.

Cly didn't care which one went down first, and he almost said so. Then he changed his mind. "Huey, which one doesn't have the antiaircraft?"

"The one to the left. To the south, I mean. The one that was moving fastest."

"I didn't see which one was fastest," the captain confessed. "Got distracted. Left craft, Early. Ready, aim, and tell the ladies when to fire."

He fixed a switch and called, "Fire!"

With a pounding sound and a protracted swish, the shell barreled across the bay and collided with the leftmost Texian patrol boat—which was bowled nearly over by the impact, and then came utterly apart when the charge caught, and blew, and sent fragments of the boat in a million directions at once. It sank almost immediately, without the stuttering hesitation of the first boat—and without the dignified fractures of the second. This boat was in bits before it went under, more kindling than craft.

Several corpses plunged in with it, lacerated and bleeding from thick slivers of timber or the charge itself. A stray limb went spinning by, slapping against the window and leaving a streak of gore that washed away quickly, swiped aside by the plant life of the bay and the pace of the *Ganymede,* which churned forward toward the remaining boat.

"Huey, does this last one have antiaircraft?"

"It looks like a support cruiser, but I don't see any signs that it's firing from the deck. It's turned the wrong direction. I can't see it clearly enough to tell for sure."

But from their own deck equivalent, Troost was shooting like a maniac—threading the bullets into the automatic firing machine with the unmitigated joy of a man who finally has something to do. He swept the water as well as he could, for the range wasn't as good as true antiaircraft, but he picked a line of men off the support cruiser's deck, or so Houjin narrated above the din of the Gatling clone above.

"He's just about blown the pilothouse clear off the cruiser!" Houjin cried. "It's falling down. The whole roof is collapsing—he hit a support, and cut right through it. That boat won't do anyone any good, not for a good long time! But, oh! Captain!"

"What is it, Huey?"

"The last boat, the one I lost before—I see it again. Coming up around the west side of the island, and it's got an antiaircraft mount, and . . . and . . . they see us, sir. They see us!" He swallowed, looked around the visor, and asked, "Sir, what do we do?"

"Where are Little and Mumler?"

"Can't locate them, sir. Wait—I see one of them, making for the south-southwest."

Deaderick said, "He's headed for the islands, the bottleneck. He thinks you've done enough damage, and he'll meet us out there. Goddamn, I pray it's the both of them."

"Can't tell, Mr. Early. I'm real sorry. But this other boat, it's coming in—not as fast as the other one, but fast. And they're dropping the antiaircraft, sir—it's pivoting on the deck. They're going to shoot us!"

Deaderick's eyes went wide. "Can they even do that? With a gun that big?"

"They're going to try," Cly predicted. "Those things are heavy as hell. I don't know if they'll be able to brace it off the side of the boat, down at us. Do you have any idea if this thing can take a hit like that?"

"No idea at all. I'd say it'll depend on how far away we are, and what caliber they're shooting."

"Tell Troost to get down from there. We're going to drop, and I don't want to drown him or blind him."

Early said, "The turret is sealed. He's in more danger of getting shot off the top than of running out of air."

"Fine, then let him stay."

Then Early second-guessed himself. "But if he *does* get blown off the hull like a wart off a frog, we won't be able to sink again—not without taking on water."

"Son of a bitch. You're right. It's not worth the risk. We'll close it up and rely on the depth charges. *Troost!*" he bellowed at the top of his lungs. "Get back down here, now!"

Whether or not Troost heard him, he couldn't say—but the engineer didn't reply, except with another thread of bullets. Their kick rocked *Ganymede* gently, but it worried the captain. "Huey, go drag him out of that turret, would you? Drop the scope for a minute and run. Early, you got coordinates on that patrol boat?"

"Setting them up. Josephine, Ruthie, line up two in a row—these guys are coming in right on top of us!"

"*Oui,* darling!"

"Fire when ready!" he yelled at them, and *ready* meant "right now," for that's how quickly the charge was sent slamming out of the chute and up to the Texian boat. It hit home, right at the seam under the prow, and when it exploded, the patrol boat dipped down, dragging water into the hull with every foot forward. "Fire a second one, do it now!"

They did, and this one hit beside the hole the first charge had made, effectively turning the boat into matchsticks that billowed underwater in a cloud—so fine, they looked like filthy smoke, or a blotch of dumped diesel murking through the water.

Houjin returned with Troost, who was covered in gunpowder or soot, but smiling from ear to ear. "Hey, I got to shoot something!"

"That you did," said Cly. "You seal that thing shut?"

"Locked it down, yes, sir. Early, you'd better keep my seat."

"I was planning on it."

The captain said, "Anyone been watching a clock?" When no one answered, he said, "By my best guess, it's been something like half an hour—and I know Early's men said we have more than that, but like Huey said, we have more people on board this time. It's getting warm in here, and close. I can't be the only one who feels it."

"You're not," Early assured him.

"We'll need to pull over and crank that hose up, and do it soon."

Houjin asked, "Why?"

"What?" the captain asked. "What do you mean, why?"

"Why do we have to pull over? Can't we just stick the thing up above the surface and let it pull down air as we retreat?"

Deaderick Early hemmed and hawed. "It's *possible,* but it's dangerous, too. You turn that generator on and the air starts sucking . . . that's fine. But if we dip, or drop—or lose the ballasting loads, or anything like that . . . if the generator starts drawing in water, we're in trouble."

Cly said, "I see why it worries you, but we've got two other things to worry about right now. For one, they've damn well seen us and they know we're here. They don't know what to make of it yet, but it won't be long before someone starts dropping bombs out of an airship, trying to knock us to the bottom of the bay. So we have to get moving."

"What's the second thing?" Houjin asked nervously.

Cly lied. "I can't remember the second thing. But I want you to shove that tube up over the waterline and start the generator. They've seen us—and that's fine, so long as we hightail it out of here. I don't much give a shit if they watch us leave. Even if they follow us, we'll lose them in the Gulf, once we've drawn down enough air to keep us down low and safe for a while."

The second thing Cly had not wanted to say aloud was that he was fairly sure it'd been nearer to an hour—forty-five minutes at the bare minimum. They were running lower than he wanted to say. He could feel it in the press of the breathed and rebreathed air on his skin, and in the moist warmth of every breath he drew. A glance over at Deaderick Early told him that Early suspected the same but was determined to ignore it.

As for the rest of them, Cly saw no reason to worry them. Not when they only needed motivating, not frightening. Frightened people breathe faster, harder, heavier. They burn up air even quicker, and that wouldn't help the situation.

The boy said, "Yes, sir, I'm on it." And he fixed the scope in a downward position, running to the air tube and its generator, deploying the one and starting the other with a pull of a crank.

"If it sucks down a little water, that won't be the end of the world. You might get wet when you bring it back down, but for now, it'll have to do us, all right?"

No one responded, so Andan Cly urged the propulsion screws to full power. Then, with Deaderick's assistance, he aimed *Ganymede* toward the bottleneck at the bay's southern entrance, leaving the worst of the fighting behind them. They wouldn't know if they'd made a difference in the battle there, not for days, but Cly was glad he'd taken a chance on it.

Maybe he was on the verge of settling down and becoming a family man, or something like it; maybe he'd go retire in the Washington Territories, leisurely swatting rotters away from Fort Decatur and the business he meant to run there.

But today he was a pirate still, and for whatever good or ill, right or wrong, holy or evil thing that word had ever meant, it felt good to wear it this one last time. Even if he wore it at the bottom of the bay, fighting the Texians by stealth and hidden in watery shadows. Even if no one would ever know he was the one who'd dropped the antiaircraft guns from the patrol ships. Even if he went down in nobody's history for this last hurrah, that was fine by him.

Pirates didn't have their own lands, or books, or histories, after all. Not much of it. Just one small island in one dark bay, off to the west of the Mississippi River.

But it was enough, and it was worth keeping.

"Early, how far off is this bottleneck—and Huey, how's the air holding?"

"Getting a little sputter, sir. Keep us higher if you can do it."

"Higher it is, kid. Watch that tube, and if you can, watch from the scope. Can you go back and forth?"

"Not really, sir."

But Troost said, "I'll watch the scope. I want to take another look up topside, anyway." He redeployed it, figuring out the levers, knobs, and cranks as he went along—and aiming it up above the water, and backwards. This meant he was off the stool and standing with his backside to the captain, Fang, and Deaderick.

Deaderick was the one who asked, "What are you doing, Troost?"

"I don't care where we're going, but I want to know where we've been. It's looking like a real mess out there, if I do say so myself."

"Good. I like making messes," Cly beamed.

"I ought to warn you, they're coming up behind us. Not fast, but steady. And—" He tipped the scope so it aimed up nearly as far as it'd go. "—I think one of the big Texian warships is turning around to track us."

"We'll lose it in the Gulf," Deaderick promised. "Sun won't be up for a while yet, and they'll never see us under the waves."

"I expect you're right." Troost nodded with satisfaction. He swiveled the scope and got up into the seat that had formerly held Houjin. "Hey, good news in this direction."

The captain asked, "How so?"

"I see both of our guys—Little and Mumler—one on each

bank. Jesus Christ, they're close together. They don't mean for us to squeak between 'em, do they?"

"They don't call it a bottleneck for nothing," Deaderick said. "We'll slow down and squeak between 'em, that's right. They'll pole us on through. Then we ought to see if we can grab them and pull them on board. I don't want to leave them out there, not with Texas coming up behind us."

Cly agreed. "Good idea. Huey—how's the air coming?"

A big burp of water sloshed inside, soaking the boy from the waist down, but he laughed. "Gotta stop for now, but that should be plenty. It was more than a couple of minutes, wasn't it?"

"Hey, Early," Troost said. "I've got another idea for an improvement on your next model."

"Clocks?"

"Damn right. You need some clocks in here."

Before long, the first tap of a pole clanked down into Ganymede's interior, and before much longer than that, they were through the bottleneck between Grande Terre and Grand Isle. With two new passengers, they struck out for the prearranged position in the Gulf of Mexico, where the Union airship carrier *Valiant* awaited—surrounded at a distance by curious Texians who were too smart to come any closer, but too wily to let it alone altogether.

When Ganymede *reached* the *Valiant,* Captain Cly and First Mate Fang held the ship steady as an enormous winch—designed to retrieve airships, should they fall into the ocean during landing or takeoff—craned out over the water and affixed itself to *Ganymede*'s hull. A series of hydraulic cinches compressed, squeezed, and, after a few false starts . . . established a secure grip on the huge steel watercraft.

A crank turned, and more hydraulics stabilized the affair, counteracting the tremendous weight of something being heaved from the water. A giant arm swung, and dropped the craft onto a platform that was ordinarily used to land and park airships.

But *Ganymede* had the same shape as an airship. And it had similar controls, so a pilot like Andan Cly could get her from Pontchartrain to the Gulf. And in the end, everything went just as Josephine had planned.

Or perhaps not *just* as she'd planned, but so close to her original scheme that she was prepared to take credit for it. This had worked out, hadn't it? It'd gone as well as anyone could have hoped—better, even. She had not merely delivered the ship, but, thanks to the captain and her brother, they could provide a detailed report of the weapons system: what parts were satisfactory, which aspects could stand improvement. How the ammunition could be better designed, and how it ought to be stored. How the controls might be calibrated for surer accuracy with every shot.

Josephine did not mind admitting that none of those things would have occurred if they hadn't made it to the bay and assisted the pirates against the Texians. So she refused to regret the delay or the spent ammunition.

With conscious, sincere effort, she declined to fret over the change in plans.

Instead, she waited until *Ganymede* had settled and been released from the winch's grasping claw, and there was no more motion except for the distant, almost undetectable flutter of the Gulf moving beneath the *Valiant*. Then she went to the ladder and climbed it, with Ruthie right behind her, and unscrewed the portal door, opening the hatch and letting the clear night air spill down into *Ganymede*'s gut.

The sky outside smelled of salt and birds, and it was littered with the peaceful twinkle of stars, shrouded in part by a faint mist that might have been cloud cover, or might have been smoke drifting out to sea.

No longer could she hear the interminable din of artillery and the crashing and burning of airships or boats. Only the murmurs of curious men reached her ears, accompanied by an official-sounding bark of, "Hail *Ganymede,* and its occupants. This is Admiral Herman

Partridge of the United States Airship Carrier *Valiant*. Declare yourself, and your intent. How do you reply?"

Casting a brilliant smile at Ruthie, Josephine flipped the hatch door back and emerged. She said, "I am Josephine Parella Rawling Early. And I am proud to deliver this Rebel device into your hands."

Sixteen

The *Naamah Darling* was four days late returning to Seattle, but Cly had sent a telegram from Denver explaining the situation. A freak late-season blizzard had come swooping down across the mountains, stranding the crew in the Colorado Territory, but they hunkered down in a boarding house on the west side of the city and made the best of it. There wasn't much else to be done, and Andan Cly figured that if Yaozu wanted to make a huge fuss about the delay, then that was his business. But until the other man could control the weather, he'd have to get used to disappointment.

Cly didn't expect it to be a problem. The business of cross-continental travel was one of luck and coincidence, fortune and ill wind. When more than a thousand miles stand between you and your destination, it's important to stay flexible. Even the railways knew that much, and the variables in the sky were considerably more troublesome. A train could bully through a thunderstorm, and push past ice and snow, if it had the right equipment. An airship must land and wait for better skies, or else risk being dashed to pieces against the nearest mountain, or into the handiest plain.

If it'd been only Yaozu awaiting them, Cly probably wouldn't have bothered with the telegram. Yaozu could wait. But he didn't want Briar to worry, so he'd sent it—and directed it courtesy of the Western Union station at the railway terminus in Tacoma, Washington Territory, to the attention of Angeline Sealth or her nearest reliable kin.

One way or another, it'd find its way to the city named loosely for Angeline's father. The captain could count on that, if not on the weather.

The flash storm that held them in Colorado was half-frozen, driving and wet, with ice building up and layering across everything immobile, like very cold frosting on an unwilling cake. Troost made some passing complaint about wishing for the Gulf Coast again, but Cly shook his head and declined to agree.

This was better. The damp and chill suited him, with the accompanying dark and low skies, and the night that fell early. The cover of darkness felt like a friend.

Colorado was colder than he wished, yes. But it was more like what he wanted, and more of what he missed, than the sunken, soaking bayous with their verdant canopies and cold-blooded creatures that never got cold. The frigid rain reassured him that he'd made the right decision when he left New Orleans all those years ago. But ultimately, it was a fine place to visit, and he was glad to have seen it again.

Furthermore, he was glad to have seen Josephine again.

It was good to know that she had survived and prospered, and that she'd become even more of the woman he'd once so desperately loved. He was happy to know that he'd never been wrong about her, and that his affection had not been undeserved or misplaced. He was pleased to learn that she was her own boss, with her own property. A pirate in her own way, still—working beyond the law, against the government, against the Republic, and anyone else who stood between her and what she wanted.

He felt strangely proud of her, and the feeling was bittersweet. She'd been easy to admire, but hard to get to know. Easy to love, but sometimes hard to like.

The nostalgia was warm in his chest, but it did not build a lump in his throat or bring dampness to his eyes when he stared off into the darkness, at the same stars that hovered above Louisiana. He remained content to know that she was there, and all was all right—or, if it wasn't, that she was fighting to make it that way.

Andan Cly wished Josephine Early well.

And he looked forward to finding his way home.

When the storm finally lifted and the last of the frozen spring rains had melted into puddles, the captain and his crew unfastened the *Naamah Darling* from its dock and set out northwest, back toward a city that had once been called the Port of Seattle, and now was called "abandoned" by almost everyone.

The Rockies were crisp and sharp, cut into the earth in razor-blade shades of white and blue, engraved with gray. All the usual drifts and currents, the tugs and shoves of the air, were rough above the mountain range—just like always. These unseen ghosts of rising and falling pressure were familiar, unthreatening even when they were a challenge.

Sometimes, without thinking, his right foot reached for an illusory lever that would lower or raise the *Naamah Darling*. Each time, he corrected himself in time to keep from doing any damage.

"This is more like it," he said under his breath, so softly that no one but Fang heard him.

Fang signed, *Back where we belong.*

And Cly nodded.

Seattle was as they'd left it, and as it would be for months yet—until summer landed, sometime toward the end of July.

For now it was chilly and dank, shielded with a gray sky so low that it touched the city wall in places . . . draping across it like moss, or an ancient and ragged tablecloth. These wispy, dangling clouds met and commingled with the dense yellow blight gas that filled the wall and sank there, settling on the streets, on the buildings, on the leftover pieces of civilization that had remained outside and exposed.

The *Naamah Darling* hovered above it while the crew members applied their gas masks, better too early than too late; then the ship descended slowly, carefully down through the clouds, through the fog, through the noxious gas, and puttered toward Fort Decatur.

They did not see the lights from the Chinese lanterns until they were nearly upon them.

The lanterns burned warm and yellow, shaded by red and orange paper, lifted on strings like floaters on a fisherman's net. These lights invited them—gave them a space to aim toward, and land upon— and the ship followed their suggested path and set down softly, expertly, into the fort's main square. Surrounded by the tall, pointed trunks of felled trees, the courtyard-type space was impenetrable to Seattle's walking dead. It was likewise safe from most of the more mindful human invaders, or curiosity seekers, or anyone else who wished to come inside uninvited.

Down the *Naamah Darling* dropped, and before there was time to affix the craft to the two fallen totem poles that temporarily served as a dock . . . up from below came the expectant residents of Seattle, to greet the ship and its crew.

Briar Wilkes and Lucy O'Gunning were there, Briar with a smile on her face that could be seen in her eyes behind the visor, and Lucy with a pair of wheeled carts that had been rigged for use in the underground's rail systems. Lucy was smiling, too, but at the prospect of rum and absinthe. The barwoman reached up and slapped the side of the *Naamah Darling,* daring the steps beneath it to open, and to hurry up about it, would they?

In response, or more likely as a coincidence of timing, the stairs did indeed come down and Cly descended them first. He ducked his head beneath the overhang and climbed even more quickly upon seeing Briar—who did not run to meet him, but stayed where she was.

Her mask hid most of her face except for those lovely eyes. It was wrapped around her head, pushing down her dark, curly hair with streaks of blight-bleached orange running through it like fine seams of gold in a boulder. Atop that mass of never-quite-contained hair sat her father's old hat, the one he'd worn as sheriff; she also wore his belt, with the zigzag *MW* for his initials, and an oversized coat that kept the blight off her skin. It, too, had been taken from his closet, before she'd gone over the wall to make herself at home inside it.

"Captain," she said.

If he'd been wearing a hat, he would've removed it. "Wilkes," he replied.

"I'm glad you're home."

Later, while Troost, Fang, and Houjin helped Lucy O'Gunning load the spoils of her wish list into the carts, Cly and Briar went downstairs—into the train station, to pass beneath its unfinished ceilings, and to walk the prettily marbled floors with their natural patterns swirling underfoot. All was alight with lamps both gas and electric; the hissing burn of one complementing the crackling fizz of the others, creating an underground chamber that was every bit as bright as a cathedral, and at least half so lovely.

Briar would not have chosen the station for a romantic walk, but Cly had promised Yaozu a report upon his return, and an accounting of both his money and the supplies it had purchased. So together they ambled, not in any real hurry, down a caged shaft via a mechanical lift, and through passageways that had once been meant to shelter incoming rail cars—which had never arrived, and never would.

This station, never completed or used for its intended purpose, now served as headquarters for what Briar considered a nefarious criminal empire . . . or at least the second incarnation thereof. Yaozu might prove better than Minnericht, or he might not. Regardless, to lend credit where it was due, she could be compelled to admit that King Street Station was a surprisingly clean and comfortable place.

"But that says nothing about the men who keep it that way."

"I never said it did," Cly noted. "It's nice down here, that's all. Looks downright civilized—like something you'd find on the outside."

"Except for the lack of windows, I'd say you're right." Her mask hung off her belt now—affixed to a leather loop she'd stitched in place for the purpose. It dangled against her thigh, tapping her pants as she walked.

"And Yaozu might not be so bad. In the long run, he'll be good for this place."

"That's what you think?"

"Maybe I'm wrong, and you'll get to say 'I told you so.' But he's helping me stay here. It was his money, mostly, that made the trip possible . . . and makes it possible to start up the dock I want, there in the fort." He did not mention that the rest of the money had come from Josephine, who had paid him—good as her word—upon his departure from the delta.

"Then he'll want something in return. Men like that, they never give anything away for free."

"He'll get something in return. More commerce. Easier access, coming and going."

"Well. I suppose we'll see."

"No one's asking you to like him."

"Good," she said. "Because I don't. And I don't trust him, either."

"Do you trust *me*?" he asked.

"More than I ought to," she said.

"Good. Then trust me to handle my end of things all right, and to keep the bargain from biting me in the ass later on."

"All right. I'll do that. Whatever it takes."

His forehead wrinkled. "What do you mean, whatever it takes?"

"I mean, whatever it takes to keep you down here. If all you need is a little bargain with the devil, it's not the end of the world. Not yet. And anyhow," she added, with a toss of her hair that was almost girlish, and almost made him laugh, "you're the one signing in blood, not me."

He took her hand so he could hold it while they walked, even though it made him feel big and clumsy to grasp something so small in his oversized fingers. He liked it anyway, how she trusted him, and how she only *looked* delicate—when he knew for a fact that she was not, and for that matter, had never been any of the things everyone else had assumed.

He leaned into her like a lion drawing close to a fire. He removed his hand from hers and instead, wrapped it around her shoulder, pulling her against him so he could hold her that way, and be warmed by her.

She slipped an arm around his waist.

When they reached the wing where Yaozu lived, Briar extricated herself without any reproach. She said only, "I'll go back to the vaults, and maybe I'll see you there in a bit. But I'm not interested in consorting with *you-know-who.*"

"Who's consorting? Good Lord, woman. You make it sound worse than it really is."

"Time will tell how bad it really is. Until then, I'll stick to my concerns, if you don't mind."

"I don't. And I'll be back at the vaults in an hour or two. Is . . . um. Is Zeke around?"

She looked at him with a flash of something sharp and bright—a wink of intensity that she didn't show him for long. She told him, "No, he's not around. I've sent him off to Chinatown with Mercy. His leg's all but healed up now, and he's paying her back for stitching him up by helping on her rounds with Dr. Wong."

"Helping?"

"I think he's sweet on her, and it's a shame. You can get almost anything down here in the underground, but girls his own age are hard to come by. Mercy doesn't have ten years on him, so I guess he thinks that'd be all right. Anyway, she's put him up next door to her father's place, and I didn't have to bully him too hard to stay out there with them."

"For the night?"

"For a night or two." Again, that spark of . . . invitation? It flashed, and returned to a simmer. "As long as I feel like locking him out. He's a big boy. He'll find something to occupy his time."

"That's . . . good to know."

She walked away from him then, and without looking back, she disappeared down the corridor that would take her back into the open areas beneath the streets, and back to the vaults.

It scrambled his thoughts and made him reconsider how badly he needed to talk to Yaozu, but those reconsiderations were undone when he heard the man's voice behind him, thereby settling the matter.

"Captain Cly, I see you've returned. I got your telegram. Angeline sent it down a few days ago, though she obviously didn't bring it herself. You know, I don't think she likes me much."

"She's . . . finicky about who she likes."

Ignoring the polite deferral, Yaozu said, "Perhaps that's one more thing I should put on our wish list, when it comes to citywide improvements. A set of taps."

"Do you think we can set one up? I don't know if it's even possible, down here."

Yaozu shrugged, the lines of his clean white outfit shifting and settling again. "I do not yet know what would be required, but I am interested in learning. Is there any chance Houjin would have any idea?"

"I don't know. But if you tell him to go find out, he'll report back within a day or two, putting one together with a couple of tin cans and a drawer full of spoons."

"Yes, I hear he's prone to such improvisations. And how was your excursion down to Texian territory?"

"It was fine. Brought back all your goodies, and everything on everybody else's list, too. It weighed us down like crazy, all the things everyone wanted. If we hadn't been so heavy, we might've missed that storm in Denver. But that's just how it goes."

"There's nothing to be done about the weather," Yaozu said graciously. "At any rate, if you're not otherwise occupied, I'd appreciate your company up at the fort. I've summoned a handful of men to help with the loading and unloading, but you're the one who knows what's what in your cargo bay."

Cly echoed his phrasing. "Otherwise occupied? Uh, no. Not right this second. I can take an hour or two to help you get all your gear in order." That's what he'd told Briar, after all. An hour or two. Though he determined on the spot that he was not going to hang around and be helpful for even one minute longer than that.

"Excellent. Walk with me, Captain."

"Sure. Listen, there's something you should know. Maybe you'll care, and maybe you won't," he said, adjusting his pace to walk with the shorter man, whose legs could not comfortably match his long stride. "It's about the sap, and what it's doing outside the city."

"I already know about the gas, and those Mexicans in Utah."

"Sure. But have you heard about the zombis in New Orleans?"

 *Seventeen*

Josephine held her breath and aimed.

She exhaled slowly as the zombi moseyed behind a stack of crates outside the warehouse down at the river's edge. This was the same warehouse she'd visited once before, following the two Texian officers—and then, of course, she'd been saved from potential disaster by Marie Laveau, may she rest in peace. But Marie could not save her now. Marie was beyond saving anyone anymore, and it was almost as if the zombis knew it.

Josephine would not have said it out loud, but it was hard not to notice, and not to wonder at how the riverbanks were more dangerous now than before the Queen had passed on despite Texas's efforts to the contrary. Patrols ran every night, in three shifts. Texian soldiers and Texian guns picked off the dead men by the score, leaving everyone to wonder just how many of the things, precisely, had been running around all this time.

Every morning there were more bodies, more corpse-corpses. Some of the zombies were recognized, named, and taken away. Most were not. Most of them were burned down to charred black scraps, and if anything was left, it was buried. Or else, the nasty remnants were dumped into the ocean—where everything eventually rusts, or warps, or is eaten away by carrion-seekers small and large.

They must be managed now, before they become unmanageable.

These days, or at least these curfewed nights, Josephine had started lighting candles and praying to no one in particular that it wasn't already too late.

Then she'd pick up Little Russia and don unfancy clothes, adding a dark brown cloak. She'd meet her escort downstairs at the door, and he'd flash his badge again and again to see them both past the anxious watchmen who kept the Quarter under lock and key between dusk and dawn.

Together, they would go down to the river, to the warehouses, to the edges of the territory trawled by the organized boys in brown—with their rolling-crawlers and air support, their well-drilled sharpshooters and lookouts. They worked the fringes as a team, without the tactical advantage of numbers . . . but between them, they did their part to keep the things contained.

And to study them, and discuss their theories, their suspicions.

Tonight, like every night, the warehouse was dark.

Its huge double doors—built to accommodate ship-repairing cranes and equipment—had rotted and fallen off, and now lay flat and fragmented across the pier, leaving the interior exposed to the elements.

And to the zombis.

A pair of them wandered back and forth, wheezing as they shambled, seemingly in search of nothing at all—and, finding nothing, they merely changed their path and searched for nothing once more, in another direction. Josephine could see them from her vantage point atop an old shipping container, upon which she had lain down flat on her belly . . . all the better to alternately watch the riverbank and its forlorn, collapsing buildings through a spyglass, and over the edge of Little Russia's barrel. Three other zombis were milling about, lurching and sagging, coughing and hunting.

She shuddered. She shook her head, braced her elbows, and closed one eye.

"Be patient," whispered her companion.

She scrunched her eyes shut and resisted the urge to hit him. "I *know*," she said instead, through gritted teeth. "And I *am*."

"Sorry. I don't mean to get your dander up. I'm just trying to tell you that if you give this one on the left a minute or two, I think it'll circle back around. You might be able to hit 'em both with one bullet."

He was right, and she almost hated him for it—except that the implication of his suggestion was that he believed she was capable of making the kind of shot that could knock down two zombis at once. And that was no small measure of flattery, coming from a Texian.

She relaxed, very slightly. She returned her attention to the scene before her, illuminated mostly by moonlight flickering off the river, and by two skinny gas lamps that were too far away to do anything but stretch the shadows.

Josephine said, "I'll take those two, and you pick off the ones hanging out on the right. If you don't clip that big one soon, he's going to topple clean over. That'll mean a point scored for an alligator, and not for you."

"I didn't realize we were keeping score."

"Everybody keeps score, Ranger Korman. Right now, I'm ahead by two. But if you can strike all three of the dead men on your right side, then you'll only be down by one. I daresay you'll catch up again, once we move down the block."

He made a *harrumph* noise that wiggled his mustache, and he used his free hand to adjust his hat—lifting the brim up out of the way so he'd have a clearer line of sight. "I think maybe you've miscounted."

"I think maybe you don't like the idea of being beat by a woman."

"I didn't say that."

"Keep your voice down, Ranger, or neither of us will do any better tonight. Look, here they come around again, like toys on a track. Not a brain left in their heads, I swear to high heaven." She took another breath, held it in, and exhaled slowly.

Then, as the zombis staggered into position—that critical point when two were both in the same line of sight—she clenched her jaw and pulled the trigger. Little Russia bucked in her hands, hurtling a bullet between two stacks of industrial crates, straight into the ear of one ambling zombi and out the other . . . and farther still, to lodge in the forehead of a second dead man right behind it. A big red circle splatted thereupon, and in perfect synchronicity, the two dead men toppled down to the planks. They dropped with a hollow, melodic *thunk*.

Before the other three shamblers had a chance to react, Horatio Korman's revolvers fired—two shots each—and all three went down within a span of as many seconds.

Both of the lurking shooters, the woman and the Ranger, exhaled happily and sat up. Neither was the type to praise effusively, and neither wanted to heap too much kindness upon the other. Both of them had their reasons. But they exchanged a set of friendly glances, which would've surprised anyone who knew either of them.

Not that anyone knew about these strange dates. No one except Ruthie, who only suspected . . . and who had obligingly spread a rumor that Josephine Early was being courted by someone in particular, someone who didn't want anyone knowing about his interest.

It was *practically* true.

Korman said, "Fine. I'm down by one. I'll catch up to you later. But for now, we've already shot down more than I can use in a week of Sundays, and the pier is clean. Let's watch another minute to be sure, and then I've got to get to work. I only have four dry plates on me, so that's all the photographs I can take." He sniffed, and pulled out a pouch of tobacco. "Between us, we've done the Quarter a favor tonight, wouldn't you say?"

"I *would* say that, Ranger. So there's one more thing we agree on."

"If we keep this up, we'll need more than one hand to add 'em up."

"Don't get your hopes too high. Why didn't you bring more plates? I thought you were supposed to be researching these things, proving they exist, or whatever it is Austin wants from you."

He rolled himself a cigarette and licked the paper to wrap it tight. Then he stuck it in his mouth and talked around it while he answered her question. "For one thing, they're heavy. For another, they break if I do too much running around. This photography equipment is a goddamn mess. It's barely worth the trouble, I tell you. I hear there's a fellow named Eastman who's working on making something lighter. I hope he hurries up. I look forward to the day I don't have to tote fifty pounds of spare parts just to get one stinkin' shot." He struck a match on the cargo crate beneath his rear end and lit the cigarette.

"Less trouble than stopping to draw pictures, I expect. You going to keep all that to yourself, or offer a lady a smoke?"

"By all means."

"Hand me the pouch. I'll roll my own."

He passed it over to her and watched as she established her own cigarette. He told her, "I'm not much of an artist. And even if I did take the time to sit around on my spurs, twiddling a pencil around a sheet of paper, everyone would say I'd made it all up. But a photograph—that's *evidence,* is what that is."

"After a fashion."

"What's that supposed to mean?"

"It means—pardon me, I'll need a match, thank you—that no one's believed you so far, despite your photographs." She inhaled, drawing the smoke deep into her chest and closing her eyes happily. "Your evidence doesn't seem to be working out so well."

He argued, "Plenty of people believe me. *You* believe me. Half of New Orleans believes me, and the other half has its head jammed up its back passage. I know a whole train full of people who believe me— Union soldiers, most of them. I wish to God I knew what they'd told their commanding officers once they got home from Utah."

"You don't know?"

"I can't get hold of anybody. For one thing, there are *political considerations.*" He said the last two words with snideness, clearly copying the tone of someone who'd raised them as a concern. "But there's at least one fellow who I think would have my back, if someone were to fight me on it. A captain by the name of MacGruder.

Problem is, he's been transferred. No one will tell me where he went to, but wherever he is, I bet nobody believes *him*, either."

"Go figure," she murmured.

"When I took my leaders back up to the pass at Provo, there was nothing left. Nothing!" he said a little too loudly. "Not a miserable trace of what had occurred, except a shell here and there, or a bullet left lying in the snow. I don't know who covered it up, but someone, somewhere, did. Someone wants it kept quiet."

"But not you."

"But not me. And not you either, ain't that right?"

"That's right. Not me either."

They smoked together in silence, the woman and the Ranger in civilian clothes, a man who'd still never be mistaken for anything but a Texian. When their cigarettes were nubs too small to hold any longer, they snuffed them out on the roof of the container and spent an awkward span of seconds in silence.

Finally, Josephine said, "I'm not trying to help Texas. You know that, don't you?"

"I'm not trying to save New Orleans. I guess that makes us about even."

"I don't even trust you."

"The feeling's mutual."

She smiled. "It's just as well. So!" She made a show of standing up and changing the subject as she changed her position. "Do you think it's safe to go down there and take your pictures? Collect your samples?"

He stood quietly, squinting out into the darkness, toward the gas lamps and their stretched shadows, and the river with its shimmering moonlight, and the stars that gave no light at all—but plenty of ambience. He said, "I don't hear anything else coming. Do you?"

"No. I don't."

"Then how about we start with these, and you keep a lookout while I do my business. Are you all right with that? Don't worry, you won't be doing a damn thing to help Texas. I promise you, Texas isn't listening to me. Yet."

"I don't mind playing lookout. As long as you don't mind losing tonight."

"Losing?"

"You're still down by one."

"I told you, there are still more of these things farther down the river."

"You also told me you're short on plates." She strolled to the ladder, built into the side of the cargo container, and began to descend it. "And the night is growing late, Ranger Korman. I have a business to run. And God knows, I have some sleep to catch up on."

He made another one of his patented grumbling noises and said, "Fine. Let me get these bastards squared away, and we'll see how late it's really gotten. We can always pick up where we left off later. We'll just say the score's been put on hold."

"Will we, now?"

"Yes," he said, looking down at her, for she'd reached the street level and was a few feet below him.

She noticed him looking down the top of her dress, but did not bother to cover herself, or pretend she hadn't seen him looking. All she said was, "Call it how you like it. I won tonight."

"It's whoever shoots best for the *week,*" he insisted.

"The week?"

"Yes, the week. It's only Thursday. We'll start again tomorrow night, and see who's on top come Sunday morning."

"You're a filthy heathen of a man, aren't you?" she asked him, watching as he turned around and began his own descent to the knotted, bleached boards of the pier. And to her.

"Ma'am, you don't know the *half* of it."

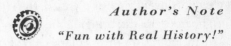

Author's Note
"Fun with Real History!"

As you've no doubt figured out by now, I'm a big fan of real history . . . and really making a mess of it. In my humble opinion, that's half the fun in steampunk—adjusting the past to better fit my personal convenience, or narrative curiosity. So it should not come as a great surprise that a healthy dose of Actual Stuff made its way into *Ganymede*.

First and foremost, I suppose, it's worth mentioning that Horace Lawson Hunley was a real person—a Confederate engineer—and the *Hunley* was a real craft. Likewise, James McClintock and Baxter Watson were Hunley's partners, but my description of their subsequent descent into murder and hypothetical treason is wholly fictitious. Although Hunley was originally from Tennessee, he relocated to New Orleans, where he lived for many years. There, he did much of his developmental work on submarines, though it was the *Pioneer* (and certainly not the fictitious *Ganymede*) that was scuttled in Lake Pontchartrain.

The *Hunley* was built and tested in Mobile, Alabama; she was subsequently seized by the Confederate Navy and put to work against the Union naval blockade of Charleston, South Carolina, drowning five men on her first outing in 1863. She killed her second crew—eight men, including Hunley himself—in a routine diving exercise later that same year. Her final voyage took place on February 17, 1864.

This time, the *Hunley* earned a spot in history as the first submarine to successfully sink an enemy ship—the *Housatonic*—in battle. That was the good news.

The bad news was that mere minutes after signaling to shore that the mission had gone as planned, the *Hunley* vanished. All eight men on board were lost, bringing the *Hunley's* final body count to twenty-six, including the five sailors who died aboard the *Housatonic*—which goes down in the history books, too, as the first ship ever successfully torpedoed into matchsticks.

The *Hunley* wasn't seen again until 1995.

And because truth is so often stranger than fiction, it was discovered by legendary author and adventurer Clive Cussler, who found it buried just outside Charleston Harbor.

Today, courtesy of the South Carolina *Hunley* Commission and a private not-for-profit group called Friends of the *Hunley,* you can see the submarine itself at the Warren Lasch Conservation Center in North Charleston, South Carolina. I recommend that you visit http://hunley.org for more information on the craft, and details regarding tour availability.

The only other historic figure of note to actually appear in *Ganymede* is Marie Laveau, renowned Voudou practitioner and cult figure of nineteenth-century New Orleans. She passed away in 1881 at a ripe old age, surely in her late eighties, but authorities occasionally differ with regards to her date of birth, so I hesitate to offer an exact figure. Laveau is allegedly interred in a mausoleum in the Saint Louis Cemetery #1 in New Orleans, but people like to argue about that, too.

As for Barataria Bay and the Lafittes . . . much of that was on point, if a bit exaggerated.

Jean Lafitte was a French privateer whose dates of birth and death are likewise in dispute, but he and his brother Pierre definitely raised a lot of hell in the Gulf of Mexico in the late eighteenth and early nineteenth centuries. After the United States passed the Embargo Act of 1807, Jean and Pierre moved their base of operations from

New Orleans proper to Barataria Bay, where they took up pirating and smuggling. In 1814, America raided the bay and seized most of its assets—despite the fact that Lafitte had actually tried to warn the States about British shenanigans. In return for a pardon, Lafitte helped Andrew Jackson defend New Orleans against the British in 1815, and later went on to take up spying against the Spanish in Galveston, Texas.

Jean Lafitte may or may not have died in 1823, but Barataria Bay was a choice spot, and persons of dubious character continued to frequent it long afterwards.

If you're from the Gulf Coast, you can probably list half a dozen things named after Lafitte off the top of your head. One of my personal favorites is the Old Absinthe House (often just called "Lafitte's") on Bourbon Street, in New Orleans. It was built in 1807, but like the above-mentioned historic quarrels, no one really knows for sure whether or not Lafitte ever owned it, visited it, or had anything to do with it.

Finally, a note about the character Ruthie Doniker, and her secret.

This ought to go without saying, but people with a variety of gender identities are not a twentieth-century invention. They are rarely discussed in traditional history books, but that doesn't mean they weren't present.

Case in point: Should you ever take the historic Underground Tour in Seattle, Washington, the gift shop at the end has a large black-and-white photo of the notorious prostitute "Madam Damnable" surrounded by several of her employees in a late-nineteenth-century parlor setting. As the tour guides will sometimes whisper to you, all is not *quite* as it appears. At least one of the ladies is a "man."

Was she a transgendered woman? Was he a crossdresser? Was the truth something else entirely? Anything's possible, and there's no way of knowing now. But there was obviously a call for her services.